DEUS EX™

IC△RUS EFFECT

D0756124

DEUS EX

ICARUS EFFECT

James Swallow

TITAN BOOKS

Deus Ex: Icarus Effect
ISBN: 9780857681607

Published by Titan Books
A division of Titan Publishing Group
144 Southwark Street
London
SE1 0UP

First edition February 2011

10 9 8 7 6 5 4 3

This edition published by arrangement with Del Rey, an imprint of The
Random House Publishing Group, a division of Random House, Inc.

www.titanbooks.com
www.deusex.com
www.squareenix.com

Book design by R. Bull.

Did you enjoy this book? We love to hear from our readers. Please
email us at readerfeedback@titanemail.com or write to us at
Reader Feedback at the above address.

To receive advance information, news, competitions, and exclusive Titan
offers online, please register as a member by clicking the "sign up" button
on our website: www.titanbooks.com

A CIP catalogue record for this title is available from the British Library.

Printed and bound in Great Britain by CPI Group UK Ltd.

DEUS EX™

ICARUS EFFECT

ONE

From the window of the great house it was possible to see the summit of Mont Blanc on a good day, a clear day when the sky was a perfect shade of teal and unhindered by clouds. There still were days like that, once in a while. Those moments that were rare and becoming rarer still, when clouds gray as oil-soaked wool graced Geneva's ornate streets with a moment of weak sunshine; but for the most part, the city remained wintry and wet, as summers became something that were spoken of by parents and grandparents to children with no experience of such things.

The house was fifteenth century, and it stood witness to the turning of the gray clouds above the city, just as it had to the republic of John Calvin, the rise of the Catholics, the fascist riots, and the gathering of nations. Like the blue sky, the house was a relic from an age so far removed from the now, it seemed as if it were something drawn from mythology. It stood undimmed by the acid rain that pitted and wormed into the bones of its fellows. The bricks and mortar of the building resisted the march of time and the polluted atmosphere, protected by a layer of polymerized industrial diamond a few molecules in thickness.

It pleased the man who lived here to toy with the idea that a thousand years from now, this place might still be standing while the rest of the city had come to dust. In his more fanciful moments, he even imagined it might become some sort of monument. The owner of the house did not consider this to be arrogance on his part. He simply thought it right, as he did about so many of the choices he made.

A trim man of solid stock, he resembled a captain of industry, a scion of blue bloods from the old country, a man of mature wealth—and he was all those things. He had a patrician face, fatherly after a fashion, but tainted by something that those who knew him well would call a sense of superiority. He walked the halls of the great house in the same manner he did the halls of the world—as if he owned them.

An assistant—one of a dozen at his beck and call, faceless and interchangeable—fell into step as he crossed the reception hall. Her shoes were beetle black, matching the discreetly flattering cut of her business suit and the cascade of her sharply fashioned hair. He registered her without a word, her footsteps clacking across the mosaic flooring.

"Sir," she began, "all connections have been secured. The gallery is ready for you."

He graced her with a nod. He expected no less.

The woman frowned slightly. "In addition...Doctor Roman has confirmed he will be arriving on schedule for your—"

"I know why he's coming." The flash of irritation was small, but any such sign from him was so forbidding that it sent his staff into silence.

He resented the small, unctuous physician and the minor indignities the man forced him to suffer each time he visited the house; but age was not a kind companion and the advance of years was taking its toll. If he were to remain at the top of his game—and more important, maintain his leadership of the group—it would be necessary for him to ensure his own fitness, and so these little moments of ignominy were his trade-off. He was no fool; all the others, his protégé in Paris first among them, watched like hawks for signs of weakness. Today would be no different.

As they reached the paneled doors of the gallery, he looked properly at the young woman for the first time and smiled, forgiving her. "Thank you, my dear," he said, the softened vowels of his native Southern drawl pushing through. "You're dismissed."

She nodded as the doors closed on her, and he heard the gentle metallic click of hidden machinery inside the frame as it sealed closed. The gallery was decorated with walls of smoky, dark wood that shone in the half-light through the arched windows. Works in watercolor, oils, some portraits, others still life or landscape, hung in lines that ranged around the room. Deep chairs of rich red leather were positioned about the floor, and he noted that a silver tray with cups and a cafetière of his favorite Saint Helena were waiting for him. He sat and poured a generous measure, savoring the aroma of the coffee as the lamps above seven of the paintings flickered in unison.

Panes of shimmering color formed in front of each of the works, shifting and changing from interference patterns to something approximating human faces. Presently, ghostly busts of five men and two women gained form and false solidity, projected from concealed holographic emitters hidden in the brass lamps. He saluted them with his cup and they nodded back to him, although he knew that none of them were seeing his real, unvarnished image. The sensor that picked up his face used software to parse the virtual avatar the others saw, advanced suites of pattern-matching programs that did away with tells and flattened vocal stress inflections; in this way he showed them only the aspects of him that they needed to see.

Data tags showed their locations in the corner of each image; Hengsha, Paris, Dubai, Washington, Singapore, Hong Kong, New York. Among them he saw the protégé, the politician, the thinker, and the businessman, the ones he distrusted and the ones he trusted to lie. He enjoyed another purse-lipped sip of the rich Saint Helena and put down the cup. "Ladies and gentlemen, welcome. Let's begin, shall we?"

As he expected, his protégé spoke first. *"The current project is proceeding as expected. I'm pleased to report that the issue we had with the Hyron materials has now been dealt with."*

"Good," he murmured. "What about the deployments of our agent provocateurs for the active phase?"

"I've staged the operatives in all the standby locations," said the politician, hissing as sibilance caught his words through the link from the American capital. *"We're ahead of schedule."* The other man cleared his throat. *"In addition, the distribution channels are now all in place."*

He looked toward the businessman. "The media?"

The man in Hong Kong nodded once. *"Our control there remains firm. We're already embedding liminal triggers in multiple information streams. I won't bore you with the details."*

He nodded. The demonstrations and confrontations they had gently encouraged were a regular feature on the global news cycle. He turned slightly in the chair and glanced at the feed from Hengsha. "What about production?"

The Asian woman's face tensed. *"Testing has proven... problematic. I've gone as far as I can, but until I have updated schematics for the—"*

Before she could finish, the dry English accent of the scientist issued from the Singaporean link. *"We've been through this. Is it necessary for me to explain once again? This is not an exact science. I told you from the start there would be delays. The work is an iterative process. In any event, I am about to acquire some new... resources that will speed things along."*

He held up a hand to silence the woman before she could frame a retort. "We all understand the circumstances. But we also all understand the importance of this project. I'm sure no one wants to be the participant who slows down the hard work of everyone else." His eyes narrowed and he gave the scientist and the woman a level look. "Solve whatever problems the two of you have and move forward.

We've invested too much time and resources in this to lose ground at this late stage."

"Of course," said the woman. The scientist said nothing, only nodded.

He felt that something needed to be said, and so he stood. "My friends. My fellow perfectibilists." He smiled again, amusing himself with the use of the archaic term.

"None of us harbor any illusions about the delicacy of our work. The burden of governance, the stewardship upon us is great, perhaps at this moment in history greater than any of our group have ever had to shoulder. Humanity is becoming malleable, and we see battle lines being drawn across our society…We alone see this where others do not, and the great responsibility, as ever, falls to us. And so we must have a unity of purpose, yes?"

A series of nods followed his words. They all knew what was at stake. The group was on the cusp of the next great iteration, the placement of the next flagstone in the path that stretched from the day of first foundation in old Ingolstadt, to that glittering human tomorrow a thousand years hence. He felt a tingle of rare excitement in his fingertips; so much of what they did was slow, so gentle and subtle that it was like a breath of wind upon the sails of society. It shifted the path of humanity by degrees, an infinitely long game that measured its turns in years, decades, generations.

But once in a while, a point of criticality would approach. A moment of importance that would act as a fulcrum for the future.

The fall of Constantinople. A sunny June morning in Sarajevo. The detonation of the first atomic bomb. The two burning towers. These and all the others. For those with foresight and the will to act for the greater good, the elite who could lead mankind through the darkness, these moments represented the rise of opportunity. The group's very existence was predicated on times such as these—and if these critical incidents did not occur in the weave of world events by a process of natural evolution, then it was only right that they *create* them.

He nodded to himself. They were the breath of wind on the sails, indeed. But they were also the hand upon the tiller.

He looked across at the face that ghosted before Turner's *Scarlet Sunset,* the other woman watching carefully from the towers of Dubai. "The... impediments," he began, with a sniff. "I'm sure we don't need to discuss names and all. Specifics we can leave to you, yes?"

The olive-skinned woman nodded. *"I have it in hand, Lucius,"* she said, showing her rank to the others with her casual use of his first name. *"The last pieces are being placed upon the board as we speak."* She smiled, and there was no warmth in it. *"The knights are in place to take the bishops and the rooks."*

None of them spoke for a moment, and he found his gaze drawn away once more to the windows. Shafts of sunshine were making a valiant effort to pierce the dreary veils of gray over Geneva, and perhaps if he had been a pious man, he might have thought it to be some sort of good omen. He was long past the point of musing on what might happen to him, should he one day be called to account by human agencies or spiritual ones for what he had done. In his time he had ordered the death of men, the warring of nations, the ruination and the aggrandizement of individual lives, each in its way a tool toward a greater end. This was simply the method at hand; it was how it had to be done, and today was no different.

They would make history happen according to their design, as they had for more than two and a half centuries.

Logan Circle—Washington, D.C.—United States of America

* * *

It was cool inside the parking levels of the Dornier Apartments, the heat of Washington's midday held back by thick concrete and air-con units that labored day and night. The walls were a uniform stone-white, punctuated every few feet by Doric columns that were more ornamental than practical. The sublevel smelled of machines; rubber, hydrocarbons, and the metal tang of batteries.

Anna Kelso glanced back over her shoulder toward the rectangle of light that was the exit, eyeing the pizeopolymer barrier bollards that had yet to retract back into the floor. The agent standing on the lip of the ramp that led up to Logan Circle gave her a nod, which she returned. He had his arms folded across his waist so his jacket stayed closed, hiding the butt of the Hurricane tactical machine pistol nestled in a fast-draw holster. The jacket was United States Secret Service issue, cut wide to hide the bulges, but those things never seemed to hang right on Anna's spare, whipcord frame. She'd long since decided to spring for the extra cash to get an Emile off-the-rack A-line modded by a tailor out in Rosslyn; still, there were days when she looked in the mirror and felt like a collection of angles cloaked in black hound's-tooth. Her dark hair framed a face that masked doubts with severity.

Anna's own firearm, a compact Mustang Arms automatic, sat high in a paddle holster in the small of her back along with two extra clips. Aside from the gun, the only other thing about her that could be considered standard issue was the discreet flag-and-eagle badge on her right lapel; the arfid chip inside today's identifier pin briefly communed with those on the jackets of the men standing in front of the elevator bank. If Kelso had been wearing the wrong pin, or if it squawked an out-of-date pass-code string, each of them would feel a tap on the breast from the tiny device to alert them to an intruder.

She gave the same nod to the other agents. The tallest of the group ran a hand through a buzzcut of steely hair and frowned. Agent-in-Charge Matt Ryan had a boxer's craggy face and a perpetually stern, on-the-job expression.

"You're late, Anna," he said, without real heat. "She'll be on her way down any second."

"Then I'm not late, Matt," she replied, and was rewarded with a smirk from one of the other agents. Kelso had a reputation to live up to.

Ryan folded his arms. "In that case, you can finish the recap for me."

"We can just draw it from the comm pool, sir," said Byrne, the youngest agent on the detail. He tapped his temple as he spoke, where a discreet hexagonal implant module emerged from beneath his hairline. "Data's all up there on the shared hub server."

Ryan shook his head. "I like to hear someone say it out loud. I'm old-school that way." He shot a look at Anna. "Go on."

She shrugged. If the senior agent was trying to catch her off guard, he'd have to do better than that. "Standard three-car detail," she began, gesturing toward the dark blue limousine idling at the curbside and the muscular sport-utility vehicle parked behind it. The third vehicle—a nondescript town car—was already out on the street, waiting for the go-code. "Our principal is one Senator Jane Skyler, and today's move is a short run out to a Cooke's

Row restaurant in Georgetown. The senator is going to take a lunch meeting, then back to her offices for a bunch of briefings." She took a breath. "We're here because she's upset some of the wrong people."

That got a nod from Ryan. "We have a credible threat here, folks. Skyler's stirred up a hornet's nest with a bunch of the West Coast triad families, and they've made it clear she has a target painted on her back."

"D.C. is a long way from California," said the other agent, a dark-skinned guy called Connor. "Do we really think Chinese hoods are going to take potshots at her on the streets of the nation's capital?"

"Whatever we *think*," Ryan replied, putting hard emphasis on the word, "we have our jobs and we'll do them, get me? Just stay focused and this will be a walk in the park."

"Sir." Connor nodded and fell silent.

Anna had to agree. The threats to Skyler's life were real enough, but she knew as well as Ryan did that the detail was there more as a favor for a woman who was a close personal friend of President DeSilvio.

Ryan closed his eyes for a moment and she heard his voice inside her skull. *"Gimme a mode check. All stations report in."* His mouth didn't move, but Anna saw the slight motion in the muscles of his throat as he subvocalized; the communications bead bonded to his mastoid bone picked up the silent whisper and relayed it wirelessly to the radio node encrypted to the protection detail's frequency.

One by one, everyone gave their call-sign code. The last was Agent Laker, who reported he had just entered the elevator and was on the way down. Ryan paused for a moment, his gaze losing focus, and Anna knew that he was using the wireless link to patch into Laker's optics, getting a look at the senator through the other agent's eyes. Then he blinked and it was back to business.

"Saddle up. We're on the move. Stay on open channel."

Connor slid smoothly into the driver's side of the SUV and Byrne clambered into the back. Anna paused, looking to Ryan for her orders as she settled a pair of military-grade sunglasses onto her nose. The elevator arrived with a melodic chime, and he nodded toward the limo. "Ride with Laker. I'll be right behind you."

"I really wasn't late," she said, suddenly feeling compelled to make the excuse. Anna thought about the careworn brass coin in her pocket and her lips thinned.

"I know." He said it without looking back.

Anna opened the limo's door as Senator Skyler emerged with Agent Laker and a man she didn't recognize at her side. Eyes narrowing, she immediately commed Laker with the sub-voc.

"Who is this joker?"

Laker made eye contact. *"Security."*

"We are her security. She knows how this goes, no last-moment changes to the detail."

"It's already been cleared with command. Guess she likes to have a backup."

The man got in the car first, and Anna saw what she expected; a corporate assistant-cum-bodyguard, rail-thin, watchful, with a humorless face. Her optics captured a blink-and-miss-it flash of something under his dark, gold-lined jacket—the grip of a hi-tech nonlethal firearm—and a discreet logo pin in the shape of a stylized bull's skull.

Belltower. As well as getting the American taxpayer to fund her security on the Washington visit, Skyler had also dropped what had to be some serious cash on a personal guard from the largest private military contractor on the planet.

The senator was speaking firmly into a vu-phone as she approached. "I don't care what Phil Mead wants, Ruthie. I don't like the man and I don't like his policies. Tell the governor he can go look for his endorsements somewhere else." Snapping the device shut, she afforded Anna a wan smile and climbed in.

Kelso was the last after Laker, and as the door thumped shut the limo set off. She didn't need to look forward to see that the town car was already on point, as the SUV slipped seamlessly into the six o'clock position behind the senator's vehicle.

Anna gave the interior of the limousine a once-over, and found herself looking Skyler in the eye. The senator reminded her of a history teacher she'd had in junior high, plump but not overweight, with a pinched face and hawkish eyes.

"I don't often see female agents with the Secret Service," said Skyler, as the convoy crossed onto Q Street and turned westward.

"There's a fair few of us," Anna replied. "It's not that much of a boys' club anymore, ma'am."

"What's your name?"

"Agent Anna Kelso, Senator."

Skyler smiled in a way that was ever so slightly patronizing. "Did they put you on my detail because I'm a woman, Agent Kelso?"

"No, ma'am," Anna replied. "They put me on your

detail because, like my colleagues, I'm very good at what I do." She could almost hear Ryan wincing in the trailing car.

The Belltower operative, who was in the middle of pouring a glass of water for the senator, shot her a look.

"That's very reassuring," said Skyler as she took the glass. "I'm sure you have a lot of people to protect, and I appreciate your hard work today." She paused for a sip and then leaned forward. "Do you mind if I ask you a personal question?"

The woman's request wrong-footed Anna, but she covered it. "I guess so."

Skyler pointed at her face. "Can I see your eyes?"

Laker gave her a quizzical look, but Anna complied, taking off the sunglasses and giving the senator her full attention. It wasn't as if she really needed to wear them— her cyberoptic implants had full-spectrum UV and solar protection built in—but they were as much a part of the Secret Service "uniform" as the black jacket and pants.

Skyler leaned closer, studying her. "Your eyes... Caidin optics, am I right? I understand your agency also requires the implantation of certain communications and enhancile cyberware as well, is that so?"

Anna was uncertain where this conversation was heading. "Yes, ma'am."

"How do you feel about that?" the senator went on. "I don't have any implants myself, I don't ask for them for my staff. How do you feel about your government insisting on such a thing for you to do your job?"

"Not every Secret Service agent is enhanced," Anna replied. "That would be prejudicial."

Skyler sat back. "Really? Tell me, how many field agents do you know who are not implantees?"

Anna frowned. "I'm not sure I see your point, Senator." But she did.

"You know what I'm doing here, don't you?" said the politician. "The president has asked me to chair a Senate subcommittee with the National Science Board on America's involvement with the science and industry of human augmentation technology. The very reason I have that job is because of what I've done to make myself a target for certain criminal groups."

The briefing on Skyler had been clear on all that, Anna reflected. Back home in SoCal, Skyler's hard, pro-science stance on tech smuggling had also led to a crackdown on something the press liked to call "harvester" crimes—the 2020s' equivalent of the old urban legend about guys waking up in a bath of ice sans a kidney... Only this time, victims were unlucky souls killed and stripped for their cybernetic augmentations. In the United States, the high price of many augs put them beyond the range of most regular citizens; trading in so-called recovered cyberware was fast becoming one of the key revenue streams for the triad gangs and their rivals, right after people-trafficking and drugs. Skyler's home state was the gateway to America for the snakeheads in Beijing, Hengsha, and Hong Kong.

As for understanding all the rest of it... well, Anna watched CNN and the Picus WorldView channel just like everyone else. People were always looking for ways to divide themselves, and the line between "augmented" and "natural" was just another take after race, religion, gender...

"My job," Skyler went on, her tone bordering on that of a lecture, "is to determine what kind of stance America should take on augmentation, to find out if this emerging technology can benefit our nation's economy."

The car slowed as they approached Buffalo Bridge. "Are you asking for my opinion, ma'am?" said Anna.

That seemed to amuse the senator. "No, Agent Kelso. But the fact is, the man I'm meeting for lunch runs the company that made those striking eyes of yours. Garrett Dansky, chief executive of Caidin Global. Tell me, did he do a good job?"

Anna resisted the urge to put the glasses back on. "I'd say so."

"And you don't feel... *diminished* by your augmentations?"

Her lips thinned. "I'm not like the panzer girls on *Ultimate Aug Fighters,* if that's what you mean." Anna kept her expression neutral; what implants she did have were mostly neural units, small-scale stuff that didn't disrupt her natural profile. "I'm good at what I do. These make me even better."

Skyler seemed to accept that and drew back, sipping her water.

"*You okay?*" Ryan's voice was a gentle pressure on the back of her head. A telltale at the corner of her optic field showed he was speaking to her on a channel isolated from the rest of the team.

"*Fine.*" She knew what he was going to say next, the question he was going to ask, about the phone call the night before; she headed him off. "*Really, Matt. I'm good.*" It was a lie.

He didn't reply. Instead, he cut the one-on-one link

as the convoy began to slow, the black iron fences of Montrose Park flashing past. They were a few moments away.

"Senator?" said the Belltower operative. He had a soft, polite voice. Skyler nodded and checked her reflection in the limo's windows.

"Dansky's there," said a voice from the lead car. *"Taking our station."*

"Copy," said Laker out loud.

Skyler's car halted and Anna was first out. Her other concerns were forgotten in a heartbeat. She was working now, her eyes scanning the street and the buildings, passing over the windows of the terraced houses with speed and care. She heard the SUV halt, heard the doors opening.

The senator was out and walking forward, Laker and the Belltower bodyguard flanking her. Dansky came up, a smile on his face, extending a hand.

When she scanned the street a second time, that was the moment when Anna Kelso felt a twist in the depths of her gut. It was an immediate, visceral reaction, and she couldn't quantify it at first. She glanced in Ryan's direction. He was looking at her with a questioning expression.

Something rang a wrong note in Anna's thoughts. She'd taken in the whole of the street scene, parsed it in a moment, just like they had taught her—and something did not fit.

Across the diagonal of Q Street, a silver Motokun sedan sat low on its shocks, as if it were too heavily loaded. The windows were opaque, and unbidden, Anna's hand slipped back under her jacket through force of habit.

She caught Byrne's gaze and he saw where she was looking; the younger agent's enhanced optics had a T-wave scanner that could peer through light cover. He peered at the Motokun and the sudden change on his face told her she was right.

"Tangos—!" Byrne's voice was suddenly lost in a roar of engine noise, and the sedan bolted forward from the opposite curb, tires screeching as the vehicle sped over the asphalt.

Anna's gun was clearing its holster as the silver sedan slammed into the back end of the town car and spun it about, ramming it up onto the sidewalk and into the line of planters ringing the restaurant's open-air terrace. The sedan's doors burst open and there were four hulking figures in black combat gear boiling out into the daylight. Each of them had a churning smoke bomb in his hand, and they threw them as one, lines of thick gray haze arcing up over the roadway.

Anna heard screaming coming from behind her, the clatter of tables being turned over and glass shattering as the restaurant's customers panicked and ran; and then she heard another sound, the familiar flat report of a grenade launcher.

She never saw the shell hit. One second she was bringing up her Mustang to bear, and in the next the hood of the limousine distorted and threw itself upward as an orange fireball consumed the front third of the vehicle.

A hot wall of gasoline-stink backwash hit Anna Kelso head-on and blew her into the lines of iron planters.

Inside her head, she could hear Ryan crying for help.

* * *

The Grey Range—Queensland—Australia

The veetol moved low and fast over the foothills, skimming the trees with barely a half-meter's clearance between the landing skids and the barren branches of the canopy. Dawn was still two hours away and the grim, moonless night drew in what little noise came from the tilt rotors at the veetol's wingtips, flattening the sound. No illumination emanated from the boxy aircraft; behind a blank, windowless canopy, the pilot guided the veetol by multiple sensor inputs from video feeds, laser-ranging returns, and a global satellite tracking system that delivered moment-by-moment data on the landscape flashing past beneath. Passing below any radar detection threshold, the aircraft rose and fell with the nap of the earth, closing inexorably on its target.

The map provided to Strike Team Six floated in the air above the metal floor of the flyer's cargo bay, projected from a holographic imager held steady in Ben Saxon's hand. He turned it slightly so he could study the patterns of the guard towers ringing the insurgent camp. Saxon had a habit of pulling at his short, unkempt beard whenever he was deep in thought, and he did it now, peering into the glowing red wire frame as if the virtual would give him some sudden new insight into the mission.

"Five minutes out, boss," said Pete Kano, nudging him in the ribs, pitching his voice to be heard over the steady thrum of the rotors. Saxon nodded, glancing at his second in command. They were a study in contrasts; the African was tall and deceptively wiry in build, big enough that he never looked comfortable inside the cramped confines of a transport helo or APC, while Saxon was stocky and of average height. Where Kano might have been an athlete, Saxon resembled a street fighter—but there was no other man he would have wanted to stand with him on a mission as difficult as this one.

Saxon had been running Strike Six for Belltower Associates Incorporated for a little over two years now, and Kano was the only man who had stayed with him for all that time. Where Saxon had been recruited directly from the British Army's Special Air Service, Kano had "liberated" himself from a Namibian crime lord's war band after a Belltower battalion had wiped out his former boss's drug-running network. The rest of the team had similarly diverse origins, men and women gathered up from national armies, police forces, criminal groups, all of them drawn in by steady pay and high rates of danger money from the largest private army in the world.

Saxon wasn't one to shy away from the word "mercenary." It was what he was, what he did for a living; calling himself a "military contractor" made it sound softer, somehow—and Ben Saxon liked the grit of the real thing. It was the main reason he had walked into Belltower's offices on the very same day the armed forces of His Majesty's Crown had told him that his services were no longer required; the idea of a life on civvie street just simply did not register with him. He liked it here in the thick; it felt *right*.

As the mission clock display hovering in the corner of Saxon's eye line dropped to the four-minute mark, Kano gave the nod to the rest of the crew, and together they ran through their final weapons and equipment checks.

Saxon hefted the weight of the Steiner-Bisley FR-27 assault rifle slung across his chest and double-checked that the ammunition carousel was locked in place, the safety catch set. Eyes closed, he ran his fingers down the grenades and gear packs clipped to his webbing vest, mentally ticking them off one by one. Then, he blink-triggered the diagnostic subroutine for his augmentations; the legs and the arm, the optics, the feed-forward system, reflex jack, all of it. A line of green dots superimposed on his vision told him he was at full operational status.

He drew a breath. "All right, boys and girls. Get ready. Everyone, take your jabs now. I don't want any of you getting the shakes or coughing up blood in the middle of this." He pulled a rod-shaped injector pen from a pocket and waggled it at them. A line of frowns and grim nods greeted him, and his team mirrored his action as he dosed himself in the wrist of his one meat arm. The injector nipped at the flesh and he felt a brief, cool rush through his veins; the drug load inside the pen was a cocktail of battlefield medicines—pan-spectral antigens supposedly strong enough to counter any standard combat toxins, antimalaria meds, and a light measure of stims, all topped off with a dose of high-strength neuropozyne. The nupoz was a necessary evil for anyone with a body full of augmentations. Without it, normal human cellular function would eventually coat any implant tech with scar tissue and corrupt the interface between meat and metal; Saxon had seen the results of it, the jitters and the pain that could turn even the toughest cog-head into a palsied wreck.

He took a moment to have a sip of tepid water from a canteen on his belt and swilled it around his mouth.

They'd been in the Australian theater now for more than six weeks, and Saxon could not get used to the dusty taste the country put at the back of his throat. He glanced at Sam Duarte, the most recent addition to Strike Six, a former gangbanger from the barrios of South America. Covered in complex street thug iconography, he looked less like a soldier and more like a stickup man—but Duarte had proven himself a lot better than just a street-corner gunsel after the team had been caught in an ambush out at Coober Pedy.

It was Duarte who had explained about the dust; it was the trees. Up north, where the Free States forces were running wild, they were torching whole swathes of countryside, sending plumes of acidic ash into the sky. What drifted down toward the southern regions was what Saxon couldn't wash out of his throat.

Belltower had been a part of the Australian conflict from the outset; at first they had just been corporate security, working for a petrochem conglomerate from Victoria drilling test wells in Aussie-held Antarctica. No one had expected them to find the biggest strike of the century under the ice shelf—and where there was oil, there was power. Fossil fuel's grip on the world still hadn't slackened, even as the fourth decade of the second millennium fast approached.

The political tensions that were already in place across the nation ground against each other, and soon the north was siding with Chinese interests after the same resources, while Victoria, New South Wales, Tasmania, and a handful of other territories hastily formed the South Australian Federation off the back of their black-gold bonanza.

And now there was a line of red across the middle of the continent, with car bombs and IEDs, camps and threats, and a conflict that would burn slow and long. While the north got on with ex–People's Republic hardware and "advisors" flown in from Beijing and Taiwan, the south had newly deep pockets, and Belltower had been right there to pick up the payday. A third of the Australian conflict was being waged by private military contractors, and the lion's share belonged to Saxon's employers.

Today they were going to earn their pay.

The mission's code name was Operation Rainbird; it was a multiple-level strike package comprising aerial bombardment of several northern forward posts and drone attacks on staging areas down the line from Cunnamulla to Quilpie, setting a column of fire that would be seen all the way to Fortress Brisbane. Strike Six had a special objective that fell into their more "direct action" remit, however—they were going to an insurgent training camp near Mount Intrepid to raze it to the ground.

Saxon and his men took the mission because they wanted it. The insurgents trained at Intrepid had killed the man whose place Duarte had filled, and they had tried to kill them all at Coober Pedy. For Strike Six, this had become personal.

Personal. The word echoed in Saxon's thoughts and he looked away. He'd been in this so long, letting Belltower take him from conflict to conflict—Brazil, Afghanistan, Lithuania, Turkey, Iceland, and all the others—that the days blurred into one. The missions…The mission and the mission and the mission, one after another, eating up his life, keeping him in the place where he did what he was best at.

But then the paper came. Real paper, a real letter, not some e-doc in his data stack. Belltower's top echelons liked to do that kind of thing, he remembered. They liked the old, traditional ways, all of them blue bloods out of Sandhurst or West Point, holding on to cap-badge rituals and honors. *Personal*, embossed on the envelope in bright red ink.

In plain and simple words the paper told him his contract was about to end. Another month, and the blood that Ben Saxon had spilled for them would evaporate. He would be free to take his pay and his shares and leave his guns behind, free to take a different path at the crossroads.

His gaze turned inward, and Saxon's lip curled in cold amusement. How could they ever expect him to do anything else but reenlist? It was a joke that they would even ask him. What purpose would a man like him find in the civilian world? The truth was, half the augmentations in him were classed as lethal weapons in more than a dozen countries. If he stepped out, what would happen to him? Would he be stripped down, *defanged*? A predator hobbled so it could fit in with the outside world?

Saxon had never connected to anyone outside; his family was long gone. He had no life beyond the unit, no loyalty to anyone but the unit. The paper made him angry. Offering him the choice was almost an insult.

"*Jefe?*" His attention snapped back to the moment; Duarte was speaking to him, and he'd tuned the young man out.

"What is it?" He covered his moment of reverie by checking his rifle once again.

Sam ran a hand over his shorn scalp, across the wine-dark lines of an intricate angel design, wings spread across his temples. "These northern guys, they're tough, yeah?"

"Not so you'd notice."

The words had barely left his mouth when the deck of the veetol tilted sharply without warning, and a scattering of loose items tumbled away. Saxon grunted as the bulkhead at his back pressed into him, and the straps holding him to the acceleration rack pulled tight, forcing air from his lungs.

The countdown clock read one minute twenty-six; they were still a long way out from the drop point. Another second dropped away and the cargo bay was filled with the dull bray of an alarm.

Amid the sound of it, every member of Strike Team Six heard the fear in the voice of the pilot as he broadcast over their mastoid comms. *"Drones!"*

Saxon's gut flooded with ice. Flying low and fast kept the veetol well out of the detection envelope of any surface-to-air missiles, but drones were a different story. Autonomous unmanned aerial vehicles, the northern forces had taken to layering them in sleeper pods along the line of the border, where they would sit dormant until something that didn't match their preprogrammed library of friendly silhouettes passed overhead.

But this sector had been swept for drones. Belltower's near-flawless intelligence corps had given Saxon the briefing. *No drones. A clear run. Direct line of assault.*

"What the hell?" Kano snarled, doubtless mirroring Saxon's train of thought.

He turned toward the African in time to see the first of the heavy rounds from the attack drone's cannon puncture the hull and the tall man's chest. Blood misted the cabin's interior as more armor-piercing shells ripped fist-size holes in the fuselage and flight systems.

Acrid smoke filled Saxon's lungs as he felt gravity snare the veetol and pull it toward the ground.

TWO

Anna rose up from where she had fallen, her arm tight with pain in a line of new bruises, all along the points where she had collided with the heavy planters. She felt woozy and her hearing was flattened and woolly from the concussion of the grenade blast. She could smell smoke and dirt and the cloying scent of crushed flowers.

The agent made it up to her knees and blinked; her optics were blurred like a poorly tuned video image, the delicate subsystems of the augmetic eyes cycling through a reset mode. Her vision hazed from black and white to color, and she saw her pistol lying among a drift of broken window glass. Anna loped forward, and stooped to gather up her weapon, eyes darting around.

As her fingers tightened around the butt of the Mustang automatic, she felt a sharp jerk at her back that dragged her off balance. Kelso saw the hood of the stalled town car coming up to meet her and she brought up her hand just in time to block the new impact. Slipping down over the crumpled fender, cursing, she saw her assailant.

It was one of the figures from the car, dressed head to foot in black combat fatigues with a zip hood that closed like a mask over his face. The man was easily twice her body mass, and protruding from the ends of his jacket sleeves were hands of dull machined metal. Her hearing was coming back by degrees, and she heard his combat boots crunching on the glass as the attacker balled a knot of her expensive Emile jacket between those steel fingers and hauled her off her feet. She struggled, but her arms felt like lead.

Blank eyes, shark-black and wet, measured her; this bastard was playing games, tossing her about like a rag doll—but now that was going to end, now he was going to kill her. The other hand came up and clamped around her bare neck and squeezed like a vise. Anna tried to scream, but the sound died in her throat, trapped there. A cascade of warning icons rained down across the inside of her eyes, fed from the implanted biomonitor tracking her vitals. She heard her bloodstream thundering in her ears.

The Mustang was heavy and dead in her grip. It was a block of iron, dragging her down. It took all her effort to lift it, her exertion ending in stifled gasps.

He saw the movement, and tried to deflect her, knock the gun away. Anna jerked the trigger by reflex and the pistol roared. The first discharge missed, but the muzzle flash flared bright across the killer's eye line and he snarled; for a moment his grip slackened and Kelso pushed away, turning. When she fired again, the round hit him at point-blank range through the base of his jaw. Her assailant dropped like a felled tree, trailing a stream of blood from the back of his head.

Anna went down with him, landing hard for the third time. She pushed away and came up in a crouch, turning away from the mess she'd made of him. A crawling, itchy gale of static was gnawing at the base of her skull—she'd lost the mastoid comm from the blast. Putting the dead man out of her thoughts, she moved off, low and quick behind collapsed tables and fallen chairs, wincing with pain at each step.

There was thick smoke everywhere; all of Q Street was wreathed in it, the drifting haze of gray mist put out by the distraction grenades churning with the dark black pall from the burning limo. The rebreather implant in her chest stiffened; she'd use it if she needed to. A strident chorus of pealing car alarms was crying up and down the street, warning lights flashing. She glimpsed Connor lying at the curb, his torso a red ruin of bullet impacts. The agent's eyes were lifeless, staring into nothing.

Anna kept moving. The crackle of automatic rounds sounded nearby, and she heard someone call out. The words were lost to her, but she knew Matt Ryan's voice when she heard it. She could make out the vague shape of the SUV—he had to be there, with Skyler. The Secret Service's first priority was always to their principal, and Ryan would be doing everything he could to get the woman out of danger.

A figure moved in the smoke, and she called to it, stifling a cough. "Matt?"

The gunshot that answered her struck Anna in the gut and she cried out. Burning, white-hot agony seared her belly and she recoiled, stumbling against a low wall. Her legs turned to water and she slipped down, a blossom of stark crimson blooming across the white silk blouse beneath her jacket. The round had gone straight through the Kevlar undershirt and buried itself in the meat of her. The agony was like nothing she had ever felt before. Her hands tightened into fists; her pistol was gone, spinning away out of reach. She felt a tightness in her chest as her biomonitor's active response system released protein threads into her bloodstream, racing to the source of the injury.

The SUV's engine rumbled, and the taillights glowed white as the gears shifted; they were going to get away, get Skyler to safety. Kelso felt panic rising in her thoughts. She was going to be left behind.

The haze was thinning, and for one random moment, a breath of clear air passed before her. She saw Byrne and Ryan with Skyler between them—the senator was slack, semiconscious—trying to maneuver the woman into the back of the SUV and keep a watch for the assailants at the same time. Dansky was staggering after them, pressing a bloody kerchief to a nasty wound on his face.

Anna tried to get up, but the pain flared in her torso like another bullet hit, and it forced her back down. She was gasping for breath when she saw the figure again.

Like the one she had killed, he was broad and thickset—a linebacker profile, black-clad and lethal. He lacked the obvious cyberlimbs of the dead man, but he moved through the smoke without pause; he had to be tracking his targets with a thermographic implant. In the assailant's hand was a large frame automatic, the length of it doubled by a cylindrical silencer.

Dansky caught sight of the armed man and cried out; the gun replied with a metallic cough and the executive went down. Anna's heart hammered in her chest as she saw what would come next. She shouted Ryan's name, the pain rising with it, and he turned toward the sound, pushing himself in front of Skyler to shield her from attack.

The next shots took Byrne in the throat and the face, ending him before he hit the asphalt. Ryan returned fire, his rounds going wide.

Anna's legs felt numb and unresponsive. She lurched forward, but the limbs were dead meat. The coppery stink of her own blood filled her nostrils and she gagged. She wanted to look away. She wanted to, but she couldn't.

The assailant went in for the kill and Ryan threw himself at the figure. There was a scuffle, and the agent tore open the zip hood. Kelso got a look at the face underneath—all fury and exertion, sallow and Nordic, with a shock of ice-blond hair. He clubbed Matt Ryan across the skull with the butt of the pistol, knocking him down. Then, with care, the killer took aim and ended him with a single shot.

Anna felt her friend die, the awful inevitability of it. She felt the horrific sense of the moment pass through her like an electric shock as Ryan crumpled into a nerveless heap and was still.

Everything about him, everything he was, the good, honest man who had done so much to help her…all of it gone in less than a second. Tears streamed down her dirty, bloodstained cheeks as she struggled to hold on to consciousness, her pain overwhelming everything. *It all seemed impossible, unreal…*

The killer halted for a long second, and she recognized the body language of someone conducting a sub-voc conversation. Then, very deliberately, he turned to examine Senator Skyler, where the woman lay half in and half out of the SUV. She tried to hold up her hands to ward him off. In the distance, sirens were approaching.

Anna waited for the next shot, but it never came. Even with all the madness unfolding around her, confusion rose in her thoughts as the assailant walked away, leaving Skyler very much alive. Instead, he crossed to where Dansky was lying on the edge of the restaurant patio, and shot the man again.

Then he turned to look toward her, and once more Anna got a good look at the sharp angles of the man's face.

It was the last thing she saw, as the thundering in her ears grew loud and dragged her down toward blackness.

The Grey Range—Queensland—Australia

Saxon never felt the impact.

A split second before the veetol collided with the hillside, jets of shock foam flooded the cargo bay with gouts of yellowy matter, reeking of chemical stink. The fluid sprayed across him, the frothing mass instantly hardening as it made contact with the air. He gagged and coughed as some of the foam made it into his mouth, his nostrils. It enveloped his body, smothering him.

The aircraft crashed down and ripped itself to bits as it drew a long black gouge of scorched earth across the tree line, the wings and rotors shearing away in puffs of high-octane flame. Somebody was screaming.

The cockpit was crushed and the fuselage torn open. Inside, Saxon was slammed around his makeshift cushion, and for long seconds he teetered on the brink of losing consciousness. He grunted with the exertion of keeping himself awake, and with a final, tortured screech of stressed metal, the wreck of the flyer tumbled to a halt, inverted, half buried in a drift of loose earth packed around the nose cone.

A wave of punishing heat pressed in on Saxon through the cowl of the solidified shock foam and he felt it running like molten wax under his hands. He dragged his left arm up through the mass and his fingers found the handle of the heavy jungle knife, lying in its holster atop his shoulder pad. The soldier lurched forward, cutting through the clogged restraint straps still holding him in his seat, then down through the thick foam-matter.

He used his right arm, his cyberarm, to peel back the curdled material. A gust of hot, putrid air washed over him. The cloying, sickly-sweet stench of burned flesh and the tang of spent aviation fuel made him cough and spit out a thick gobbet of bloody phlegm.

Fire beat at him; the cargo bay was open to the night on one side where an entire quadrant of the fuselage had peeled back off the veetol's skeletal airframe. The rest of the space was filled with black smoke and sheets of orange flame. Seats where men and women had been strapped in were now little more than charred, indefinable things. The smoke was thickening by the moment, and he wheezed, cursing, calling out their names as he sliced through the straps still holding him upside down. The knife cut the last and he dropped, falling badly. A shard of agony shot up from his right hip and he howled.

The flames were all around him now, and Saxon felt the hairs of his rough beard crisping with the heat. He stumbled forward, reaching for spars of broken steel, searching for a foothold to get him up and out of the wreckage. The metal was red-hot and he hissed in pain as it burned his palms through his combat gloves. The smoke churned around him, clogging his lungs. It was leaching the life from him, dragging on him. His chest felt like it was full of razors.

Saxon gripped the fire-scorched spars and dragged himself up the side of the fuselage, ignoring the singing pain from the places where jagged swords of hull metal slashed his torso and his meat arm. Then he was out, falling into the dusty brown loam churned by the crash. He grasped for his canteen, and through some miracle it was still clipped to his gear belt. Saxon thumbed off the cap and swallowed a chug of water, only to cough it back up a second later. Panting, he staggered a few steps from the wreckage.

The tree-lined hill extended away, becoming steeper, falling to a fast-flowing creek bed a few hundred meters below. A black arrow of smoke was rising swiftly into the night air. There was little wind, so the line was like a marker pointing directly to the crash site.

He stopped, fighting down the twitches of an adrenaline rush and took stock, running the system check. Red lights joined the green, and there were more of them than he wanted to see.

He couldn't stay here. The drone that had shot them down would be vectoring back to scope the crash site, and if he was here when that happened...

Kano's face rose in his thoughts and Saxon swore explosively. He glared back at the burning veetol. *Am I the only one who survived?*

"Anyone hear me?" he called, his voice husky and broken. "Strike Six, sound off!"

At first he heard only the sullen crackle of the hungry flames, but then a voice called out—wounded, but nearby. He turned toward it.

Pieces of hull were scattered over a copse of thin, broken trees, small fires burning in patches of spilled fuel. Saxon blinked his optic implants to their ultraviolet frequency setting and something made itself clear against the white-on-blue cast of the shifted image.

A hand flailed from underneath a wing panel, and he moved to it, crouching to put his shoulder under the long edge. Bracing against a boulder, Saxon forced it away and heard a moan of pain.

Sam Duarte looked up at him from the dirt, his tawny face a mess of scratches. The young mercenary's legs were blackened and twisted at unnatural angles; he'd likely been thrown clear of the veetol when it plowed through the trees, but the luck that saved him from being immolated had left him broken.

"*Jefe...*" he gasped. "You're bleeding."

"Later," Saxon said, and bent down to gather Duarte up, hauling him to his feet. The other man grunted with a deep hurt as he put weight on his right leg, and Saxon frowned. "Can you walk?"

"Not on my own," came the reply. "*Madre de dios,* where the hell did that drone come from?" Duarte looked around, blinking. "Where...Where's Kano and the others?"

Saxon could smell the burned meat stench on himself and he couldn't say the words; his silence was enough, though, and Duarte shook his head and crossed himself. "We have to move," said Saxon. "You got a weapon?"

The other man shook his head again, so Saxon drew

the black-anodized shape of a heavy Diamondback .357 revolver from a holster on his belt, and pressed it into Duarte's hands. "That vulture, he'll be coming back," he said, checking the loads.

Saxon nodded, casting around, scanning the drift of wreckage. He'd lost his FR-27 in the crash, but the veetol had been carrying cases loaded with extra weapons for Operation Rainbird. He spotted one off to the side and made for it.

Rainbird. The mission had been blown before they even reached the target zone. Saxon's mind raced as he ran through the possibilities. Had they been compromised from the start? It was unlikely. Belltower's mercenary forces were the best paid in the world, and there was an unwritten rule that once you wore the bull badge, you were part of a brotherhood. The company did not tolerate traitors in the ranks. Belltower policed itself, often with lethal intensity.

He reached the case and tried the locks, but they were stuck fast. The knife came out again, and he worked the tip into the broken mechanism.

"The intel... " Duarte said out loud, his thoughts mirroring those of his squad leader. "The mission intel had to be bogus..."

"No," Saxon insisted.

"No?" Duarte echoed him, his tone changing, becoming more strident. "We had a clear highway, *jefe*! You saw the data. No drones for twenty miles."

The lock snapped and Saxon cracked the case. "Must've been a mistake..."

"Belltower intel never makes mistakes!" Duarte

snapped, coughing. "That's what they always tell us!" He tried to lurch forward on his one good leg. "Whatever happened, we're screwed now... "

Saxon shot him an angry glare. "You secure that crap right now, *Corporal,*" he said, putting hard emphasis on the young man's rank. "Just shut your mouth and do what I bloody well tell you to, and I promise I'll get you back to whatever barrio rattrap you call home."

Duarte sobered, and then gave a pained chuckle. "Hell, no. I joined up to get out of my barrio rattrap. I'll settle for just getting away from *here.*"

"Yeah, I hear you." Saxon dragged a bandolier of shells from the case and pulled a heavy, large-gauge shoulder arm from the foam pads inside. The G-87 was a grenade launcher capable of throwing out a half-dozen 40 mm high-explosive shells in a matter of seconds; the Americans called it "the Linebacker." He cracked open the magazine and began thumbing the soda-can-size rounds into the feed. He was almost done when he heard the low whine of ducted rotors overhead.

"Incoming!" shouted Duarte, and the soldier stumbled toward a twist of wreckage.

Saxon looked up and shifted the optics to low-light, instantly painting the whole sky in shades of dark green and glittering white. He caught movement as something ungainly and fast wheeled and turned above them. The wings of the drone changed aspect and folded close to the spindly fuselage as it dove at them. Saxon glimpsed a ball festooned with glassy lenses tucked underneath the nose of the robot aircraft as it turned to single him out.

He broke into a run and vaulted away over fallen tree

trunks just as the clattering hammer of heavy-caliber bullets ripped into the place where he had been standing. Saxon rolled, hearing the deep report of the Diamondback as Duarte fired after the drone. The aircraft's engine note throbbed and changed as it went up into a stall turn and came about.

"The trees," Saxon shouted, working a dial on the grenade launcher. "Get to the trees. We stay in the open, we'll be cut to shreds!"

Duarte didn't reply; he just ran, as best he could, half-staggering, half-falling. Saxon looked up, finding the drone as it came hunting once more. He pulled the G-87 to his shoulder, almost aiming straight up, and squeezed the trigger. With a hollow grunt, the weapon discharged a shell in an upward arc. The dial set the grenade fuse for a half second, but even as the drone passed over him, Saxon knew he had misjudged the shot. The shell exploded and the robot flyer bucked from the near hit, but maintained its dive.

His blood ran cold as the aircraft put on a burst of speed and fell toward Duarte, like a cheetah zeroing in on a wounded gazelle. "Sam!"

The soldier twisted and raised the revolver, the bright stab of discharge from the muzzle flaring in the low-light optics. The heavy cannon, slung in a conformal pod along the length of the drone's ventral fuselage, opened up with a sound like a jackhammer—and Sam Duarte was torn apart in a puff of white.

"*Bastard!*" Saxon rose from cover, screaming his fury at the machine as it looped and turned inbound once more, preparing to finish the job at hand. He broke out and ran as fast as he could toward the steeper slope where the trees were denser, the grenade launcher bouncing against his chest, his every breath a ragged, gasping effort. The cannon started up again as he reached the perimeter of the tree line, and Saxon turned as he ran, mashing the trigger. The remaining three rounds in the magazine chugged into the air one after another, exploding barely a heartbeat apart at a height just above the canopy. The drone's delicate sensors were blinded by the flashes and the scattering of shrapnel, and it lost its target. The flyer drifted off course and clipped a tall tree; in seconds it was spinning and coming apart, shredding into a new firestorm of burning metal.

The detonation sent Saxon sprawling and he lost his footing. The soldier slipped over the lip of the hill and tumbled headfirst down the steep, crumbling face, bouncing hard. Unable to arrest his descent, he fell pinwheeling over the edge and into the muddy waters of the creek below.

Washington Hospital Center—Washington, D.C.—United States of America

Sensation returned to her by degrees, assembling itself piece by piece, line by line. She had the sense of being in a bed, the cotton sheets pressing against her legs, the prickly feel of the mattress cloth beneath. Her lips were cold and dry, a steady breath of oxygen flowing from a plastic mask resting on her face. Anna felt worn and old, broken and twisted. Her body seemed dislocated from her; she expected pain. Why wasn't there any pain?

With difficulty, she turned her head on the pillow

beneath it and felt warmth on her face. Licking her lips, she tried to speak, but all that emerged was a hollow gasp. It was dark all around her, a strange dimensionless void that she couldn't grasp.

Then footsteps, people nearby. A voice. "Anna? Can you hear me?"

"Yes."

"Okay, just lie still. You're in the hospital. Try not to move."

The oxygen mask was pulled away and she licked her lips. "Why...is it dark?"

"Okay, nurse, thank you." Someone else coughed and she heard the familiar shuffle of expensive Italian loafers, a door closing. "Hey, Anna. It's me, Ron. I'm here with Hank Bradley from Division. Just take it easy."

"Ron?" Agent-in-Charge Ronald Temple was Kelso's supervisor, a decent guy with a long career in the Secret Service. She hadn't expected to hear him. "What's wrong?"

"Agent Kelso..." The next voice was Bradley's. Anna didn't know the man as well as Temple, just by hearsay and reputation as something of a hard ass; he was a senior agent working liaison with the Secret Service and the Department of Justice. His presence underlined the gravity of what had happened. "I'm afraid we had to take your eyes."

"What?" Her hand automatically reached upward. Pads of gauze covered her face, and in a sickening moment of understanding, she realized that the orbits of her skull were empty. Something hard and plastic protruded through the bandages from one of the sockets.

"We can't talk like this. Wait a second." Bradley came

closer and Anna heard the whisper of a cable uncoiling. Something connected with a snap and she felt a sudden giddy rush of vertigo as an image exploded before her.

She saw a strange figure swaddled in bandages and crowded by electronic devices, like a hi-tech mummy. Monitors and an oxygen cylinder framed a bruised, puffy face. "I can see again." The figure mimed the words as she said them, and then the point of view shifted, taking in Ron Temple at the window, framed by sunlight. His round face was tight with concern. "Me. I'm looking at me."

The view bobbed. "I'm running you a feed from my optic implants," said Bradley. A thin, brassy cable extended from inside his right-hand cuff and into a socket on the temporary eye interface.

"I look like shit," she managed, swallowing a sob.

Temple came to the bed and perched on the edge, taking her hand. "Yeah, sweetheart, you do. But you'll be okay. The doctors got the round out of you, it didn't hit anything vital. Tissue damage mostly. The Kevlar took the brunt of the impact, slowed it down some."

The next words fell from her in a breathy rush. "Matt's dead. Byrne and Connor, too…"

Temple gave a shallow sigh. "Anna…They're all dead. You're the only one in the detail to make it."

"We hoped Hansen, the Belltower guy, might pull through," said Bradley. "They lost him on the operating table."

"How long have I been in here?" She gripped Temple's hand hard.

"Four days."

"The senator?"

Bradley's point-of-view nodded again. "She's okay. We already got a statement from her. That, plus imagery from the traffic cams, and we're assembling a model of the incident. But that's why we had to subpoena your optics. You're the only one who got a good look at a face. I had tech forensics from the FBI reconstruct a few stills from the data in the image buffer."

"We'll get you replacements," Temple noted. "Good stuff, new Caidins or maybe Sarif..." He handed her a sip-bulb of water. "I'm sorry you had to wake up blind..."

"Thanks for being here, sir," she said, taking a drink of the cooling fluid. "Has someone—" Anna took a shaky breath and started again. "Has someone told Jenny?" Jennifer Ryan was Matt's wife of some sixteen years. They had two girls, Susan and Carole. She remembered their house as a warm, welcoming place.

Temple nodded gravely. "She knows. I'm sorry, Anna."

"I understand you and Agent Ryan were close?" asked Bradley.

The other man answered before she could. "Ryan was her...mentor."

"Something like that," said Anna, the words barely a whisper. She swallowed and straightened up. "Do you have the images with you? Can I see them?"

Bradley and Temple shared a look. "Okay," said the agent, and he drew a folding Pocket Secretary PDA from his jacket; it opened up, blooming like a metallic flower. Bradley hesitated, then held it in front of him, tabbing through the virtual pages. "We're sifting through witness statements at the moment, still building the picture."

"Leads are coming together," Temple offered. "We don't have any suspects as yet…These creeps just melted into thin air."

"We had a report about an unmarked helicopter putting down briefly in Montrose Park, but D.C. air traffic control have nothing on that," noted Bradley distractedly.

"I never saw anything," said Anna, her thoughts churning. "What about evidence at the scene?"

Temple shook his head. "No shells—they used caseless ammo. Fiber traces are a dead end, too. We did get a line on the car they used, though. License was fake, most of the registration marks were lasered off, but we got a partial from the engine block. Turns out it was listed as stolen from a shell company that's a known front for the Red Arrow triad."

"I killed one of them," she insisted.

"They torched the corpse before they left," he said. "Thermite grenade. All we got left is a heap of burnt scrap metal and some biological traces that come up blank on the Interpol register."

Bradley gestured with the PDA. "Here's the picture of the shooter."

Anna studied the grainy, ghostly image through the other agent's eyes. The blond hair, the hard, pitiless gaze of the man who killed Matt Ryan caught in midturn.

Suddenly she was back there again, collapsed in the street, wet with blood, racked with agony. Waiting for death. A shudder ran through her.

"Why…Why didn't he kill me?" she breathed.

Temple squeezed her hand. "Best guess is, you lucked out. Black-and-whites from the Georgetown precinct were maybe ten seconds away at that point. Blondie there probably thought you weren't going to survive a gut shot and decided to buck out instead of hanging around to make sure."

"But he didn't kill Skyler," she insisted. "Matt, Byrne, the rest of the team, even the guy the senator was meeting, Dansky…They murdered all of them, but not her. If it was the triads, why the hell is she still breathing?"

"A warning," said Bradley. "This is the Red Arrow telling Skyler to back off from chasing down the harvesters in SoCal. They're showing her that she can be got to, no matter where she is, or who's protecting her… " He trailed off and ran a hand through his hair. "This whole thing is a mess. These people have made the Service look incompetent. Even Skyler's started distancing herself."

"Sure she has. This is Washington," said Temple, with an irritable snort, as if that were explanation enough.

"No," Anna shook her head. She placed her hands flat on the bed and tried to gather her thoughts, tried to screen out the howling emotional pain clawing at the inside of her, forcing herself to think like a federal agent and not like a woman who had seen one of her closest friends brutally gunned down in front of her. "You saw that creep in the picture. He's whiter than I am. I worked on a counterfeiting investigation against the Wo Shing Wo triad in Detroit, back in 2021. Those guys don't hire contractor muscle to send messages, and the Red Arrow are no different."

"You can't be certain of that, Agent Kelso." Bradley was studying her closely. "Skyler's people have already had the Red Arrow taking shots at them back in Los Angeles. This is an escalation." She saw her own expression tighten as he spoke.

In her mind's eye, the moment was unfolding again, and she grimaced. "He shot Dansky," Anna insisted. "There was no reason to do that. The man was unarmed, no threat, not like the rest of us. And then the shooter went back, and *he finished him off*. He *executed* him."

Bradley was quiet for a moment. "We've already interviewed the staff at Caidin."

Temple nodded. "It was like someone kicked over a hornet's nest in that place…"

Bradley continued. "Garrett Dansky was meeting with Senator Skyler to discuss some details of…" He drifted off, glancing down at his PDA again. Anna saw panels of notes, the words "United Nations" and "rumors" leaping out at her. He looked away before she could read more. "Apparently, the Caidin corporation are concerned about the possibility of some discussions going on at the UN. Something to do with the regulation of augmentation technology production. Pretty dry stuff. I don't see the Chinese mob having much stake in that kind of thing. Right now, we don't have anything to suggest that Dansky's death was anything more than just a collateral."

"The fact is," Temple said, "we've got to work to keep on top of this. And you surviving is a break, Anna. I've got a couple of techs outside ready to debrief you if you're up for it. The more you can tell us, the more we can do about getting these guys. Okay?" He gave her a supportive smile.

Anna tried to return it, and she felt a sob rising in her throat again. Perhaps if they hadn't taken her eyes, she would have cried right then and there. She hated herself for feeling like this, barely able to control her emotions—the rage and the fury, the anguish and the sorrow that swept about her like a silent hurricane.

Matt Ryan is dead. The one person she trusted more than anyone else in the world, the man who had saved her life. The man who had given her a second chance. He had died and Anna had been unable to do a thing to stop it. Her hand instinctively reached for the pocket where the brass coin would be; but it wasn't there, and her fingers tensed. She thought about the call she'd made, the night before the incident. Matt had always been there for her, and asked for nothing in return.

"The Service will not stand to let this pass, Agent Kelso," said Bradley. "We will not let these men walk free."

She took a shuddering breath and gave a long nod. "Yes, sir. I'll do everything I can to assist the investigation."

"Good—" Bradley leaned in to remove the wire, but she halted him.

"Before we do that, could I... Can borrow a cell? I need to talk to Jennifer Ryan. She needs to hear it from me."

Temple handed her his vu-phone. "Go ahead. Take your time."

When she was alone, and everything was dark again, she spoke the number for the Ryan household into the device and listened to it dial.

Inside her thoughts, something hard, cold, and beyond anger began to crystallize, like black diamond.

Station November—New South Wales—Australia

He remembered bits of what happened in the time between the drone exploding and awakening in an SAF field hospital just south of the redline.

He remembered drowning, or something near to it. The slurry of muddy orange-brown water in the fouled creek smothering him like the shock foam. He remembered the horrible ripping sound of Sam Duarte's execution at the guns of some autonomous robot predator. And he remembered the shadow, the hulking shadow that waded into the river and dragged him out over the rocks. The voices, talking in languages he didn't understand.

Saxon lost a lot of time there, or so it seemed. Days and nights blurred into one another. He found it hard to keep the passage of them straight in his head. Dimly he was aware that they had medicated him. The doctors talked about how the burns that the crash had inflicted on him were severe. They talked about the damage his cyberlimbs had suffered from the fall into the creek. The Hermes leg augmentations were shot, little better than scrap metal now; and then there was the litany of malfunctions with his internal implants, the optics and the reflex booster, the commo and all the rest. All this, without even a mention of how the meat, the human part of him, was faring.

All these things seemed faint and far distant, though. Each time he slept—if you could call it sleep—there were ghosts waiting.

Sam, Kano, all the others from Strike Six, all watching him. They never spoke, they didn't curse him or cry out. Sometimes they were intact, the black tri-plates of their flexible armor vests pristine and bloodless, gold-faced helmets raised visor-up as if they had just walked in off the parade ground. Other times, they were burned things, shapes of red and black flesh on charred bones.

They didn't blame him or forgive him. They just watched.

Sometimes, in those moments when he couldn't be sure if he was dreaming it or if he was seeing the real thing through a veil of painkillers, they would be in the room with him. Sitting on the beds, smoking a cigarette, sipping from a cup. And the shadow was with them. In the room, watching him like they did.

Saxon had lost men before. He wasn't a stranger to it. But he wasn't used to the idea of being a survivor, of being the *only* survivor. It gnawed at him.

One day he drifted back to the surface of consciousness and found the shadow sitting in the chair next to his bed. Saxon knew he was real because he could smell him. The shadow smelled like rich, strong tobacco, and the scent triggered a sense-memory in the depths of Ben Saxon's mind. He remembered being a boy, maybe five or six years old, his grandfather taking him through the streets of London past impossibly old buildings, to a gilt-edged hole-in-the-wall shop, all paneled with mirrors and advertisements for cigars. A man in there, selling packets of raw pipe tobacco, and the strange exotic textures that smelled like the air of distant lands.

The memory evaporated and Saxon blinked. The shadow was a man, a few years his senior, but intense and muscled, with an angular face like carved wood. Rugged, handsome after a fashion... but hard with it. Saxon sensed that about him more than anything, like a ghost aura. The shadow was a soldier and a killer.

"You..." he managed, licking dry lips. "You're the one... pulled me from the creek bed."

That earned him a nod. "You would have died," said the other man, the trace of an Eastern accent threaded through his words. "That would have been a waste."

Saxon eased himself up a little, blinking away the last of the fog from his chemical sleep. "Thanks."

"I did it because it was the right thing to do," he went on, fixing him with an intense look, his right eye a striking silver-blue augmentation. "And, it seems, because fate deemed it right."

Saxon shook his head. "Never believed in that stuff myself."

"No?" The man drew out a cigarette, offered one that Saxon refused, and then proceeded to light his own with an ornate petrol lighter. "I am a great believer in the notion of 'right place, right time, right man,' Mr. Saxon." He took a long drag. "And that is you, at this moment."

Saxon noticed the man's arms for the first time; they were like images from old medical textbooks, skinless limbs packed with dense bunches of artificial musculature over steel bones. Top-of-the-range, mil-spec cyberlimbs. For a moment, he measured himself against the stranger, wondering if he could take him on. Saxon concluded that at best, they might be evenly matched.

He looked away, glancing around the ward. They were alone. "Who are you?" He studied the man for a moment. He was wearing a nondescript set of black fatigues completely bereft of any identification tags or insignia. He was also unarmed...but then he showed a kind of careful poise that made Saxon suspect he didn't need a gun or a knife to be lethal. "Are you Belltower?"

"I have a far wider remit than Belltower Associates."

He smiled and exhaled. "You wouldn't know the name of my... group. And that's exactly how we like it to be. I suppose you could call me a freelancer, if you really felt the need to hang a label."

Deep black. Saxon had crossed paths with men like this before, in his time with the SAS. Soldiers whose missions were so far off-book that they didn't exist on any official documentation, groups that simply did not show up on the radar. He had to admit, he was intrigued. If a unit like that was operating in the Australian conflict zone, what did it mean? Was this man even fighting for the same side as him?

"My name is Jaron Namir," he said, at length. "We share a similar past, you and I. Both of us have worked under, shall we say, *special conditions* for our respective homelands."

The accent suddenly clicked with Saxon and he placed it. *Israeli. Which makes him, what? Former Mossad? Someone who got out of there before the war with the United Arab Front flattened everything?*

Saxon tried to keep the tension he was feeling from showing. This man knew who he was, and he'd revealed key information about himself, or at least laid out some false trail; that meant there was a good chance Namir never intended to let Saxon live.

"I wonder, would you let me make an observation?" Namir went on. He asked the question with all the certainty of a man who knew he would not be refused.

Saxon watched him carefully. "Feel free."

"You're wasting your potential here. Belltower offers a good career for men like us, I don't dispute that. But the chance to really accomplish something? To make a difference, to bring order to a chaotic world? Belltower can't do that."

A chill ran through the soldier's veins. "You're trying to recruit me?"

Namir studied him. "I read the after-action report on the failure of Operation Rainbird. You survived against very long odds, Mr. Saxon. I am quite impressed." He stubbed out the cigarette. "I could use someone with your skill set. I find myself a man down after a recent incident, and you make a good candidate. Interested?"

"Maybe if you told me who the hell you are."

"I told you, the name would not—"

"Try me."

Namir gave a shrug. "I am field commander of a nonaligned special operations unit known as the Tyrants. We are an elite, independent, self-financing group dedicated to maintaining global stability through covert means."

"A rogue cell?" Saxon frowned. Like any other, the spec ops community had its own share of urban legends, and in his time he'd heard stories of so-called rogues, operators who had dropped off the grid and gone into business for themselves; but the idea had always seemed a little too far off the beam to be truthful. Saxon had never believed anyone could run alone out there in the thick for too long, not without backup. "Tyrants…That name doesn't exactly have the ring of righteousness to it."

"I beg to differ," said the other man. "The true meaning of the word stems from the Greek *turannos*. It was only later the name gathered its negative connotations…In its original form, the term describes those who take power by their own means, instead of being awarded it through birthright or elective. That is what we do, Mr. Saxon. We take power from those who abuse it. We restore the balance."

"Out of the goodness of your heart?"

"Belltower's failures cost you the lives of the men and women in your unit," Namir said, his tone becoming grave. "Are you really ready to go back to them, knowing that? Be honest with me, Mr. Saxon. Are you ever going to trust your employers again?"

Saxon closed his eyes, and for a second he saw the ghosts. "I have a responsibility. I signed a contract..."

"One that is near to ending." Namir made a dismissive gesture. "We can deal with that. If only a piece of paper is stopping you, believe me, I can make that go away." When Saxon didn't answer, he got up and straightened his fatigue jacket. "This offer won't come again," he said. "And if you decide to go looking for us after the fact, I warn you...there will be consequences."

Saxon looked down at his hands, one scarred flesh, the other scratched steel. Everything Namir had said about trust, about Belltower—all of it was as if he had plucked the thoughts straight from his mind. Each day that had passed here, each day he sat surrounded by his ghosts, every passing hour was eroding something deep inside him, and in its place it left only a cold hollow. That, and a slow-burning, directionless desire to claim a blood cost back from the people who had murdered Kano, Duarte, and the others.

"We can give you what you need, Ben," said Namir. "The Tyrants help their own."

When Saxon said the next words, they seemed to come from a very great distance. "I'm in."

THREE

Kelso pulled the black microfleece hoodie tighter over her head, grimacing into the cold wind sweeping in from the Hudson River, her nerves ringing like struck chimes. She moved like she had purpose, ignoring the urge to look over her shoulder, negotiating the debris and cargo containers placed across the width of the pier in what seemed a casual fashion; in fact, the junk had been arranged to provide bottlenecks to stop anyone from rushing the big ship moored at the 86 from the shore. In the bleak light of the evening, the vessel was a wall of gray steel curving up and over her head, frozen there like a wave cast in metal. Chains of fairy lights hung down from rusting gantries, flapping in the breeze, and while the upper deck was mostly dark, she could hear the sounds of people running around up there, and the occasional crunch of metal on metal. They had a regulation-size basketball court made of scrap iron and chain link on the deck—she'd seen it in the distance as she crossed the bridge over 12th Avenue—and there was a game on, lit by bio-lume sticks and fires burning in oil drums.

Ahead she glimpsed the name of the venerable old vessel. Image patterning software in her Sarif optics picked out the letters defaced but still standing clear of the go-ganger tags painted over them: *Intrepid*.

Anna kept walking, approaching the covered gantry that extended up into the hull. Once upon a time, this old warship had sailed the world, projecting American sea power in the Pacific, Cuba, and Vietnam; fate and rich men had saved her from becoming a billion razor blades, and for a while the aging aircraft carrier had stood at dock, hosting stories of old wars, even serving her nation once again when the towers came down. But that was almost thirty years dead and gone, and recession and stock crashes had sent the old warhorse into darkness. The relic planes that had once stood on her decks were gone, sold off to collectors, and the ship itself had been left to rust. But like so many things, the people at the fringes of the city had found a use for her.

Anna had paid enough bribes to get the word of the day that let her on board. From the aft of the hangar deck, the sounds of a hammer-speed DJ resonated down the echoing hull. Between here and there, the place they called "the wet market" blossomed like a multicolored fungus, dozens of makeshift stalls selling pirated datasofts, old tech, and recovered cyberware alongside oil-can cook plates crackling with hot fat and pungent foods from India, the Caribbean, or the African Federation. There was no law at the 86, but the New York Police Department tended to let things lie, providing that the residents kept themselves to themselves and made sure that any bodies washed up inside New Jersey's jurisdiction.

Anna skirted past the marketplace and found a corroded set of ladders that led up to the next level. The corridor she emerged in was gloomy. It smelled of rust and seawater. Following lines of peeling lume tape, she ascended again and emerged somewhere near the bow. A large section of the forward deck had been cut away and in its place there were a couple of jury-rigged geo-domes made of smart fabric. The sea smell gave way to the faint whiff of ozone and battery acid.

Inside the dome there was a parade of cowboy electronics; server frames modified like hot rods, chugging gasoline generators and fat trunks of cable snaking from fans of solar panels or military-issue satellite antennae. Monitors and holoscreens lit the space with cold blue illumination, and here and there, faces rendered ghost-white glanced up at her from laptops or gamer pits.

"Kel." She turned sharply at the sound of her cover name and saw Denny walking toward her. So dark-skinned as to seem almost coal-black, he was a short and stocky hacker with a shorn skull and an unkempt soul patch on his narrow chin. He had mirrored Kusanagi optics that gave his eyes the look of steel spheres. Following a few steps behind was a tall, rail-thin woman inside a doublet a size too large for her. She had thumbless spider-hands the color of old terra-cotta.

Anna gave Denny a nod from beneath her hood, watching the woman's face grow more sour the closer she got. In better light it was difficult to be sure how old the taller woman was. Interface sockets glittered in the half-light, making a line over her right temple.

"This is Kel," Denny was saying. "She's in the market for some intelligence."

He was going to go on, but his companion waved him

into silence. "I am getting a distinct taste of blue in my mouth," she hissed. "You bring a cop on the boat? Are you an idiot?"

"Widow—"

"What?" Anna gave her a disgusted look, then glared at Denny. "This again? I thought me and you had gone through all that *who-the-fuck-are-you* crap already." Kelso had targeted Denny through some files she'd skimmed from a contact at the DOJ, and worked him to get under this cover as "Kel," an out-of-towner looking to buy some information. She turned away. "Forget it. I don't have time for this."

"Kel, wait." Denny turned to Widow and glared at her. "She's clean. I ran her jacket. Not even a touch of blue."

Widow folded her thin arms. "Then she's definitely a cop."

Anna put on an angry snarl that wasn't all fake. "Who the hell is this skinny bitch and why am I listening to her talk? Didn't we have a deal, Denny?"

"You know who I am?" Widow snapped back. "Go-Five, that's who I am. I'll rip your life open in ten seconds. Zero everything you ever owned!"

Go-Five meant GO5, also known as the Gang of Five. They were a collective of hacker guns-for-hire well known by the FBI's cybercrime division, with a lengthy rap sheet packed with all kinds of interesting digital larceny. The other interesting thing about them was that the Gang of Five were all faceless ghosts, which made it easy for someone to wear their name and reputation with little fear of being proven a liar.

"Bullshit," Anna retorted. "Go-Five are all Koreans, everyone knows that."

Widow snorted, and it was then that Kelso knew she had her on the line. The hacker community was driven by rep, and any one of them was only as good as their last score. Studying Widow in the actinic glow of the screens, Anna saw a woman trying to hide her age, running hard to keep up and not quite making it. She was maybe twenty if she was a day; old for a keyboard queen. All it would take to turn this around was to apply pressure to her vanity.

"I'm better than any K-towners," Widow said, doing the job for her. "Better than those Juggernaut dinks and that day-player Windmill."

Gotcha. "Prove it," Anna demanded, handing her a data spike. "Denny asked me to come here because he said you people could cut ice for me. Can you do it or not?"

Widow snatched the spike from her hand, pale fingers with red enameled tips flashing. Inside it was every piece of information Kelso had, carefully stripped of any identifying markers that might show its origins from a law enforcement agency database.

"Get her money," growled Widow at Denny, and stalked over to a desktop setup.

The other hacker blew out a breath. "So we do it like you asked, right? Run the face on the file through the net, see what comes up."

"I need to know who he is."

Denny shrugged. "No guarantees, Kel. It's pay-for-play. Outcome is what it is. I told you that already."

"I need to *know*," she said, nerves bunching. Anna felt her mask of self-control slipping and took a moment to center herself. "If she's as good as you said..." Her mouth went dry and she drifted off for a moment. The jittering in her hands was coming back again, and she buried her fists inside the pockets of the hoodie. The other tell, that weird chemical taste in the back of her throat, like dry earth, was getting stronger.

Anna resisted the urge to reach for the ampoule pen in the pocket on the arm of the fleece and hunched forward. "Are we doing this or not?" she demanded, off the odd look Denny put her way. "Tick tock," she added, irritably.

Denny held out his hand. "Cross my palm."

She fished inside an inner pocket and came back with a credit chip imprinted with the logo of the People's Republic. The arfid strip in the card had been scrambled—a low-tech approach, to be certain, but enough that it rendered the transaction untraceable. The hacker made it vanish. "How long is this gonna take?" Anna went on, her tone turning brittle.

"Not long," he offered, eyeing her, catching her manner. "Hey, Kel…If you, like, *need* something, I can speak to some of my people—"

She turned away, walking toward the fabric walls of the dome. The offer tempted her more than she wanted to admit. "You know what I need, Denny," she said over her shoulder. "I need a name for that face."

Aerial Transit Corridor—Smolensk Oblast—Russian Federated States

Through the oval window of the pressure door, Saxon could see the morning light crossing the landscape far below, chasing the aircraft as it flew eastward. By the time they reached their destination, the dawn would have overtaken them, but for now the rising sun was still at their backs, visible in lines of color that illuminated the thin strips of clouds passing beneath. The view tilted as they banked gently, and Saxon put out his right hand to steady himself. He was still being careful with the cybernetic limb; it was a military specification model manufactured by Tai Yong Medical, one of—if not *the*—biggest augmentation conglomerates on the planet. Along with new Hermes legs to replace those he'd damaged in the veetol crash six months ago, the upgraded Samson-series arm and a few other implants were all part of what Namir had called his "welcome bonus" for joining the Tyrants. The arm could be twitchy, though. Twice now, on the first few operations Namir had deployed him on, the Samson had shown a trigger delay. Saxon reckoned he had it tuned well enough by now, though. Still, he resolved to up his neuropozyne dose a little, just in case.

"Thinkin' about a skydive?" said a voice. "You itchin' to try out that new high-fall aug?"

He turned. Filling most of the corridor behind him, Lawrence Barrett had Saxon fixed with a wolfish grin. The American was big, and he was ugly. A flat buzz cut framed features that were burn-scarred and bold about it. The only part of the man's face that was unblemished was the synth-skin along a reconstructed jaw. Saxon understood that Barrett's looks had been given to him by close proximity to a bomb blast, but he knew little more than that. The big man wore his disfigurement like a badge of honor, highlighting it with a brass bull ring through his nose.

Saxon wasn't a small guy by any means, but he carried himself differently from Barrett, with this thuggish swagger;

he didn't feel the need to look threatening every second of every day. But then again, men who looked as tough as they were could be a useful tool in the spec ops game. Saxon was more a student of the subtle approach, though.

"I don't like flying," he offered. "Bores the hell out of me, yeah?"

"I hear that." Barrett nodded, toying with the wrists of his black-and-steel cyberarms. "This is the shittiest airline ever. No damn stewardess and the in-flight movie sucks." Outwardly, the jet they were aboard resembled any one of a number of conventional private airliners—but under the mimetic fuselage was the mobile operations center for the Tyrants, easily the rival of any military forward air command unit in the world.

Barrett wandered toward the galley and Saxon fell in behind him. He'd been on a couple of sorties with the American—surveillance jobs in Bucharest and Glasgow—and all along he'd felt like he was being watched himself. It wasn't surprising, Saxon thought. They'd invested time and money in headhunting him from Belltower, so it made sense to have him pass through a few rookie assignments before stepping up to the real thing—but to be honest, he chafed at it. He wasn't just some grunt in off the street. He knew how to do the job as well as any of them. He was tired of the small-scale, low-threat gigs. Still, the Tyrants paid well, and they had good funding, that was clear—although he'd learned straightaway that asking questions about that side of things was off-limits. Namir had made that very plain.

He'd seen some of the other Tyrant operatives here and there over the past couple of months, usually just in passing—but this was the first time they'd all been gathered together for a mission. Saxon felt an itchy tingle of anticipation in the palm of his gun hand. The gloves were going to come off when they got to Moscow—he could sense it.

They emerged in the open common area on the aircraft's upper deck. A gleaming steel galley ranged along one wall, and there were chairs and monitors facing it. Barrett pawed through a food locker like a hungry bear and Saxon glanced away, finding another member of the team engrossed in maintenance on a heavy cyberhand.

The German was the other new guy in the Tyrants, although he'd been in a while before Saxon's arrival. Beneath a dark jacket he had the spare, rippled physique of a bodybuilder, a thick neck and natural eyes that still seemed somehow lifeless. A black watch cap was pulled down over his hair. He didn't show many augmentations aside from the hand, but Saxon had seen him moving and was willing to bet the legs were metal. The guy was the youngest of them, somewhere in his twenties.

"You're Saxon," he said. His accent was deep and resonant. "We have not formally met." He nodded at the dismantled mechanism at the end of his arm. "Forgive me if I do not shake your hand. I am Gunther Hermann."

"I know." Namir had mentioned Hermann in passing; from what Saxon had learned, the younger man had been part of Germany's GSG-9 police counter-terror unit until the Tyrants had recruited him. Something in the way that Namir had glossed over that fact made Saxon wonder about the reasons for Hermann's departure from the Bundespolizei.

Hermann put down his tools and took a careful drink from a can of orange soda. "You are the replacement for Wexler, then?"

"I guess so." There had been little said about the operator whose boots Saxon was filling. He hadn't wanted to push the issue. People died in this line of work as a matter of course.

"He was slow," offered Barrett. "Got himself killed 'cause of it."

He decided to venture the question, caution be damned. "What happened?"

"Now, why do you need to know that?" Saxon looked up as a third man entered the common area from the forward compartment. His lips thinned. In any group there was always a place where the dynamic created friction, and it was right here, between Ben Saxon and Scott Hardesty, the team's dedicated sniper.

Hardesty was rangy and tall, so much so that he seemed in danger of scuffing the top of his bald scalp on the ceiling. Saxon never saw him wearing anything other than a combat overall, sometimes with a gear vest or equipment belt. He was long and thin, like the spindly extreme-range rifles he carried on-mission, and augmented across all his limbs. His eyes were high-specification optics of a kind Saxon had never seen before.

At first Saxon had found it difficult to adjust from being a team leader, as he had been with Strike Six, to being a line operator once again—and Hardesty seemed determined to make it harder by being as big a pain in the arse as he possibly could. The man had taken a strong dislike to him, but the reason why wasn't clear.

"Just making conversation," he demurred.

"Joe Wexler was good," Hardesty insisted. "I could trust him. I don't know you. So I don't trust you."

Saxon moved to the cooler and took a bottle of water. "Trust this; Namir didn't invite me in because of my sparkling personality."

"Dead weight gets cut loose very fast around here," said Hardesty, pushing past as he made his way down the compartment. "Keep that in mind, limey."

As the aft door closed behind him, Saxon shrugged. "Friendly fella."

"Wexler was ex-CIA, like Hardesty," Barrett noted. "You know spooks, they like to stick together."

"Right."

Hermann blew out a breath, his hand folding closed once again. He gave it an experimental flex, and Saxon saw where the knuckles and the proximal phalanges were heavily reinforced. Hermann noticed his attention. "A custom-designed modification," he explained. "In time, I hope to enhance the rest of myself in a similar fashion."

"Metal, not meat, eh?"

Hermann nodded, as if any other idea would be foolish. "Of course."

A soft chime sounded from the intercom, and Namir's voice issued out of a hidden speaker in the wall. *"Final approach in ten minutes,"* he said. *"Prep your gear and be ready. We're on the clock for this one, so mission brief starts the moment the wheels stop. That is all."*

Saxon glanced out of the window. The outer suburbs of the Russian capital flashed by, the city below shaking off sleep and awakening.

Pier 86—New York City—United States of America

Widow leaned back from the monitor and made a low, self-amused grumble in the back of her throat, the spider-hands reordering themselves into something closer to the order of human fingers. She looked up at Kelso and gave her a sour smile. "Thanks for the paper," said the hacker, nodding toward where Denny stood off to one side. "I always love doing these fun little jobs." Her tone made it clear the opposite was true.

Anna kept her hands inside her pockets. Jags of annoyance pulsed through her like twinges of pain from a pulled muscle, and she thought about how much she would enjoy slapping the smirk off the thin, spindly woman's face.

Widow gestured at the screen, where the captured image of Matt Ryan's killer was surrounded by a halo of search windows and subroutine panels. "This guy is a ghost."

"A name," she snarled. "I paid you for name."

"No." The hacker got up, pointing a too-long finger. "You paid for a *search* for a name. Not the same thing."

"Did you even do anything with that data?" Anna retorted. "Or did you just sit with your virtual thumb up your virtual ass for the past hour?"

Widow's face darkened. "Pay attention, slow-drive, because I'll only explain this once. I did a webwide trawl of all public-access video databases, plus a thousand more private imaging servers, parsing a data mesh based on Blondie here"—she waved at the screen—"and ran a match search using a collective of bloodhound info-seeker programs. The fact that he didn't even get the slightest of hits should be a wake-up call."

Kelso paused, the hacker's words catching up with her. Widow had a point; even the *absence* of data was a kind of data itself. The problem was, the absence of data was all that she had to go on, a whole damn pile of it.

"He gotta be high military or corporate," added Denny. "To cull someone's past like that? Outta our league." That drew him a sharp glare from Widow.

Everything they were telling her dovetailed with her own information. Whoever this man was, he had never been muscle-for-hire working kills for the Red Arrow triad. But who, then? The old, familiar frustration bubbled up inside her, the tension gathering at the base of her skull.

And then Widow did something Kelso didn't expect. She grinned. "Do you want to know how good I really am?"

"You do have something." Anna stepped closer. "Let me guess, you're gonna shake me down for more yuan?"

Widow gave an arch sniff. "No. I got standards. You paid top dollar for the gold service, so you get it." She giggled. "I just like, ha, building a sense of drama."

"A name?"

"Yeah," Widow said, "but not this guy's, not exactly." She returned to the monitor and pulled up some panels. "Got some puzzle palace stuff here, up on the Konspiracy Krew boards and over at Glass Curtain. Your mark, the data on the hit he was part of? The tactics match an open search those guys got running at their end."

Anna had heard of the groups Widow mentioned; they were fringers, part of the wide-eyed and credulous flying-saucer crowd, busy posting proofs that the moon was hollow or some other *Twilight Zone* crap. "You're not taking those mouth-breathers seriously?" The jitters were in her hand again, and she tightened her fingers, the nails digging into her palms.

Denny chuckled. "Even a stopped clock is right twice a day, neh?"

"Ever heard of the Tyrants?" Widow cocked her head.

She shook her head. "I quit listening to the Top 40 the same time I stopped wearing a training bra. *Talk to me!*" Anna's temper flared again. She could feel her tolerance level dropping along with her focus.

"They're a black-ops cartel," Denny offered. "No oversight, so it's said. Richer than shit. And hard-core, like you wouldn't believe. Stone killers through and through."

"Glass Curtain have them linked to a bunch of spook house stuff," Widow explained. "Regime change. Political murder. Intimidation. Corporate assassination."

The last phrase brought Anna up sharp. She thought about Dansky, there on the sidewalk. The killer going back to him, the second bullet placed to end his life instantly. She could feel the synchrony of the act in her mind's eye all over again. Everything Widow was saying fell into line with all the information Kelso's investigation had uncovered to date. It couldn't be a coincidence.

The earthy taste in the back of her throat was strong and she wanted to make it go away. "I want all you can get me on them," she said.

Widow smirked. "That'll cost extra."

In the next second, the million-candlepower glare of a night sun blazed through the thin ballistic fabric of the dome's roof, turning the gloomy interior into a starkly lit arena filled with sharp-edged shadows. A booming voice resonated through her rib cage, broadcast from overhead.

"This is the NYPD. Stay where you are. This area is under lockdown. As of this moment, all rights have been suspended." Beneath the words, she heard the familiar rising hum of sonic screamers winding up to discharge.

Denny broke into a run, but Widow was red-faced and shouting. Anna lost her words in the building wall of sound, but she knew that the hacker was blaming her for this. She thought Kelso had brought the police here.

Widow grabbed at her, knife-sharp nails emerging from the tips of the spidery fingers, but she punched her down, vaulting away through the panicked mass of the dome-dwellers as they ran about her. They tore up their decks from where they were mounted and yanked fists of glowing fiber-optic cable out of server farms, desperate to leave nothing behind that would incriminate.

Anna had just as much reason to run as all the rest of them. She reached the dome wall and slashed a new exit for herself with the collapsible push-dagger that dangled from a lanyard about her neck. Falling out onto the deck of the *Intrepid,* she was deluged in the white glare; overhead, a pair of silent police blimps drifted in the breeze. Clusters of cameras, sensors, and guns were barely visible amid the drowning wash of hard light. Down on the river and on the shoreline, red and blue strobes came on. For one long moment, she found herself wondering if Widow was right—had she brought this with her?

Kelso joined a throng of people running toward the old carrier's fantail just as the screamers went off. The wave of noise slammed into them and she fell as they did, her skin crawling with the burn of infrasonic sound.

The cops came across the deck of the old warship in a line, heads concealed by the mirrored masks of riot helmets, webber guns and restraint dispensers in their hands.

Sheremetyevo International Airport—Moscow—Russian Federated States

The aircraft parked at a discreet hangar on the far edge of the airport, distant enough to be out of sight of any prying eyes. The fuselage currently displayed the livery of Skye Secure Aviation, a transport subsidiary of Belltower typically used for the transit of sensitive cargoes; it was the ideal cover, but the mimetic hull could just as easily mimic the insignia of any civilian airline or military air force.

The operations room was a high, narrow chamber that filled both decks. Thinscreens were arranged on every surface, and hanging down from above, a cluster of holographic projectors resembled the splayed legs of an impaled insect. Folding seats among the control consoles and comm desks provided space for everyone to sit, but most of the Tyrants stayed on their feet. The air of barely contained tension was thick in the room; all of them wanted to hear the go-command.

Namir worked a panel, bringing the holograph to life. Nearby, seated in a way that communicated casual disinterest, the sixth member of the Tyrants toyed with a loose belt length, hanging from a half-jacket patterned with triangular armor plates. If Yelena Federova was actually capable of speech, she made no effort to show it. When Saxon saw her, the woman was padding silently around the aircraft, almost a ghost. Most of the time she kept to Namir's company, and Saxon had been content to leave it at that; still, he couldn't escape the sense that she, too, was measuring him.

The dusky-skinned woman graced him with a cool nod, sullen eyes briefly looking up from under a cascade of dark hair that hung down over her face from a half-shorn scalp. Federova had a dancer's physicality to her, an aura that Saxon could describe only as "grace"—but she hid a lethal edge beneath it. Her augmented legs were crossed in front of her; long and perfectly machined, they resembled the framework of racing motorcycles, curved and finely balanced. Standing, she seemed to balance *en pointe* like a ballerina.

The mutter of the holograph's activation pulled Saxon's attention away, and he watched as a vector-scan model of a blunt, modernist building sketched itself in the air before them.

Jaron Namir stepped up to the edge of the nimbus of laser glow; the colors threw stark highlights over his craggy features. "Intelligence has located one of our high-value targets," he began. "Here. The Hotel Novoe Rostov, off Zubovskaya Square." He touched a control and the image blurred, re-forming into a series of phantom panes. Several of them showed digital photos of a heavyset man with a beard and thinning hair. "This is the mark. Mikhail Kontarsky, a minister of the Russian federal assembly, and senior administrator of the RFS committee on human augmentation policy."

Saxon raised an eyebrow at that, but said nothing.

"This man is corrupt to the core," Namir went on. "He's betrayed his country and the people who elected him. Kontarsky has been suborned by an organization called Juggernaut. What we know of them is this: they are a decentralized anarchist terror group that uses information warfare to further an antiglobalization agenda. Neutralizing Kontarsky is a first step toward eradicating these dangerous militants, and it will deny them a conduit into the Russian Federated States."

The Juggernaut name was familiar to Saxon. He recalled intelligence briefings from his time with Belltower; one of the targets of the group had been Tai Yong Medical, a major client for the PMC's security division.

"So the Russkies are incapable of dealing with Kontarsky themselves?" said Hardesty, throwing a look toward Federova, who ignored it. "Why do we have to intervene?"

"Because the man is a point of instability, in a kleptocracy masquerading as a government." Namir paged through more images. "Kontarsky is a wild card. He has many friends in the duma—the parliament…That's why Juggernaut has turned him. He has to be removed."

"That would mean *terminated*," Hermann asked, "if we are being clear?"

Namir nodded once. "Make no mistake, we are dealing with a dangerous man here. Kontarsky is connected to several Russian organized crime syndicates. He's no choirboy."

Saxon peered at the screens, catching glimpses of elements from the politician's file, evidence of corruption and money laundering scrolling past his eyes.

"Mission data is being downloaded to your personal stacks," said Namir. "Draw weapons for a covert urban assault from the armory, and assemble on the tarmac in five minutes for deployment."

Saxon followed Hermann aft, turning the briefing over in his mind. "Taking down a member of the Russian ministry... Am I the only one who has questions about that?"

The German threw him a look. "If Kontarsky is a target, I trust the reasons are sound."

"Do you?" Saxon hesitated. "You've been with the outfit longer than me. Don't you wonder who gives the orders?"

"Namir gives the orders," Hermann said flatly.

"But who gives them to Namir?"

The other man walked on. "It is not something I trouble myself with, Saxon. Sometimes it is necessary to operate in the shadows to maintain the status quo. That is what we do."

"But still—"

"Still *what*?" Saxon turned to find Namir standing behind him. "Do you need a reason, Ben? Look at Kontarsky's files. He's not an innocent man."

Saxon paused, studying the Israeli. "Who is?" In such close quarters, his thoughts couldn't help but turn again to wondering who would prevail if the two of them faced off. *It would be an even match,* Saxon thought. *At first.*

Namir glanced over Saxon's shoulder as Hermann passed through into the aft compartment, leaving them alone for the moment. "Juggernaut is a clear and present danger to global stability. They have to be dealt with. You understand that, yes?"

"I understand that *someone* is threatened by them," Saxon replied. "Tai Yong Medical? Others, maybe?" It was a clumsy attempt to gauge a reaction, and he knew it, but Namir gave him nothing.

"Have you ever wondered why Belltower's intel during Rainbird was so wrong?" The question came out of nowhere, and Saxon blinked. "Juggernaut are info-terrorists, Ben. Along with all the other brushfire wars and proxy conflicts they have a hand in, they're working with the Australian Free States. Conducting pay-for-play cyberwarfare on their behalf, compromising data security, disrupting intelligence gathering. The men Kontarsky is working with are the ones responsible for your squad dying out there in the desert." Namir paused to let that sink in. "Is that reason enough for you?" he asked gently.

FOUR

NYPD 10th Precinct—New York City—United States of America

The coffee helped, but not enough. It was strong and tar-black, and it tasted awful, but the stew of day-old caffeine and stale sugar gave Kelso something to focus on.

The metal chair she sat upon, its twin across the way, and the table bolted to the floor were all the interview room had that could be considered furniture. The polymer cuff around her right hand was tethered to a loop in the tabletop, her other hand free to toy with the paper cup. Light came from a glow strip sealed behind armored glass, and high up over the lintel of the door across from her, the glassy fish-eye dome of a camera pod watched her, unblinking.

Anna knew things were going poorly when the cop who escorted her up from general holding didn't ask any questions. He just secured her, gave her the coffee, and left. Now she was marking time until the door opened again.

As if the thought of it were enough to make it happen, the metal hinges creaked and there stood the man she least wanted to see in the world.

Ron Temple threw a weak smile at the man by his side. "Thanks, Detective. I'll take it from here."

The other man eyed Anna, and walked away without a

word. Temple dropped heavily into the vacant chair as the door locked shut behind him, placing a silver briefcase on the desk. He was tired, eyes bloodshot, still wearing the big, high-collared greatcoat he sported on the streets of D.C. Anna imagined he'd come straight here, after he heard.

"What the fuck are you doing, Kelso?" he asked in a low, weary voice. Anna blinked; she couldn't recall Temple ever cursing like that before in front of her. He went on. "Do you have any idea of the kind of depths of shit you are in? No, don't bother to answer that. Of course you do. Because you're an agent of this nation's highest-profile law enforcement agency, and not an idiot."

"I had my reasons," she managed.

"This is not a conversation!" he thundered, his annoyance bubbling over. "You do not get to justify this kind of stupidity!" Temple hesitated, and looked up over his shoulder at the camera eye. The indicator light showing that the monitor was active winked out, and he turned back to face her. His expression was conflicted; anger in there along with disappointment, sadness, and other things she couldn't read.

"You've put the Service at risk, Anna. Not just yourself, but all of us. I've had to call in a dozen markers from the NYPD to make this go dark, do you understand? As far as our flatfoot cousins are aware, your little excursion up here was a deep cover surveillance operation, and that's how it's going to stay. I'm damned sure I don't want New York's finest figuring out that an agent of the United States Secret Service was conducting an illegal, unsanctioned investigation!"

"It was the only way…"

He went on as if she hadn't spoken. "I know about everything. After I got the call, it all started to make sense. I had Drake and Tyler trawl your files. You've been using your access to the DOJ network and Nat Crime databases to pursue unlawful searches, hiding it from all of us while you let your actual assignments slide."

She didn't look away. Every word of what he said was true. For the past few months, ever since she had signed back on to active duty after the shooting, Anna Kelso had been digging into the investigation surrounding the Skyler hit and the identity of the assailants—despite orders to leave it to the team handling the incident. The case was closed; good leads took the agency to three associates of the Red Arrow triad, but they had all perished in a police shootout before arrests could be made. Strong evidence mounted up after the fact, placing the suspects as the black-armored men in Washington.

Kelso hadn't believed any of it. The triad connection was a blind, she knew it in her gut.

Someone else had been responsible for the murder of Dansky, Matt Ryan, and a handful of other good agents; but that was a minority opinion in an agency that just wanted to bury its dead and move on.

Temple's ire lessened, and he sighed. "I blame myself for this. I should have seen the signs. I should have known you weren't ready to return to operations."

"Don't talk about me like I'm..." She stumbled over the word. "Weak."

"Do you really think raking over the ashes of what happened six months ago is honoring Matt Ryan's memory?" He shook his head. "Can you imagine what

Jenny and her kids would think about this?"

"You don't understand!" she insisted.

"I do," he insisted. "I know what Matt did for you, Anna. I know how much he meant to you." Temple opened the case and drew out an evidence packet containing her personal effects. He fished inside and came back with a clear plastic bag; within was the rodlike shape of an injector pen, along with a couple of drug ampoules. "And I know how disappointed he'd be to see *this*. How long have you been back on stims?"

Kelso's mouth flooded with saliva at the sight of the injector, and it took a physical effort to look away. "I'm not using again. It's not the same." Her cheeks burned. "I just needed to stay on top of things..."

"I would like to believe you." He tapped the bag. "Frankly, this alone is enough to have you cashiered, maybe even net some jail time." Temple pulled out a data slate, and studied it. "Ryan got you a second chance after you were suspended for use of stimulants three years ago. If not for him, your career would have been over." He put it down. "This is worse than just backsliding, Anna. This is a lot worse. You've become erratic, even obsessed. You're unstable."

"I want justice!" she shot back, pulling against the restraint. "The attack on Senator Skyler was a false flag operation! She was never the target, it was Dansky all along, and we got caught in the cross fire!"

"I read your report," Temple said. "There's nothing to back that up. And the case is closed. The men who killed Ryan and the others are dead."

"I don't believe that." Anna leaned forward. *Why can't*

he see? "Division turned down my requests to reopen the case, so I looked into it myself. Dansky wasn't the only one…There are others, important people, scientists and corporate executives, other politicians, even United Nations ambassadors…all of them targeted by assassins with a similar MO—"

"You can't know that!"

"The same men who killed Matt are still running free!" she spat. "I've been trying to find something, anything, a name…" Anna suddenly realized how she had to look, the wild intensity in her eyes; she swallowed hard and tried to calm herself. "That's why I came here, to deal with the hackers on the *Intrepid*. They could get me data that was off the grid. Get me names."

"Or maybe they were just playing you?"

"Tyrants." She said the word like a curse.

Temple eyed her. "What?"

"That's what they call themselves. The killers." She frowned. "If I can track them, find out who they are working for—"

"That's enough!" Temple slammed his hand down on the table. "Those hackers you were caught with? Half of them are known associates of a global cyberterrorist cell, a group called Juggernaut. They're on the National Security Agency's most-wanted list, for god's sake. *Think*, Kelso! Can you imagine what would happen if a Secret Service agent was connected to people like that?" He shook his head again. "I saw your requests to Division, that paper-thin garbage you called evidence. You were turned down because you have nothing but supposition and hearsay. At best, you've got a half-baked conspiracy theory! I kept the heat off you out of respect for Matt, because I knew his death hit you hard. But you've crossed the line."

Anna felt a chill run through her. "So...What happens now?"

Temple folded his arms. "If things were different...I'd charge you myself. But the fact is, what with that pit bull sniffing around the Service looking for some dirt, the agency needs to keep this in-house." The "pit bull" was Florida governor Philip Riley Mead, who was working the angles on Capitol Hill, using every trick he could— including pouring scorn on the DeSilvio administration by shining a light on every mess he could find. Some people called him a crusader for good, speaking about him taking the Oval Office for himself one day; but Kelso just saw a bland, opportunist politician who was nothing but good teeth and hollow platitudes. "We're going to deal with this quietly," Temple went on.

He handed her the packet and then drew a thin envelope from the pocket of his coat. Inside there was a credit chip and an airline ticket.

Temple fixed her with a steady, measuring gaze. "Your badge and ID have already been deauthorized. I've reclaimed your service firearm. As of this moment, you are officially on medical suspension. In a month, when this has all been forgotten, a closed-session review of your conduct will be held, and you will be discharged from the Secret Service, forfeiting pension and all privileges. At the very *least*." He stood up. "The ticket will get you back to Washington. Do yourself a favor, Agent Kelso. Go home. Let this go. Let *Matt* go." He gathered up the evidence bag with the stims and grimaced at it. "And don't make things any worse for yourself."

After he left her alone, the restraint loop gave a buzz and fell off her wrist. Anna picked up the packet and something slipped out. A brass coin clattered to the table; her sobriety chip. For a long moment, she thought about leaving it where it had fallen.

Angrily, she snatched it up and jammed it in her pocket.

Zubovskaya Square—Moscow—Russian Federated States

The night-black helo circled once over the buildings along Burdenko Street, the ducted rotor-rings turning, the sound-deadening baffles humming. The boxy little flyer hugged the angular tops of the offices and apartment blocks, skimming over old tiled roofs cheek-by-jowl with modern polyglass domes and sheets of solar paneling. The nose of the craft dipped as Hardesty dropped from the starboard side; then they were rising up and away, describing a wide circuit around the lines of the plaza at Zubovskaya.

Saxon straightened the Kevlar balaclava over his face and peered through his polarized eye-shields. Ahead he could see the roof of the Hotel Novoe Rostov. The team had reviewed the deployment on the way from the airport, and they were ready.

He took a breath and ran through his own internal checklist, ending it with a last look at the ammo selector on the Hurricane tactical machine pistol that hung from his shoulder strap. The compact submachine gun was all ABS plastic and black-anodized steel, the blunt muzzle lost behind a triangular suppressor.

"Twenty seconds." Namir's words came over his

mastoid, buzzing in Saxon's skull. The subvocalized radio message had the peculiar echo to it that made encrypted comms sound as if they were being beamed down from space.

Saxon frowned. They were cutting it fine. The sun was rising, and the morning light would cost them good cover if they didn't move fast. Then Hardesty spoke over the general channel.

"In position," he said. *"Three targets. Green light."*

Namir gave an imperceptible nod. *"Execute."*

Saxon turned to the window in time to see a man on the roof of the Rostov looking up at them, raising a handheld to his ear; in the next second the man jerked violently backward as if pulled by an invisible wire, a jet of red spurting from his chest. As the helo descended, he spotted the other guards on the roof, collapsing in puffs of pink mist.

The helo fell into a hover ten meters up, and the rest of the Tyrants deployed, Barrett and Hermann leading, then Namir and Saxon, with Federova last.

Saxon tensed; he was used to fast-roping, but his new high-fall aug—part of the "recruitment package"—meant he could drop straight into the thick without a descender cord. The whole thing was counterintuitive, but it worked. He jumped, and a moment before he landed, a brief pulse of electromagnetic energy flared around him, cushioning his fall. He landed squarely, the crackle of the effect generated by the augmentation taking the shock and bleeding it off to nothing.

Federova put down a heartbeat later, cat-falling with little more than a crunch of gravel. She had her hair back behind an Alice band studded with data loops, but no hood. Federova saw him looking and gazed back, languid and unconcerned.

With a gust of downwash, the helo powered into the sky. He looked away, scanning the rooftop. The Rostov was a shallow, three-lobed tower that had been thrown up in the boom years of the early 2010s, but never completed. There were whole floors of the building that were locked off, still unfinished over a decade later.

"Blue, Green," said Namir, using Barrett and Hermann's call signs. "Secure the roof. Check for stragglers." He glanced at Saxon. "Gray, with me."

"Roof is clear," Hardesty said, from his firing nest across the square. He didn't like the suggestion that he'd missed someone.

Low and quick, Saxon followed the Tyrant commander toward the boxy service shack in the middle of the roof. He passed the corpse of the man the sniper had shot in the chest, and scanned the body. The dead man had a look of frozen surprise on his face, a foam of red froth on his lips. Hardesty's bullet had punctured the heart, the exit wound ripping open the guard's back.

The man's face triggered a connection to the mission data Saxon had shunted to a temporary memory store in his implanted neural hub; the modified wet-drive was another "bonus" from the Tyrants. He blinked up an image from an arrest record. The man lying in the pool of crimson was immediately identified as Oleg Pushkin, a minor enforcer with the main Moscow crime syndicate, the Solntsevskaya Bratva. "This guy's a mob hitter," Saxon murmured.

"They all are," Namir replied. "Keep up."

Barrett was at the service shack as they reached it. Air-conditioning equipment, heat exchangers, and cable gear for the Rostov's elevator banks hummed inside.

Namir nodded at a secured maintenance hatch on the side of the shack. "Open it."

Hermann leaned close and used a digital lockpick to neutralize the security latches; when he was done, Barrett stepped in and curled his fingers around the lip of the hatch with a grimace. The bunches of myomer muscles in his arms stiffened, gathered—and then with a low howl of tortured metal the hatch came away, shearing the bolt heads clean off.

As Namir peered inside, Saxon glanced over his shoulder and his brow furrowed in confusion. "Where's... Red?" There was no sign of Federova anywhere on the rooftop. She had been only a few steps behind him.

Barrett chuckled. "She's around."

"Green," said Namir. "Deny their communications."

"Complying." Hermann nodded, drawing a thick, disc-shaped object from his backpack. It resembled a land mine. Acting quickly, the German set it on the ground and flicked a yellow-and-black-striped activation switch. A flicker of interference momentarily stuttered across Saxon's cyberoptics.

"Target comms are dead," reported Barrett, cocking his head like a dog hearing a whistle. "Ready."

"Insertion," said Namir. "Go!"

One after another, they threaded in through the torn-out hatch and into the mass of machinery crowding the interior of the service shack. Inside, a triangular cluster of running gear fell away into a series of shafts that ran the length of the Rostov, down to the basement parking levels sixteen stories below. Saxon toggled his optics to low-light mode and the space became visible in shades of green and white. The shapes of elevator cars were visible, most of them static, others gently rising or descending.

Namir and Saxon took point, working their way down past the slowly turning drums of support cables and the rumbling lift gears. According to their information, Kontarsky and his people were on floor thirteen; outside, the pilot of the helo was watching the windows of the apartments on the thirteenth floor, scanning through the vision-opaque glass with a thermographic sensor, watching the body-heat traces of the minister and his staff. At this time of day, most of them were asleep; only the guards were supposed to be awake. They had to take care, though; their intel wasn't clear on how many, if any, civilians were in the building. Collateral damage was to be kept to an absolute minimum.

Securing nylon cords to the cable frames, the two of them fast-roped down in silence, pausing at each level to sweep for magnetic anomaly detectors or beam sensors. Saxon watched Namir work with speed and delicacy, rendering security systems inert with the skill of a veteran.

The central lift of a three-block cluster was locked in place at the thirteenth. The plan was to enter through its roof and fan out along the three radial corridors—Namir, Hermann, and Saxon taking one each, Barrett holding the core as backup.

"Prep for breach," Namir subvocalized. Saxon lowered himself to the top of the elevator car, disconnected his

tether, and drew out a pressurized canister of det-foam. Dialing the nozzle to narrow feed, he put marble-size blobs of the khaki-toned chemical in the corners of the car's roof, then thumbed a set of slaved microdetonators into the congealing foam.

As he finished, he felt the elevator move slightly beneath him and heard voices. Three men, speaking in Russian. Through an air vent, he could see a sliver of what was going on.

"*Shto slúchios?*" said one of them. He was tapping the radio headset at his ear, frowning.

Another man, out of Saxon's sight line, spat in irritation and followed his cohort into the lift. They were leaving their posts; Hermann's trick with the communications blackout had spooked them.

Then the man with the radio gave a slow, owlish blink; Saxon recognized the action. He had implanted optics—he was changing vision modes. The guard looked up, and for a fraction of a second Saxon saw a bluish glitter in his right eye. The tell gave away exactly what kind of optic the guard was using; a terahertz lens that could see right through light cover.

In the next few seconds, everything happened with bullet-fast rapidity. The guard swore explosively and slammed his fist into the control pad, sending the elevator into an express plunge to the lobby. The other men in the car dragged their guns up, but they were armed with cut-down assault rifles and inside the close confines of the elevator, the size of the guns made them unwieldy.

Saxon held tight to the car's frame and felt his stomach turn over as the lift dropped away; in the next breath the guards would have a bead on him. A spray of blind fire, and he would be ripped to shreds.

He cursed and did the only thing he could, tapping the detonator key on the control bracelet around his wrist. The blobs of det-foam combusted with sharp, smoky reports and the roof of the elevator car collapsed inward, Saxon falling with it. The noise deafened him.

The confined space became chaotic. The guards cursed and struggled to deflect the debris, lashing out. Saxon had no time to draw a weapon; it was like fighting inside a coffin, with no room to maneuver; nothing to do but strike fast and give no quarter.

He punched the man with the t-wave optic into the wall and the guard's rifle snarled, discharging a three-round burst into the door. Then, spinning in place, Saxon drove the armor-plated pad on his elbow into the rib cage of the second guard. He shoved him into a thinscreen along the back wall and it fractured, webbing with cracks.

The third guard was still struggling with his rifle, shouldering aside the remains of a collapsed lighting rig. He launched himself at Saxon and slammed the frame of the weapon into his face, cracking his eye-shields. The soldier hit back with a punch from his augmented arm, and connected with the guard's ribs. Bones fractured with a sickening crunch and the assailant staggered backward, wheezing.

Then all three of them attacked him at once, using their guns like clubs to beat him about the head and shoulders. Saxon felt an impact at the base of his spine and he stumbled, losing his balance as the elevator continued to drop toward the ground floor. He had no doubts that the guards had reinforcements waiting there; he had to finish this quickly.

Locking his legs, Saxon pivoted and let his reflex booster implant ramp up to full. His nerves jangled with the sudden new input, the influence of the neuromuscular accelerator coursing through him. The guards were crowding in and he struck out once more. The man with the cracked ribs went back into the doors, slammed into place by the torso of the first guard. Saxon fired a low, fast kick at the leg of the other man and was rewarded with a pain-filled yelp. Natural bone broke easily under the turned steel of a heavy augmentation.

The giddy rush of speed made Saxon's skin prickle; he felt heat wash over him, and in a moment of sudden, shocking scent-memory, he smelled aviation fuel and smoke. The crackle of the fires around the crashed veetol were abruptly there in the front of his thoughts, the horrible tearing noise as Sam died in front of him—

Fury spread through Saxon like a wave, and he went in for the kill. The throat of the fallen guard he crushed with a brutal, stabbing blow from his cyberarm; then he pulled a broken piece of roof support up from where it had landed and used it to beat the next of the guards bloody. The last man, who fought back as he coughed and spat, struck out with a cyberhand that sprouted a fan of blades. Saxon took a cut across his cheek, but the pain seemed distant, edited from the moment. He took the guard's arm—a spindly model sheathed in pink, flesh-toned plastic, doubtless Federal Army surplus—and bent it back against the joint, fracturing the casing. The guard tried to struggle free, but Saxon took a clump of his hair and beat his head into the walls until he fell.

The elevator chimed and Saxon let the guard's body go, allowing it to fall out and onto the dusty marble floor of the lobby.

Three more men were waiting for him, standing in a semicircle around the elevator bank, each with a heavy-caliber automatic raised and aimed. The data feed from the wet-drive helpfully told him that these men were also members of the Bratva, each with a lengthy police record; but the tips of the prison tattoos that emerged from the open collars of their shirts made that clear enough.

Saxon slowly raised his hands, panting, the moment of animal fury he had felt in the elevator fading as fast as it had come. For a few seconds there, he had become lost, absorbed in rage-fueled guilt over Sam, Kano, and all the others. The edges of the dark anger he had first felt in the field hospital boiled inside him.

He knew enough Russian to understand that the men with guns wanted him to kneel down. Carefully, he did what they asked, biding his time. One of them would have to come close enough to take the Hurricane from him, and then, if there was a chance—

Something shimmered like oil on water in the corner of Saxon's vision and he turned toward it in time to see a shape emerge out of the air, a glassy, swift figure blurred by motion, abruptly becoming solid, *real*.

The military called it "mimeoptical active camouflage"; Saxon wasn't up on the full technical specs for the augmentation, but from what he knew, the system used a matrix of molecule-thin induction wires implanted beneath the epidermis and across cyberlimb plating that when activated, generated a local electromagnetic field that could render a human being into a walking stealth weapon. It was prohibitively expensive and delicate under battlefield conditions, and difficulties with the human augmentation interface meant that it was rarely deployed in combat. Full synchrony between the user and the system was hard to achieve; to use it well, you had to be someone with a near-pathological focus of will.

The ghost figure became Federova, and she killed the first man with a slashing knife cut to the throat, dispatching the other two with quick, silenced bursts from her machine pistol. She trembled slightly as the camouflage effect bled away, the focused EM field dissipating.

Federova looked across at him as he stood up, her scalp beaded with sweat; and then she smiled.

"Go tactical," ordered Namir.

The elevator doors came off their mountings in a screech of torn steel, and Barrett swung out behind them, snorting with effort. He dealt with the guard closest to him with a savage backhand punch that drove bone shards up into the man's forebrain. The guard dropped to the unfinished concrete floor, twitching as he died. Namir and Hermann came in a heartbeat later, their machine pistols snarling. Armor-piercing rounds sprayed in fans, taking more kills.

One of the guards was still alive, and he stumbled toward a side corridor, bleeding heavily. The German was on him in a moment, and with a haymaker punch from his armored fist, he crushed the man's skull with single blow.

"Move," snarled the commander. The mission was entering its full active phase; now speed, not stealth, was of the essence. Namir glanced around, his eyes narrowing.

The thirteenth floor did not match the spy photos captured by the intelligence sources of his patrons. Instead of fitted deep pile carpets and bright walls patterned with subtle murals, the surroundings were bare and undecorated. The floor had the dusty scent of old concrete and ozone. Where mahogany doors should have led the way to opulent suites and apartments, there were yawning open frames walled off by ragged sheets of industrial polythene.

Hermann gave him a quizzical look. "This is not right."

"No," admitted Namir. "Proceed. And stay alert."

"Company," snapped Barrett, raising his arm. A group of four more thugs sprinted into view from along one of the radial corridors, each of them armed with a heavy rifle.

"Take them," said Namir.

Barrett's right arm came apart on expanding frames, the plating folding back, the hand turning aside to allow the mechanism within to emerge; he tugged an ammunition belt from a hopper in his backpack, swiftly slotting it into the feed maw on the base of the reconfigured limb. From the wrist emerged the triple-head barrel of a minigun. The muzzles spun into a blur, and with a sound like the buzz of a heavy electric generator, the cyberweapon ejected a gout of yellow fire and a storm of bullets. Grinning, Barrett panned the cannon across the corridor, ripping through the flimsy flakboard the guards used for cover, tearing into them, blowing craters in the surface of the unfinished concrete.

"Advance! Kontarsky's rooms are just ahead." Namir surged forward, and the others went with him. Reaching the space where the grand suite should have been, the Israeli reached up and tore aside a curtain of plastic.

Inside there was only another echoing, half-built space.

Festoons of cables hung from the ceiling or snaked across the floor from drumlike power cells; the room was hotter that the corridor outside, blood-warm and dry.

"What the hell...?" Barrett scanned the room, his scarred face souring. "This is the wrong goddamn place! He's not here...nobody is here!"

"Negative," insisted Hermann. "This is the correct location. Kontarsky should be in this room. We saw the thermographic scans..."

"Why would six men guard nothing?" Namir demanded. He stalked across the open space, his footfalls echoing. Something about the dimensions of the room seemed off; in front of the windows that looked out onto the Moscow dawn, there were long glassy panes arranged in a barrier, running wall to wall and floor to ceiling. The power cords ran to connectors, and as Namir came close, he felt a steady surge of warmth radiating from them.

"White," he said to the air. "Go to thermal. Target the thirteenth floor. Tell me what you see."

"I have three unit indicators," came the reply from the sniper. *"Silver, Blue, Green. Multiple unidentified targets same location."* He paused, a note of confusion entering his tone. *"You're in the room with them... "*

"No," Namir growled, reaching down to grab a bunch of the cables. "We are not." He gave the cables a violent yank and they tore free from the glass, spitting sparks. The glass panes shimmered and went transparent as power bled out of them.

Hardesty's gasp of surprise was transmitted over the open channel. *"What the hell...? Silver, all unidentified targets have vanished. Repeat, vanished."*

"They were never here," Hermann said aloud. "The panels. They were some form of thermal blind, projecting a decoy image."

"Real smart," muttered Barrett. "So where is this creep really hidin' out?"

"Find him," demanded Namir.

Saxon nodded distractedly, and glanced around the marble lobby. It was gloomy in here, the only light a weak morning glow through the fan-shaped windows above the high front doors. Aside from Federova, the area was deserted.

He glanced back to find the Russian woman down on one knee, rifling through the pockets of one of the men she had just killed. A gasp escaped the guard's mouth as she turned him over, a last breath leaving his lungs as she shifted the body.

"If the target's not on thirteen, then he's got to be on a different floor, shielded from thermographic scan." Saxon gave voice to his thoughts, following them through. He cast around the lobby. "There are multiple lift shafts. One of these has to be a dedicated express elevator... *Here.*" He found a single set of doors off to one side, in a discreet alcove; everything about the positioning of it screamed *Restricted Access.*

"Use it," Namir ordered. *"We'll track your locators, vector to you."*

"There's no call button here," he noted, finding a glass panel set in the wall. "It may need some kind of key, or maybe palm print recognition—"

A heavy, wet crunch sounded behind him, and a blade edge clanked against the marble; then Federova was sprinting to his side. In her fingers she carried something fleshy that left a trail of red droplets all across the tiled checkerboard floor.

"Never mind," Saxon reported, as she pressed a severed hand into the panel. "Red has, uh, improvised."

The elevator gave a hollow chime and opened itself to them.

It let them out on ten, right in the line of fire from a pair of security-grade boxguards. The machines were steel cubes the size of a washing machine, inert in a monitoring mode; but when their sensors detected something that did not match their programmed security protocols, the mechanisms unfolded like a complex puzzle, extruding weapon muzzles and targeting scopes. They were the smaller cousins of the large, vehicle-size versions deployed by the military or law enforcement, but they could still be lethal.

Saxon rolled out into the lavish corridor, bringing up his machine pistol as he moved. Federova launched herself from the elevator car on those racehorse legs of hers, so fast she was almost a blur of motion. The boxguards dithered, the simple machine-brains of the basic robots hesitating over which target to attack.

Saxon used the moment to his advantage, coming up in half cover behind a cockpit leather armchair. He aimed with the Hurricane and squeezed the trigger, marching a clip of armor-piercing rounds up the frame of the closest boxguard, ripping it open. It stumbled into a wall and collapsed.

Federova was on top of her target, and she took off the machine's primary sensor head with a spinning crescent kick. The robot reeled, and the dark-skinned woman rammed the muzzle of her machine pistol into a gap between its armor plates, and fired point-blank.

"Tenth floor," Saxon reported. "We're splitting up to search for the target." He looked toward Federova, who gave him a curt nod and set off down the southern corridor.

"Copy, Gray," said Namir. *"We're coming to you. Isolate and neutralize."*

Saxon chose the northwest arm of the Y-shaped corridor and moved forward, low and fast, from cover to cover.

Something moved ahead of him, and he saw a squat, thickset shape roll out from a shadowed alcove. It was an ornate machine, plated with steel and sheathed with ceramic detailing—an elegant hotel service robot modeled on some arcane, pre-twentieth-century artistic ideal of what an automaton should be. It moved on fat gray tires, turning like a tall tank. A speaker grille presented itself to Saxon and spoke in Russian, then Farsi and finally English. "This area is off-limits to guests," it declared. "Proceed no farther."

A fan of green laser light issued out and scanned the hallway, catching Saxon by surprise. The machine caught sight of his drawn weapon and reacted instantly. Ceramic panels opened up to allow the vanes of a pulsed energy projector to emerge. "Mandatory warning delivered," it said. "Deploying deterrent."

A throbbing wave-front of force hummed from the robot and blasted down the corridor. Saxon went down as the pulse threw freestanding tables and flower vases into the air with the force of the discharge. The rush of the knockdown effect was powerful, like the undertow in an ocean wave.

He leapt from where he had landed, firing as he went. Bullets sparked off metal and inlaid wood, marring the elegantly worked surface of the machine. It fired again, dislodging pictures from the walls, blasting open the doors to empty rooms.

Saxon's free hand closed around a cylindrical object on his gear vest and he tugged it free with a jerk of the wrist. By feel alone, he found the primer tab and pulled it. The weapon buzzed in response and Saxon threw it hard, diving for cover behind a damaged door.

The Type 4 Frag-k grenade clanked off the casing of the robot and bounced to the carpet beneath it; a moment later the explosive core detonated, blasting the machine off its supports and into a smoking heap.

Bursting from cover, Saxon raced through the cloud of cordite smoke and the humming after-note of the explosion. He took down the door to the corner suite with a kick from the heel of his tactical boot and pushed through, leading with the Hurricane.

Inside, the room was wide and devoid of angles, all soft furnishings and bowed windows. A thick layer of metallized plastic sheet—doubtless some kind of sensor baffle—coated the window glass, bleeding out all the color and warmth of the dawn rising over Zubovskaya Square. Saxon found the power feed for the baffle and disconnected it.

Off to one side, folding panels opened out into a range of rooms bigger than the house Saxon had grown up in; on the other side of the suite, a second bedroom had been gutted to accommodate the racks of a compact server farm, an orchard of data monitors, and a complex virtual keyboard.

A man in a dark jacket rushed Saxon from a doorway leading to the bathroom, the lethally compact shape of a Widowmaker shotgun in his hands. The machine pistol in Saxon's ready grip chattered and the thug took the burst in the chest, crashing backward onto the tiles in a welter of blood. He ejected the clip, slammed a fresh load into place, and crossed into the bedroom.

Mikhail Kontarsky, his face lit by sheer animal panic, recoiled from the keyboard console and fumbled for a nickel-plated heavy-frame automatic pistol lying on top of one of the server pods. Saxon brought up the muzzle of the Hurricane and aimed it at Kontarsky's chest. "Don't," he told him.

The Russian wasn't the man he'd seen in the briefing picture anymore. That grim face and distant gaze were gone, replaced by raw terror. He gave a brittle nod and held his hands to his chest. "Please," he began, his voice heavily accented. "You must not stop me."

Something in Saxon's peripheral vision shimmered, and he realized that beneath the panes of complex, scrolling data on the screens, there was a recognizable shape, the ghost-image of a human face, peering out through layers of static. *"He's here to kill you, Mikhail,"* it said. The voice was toneless, sexless, flattened into a brittle machine-timbre that was utterly anonymous; the only thing that could be considered any kind of identity was a data tag showing a name, *Janus*.

"You told me I would have more time!" Kontarsky spat, his lips trembling. He gave Saxon a pleading stare. "Please, I have to finish what I started, or—"

Saxon took a warning step forward. "Touch that console and it will be the last thing you ever do, Minister."

"Mikhail," said the video-masked figure. *"This is bigger than you. We need the data on the Killing Floor, you must complete the upload—"*

Saxon sneered and put a burst of rounds through the big screen, silencing the voice. Kontarsky howled and stumbled backward. "Enough of your pal." He grabbed the man by the collar and dragged him forward, propelling him out of the room.

"No." There were a dozen other monitors in the gutted bedroom, and screens in the main part of the suite; each one flickered into life, repeating the image of the static-shrouded face. The word repeated over and over as each one activated. *"No. Not yet."*

"It's over," Saxon told him, ignoring the voice.

A flash of resentment and defiance crossed Kontarsky's face, and he struggled in Saxon's grip. "You're not here to arrest me...You're not a policeman! What authority do you have?" The moment passed just as quickly, as the man's eyes fell to the machine pistol. "Please, I beg of you. Do not kill me. I only did what I thought was right!"

"He is not a criminal," insisted the voice. *"You cannot judge him."*

Saxon's jaw stiffened. "You're part of a global terror network!" he spat. "You're part of Juggernaut! And the people you sold out to are responsible for the deaths of my men!" The anger was coming back, and he felt the burn of it. "Operation Rainbird." He snarled the words at the cowering man. "You know that name? You know what happened out there? They were soldiers, doing their jobs—it wasn't even their damn war!" Saxon clubbed Kontarsky with the butt of the gun and sent him stumbling into the door frame. "Now move! I'm taking you alive! You can answer for what you've done!" He glared at one of the screens. "Are you watching this? Because we're coming for you next."

"N-no, no, no…That's not true," Kontarsky stammered, turning to the monitor. "Please, Janus!" he implored the video-ghost. "Help me…"

But the image's attention was on Saxon. *Do you know what you are doing, mercenary?* He thought he detected a faint edge of reproach in the words. *Do you know what master you serve?*

The question made Saxon hesitate and he shot Kontarsky a hard look, hauling him up to his feet, pushing him forward into the middle of the room. The man staring back at him was pale with fear, his eyes betraying no duplicity, no deception. "I don't know anything about your men," he whispered. "You must believe me!"

And for a moment, Saxon *did*. He was a good judge of liars; he'd met enough of them in combat and elsewhere, and he knew the look of a man too afraid to lie. And if "Rainbird" meant nothing to him, then—

"Green light."

Saxon heard the voice over the general comm channel a split second before the plastic-coated window crackled with fractures. Hardesty's bullet entered Kontarsky's head through the nasal cavity, blasting bone and brain matter across the wood-paneled walls. His body fell, jetting red, collapsing across a rosewood table.

When Saxon looked up again all the screens were dark.

FIVE

The autocab let her out at the curbside outside her apartment block, and Kelso glanced back to watch the driverless vehicle nose its way back into traffic, the sensor antennae along the hood of the car feeling the air. The fare from the airport had claimed the last of the money on the discretionary credit chip Temple gave her. The flight back had passed in a blur, Anna's gaze turned inward, passing the time with the ebb and flow of the same emotions over and over again. She felt disgusted at herself for her weakness, angry at getting caught, sad at the thought of letting Matt down, numb and furious, full of regret and fear.

But mostly she felt hollowed out inside. All the work, everything she'd done in the endless days and weeks of her clandestine investigation, now was unraveling all around her. She had destroyed her career for the sake of something that only she seemed able to see, for a truth that no one else wanted to face.

As she walked the short distance to the lobby of the building, the question echoed in her mind. *Was it worth it?*

Inside, she thumbed the entry pad to her apartment and ignored the glow of the messaging system, dropping the packet she had carried all the way from the 10th Precinct on the sofa. In the living room, the television activated automatically, blipping to the local Picus News affiliate preset. The screen showed a report about the upcoming National Science Board caucus on human augmentaion; the conference was getting a lot of heat from the pro-human, anti-enhancement lobby, and it seemed like every day a new busload of protestors arrived in the capital.

She ignored the low burble of the screen and fished out her vu-phone, leaving it on the countertop in the small, plastic-white kitchen, mechanically moving through the motions of swigging milk from a carton in the refrigerator. The apartment was dim; the sunny magnolia colors did little to lift the tone of the gloom leaking in from the dull, low cloud smothering the sky.

Anna grasped the carton in her hand, her fingers deadening with the cold. *Was it worth it?* The question hammered at her in the silence.

A grimace crossed her face and she went to the alcove where her laptop sat inside an old cedar bureau. The computer woke at her touch, and she pulled her federal ID from her pocket; the machine automatically pinged the arfid in her badge, but the data chip did not reply. Instead, a small panel opened on the screen. The text it contained was a paragraph of legal boilerplate reiterating what Temple had told her in the holding room, but the meaning was clear. *Access denied. Clearance revoked.* Even the most basic level of entry into the agency network was sealed off from her.

She sat in the dimness, lit only by the glow of the screen, and began to wonder what else had taken place while she was in New York. Temple had reamed her files, that much was certain...but had he sent agents to her home as well? Anna looked around. She saw nothing out of place.

A sudden impulse pushed her up from the chair where she sat, and she crossed to the closet. Inside, hidden behind the hanging clothes, the safe-locker she'd installed back when she moved in was visible, the door still sealed shut. She typed in the entry code and found the contents as she'd left them. A box of what little jewelry she had, some cash and papers—and in a separate section, a short-frame Zenith 10 mm automatic, two full ammo clips, and a small flash drive.

Anna took the gun and checked it before loading. The weapon was legal, licensed and clean. If anything, the flash drive was the more dangerous item; inside it was an encrypted copy of everything she had worked on, every bit of data gleaned along the road to this moment.

She turned the memory module over in her hand. All that work, all the lies and secrecy, the nights she stayed late at the agency offices digging into files she should never had accessed, the legacy of the stims she'd taken to keep awake, to keep going...

Was it worth it?

A chime sounded though the apartment, and Anna flinched in surprise. The house was announcing a call on her vu-phone. She left the gun and the drive on a shelf in the closet and went to the handset.

The caller ident read *Matt Ryan*. Anna had been maudlin about deleting his name and number from the phone's memory. It was a foolish, silly thing, but she'd kept putting it off; perhaps on some level she was denying the reality of what had happened six months ago on Q Street.

She gripped the handheld, her knuckles turning white around the silver casing. Slowly, Anna raised it to her ear, tapping the answer pad. "Who is this?"

The voice at the other end was electronically distorted, all trace of identity bled out. *"You and I need to have a talk."* Kelso's training instinctively kicked in; she tried to listen *through* the masking filter, looking for the cadence and pattern of the voice, profiling the speaker in her mind.

"Whoever you are, you're not Matt Ryan. So I'm hanging up—"

"That would be a mistake," said the voice. *"I spoofed the caller ID so you'd pick up. Because I'm guessing right now that you're not in the mood to talk to people. Not after what happened at the pier."*

Her throat went dry. "What pier?"

"Don't talk to me like I'm stupid, Agent Kelso. I really hate it when people do that."

"Then show me the same courtesy," she snapped, her patience wearing thin. "Who the hell are you and what do you want? Answer that or get lost."

Anna heard a faint sigh. *"You can call me D-Bar. And like I said, I wanna talk to you."*

"We are talking."

"Well, when I say I want to, I really mean we want to. And not over an open line. In person."

She drifted back toward the closet, reaching for the pistol. "Uh-huh. And who is 'we'?"

"A group you may have heard of. We call ourselves the Juggernaut Collective. We're kind of a big deal."

Anna's hand froze on the gun. "If you know who I am and what happened out at the pier, then you know the last thing I'm going to do is talk to a terrorist." She should have disconnected, right then and there; but instead she waited.

"*One man's terrorist is another man's freedom fighter. Yeah, trite, maybe, but true.*" The sigh came again. "*Look, let's cut to the chase, 'cos I'm not sure how much longer I can keep this conduit secure. You went to that wannabe Widow and her crew and they gave you some scraps. But the fact is, she's a bottom-feeder and she was never going to get you what you need. We can. We're looking for the same thing.*"

"I don't know what you're talking about—"

"*The Tyrants. Do you want to know who they are or not?*" Anna said nothing, and after a moment the voice returned. "*I'll take your silence for a yes. Check your messages. If we see anyone but you, that name will be all you'll ever get.*" The connection cut with a click; a moment later, the vu-phone beeped. In the message cue was a street address in downtown Washington, D.C., and a meeting time two hours hence.

In the bathroom she paused to splash a handful of cold water on her face. Two hours; that barely gave her enough time to throw on a fresh set of clothes and bolt out the door.

And she was tired. The events in New York, the time in the cells, the nervous tension of the flight home... The fatigue from all of it was exerting a heavy, tidal drag on her. She couldn't afford to do this half-awake. She couldn't afford to miss something.

Anna reached for the door to the medicine cabinet without looking in the mirror.

Knightsbridge—London—Great Britain

The town house had once been a hotel, an exclusive boutique lodge in a shady mews just a few blocks away from the greensward of Hyde Park. Like so much of the city, it sat in unconcerned contrast with the sheer-sided corporate towers emerging from the streets around it, the pale stone of the five-story exterior understated, the rectangular windows lit from within by a warm glow not lost through the thickness of armored polyglass. From the outside, it seemed no different from any of its neighbors; but the structure of the town house was reinforced and hardened against anything up to a rocket attack.

Saxon glanced around the fourth-floor room and took in the clean, sparse décor; white walls and chrome-framed furniture. A print of Rubin's *The Flute Player* hung on one wall, a large thinscreen monitor mirroring it on the far side of the room. The six operatives sat around a long, glass-topped conference table, each dressed in what passed for civilian attire—although to a trained eye none of the Tyrants could shake the aura of a soldier, even when armor and weapons were out of reach.

At first, Saxon thought the town house was some sort of operations center, perhaps the London base for the Tyrants; but then he had glimpsed slivers of the rooms on the lower floors through half-open doors. He saw living spaces, a study, a kitchen—and dotted around, the touches that showed a family lived in this place. On the third-floor landing, Saxon passed a framed photo and had to look twice; Jaron Namir gazed back out at him, dressed in a suit and wearing a yarmulke, smiling broadly. A woman in yellow and two children, a boy and a girl, shared his good cheer. The image was jarring; try as he might, Saxon couldn't connect the man in the picture with the man he had seen kill silently with no pause, no flicker of remorse.

They were in Namir's home. Something about the idea of that ground against Saxon's every ingrained instinct. The idea of a man like him, a man like Namir having a life and a family outside the unit, seemed false. Somehow, *unfair*.

In the wake of the mission in Moscow, the team had gone through a cursory review aboard the transport plane as it flew west, back into European airspace. As with every other operational debrief, Saxon had felt as if they were going through the motions, not just for themselves, but for some unseen observer. The people who gave the orders were watching, he was certain of it. Not for the first time, he wondered if they would ever show their faces.

Seated around the table, Namir led them through the postmortem once again. On the plane, they had given their reports one at a time; now, with all of them together, Saxon felt the pressure of the unanswered questions in his thoughts.

He leaned forward. "I could have brought Kontarsky in alive."

Hardesty gave him an arch look. "Was that ever the objective?"

Saxon ignored him, turning to Namir. "You said Kontarsky was working with Juggernaut. He was a high-value target. He must have had intel we could use."

"The minister was compromised," Namir replied. "Anything we'd have been able to compel from him through interrogation would have been marginal at best. We didn't need what he knew."

Saxon's eyes narrowed. Despite what Namir had told him earlier, he was sure of Kontarsky's reaction when he mentioned Operation Rainbird. The name meant nothing to the man.

Namir saw his train of thought and headed him off. "You need to see past this, Ben. Don't make it personal. Kontarsky was a cancer in the Russian federal government. We cut him out."

"Sends a message," offered Barrett in a languid tone. "Anyone deals with Juggernaut, they're not protected."

"We're not in the business of taking prisoners," Namir went on. "You know that."

Hardesty leaned back in his chair. "As we're on the subject, maybe the limey can explain why it is he didn't just double-tap the creep the moment he found him?"

"I told you. I could have brought him in."

"You don't get to make that choice," Hardesty replied. "You're not in command of this unit. We're not your little PMC scout troop, Saxon. You lost that, remember?"

Saxon studied the other man. "Maybe if you were actually on the deck with the rest of us, instead of hiding behind a camo net four hundred meters away, I might have some respect for your opinion, *Yank*." He gave the last word a sneer. "Don't make the mistake of thinking you see everything down that rifle scope."

"What I did see was you talking to the mark," insisted the sniper. "And someone else, too, maybe?"

"Kontarsky was the only one in the room," Saxon replied, a little quicker than he would have liked. From the corner of his eye, he saw Hermann, Federova, and Barrett watching the exchange, gauging his reaction.

Do you know what you are doing, mercenary? The ghost-voice's questions returned to him. *Do you know what master you serve?*

The misgivings muttering at the edges of his thoughts were there, clear and undeniable. Saxon broke eye contact with Hardesty as Namir stood up and crossed the room to a window.

"I understand your intentions," said the commander. "But I need all of you to follow orders when I give them. We may not have allegiance to a flag anymore, but we all must share allegiance to the Tyrants. If we don't have that, then we're no better than Juggernaut or any of the other anarchists out there." He threw a look toward Saxon and Hermann. "You two are our newest recruits. You both understand that, don't you?"

"Of course," replied Hermann, without hesitation. In turn, Saxon gave a wary nod.

Namir went on. "There are reasons for everything we do. Reasons for every order I give you. Every mission." He smiled slightly, the craggy face softening for a brief moment. "We cannot bring stability if we don't have equilibrium in our ranks." Namir's gaze crossed to Hardesty, and his tone hardened again. "Clear?"

The sniper pursed his lips. "Clear," he repeated.

He will never tell us, Saxon realized. *Whoever is pulling the strings, he's never going to pull back the curtain on them.* The question that came next pressed to the front of his thoughts: *Can I live with that?*

In the months since Namir had plucked him from the field hospital in Australia, Saxon had earned more money than he had in years of service with Belltower and to the British Crown. The Tyrants had fitted him with high-spec augmentation upgrades, given him access to weapons and hardware that had been beyond his reach in the SAS or as a military contractor. Downtime between missions was spent at secure resorts, the likes of which were open only to corporate execs and the very rich. And the missions... the missions were the most challenging he'd ever had. Putting aside Hardesty's irritating manner, Saxon meshed well with all the Tyrant team members. He couldn't deny that he liked the work. They were free of all the paperwork and second-guessing he'd waded through as someone else's line soldier. None of the Tyrants wasted time saluting and sweating the trivial crap; they just got on with the business of soldiering, and the appeal of that simple fact held Ben Saxon tight.

He liked being here. Despite all the doubts, it still felt *right*. After all the two- or three-man operations, the tag-and-bags, the terminations and infiltrations, and then the Moscow gig, Saxon felt as if he had *graduated*. He was in; but part of him remained troubled, and it annoyed him that he couldn't fully articulate it.

Was it the secrets? It seemed foolish to consider it; as a spec ops soldier, he'd spent most of his career working in the dark...but with the British Army and then with Belltower, he'd at least had some grasp on what he was risking his life for.

In the humid night air of the field hospital, Namir

had offered him a second chance. He had offered the opportunity to make a difference, but more than that, Namir had offered Saxon *trust*.

Or perhaps, just the illusion of it. There were other operations going on, he was certain. Tyrant missions that he wasn't supposed to be aware of; he knew for a fact that Federova and Hardesty had been deployed to the United States, Japan, and India on untraceable black-bag jobs. Once more, any question about who chose their targets or what they were was not going to be answered.

Do you know what master you serve?

He decided then that for the moment, the questions the shadowy hacker Janus had posed would go no further.

Namir turned from the window. "It's clear to me that we've reached an important juncture here." Hardesty, Federova, and Barrett abruptly stood up, with Saxon and Hermann reacting just a second later. For a moment, the ghost of a cold smile danced on Hardesty's lips.

"About time," said Barrett.

Namir nodded to the big man. "Open the study, will you?"

Barrett nodded and crossed to the wall where *The Flute Player* hung. He whispered something Saxon didn't catch and a seam opened on silent hydraulics. The wall retracted into itself to reveal more rooms beyond. Saxon caught sight of a dark, windowless space, weapons racks, and workstations.

"Yelena?" Namir inclined his head toward Federova.

The woman's hand blurred as she pulled a weapon from a pocket, a boxy plastic handgun lined with a yellow-and-black hazard strip. She turned it on Hermann and pulled the trigger.

A thick dart buzzed from the muzzle and hit the German in the neck; Saxon heard the hum of a tazer discharge and Hermann moaned, his body going rigid. The younger man fell, his watch cap falling from his head.

"What—?" Saxon looked up as a second dart struck him in the chest. He had an instant to register the bite of the contact needles in his skin before a second stun charge lashed into him.

The Obama Center—Washington, D.C.—United States of America

The message brought her to the doors of the conference center, the fading light of evening lit by the glow from inside the glass-and-steel building. A gallery of holograms formed a promenade from the street to the main doors, each of them moving through cycles showing venue information and events listings.

She moved closer, her senses sharpened and acute; for the moment, the fatigue gnawing at her had been beaten back. Kelso knew she'd pay for it later—but for now she was focused and alert.

Over the entrance, a banner announced the name of the seminar that was about to begin: *No Better—The Myth of Human Augmentation*. She immediately recognized the title. The ebook that it was based on had been hovering around the top ten of the Picus Network best-seller list forever, along with its various audio and video versions, not to mention the frequent references to it on the chat-show news circuit. She glanced up to see the face of the author smiling down from one of the holoscreens. William

Taggart's warm, fatherly eyes watched her from behind a pair of understated glasses, wearing the same expression of compassionate concern that graced the back cover of every copy of *No Better,* and every flyer for his lobby group, the Humanity Front.

Taggart had founded his organization with one goal in mind—to disabuse society at large of the idea that human augmentation technology was a positive development. As Taggart's people would put it, cybernetic implants served only to dilute a person's humanity, making them less than what they were instead of more.

Anna found the Humanity Front's rhetoric a little hard to take, though. The augmentations she possessed had improved her, and that was something she'd never been in doubt about—and when she thought about the facets of her life that made her feel less human, her implants weren't at the root of it. She frowned and pushed that thought away.

Smartly dressed young men and women were handing out flyers to the attendees and anyone who walked within arm's reach. Anna noted that a fair few of them were sporting simple mechanical prosthetics in place of limbs. These were people who had taken to what some called "disaugmentation," freely giving up cybernetic implants in an attempt to move back to being fully human again; the only thing was, losing an augmentation wasn't like getting a gang tattoo removed or ditching your piercings. She didn't know quite how to take someone who'd made that choice willingly. Maybe life with a basic leg prosthesis was easier, with less maintenance to deal with and no weekly regimen of neuropozyne doses to keep the nerve contacts crisp, but Anna wasn't buying it.

Here, though, she seemed to be in the minority. A lot of the downtowner crowd were filing in to hear Taggart give his lecture, and after having heard the man on television, Anna had to admit he had charisma enough to hold your attention, and the kind of academic gravitas that many people admired. Along with plenty of his supporters, he was here to make his voice heard at the National Science Board meetings, to continue his campaign to decry augmentation; he would doubtless be a fixture at the pro-flesh demonstrations taking place over the next few days.

As she entered the conference center atrium, as if on cue, a recording of Taggart's voice issued out of a hidden speaker. *"Some people believe augmentation is the wave of the future. That replacing part of yourself with machines will make you superhuman... But the truth is, for every part of yourself you sacrifice, you are less than you were before. That's why I created the Humanity Front. Tonight, I'll tell you why you should be a part of it, too."*

Anna scowled slightly. The name made Taggart's anti-aug crusade sound like a paramilitary group, and Anna wondered if that might have been a deliberate choice. Some of the people who shared Taggart's views did a lot more than write books or give speeches; episodes of violence against augmented humans fanned the flames of a new breed of intolerance. Groups like the militants of Purity First were more than happy to twist Taggart's message toward aggressive ends.

There were more than enough people who couldn't afford augmentation in the States and elsewhere—and she doubted any of them could have paid the extortionate ticket fee for the seminar either—as well as those who felt threatened by the new technology, just like they were by anything unfamiliar to them. The Humanity Front was selling itself as two things: a caring group out to show augmentees the error of their ways, and a force for retaining the status quo. Anna wondered if men like Taggart would ever understand that you couldn't put the genie back in the bottle.

"Can I help you?" A tanned young guy sporting a blandly neutral prosthetic hand stepped up to greet her. He gave her a once-over, immediately spotting her cyberoptics, and his expression became almost pious. "Everyone is welcome."

Over his shoulder, a shimmer passed through one of the holograph banners, the text changing. A new string of words formed: *Kelso. Upper tier. Section G. Box 3.* She gave him a tight smile. "Actually, no. I know exactly where I'm going."

Anna had her hand on the butt of the Zenith as she entered the skybox. It was well appointed, with an excellent view of the stage below. The house lights were just starting to grow dim, and as the door closed behind her, William Taggart stepped out into the pool of light cast from above, to a tide of applause. She hesitated; the skybox's illumination was low and there were deep shadows everywhere.

Down on the stage, Taggart began with some carefully rehearsed platitudes, and from the shadows, Anna heard someone make a spitting noise. "Yeah, that's enough from you, Billy." The voice was young and male.

She went to low-light and a figure in a bulky jacket and baseball cap became clear in one of the low, dense seats.

With a wave, the youth cut off the sound feed from the auditorium and turned to face her. "Let me guess. You're D-Bar?" He was a youth, no more than nineteen, slouching and cocksure.

"Wow," he replied. "You're more of a looker in the real."

"Whereas you are far more disappointing." She backed off a step. "I'm not in the mood for games, kid." Automatically, she started to profile him in her thoughts. He had an accent that didn't fit; it had a European twang, maybe French-Canadian.

D-Bar stood up. He was gangly, and the puffed-up jacket hung badly on him, making him look even thinner than he was. A collection of data goggles and audio buds lay in a complex tangle around his neck. "*Kid?* Oh, come on, Agent Anna Kelso. Book by a cover and all that static? And here I was thinking you were a professional… "

She looked around the room, searching for anything that screamed out *ambush*, and found nothing. "Fair point," she conceded. "It's just that the name 'Juggernaut'… well, it conjures up a different kind of person than you."

D-Bar nodded sagely. "Oh, I hear you. I get that a lot."

"Where's the rest of the 'we' you mentioned on the phone?"

He tapped his hat, and she saw what looked like a minicam clipped to the bill. "Watching. If you try to ice me or anything, they'll wideband the pix to every screen in a five-block radius."

"Cute trick." It was likely a threat he could make good on; Anna had read up on the Juggernaut Collective's impressive hacking expertise. It was a matter of public record that they had bankrupted two Fortune 500 companies, crashed the Syrian intelligence agency's mainframe, and brought the Seattle traffic grid to a standstill. "Maybe I should just arrest you, then. I could use a win right about now."

That got her a flash of real worry; but then the youth shuttered it away. "You don't want to do that, Anna. We're the good guys, yeah? Like you. Serving the cause of justice and all that stuff."

This time she snorted. "Now who's being patronizing? You expect me to buy into the whole 'white hat' hacker thing? Juggernaut are information terrorists. You're not Robin Hood, you're a cybercriminal. "

D-Bar gave a mock shudder. "Ooh, yeah. Don't you think things always sound cooler when you put the word 'cyber' in front of them?" He gave a short, nasal laugh. "Okay, so we rob from the rich and we keep it. Can't deny. But what we also do is oppose inequality."

"By breaking the law?" she snapped.

"We're the thorn in the side of heartless megacorps who wanna turn the world into their personal chum-bucket!" he insisted.

"What, is that your recruitment speech?"

D-Bar chuckled. "I don't have to recruit you. You're already on our side."

"Don't count on it." Kelso licked her lips, an earthy taste in the back of her throat. Her hands tightened as her annoyance built. "You've got ten seconds to tell me why the hell I am here, or I'm dragging you out in cuffs."

"I thought the choice of locale was, y'know, *ironic.*" When he saw the hard edge in her gaze, he paled a little.

"Okay, okay. Look, for a while now, we've been bumping up against the edges of something..." D-Bar paused, feeling for the right word. "*Shadowy*. There's a group out there. An organization with a long reach and a lotta patience. They've been systematically using info-war and assassination to target midlevel corporates—"

"Isn't that what you people do?" she broke in.

The youth's eyes flashed. "Juggernaut doesn't kill people, lady. And if you let me finish, I was gonna say it's not just corporations getting the knife. Other free groups like us are going dark. These bad guys are taking people down with blackmail, extortion, entrapment, absorption..."

Anna's patience was wearing thinner by the moment. She folded her arms across her chest. "And this concerns me how?"

"The Tyrants," D-Bar sounded out the name, and she couldn't stop herself from reacting to it. "Yeah, that get your attention? The Tyrants are their attack dogs, Agent Kelso. This...group, whoever they are? Those black-ops bastards are doing their dirty work for them." He leaned closer. "We're both looking for the same thing. We're both asking the same question."

She was silent for a long moment, her irritation warring with her curiosity. Finally, she gave it voice. "What do they want?"

Knightsbridge—London—Great Britain

Saxon felt cool, clammy concrete against his back and he rolled slightly, his head swimming, clearing from the effect of the stun-dart.

He heard a woman's voice, distant but light and playful. Gradually, he leaned up from where he lay and caught sight of a short, unfinished corridor stretching away from him. He was inside the hidden spaces behind the picture on the wall, under the stark light of a fluorescent bulb. At the edges of the shadows around him, he glimpsed Barrett, Hardesty, and the Russian woman. Hermann was nearby, slowly pulling himself into a pained crouching position. The chamber they were in was no bigger than the conference room, but it was sparse and had the feel of a place one might use for a purpose that needed a little space, like a sparring court. Or an interrogation room.

Hermann tried to get up, but that drew a guttural, negative noise from Barrett. "You stay right there, son," he told him. The German frowned and ran a hand through his short, dirty-blond hair.

The woman at the far end of the corridor was talking to Namir, and in that moment he knew who she was: *the wife*. He didn't understand Hebrew, but he recognized the rhythm of it. Their voices had the casual, easy pace of two people who knew each other intimately. Saxon closed his eyes for a moment and tried to marry the voice he heard with the Jaron Namir he knew from firsthand experience. Just as with the picture on the landing, the two things refused to mesh. He was listening to a warm and personable man, a father joking with the mother of his children, not the stone killer he knew from sorties into the deep black. Saxon had seen Namir kill men in the time it took him to blink, and do it calmly and cleanly. He wondered how he could be both of those people at once.

A child called out and the wife stepped away. After a

moment, Namir came back down the corridor and Saxon saw Hardesty grin in the darkness, in anticipation of something.

Namir saw it, too, and drew a handgun, throwing the American a flat look. "Scott. Go see to Laya and the children, would you?"

The sniper's face fell. "I thought—"

"Do it now," said Namir. "I'll handle this."

There was a moment when it looked like Hardesty might argue; but then he grimaced and walked away. Saxon heard the sniper call out and a child laugh in reply; then the hidden door closed and the sound died.

Namir worked the slide of the automatic pistol and ejected all but one round into the palm of his hand, then pocketed the bullets.

At last, Saxon spoke. "What's going on?"

"One of you is disloyal," Namir said, without looking at them. "I know which. And the other needs to prove himself." He gestured with the gun. "So, two birds and one stone."

"One bullet, more like," Barrett noted dryly.

Hermann gave Saxon a fierce look. "I am no traitor!"

Saxon got to his feet. "Are you serious? Disloyal how, exactly?"

Namir tossed the loaded pistol onto the floor between them. "I'll explain it to you if you live past the next five minutes."

"You actually expect me to—" Hermann never let him finish. The German was swift and he came up hard, striking with that armored fist of his in a short, hammer-blow punch. Saxon barely had time to deflect it.

He was aware of the others drawing back and away as Hermann moved in and came at him again. This time, Saxon was a half second too slow and the metal-clad fist clipped him across the shoulder. Even a glancing impact was enough to rob him of a little balance and Saxon shifted his weight. Even if he wasn't sold on this sudden, enforced bout of trial-by-combat, the younger man certainly was. Hermann glared at him, sizing him up; the way he did it made it clear to Saxon that the German had given plenty of thought to how he would fight him if the opportunity arose. He had a sudden mental image of Gunther taking him down, stripping his corpse for parts to bolt on to himself like a hunter taking the skull and pelt of a kill.

Saxon dodged the next punch, and the next, but then his luck ran out. Hermann connected with a heavy strike to the sternum that rattled Saxon's rib cage and ghosted the taste of blood up his throat. The other man glimpsed the flash of pain in his eyes and for the first time since he'd met him, Saxon saw something approximating a smile flicker briefly over the German's face. He came back in like thunder, a flurry of fast kicks and faster punches that Saxon had to work to deflect, never once getting the chance to attack in turn. The young man's nerve-jacked speed was far in advance of Saxon's own reflex booster, maybe a custom model or something the Tyrants had granted; it didn't matter. Trying to match Hermann blow for blow wouldn't work.

Instead, Saxon let the other man's overconfidence take the lead. He let his guard go loose, and the hammer-blows started to land. Finally, Hermann connected with a punch that sent Saxon reeling, down to the concrete floor.

He blinked away pinwheels of pain from behind his eyes. Hermann went down in a looping sweep, grabbing for the pistol; he took his gaze off Saxon in that moment, chancing that his opponent was winded. *His mistake, then.*

As the German snatched up the weapon, Saxon rocked off his augmented legs and collided with Hermann, sending him reeling toward the edge of the light cast from the overhead bulb. The hand gripping the gun came up and it turned into a wrestling match.

For long moments they both strained for the superior position, but Saxon had the power, and the will to take the long road. Finally, with a savage twist of his wrist, he pulled the pistol away and elbowed Hermann hard in the throat, putting him on the ground.

Saxon weighed the gun in his hand.

"You gonna do it?" asked Barrett.

At the periphery of his vision, Saxon saw Namir shift slightly, his hand moving out of sight. Hermann looked up at him, silently furious.

"No," Saxon said at length. "I'm not going to do it. Because there isn't any bloody traitor, and I don't play games like this. I'm a professional." He flipped the gun over and held it out, butt first, to Namir.

The Tyrant commander took it with a nod. "The right call, Ben. If you had pulled the trigger, I would have shot you myself."

Hermann got up slowly. "Then both of us would be dead."

"Rounds in the gun were blanks," said Barrett. "We've done this before. We ain't stupid." A smile crossed his scarred face. "You did good there. You got steel. I'm impressed."

Saxon frowned. "A test?"

"In a way," said Namir. He nodded to them all, and when he spoke again his tone was all command. "We've got another assignment, in America. We fly out tomorrow, so make the most of your downtime tonight and be sure to prep your gear."

"That's it?" Saxon took a step after him as he walked away. "You got nothing else to say?"

Namir glanced over his shoulder. "What do you want, Ben? A membership card? You both proved yourselves. You're part of the Tyrants. Until death."

SIX

Wdon't have all the answers." Anna watched the hacker as he crossed to the minibar behind the skybox's line of seats and did something to the lock to make it open, fishing inside for a slender can of Ishanti. He popped the cap and drained the energy drink in a single, long pull. "Ah. Better."

Beyond the sound-screened window, she saw William Taggart bow slightly as something he said earned a round of applause from his audience. The resonance of the clapping was distant, like faraway waves.

"What do you know?" Anna demanded. "I'm tired of your games."

"Games haven't even started yet," said D-Bar. "Not for you, anyhow." He sighed. "Let me put it another way... You ever heard of something called 'the Icarus Effect'?"

"Sounds like a Las Vegas magic show."

The youth chuckled and discarded the empty can. "Yeah, I guess. The Tyrants certainly have a way of making people vanish, that's for sure." He came closer, became more animated. "You know the story of Icarus? Guy and his dad build a set of wings, guy gets bold and flies too high, too close to the sun, guy gets dead. Same idea. It's a sociological thing, see? A normative process created unconsciously by a society in order to maintain the status quo, keep itself stable." D-Bar talked with his hands, making shapes in the air. "Whenever someone threatens to do something that will upset the balance, like flying too high...the Icarus Effect kicks in. Society reacts, cuts them down. Stability returns." He sighed. "That's what the Tyrants do. They enforce that effect for their masters, only they don't wait for it to happen naturally. They choose whose wings are gonna be clipped, if you get me." He jabbed a finger at the air. "These creeps, they're all about power. Anyone who threatens them, anyone who makes waves, gets dealt with."

"Threatens them how, exactly?" said Anna.

"You know what they say; if you wanna make enemies, try to change something. People invested in keeping things the same don't like it when you make waves." He fished in his pocket and pulled out a data slate. "Look at this. These places and faces mean anything to you?"

Anna glanced down and images scrolled past her: a highway accident in Tokyo that claimed the life of a cybernetics researcher; a string of missing-persons reports from a Belltower law enforcement detachment in Bangalore; the violent mugging of a senatorial aide in Boston; an augmented teenager killed by police snipers in Detroit.

At first, she saw nothing that registered with her; then a face she recognized from her own investigations passed by—Donald Teague, an advisory staffer at the United Nations, shot dead in Brooklyn by unknown assailants. An eyewitness report talked about an ambush of Teague's car and three men in black combat gear, and of the almost military precision with which the kill had been made...

She blinked, and for a moment the dark memory of a day in Georgetown pressed in on her thoughts, threatening to overwhelm her. Anna stiffened, forcing the recall out of herself. She read on. There were other points where the files connected to those she had discovered on her own. Men and women from corporations, government figures, those with international or UN connections like Teague. All of them either dead, missing, or assaulted. She halted on one image in particular; Senator Jane Skyler, caught by a stringer's camera six months ago as she was wheeled through the doors of a private D.C. medical clinic. Matt Ryan's blood was rust-red on her expensive silk blouse.

"And there's more we don't even know about," D-Bar told her. "The ones who were leaned on instead of getting roughed up or murdered. The ones who buckled, who did what they were told to."

"Assassination, extortion, coercion..." Anna said aloud. "The Tyrants are behind all these incidents? How could they be doing that? They would need global reach, unparalleled access to secure information—"

The hacker seized on her words. "Ah, now that, that we *do* know something about. The group, the guys with their hands on the leash of the dogs...they've penetrated hundreds of agencies. They got a spy network that spans the world." He nodded to himself. "That Skyler thing, fer'ex. How'd they explain away the shooters knowing exactly where and when to find the senator?"

Anna frowned. "The FBI investigation turned up evidence that one of Skyler's maids was paid off by the Red Arrow triad."

"Pled innocent, though, right? Then what?"

Kelso recalled that the woman had died in prison, killed during a violent scuffle. Like so much about the Skyler hit, Anna had never accepted what had become the official version of events.

D-Bar went on. "The Tyrants got their info someplace else. I reckon you've probably been thinking that for a while, but you don't wanna go there, do ya?"

She glared at him. He was perceptive—she had to give him that. "If you're so goddamn clever, say it."

"I can do more than that," he told her. "I can show you. *We* can show you the truth about what you've suspected all along. That the Tyrants have a source inside the United States Secret Service."

"It's not possible," Anna said, without conviction. A chill ran through her. The very real possibility of someone being compromised within the agency made her feel sick inside.

D-Bar studied her carefully. "We came to you, Agent Kelso, because we can't prove any of that. But *you* can."

She shook her head. "I can't do anything. Even if you're right, I'm suspended."

"I'll get you back inside," he told her, with absolute, unshakable confidence.

"All right." It was a second before Anna realized she had spoken.

Knightsbridge—London—Great Britain

Namir gave him a room at the top of the town house, in the converted attic where white pine floors ranged up to tall, arched windows that looked out onto the London skyline.

Saxon left the lamps off and cracked open the window a little, letting in the night air along with the steady rush of the traffic out on Kensington Gore. The distant rattle of a police aerodyne reached his ears, and he saw a saucer-shaped advertisement blimp caught like an errant cloud, drifting east toward Mayfair. The glow of the video billboards flanking the airship reflected off the rooftops, strings of commercials for high-end fashion, cybernetics, and consumer electronics raining silently down over the city.

The night was uncharacteristically warm, and as soon as he had settled in the room, Saxon stripped to the waist and found a place to sit cross-legged by the freestanding mirror, checking himself over in every place that Gunther Hermann had laid his punches and kicks on him. He had a collection of ugly bruises, shallow cuts, and minor contusions, but nothing that could have been a broken or chipped bone. Saxon ran his flesh hand down the length of his cyberarm, checking maintenance seals and actuators. He made a few practice moves; the arm felt slightly off-speed.

With a grimace, Saxon filled a tumbler of water from the filter carafe on the nightstand near the wide, shadowed bed; then he loaded a fresh dose of neuropozyne into an injector pen and took the shot in his arm.

He drained the glass as he stood at the window. *What the hell just happened?* he asked himself. For a moment, it seemed as if he was hanging over the ragged edge, that everything he was or could be was about to be snuffed out in an instant; and then the gun and Gunther's life had been in his hands.

Were the rounds in the pistol really blanks? If I had pulled the trigger, put a shot between the German's eyes, what would they have done? It chilled him to consider a different truth from the one Namir had laid down as he took the weapon from him. Saxon's disquiet should have been silenced; he had passed a test down there in that room. In some strange way, he had bonded with the rest of the Tyrants.

So why doesn't it sit right? He almost asked the question out loud.

Saxon glanced up and saw the airship drift overhead. Up there, a woman's face was lit by rainbows of color, showing off a cascade of diamonds around her wrist. Her mouth moved and a marquee of words appeared in sequence on smaller video-screens all around her. *What master do you serve?*

He blinked, uncertain if his eyes were playing tricks on him.

The woman on the screen, flawless and fashion-model perfect, was looking right at him, as if the billboard was a window through which she was peering. Over her shoulder, he saw a virtual skyline mimicking the view from the tenth floor of the Hotel Novoe Rostov.

What master do you serve? she asked once again. The words shifted and changed like drifts of sand, transforming into a string of numerals. The groupings matched an international sat-comm code.

Before he was even fully aware he was doing it, Saxon reached for his gear pack and recovered the spare vuphone he kept for emergencies. It wasn't the slick, cutting-edge device the Tyrants had given him, just a store-bought disposable. He entered the digits and thumbed the dial key. A string of swift tones sounded from the earpiece, followed by a hum as the line connected—

Behind him, the bedroom door clicked open, and he spun from the window, cutting the call short, letting the phone drop.

In the light cast from the airship's advert-screens, Yelena Federova resembled some kind of shadow-wraith, a creature made out of flesh and darkness straight from fable. She stalked silently toward him, her black-and-steel legs catching the glow. Her eyes were hooded and he could not read them. Slowly, like a knife being drawn from a sheath, a low smile crossed her lips. The sullen glower that characterized her neutral mode of expression was gone, and instead Saxon saw an echo of the predatory thrill Federova had shown in the Rostov's lobby, after cutting down three men in as many seconds.

It came to him that he had failed the test. She had come to kill him, quietly and discreetly. Sparing Gunther's life had marked him as weak; he was going to be cut from the pack...

She halted a few steps from him, and then, with care, Federova pulled at the tabs holding the ballistic-cloth blouse closed over her chest. She let it fall free to the floor; beneath she wore nothing, and Saxon's gaze was drawn to the rise of her breasts, a small ebon cross hanging in the valley between them. Her tawny skin was marred only by the scarred disc of an old bullet wound. Then she shrugged off her short breeches and crossed the rest of the distance, her hands reaching for him.

Saxon let her draw in, let her find her own way; and when their lips met, hers were as cool as fresh water. Together, they drifted out of the light and into the shadowed corner, descending into darkness.

U.S. Secret Service Headquarters—Washington, D.C.— United States of America

At this time of the evening, the building was sparsely populated; but then, cops never slept, and the agents of the Secret Service were no different. There would be more than enough people still on duty or working late to steal a march on their investigations, others preparing details to deal with VIP escorts while the demonstrators were in town. More than enough of them to make this a difficult endeavor for Anna Kelso. Everyone on her floor, at the very least, had to know about the cover story Temple had put in place—Kelso's so-called medical suspension. She knew that others would have been told everything, and how those people would react if they saw her here... It would not go well.

All that she pushed aside as she went in through the front doors. In her head Anna was going through the same warm-up techniques she used for undercover work; it was peculiar to do it here and now, but she was pretending to be something that she wasn't—an agent with a right to be there.

The security guard at the desk gave her a wan smile. Anna cursed inwardly; he knew her, in a nodding kind of way. She had hoped someone else would be on duty tonight.

"Agent Kelso." His face showed faint confusion. "I'd heard you were taking some medical leave?"

She smiled back at him, playing into the moment. "That's right. But I've got to drop some paperwork off for the guys picking up my caseload."

"I'll need you to sign in." He offered her a touch pad, and she ran a stylus over it in a quick scrawl. Anna couldn't help but glance over her shoulder, back out to the parking lot where her car was waiting. She thought about running.

A soft beep sounded from the guard's panel. "Thanks."

She was through the security arch before it caught up to her that she had been allowed in without question. Anna resisted the urge to reach up and touch the badge in her pocket; whatever D-Bar had done to it on the drive from the conference center had worked.

The elevator took her to the seventh floor, and all the way up she fought back the twitchy sensation in her fingers, folding her arms, unfolding them, shifting her weight from foot to foot. The dose she'd convinced herself she needed, the shot of stims that had propelled her through her confrontation with D-Bar, was waning. She could sense the dark clouds of the comedown encroaching, like a thunderstorm just over the horizon. Anna blinked; her eyes were tired and gritty.

When her phone hummed in her pocket, she almost jumped. Quickly she thumbed the wireless headset from the dock on the back of the handset and inserted it in her ear; she wasn't about to let D-Bar access her mastoid comm. "Talk to me," she said.

"*Are you there?*" asked the hacker. "*I ghosted you via the entry subnet, blanked the sign-in as soon as you were through. Can't go any further without your help, though.*"

"Working on it," she replied. "Now shut up and let me concentrate." Anna muted him as the elevator let out a melodic chime and the doors opened. She stepped out, and for a second, force of habit took her in the direction of the main office bullpen. Across the tops of the open cubicles, the desks and glassy partitions, dimly lit by glow strips and the occasional active monitor screen, she saw her work area. A bright orange storage crate was on top of it, crammed with her personal effects. She thought about the marksmanship plaque, the photo of her and the rest of the team after the Anselmo case bust, and fought down the irrational urge to risk discovery in order to salvage those little, trivial mementos.

Then she saw Agents Tyler and Drake walking between the desks toward her, and Anna's purpose snapped back into sharp, cold focus.

Chiding herself for the moment of inattention, she turned on her heel and went back around the elevator bank, heading away. The corridors leading to the server room on floor seven went past the conference areas, and they were all dark and unlit. Anna hoped that Tyler and Drake would enter the elevators, but they were coming her way, their conversation reaching her. They were talking about the Redskins game, both men dour and serious about matters of yardage and field goals.

Fear bubbled up inside her, threatening to flood out into panic. She pressed it down, and her hand found a door.

Anna slipped into an empty conference room and closed the door behind her, pressing her back to it. She held her breath.

It seemed to take forever for them to pass, the echo of their mundane discussion hanging in the air; then they were gone, and she was moving again.

The server room needed another identity pass, and Kelso showed the sensor her badge. The door opened with an obliging click and she was inside.

"I'm there," she said, toggling the mute on the headset. On the drive over, D-Bar had told her what to look for. From her pocket, she fished out a data rod the size and thickness of her thumb.

"You know what to do," D-Bar said, his tone a mix of eagerness and annoyance.

"Here we go." She found the correct input socket and slid the rod home. A sleeping monitor screen immediately flashed into life, and a cascade of information panels unfolded across it.

In her ear, the hacker muttered under his breath. *"Wireless link established. Greentooth is handshaking... Okay, here we go... "* He cursed and she heard the distant rattle of a keypad. *"Damn it. You know, this would be a lot easier if I had both hands free."*

Anna eyed the door. "What can I say? I'm the cautious type."

On the drive from the conference center, D-Bar had brought out a customized laptop from his backpack; the thing had the shell of an off-the-shelf business machine, but even her inexpert gaze could tell it was tricked out with multiple hardware modifications and bespoke black-market tech. The airstream casing was ruggedized and covered with laser etching and decals; it reminded her of a racecar.

She pictured D-Bar out there in the parking lot, hunched over the keyboard in the passenger seat, watching the feed as his machine talked through the rod's encrypted wireless link to the Secret Service mainframe. Before she had left him in the car, Kelso had asked the youth to show her his right hand; with a flick, she'd snapped a cuff around his wrist and tethered him to the steering wheel. After all, she was putting a lot of trust in the Juggernaut hacker, and there was nothing to stop him from copying what he needed from the secure server and leaving her to take the rap.

"Okay," he went on, "I'm injecting the seeker worm program...now." One of the information panes on the screen flickered red-white and vanished. "Search routine is running. I've preloaded the seeker with parameters related to the leaked information and the Tyrant targets. It'll automatically flag anything it finds and upload it to a saved file."

"Good." Anna's hand snapped out and she yanked the data rod from the interface socket. D-Bar called out in surprise as he lost his remote feed, but she ignored him, dropping the rod to the floor and breaking it in two with the heel of her shoe.

"Was that you?" D-Bar demanded. "What did you just do?"

Anna's hands twitched, making it difficult to gather up the broken pieces in one go. "Cut you off," she confirmed, dropping the fragments into a cup of cold coffee some errant technician had left on a nearby desk. "This is not my first rodeo, kid. I let you drop the seeker, but I'm not letting you keep an open conduit into a federal law enforcement agency's mainframe, not for one second more than I have to."

"And how exactly are you going to get the data out?" he retorted.

"Way ahead of you." Anna rooted through a storage locker and found a case of blank media units, flash drives of the same model she'd used to store her own information. Working as swiftly as she could, she connected a drive in place of the data rod and let the unit fill with the seeker program's digital harvest.

D-Bar was too interested to stay silent for long. *"What are you seeing?"*

"A lot," Anna admitted. Data flashed past her eyes, much of it in formats unfamiliar to her, some immediately recognizable as U.S. Secret Service and Department of Justice files. There were operational schedules, transport routes, profiles of agents on duty and principals to protect; but there were other documents as well, evaluations and surveillance records, the kind of materials that Kelso's agency didn't use. Then she saw information that bore digital watermarks from Homeland Security, the Federal Bureau of Investigation, the Diplomatic Corps; other pages were not even in English, and it took her a second to realize that she was seeing memos and documentation from security agencies outside the United States. Whoever the leak was inside the service, they had been tunneling through the agency's link to the DOJ, and from there out to the shadowy nexus of information shared by the global law enforcement community.

As abruptly as it had begun, the search ended and the data parsed itself into the flash drive. Anna felt a cold impulse down her spine and she reached for the keyboard in front of the monitor, inputting the name "Skyler" and a date string as the parameters for a sweep of the stolen data. Instantly, the complete scope of all the supposedly secure transit information about Senator Skyler's detail on that fateful day was there in front of her. Every last bit of it, from details of what pool vehicles would be used and their maintenance records, through the receipts showing how many bullets the agents on the detail had logged out from the agency armory. Everything an assassin would need to prepare a flawless attack.

The file bore a validation code, a digital fingerprint tying the requested data to the terminal and agent identity of the person who had copied them. Anna knew the code; she'd seen it a hundred times appended to her own after-operations debriefs and memos. But still she clicked on the text string, hoping that she had read it wrongly. Hoping she had made a mistake.

The display opened a panel and showed her Ron Temple's authentication.

"You son of a bitch." The words slipped out of her in a shallow breath, drained of all anger and fury. Anna felt nothing, just a chill numbness at the core of her gut.

A man she had trusted, a man she had served with, and before her lay proof that he was a traitor, proof that he had sold out whatever integrity he had to the faceless figures who had their hands on the leash of the Tyrants.

Then the emotion came, breaking the icy dam of the dead feeling in her chest, engulfing her. Anna's eyes prickled and her vision misted. She staggered a little and reached out a hand to steady herself. Temple had sold them out—Kelso and Ryan, Byrne, Laker, and Connor, everyone on the Skyler detail, along with all those other men and women he had given up. Her hands drew into hard, tight fists. She wanted to know *why*. More than the fury, more than the rush of potent despair, Anna wanted to know the answer. How a man could betray his oath and his colleagues. For money? Out of fear? No answer she could imagine seemed good enough.

A repeating tone dragged her back from her reverie, and she blinked owlishly. D-Bar was yelling in her ear, and Kelso glanced back at the server monitor; a warning panel was blinking there, a string of text in livid red letters telling her to stand by and wait for security.

"Are you listening to me?" D-Bar shouted. *"Kelso, can't you hear that?"*

She pulled out the connector leading to the flash drive, then shoved the data device in her pocket, moving swiftly across the room to the door. Outside she could hear voices.

Fighting down the tremors in her fingers, she stepped out calmly into the dim corridor and walked at a steady, unhurried pace toward the elevator bank. Every nerve in her body screamed at her to *run,* but she knew that the agency's internal security monitors possessed subroutines that looked for abnormal body kinetics—if she ran, they would see it. She smothered the urge with a grimace and metered her pace. Just a few more steps.

Behind her, she heard a voice call out. *Drake.* She knew it was him without having to turn around. Anna ignored him, kept moving. In a few more seconds, she'd turn the corner and be at the elevators.

"Hey, stop!" called the other agent. "I'm talking to you! Stop right now!" Anna heard the rustle of a holster being snapped open, the click of a safety catch flicking off. "I won't tell you again!"

She fled. It wasn't a conscious choice on her part, not something she was aware of doing on anything but the most base, animal-brain level; but suddenly she was sprinting the rest of the distance down the corridor, her thoughts clattering inside her mind, the rush of new adrenaline warring with the tidal drag of the stim crash. She couldn't think straight, she couldn't process. All she could do was run, run, *run*—

Anna raced around the corner and came face-to-face with Agent Tyler, wandering out of the break room past the elevators, stirring a cup of dark coffee. "Kelso?" His face registered a moment of confusion.

"Stop her!" shouted Drake. That was enough to galvanize Tyler into action, and he let the cup drop, going for his service weapon.

Anna ignored him and dove for the open doors of the elevator, hand reaching for the controls. Her feet were just across the threshold when Tyler snatched at the collar of her jacket and pulled hard. Some of her hair caught in his grip and sent a shock of pain through her head. A kick landed in the back of her right knee and her leg buckled. She went down, catching a glimpse of herself falling and Tyler right on her in the mirrored back of the elevator car.

Then she was on the floor, half in and half out of the lift, with a federal agent's handgun pressed into the small of her back.

"You're under arrest," said Drake.

Romeo Airport—Michigan—United States of America

The aircraft put down on the runway just as the sunset bled away across the landscape. No visible-spectrum landing lights were in operation, and the pilot brought them in using a virtual headset rig that made it seem to him as if he were touching down in the middle of the day.

Romeo had gone back and forth between active and inactive over the last four decades, until it had quietly slipped into the hands of a minor corporate consortium that, via a labyrinth of blinds and shell companies, was one cog in a far larger machine. The surrounding area was remote enough that the local populace were sparse, but it was close enough to Detroit for the glow of the city's skyscrapers to be visible on the horizon, the colors reflecting off the bottom of the low cloud base.

Inside the hangar, a staging area had already been set up alongside a fuel bowser for the jet and a line of utility trailers. Robot forklifts swarmed around the rear of the plane, peeling back the vast curved blades of the cargo doors to gather up the helo nestled in its storage cradle.

In defiance of common sense and regulations, Hardesty stood at the thin sliver of open air between the tall hangar doors and smoked a cigarette. Saxon caught the pungent smell of the nicotine as he crossed the space, taking the opportunity to exercise his legs after hours aboard the jet. Federova was at the back of an unmarked van, picking her way through a set of armored, olive-drab cases. She was considering different models of grenades, picking them up, weighing them, exchanging them for others. He smiled thinly; she reminded him of someone at a market stall buying fruit.

After that night in London, he hadn't known what would come next. Even in the throes of their quiet, animated sex, he had still been on alert, waiting for the moment when she tried to stick a knife in his ribs or snap his neck. But that moment never arrived; and when they were both spent she left him there, as silent as ever. He couldn't help but wonder if Hermann had got the same treatment when he joined up.

On the flight, Federova looked right though him, her manner utterly unchanged from the one she had shown him before. Saxon decided to file their night together away as some kind of opportunist incident and think no more about it; but it wasn't easy. She had been... a challenge.

"Saxon." He turned to see Namir beckoning him from a temporary workstation set up near the nose wheel of the jet. As he approached, he saw Barrett and Hermann there with him, peering into a virtual map of the city of Detroit.

The young German's manner also remained unaffected toward Saxon, despite the moment in the fight room; but unlike Federova's cool affect, Saxon could see the chink of something through Hermann's metaphorical armor. *A new respect, maybe?* Or perhaps it was something else: some kind of jealousy. Saxon had beaten him because of two things—endurance and superior augmentations. The former was something that had to be taught, but the latter...that could be bought. He wondered how badly Gunther Hermann wanted to surrender a little more of his meat to the machine. Saxon guessed he wouldn't hesitate if the offer was made.

He studied the map as he came closer. On the flight in, Namir had discussed the next operation in brief. Detroit was home to a corporation called Sarif Industries; Saxon had heard of it, a cutting-edge cybernetics research and manufacturing concern that specialized in boutique tech off the axis of most people's budget. According to Namir, Sarif had forcibly indentured a group of scientists, who were now being held against their will in the company's main research and development facility. The Tyrants were going to go in and extract these people, and "restore the balance." He wondered how much of that was true.

Barrett played around with the map control and shifted the image to a plan view of the Sarif facility. They were planning a rooftop assault, and the timing had to be perfect.

"We have a narrow window of opportunity to breach their perimeter," said Namir. "Some of the Sarif staff are heading out to Washington for a meeting with the National Science Board, and there's a weapons demonstration taking place on-site for a representative from the Pentagon. As such, their focus will be split on that and preparations for the trip. We also have an electronic interdict ready to deploy, but for now, we'll wait here for the word before we move to the forward waypoint in the city."

"Weapons?" echoed Saxon. "I thought Sarif was all neural implant tech and athlete-grade cyberlimbs."

Namir gave him a long look. "That's part of the reason we're going in." He pulled the map back out to a higher scale, and Saxon got the message that he wasn't going to give him any more details. "Some of our...associates have secured a holding area for us here." He pointed a slender steel finger at a location out in the city's industrial wastelands. That's our waypoint once we clear the objective and exfiltrate. There will be some postmission cleanup to go through at that location, then we'll decamp and return here for departure."

"What kind of threat force will we be facing?" asked Hermann.

Barrett answered before Namir could speak. "A bunch of rent-a-cops. Some embedded security tech. Nothing that'll make you break a sweat." He shrugged, the action exaggerated by his augmented arms. "Hell, I could do this number on my own. We could leave half of you on the bench for this one."

Saxon met Namir's gaze. "Is that right?"

The Tyrant commander released a sigh. "I'm still working out the tactical details. The information we have received on the objective so far has been...incomplete. I decided to mobilize the whole unit in case it is needed." He smiled thinly. "After all, it's better to have an asset and not need it, than to need an asset and not have it, don't you agree?"

"Can't argue with you on that score," Saxon admitted. Next to the display there was a data slate showing what seemed to be personnel files. He picked it up and studied them. "These are the marks?"

Namir reached over and took the screen from him. "That's right. Along with some other actives who may be encountered in the area of operations." He hesitated, then called up a different file and showed it to Saxon. "Take a look at this. Give me your first impressions."

"All right." Saxon studied the screen, a little warily.

Looking back up at him was a younger man with a narrow, angular face and hard eyes. A loop of footage a few seconds long ran past, perhaps snagged from a security camera feed. The guy had no visible cyberware, but the way he carried himself immediately set off a warning in Saxon's mind. "This guy's not a rent-a-cop," he said. "Trained. I'd bet on it. Not military, though, not a spook either. A federal agent? Some kind of copper?"

"That's a good read. He's a former officer of the Detroit police department, Special Weapons and Tactics unit. Currently heading up physical security at Sarif Industries."

Saxon read the man's name out loud. "Adam Jensen." He scanned the other pages in the man's file. His eye dithered over marksmanship records, details of Jensen's police career, and information about a discharge from the force that said more by what it left out than what it didn't. What he read there crystallized his thoughts. "He's no day-player."

Someone made a spitting noise behind him, and Saxon turned to see Hardesty approaching. "Jensen's a flatfoot," he sneered.

"An *ex*-flatfoot," Barrett added, with a derisive snort.

"My point," Hardesty replied, nodding. "He's not even that. He's just a broke-ass cop, out of his league. No threat to us."

Saxon answered, keeping his eyes on Namir. "You shouldn't underestimate this guy. Read the file. He's tenacious. Men like that don't go down easy."

"Like knows like, is that it?" Hardesty came closer.

"I guess." He shrugged and handed back the data slate, glaring at the other man. "Let's just say I can tell the difference between someone who is a professional, and someone who pretends to be."

For a long second, Hardesty balanced on the edge of the veiled insult; then he gave a humorless smirk. "Useful. You gotta teach me that sometime, limey."

Namir blanked the holograph map with a wave of his hand. "Get your gear together and stand by. We need to be ready to deploy at a moment's notice."

U.S. Secret Service Headquarters—Washington, D.C.— United States of America

In the basement of the agency offices there was a holding area with cells and a processing office. It didn't see much use on a day-to-day basis and it was a lot cleaner and well appointed than its NYPD equivalent, but the function was the same. A cell was a cell was a cell.

They took all her gear, including the flash drive, the doctored badge, and her car key; Agents Drake and Tyler were dogged but they were smart, and she guessed that sooner or later one of them would head outside to the parking lot to go looking for her vehicle. Anna found herself hoping that D-Bar had been quick enough to hot-wire her nondescript Navig sedan and get the hell out of there when he'd heard the scuffle over the headset; she'd left the line open all the way.

They took her watch, so she had no way to reckon the passing of time. Maybe under normal circumstances she might have sat there on the plastic mattress and fretted about what was going to happen; but the crash was on her and she surrendered to it. Anna let herself go and fell into a deep, dreamless slumber.

When Tyler woke her, it was like dragging herself up from the bottom of the ocean, as if her conscious mind were wrapped up in anchor chains that kept trying to pull her back to the dark and to sleep. Shrugging it off, she rose and followed him, grim-faced, down a corridor to an interview room. This, too, mirrored the one she'd been in at the 10th Precinct.

Inside: a plain table and a few chairs, the console of an audio and video recording system built into the wall, and Ron Temple. His arms were folded in front of him, and his face had an expression on it she'd never seen before. It wasn't fear or anger, but some strange merging of the two.

Anna couldn't help herself. The moment she saw him, she went for him. "You fucking bastard—!"

Tyler was right there to stop her, and he caught her in an armlock, twisting the limb back until Kelso grunted in pain. "Calm down, Anna."

"Go screw yourself, Craig!" she retorted.

"Sir?" Tyler gave Temple a questioning look, and his superior nodded toward the other chair. In quick order, the agent pushed her into the seat. Anna's cuffs slammed into the tabletop and were held there by an invisible electromagnetic inductor coil.

"I'll take it from here," said Temple. "Wait outside."

Tyler gave her a last look and then did as he was told.

Before Temple could speak again, she snarled at him. "I know what you did, you goddamn rat! You sold out your own people! You got Matt killed—"

Temple reached across the table and silenced her with a hard slap across the face. "Shut up," he said tightly.

"You stupid, stupid bitch. I warned you! Didn't I warn you to stay away from all this? But you couldn't just let it go, could you? You dosed yourself up and came right back."

Her head rang with the impact and pain flared on her cheek. "I know you're part of it. The Tyrants. All of it."

"That name doesn't mean anything to me," he replied, too quick, too practiced. "You don't understand anything."

"I understand you abused your position!" she spat, pulling at the cuffs. "I understand that you took money to give up confidential information, information that got people hurt or killed!" She drew a sharp breath. "They were your colleagues. Matt and all the others..."

When she looked up, she saw fear in his eyes. Temple was shaking his head. "You don't know. They have people everywhere. It's not like there was a choice, Kelso! It was my life, the life of my family, my kids!" Anna recalled he had an ex-wife and three children living in Toronto. "This is the way things work!" he spat, the anger returning again. "You're too naïve to see it, and now you're going to pay for that. Because I am damn well not going to take the fall!"

"Who are *they*?" Anna demanded. "The government? Corporates?"

He gave a harsh laugh. "Too small. It's more than just flags or dollars! These people are so big you don't even see them!" He was trembling, and he seemed to realize it. After a moment, Temple took control of himself. When he spoke again he was formal and guarded. "You've destroyed yourself, Anna. The drugs, collusion with terrorists, breaking in here and stealing classified data... " He produced the flash drive from his pocket and showed it to her. "You gave me everything I need." He shook his head. "If you had just listened to me, you could have walked away. But not now." Temple stood up. "You're going to disappear. Everything about you will be destroyed, and when they're done, it will be as if Anna Kelso never existed."

"You can't hide this!" she shouted.

"They already have," he said, without looking at her.

SEVEN

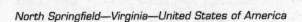

North Springfield—Virginia—United States of America

The unmarked van rumbled along the central lane of Interstate 495, heading westward into the evening. If any of the other drivers in the sparse traffic had given it a second look, they might have noticed the opaque polyglass slits along its flanks and the air vent in the roof; but there were few people driving at this time of day, and for the most part the 495 was the domain of unmanned cargo haulers. The blank-faced, slab-sided machines hummed past the van, running lights bright around prows that had a whiskered look, like dogfish. Some of them had thinscreens along their flanks denoting cargo and livery, lighting up the road as they passed.

Shafts of color penetrated the interior of the van and made Anna Kelso blink and turn away. She shifted uncomfortably. The orange detainee jumpsuit she wore was scratchy, the fiber-paper material rough in the places where it rubbed on her skin. Restraints around her wrists and ankles gave her limited freedom of movement, but not enough to sit up or appreciably change position.

The only other person in the back of the van was Craig Tyler. His narrow face and small eyes were set in a professional expression of detachment, but Anna knew him well enough to see that he was uncomfortable with the job he'd been asked to do. Temple had charged Tyler and Drake to personally convey her from D.C. out to whatever holding facility they had lined up; the other agent was in the driver's seat, on the far side of the armored bulkhead isolating the rear section of the van.

At first, Anna had been afraid that they were taking her out to some remote spot in the projects, somewhere that they could put a bullet in the back of her head and leave her for dead; but it soon became clear things were not going to be that simple.

All she'd been able to draw out of Tyler was that the agents were taking her to a rendezvous, where she would be transferred into the care of "contractors." The word had an ominous ring to it; anyone who had worked inside the Beltway for more than a few months knew that behind that term lay a multitude of sins. Temple had been right; she would end up inside some ghost prison, a "black site" facility off the grid, and that would be the last anyone would see of her.

"They're going to interrogate me," she said, her fear giving itself voice. "Some faceless mercenary, someone with no legal oversight, no due process." Anna stared at Tyler, who wouldn't meet her gaze. "And when they're done, when they get all they want from me, I'll be executed." She stamped her foot on the metal floor. "Right here, Craig. On American soil. You know that's not right!"

He was silent for a moment. "What I know is that you're a terrorist sympathizer, Anna. You've been classified an enemy combatant."

"Bullshit!" she snapped. "You know me! You know

what I was doing was not about terrorism! It's about Matt Ryan—"

"Maybe so," he retorted, speaking over her. "Maybe, yeah, that is what *you* think you're doing, breaking the chain of command and conducting illegal operations without sanction...But you're in bed with international criminals! You're working with Juggernaut! They're wanted by Interpol, the NSA, FBI—"

"I..." She tried to find the right words. "It's not what you think!"

Tyler reached into a pocket and pulled out a data slate. "D-Bar. You know who he is, right? Your hacker buddy?"

The name brought Anna up short. *How does the agency know about D-Bar?* She'd kept that information to herself. They had to have been listening in on her calls. More than likely, her apartment was wired as well.

Tyler ignored her, reading from the slate. "Patrick Couture, also known as P-C, also known as D-Bar, from the French word meaning 'to unlock...'" He frowned. "Escaped capture by RCMP forces in Quebec, currently wanted in connection with numerous data-crimes on three continents, known to be an active member of the Juggernaut Collective. Designated priority target." Tyler waved the slate at her. "This isn't some kid pirating software or deep-sixing parking tickets. He's part of an international criminal conspiracy! And now so are you."

For a moment, she couldn't find anything to counter his accusations, and Anna began to wonder if she had been played all along. What if Juggernaut had been tracking her, watching while she conducted her covert investigation? What if they had used her, twisted her to their own ends?

She bit down on her lip, feeling sick inside. *Another lie on top of all the others?* "No," she managed, shaking her head. "It's Temple. He's the traitor! He's been using his access to the DOJ network to pass classified data!"

"To who?" Tyler demanded.

"I...I don't know!" she said angrily. "All I know is that he's responsible for the deaths of a half-dozen Secret Service agents, men you and I worked with!"

Tyler sat back, his expression souring. "I'll tell you where you are going, Kelso. You're being transferred to a secure psychiatric unit out of state. Maybe there you can get some help. If Juggernaut were just using you—"

"Don't talk to me like I'm delusional!" Anna snapped, pulling against her restraints. "I know what I saw!"

Tyler's hand slipped to the stun gun on his belt. "Sit back," he ordered. "Don't make me knock you out."

She sagged and fell against the metal bench as another truck hummed past, the light cast from the screen-panels along its flanks moving slowly along the inside of the van. Something made her look up, and for a moment Anna thought that the stims, the stress, and the lack of proper sleep had all conspired to make her hallucinate.

Visible through the slit-windows, she saw a line of text marching along the side of the driverless truck as it paralleled the van. *Brace Yourself, Kelso,* it read, *This Is Going to Hurt.*

Her jaw dropped just as Tyler caught on, and the agent turned to look out the windows, catching sight of what she had seen. He tapped his mastoid. "Drake, do you see—?"

Before he could complete the thought, the wheels of the computer-controlled hauler gave a savage screech and the glowing screen-panels loomed through the windows. The robot truck broadsided the van and the vehicle resonated with the force of the impact. Tyler was knocked aside, but Anna was ready, riding out the collision. Through the security panel in front of her, she heard Drake swearing as he tried to stop the van from spinning into a wild skid. Then the truck veered across the lanes a second time and Drake lost control as they collided. The vehicle fishtailed across the freeway and momentum turned it sideways. There was a moment of stomach-churning vertigo as the van flipped over and crashed onto its side. A horrible grinding shriek sounded out as the prisoner transport scraped to a halt along the asphalt.

Anna recovered quickly, ignoring a cut over her right eye. Tyler was lying on his side, his breathing shallow but ready. She pulled as far as the restraints would let her and grabbed at him, dragging him closer. Her hands snagged the magnetic key rod on his belt and she tapped it on the cuffs; they fell away and she immediately felt a prickling sensation as proper blood flow returned to her extremities.

Someone banged twice on the rear doors. A hissing, fizzing glow appeared where the lock was mounted and she turned away. Metal parted with a heavy cracking sound and the doors fell open.

The bright beam of a torch engulfed her and Kelso held up a hand to shield her eyes. "You gonna sit there and stare, or are you gonna get the hell out?" said a voice.

Anna lurched onto the highway, panting, and found D-Bar standing there, a manic grin on his face. The unmanned truck was idling nearby, blocking the view of the wrecked van from passing traffic. The hacker jerked his thumb at a sporty Redline roadster parked nearby on the hard shoulder. "C'mon, your ride's here."

"You did that?" She blinked. "Tyler... Drake... You could have killed them!"

D-Bar gaped. "Excuse me, but weren't they taking you off to some deep dark hole, never to return? And *you're welcome*, by the way!" Anna took two steps toward the front of the van, but D-Bar grabbed her arm and pulled her back. "The driver is okay, I checked. Don't worry, I don't want a murder rap any more than you do."

Limping, she followed him to the sports car; it was a Falcon GTG, worth maybe ten times the sticker price of Kelso's commonplace sedan.

"I hadda dump your wheels," he said, before she could ask. "Which I managed to do, despite the whole handcuffing thing..." He drifted off, and paused. For the first time, Anna noticed he was wearing an earphone. "Yeah, okay," he said, speaking to the air. "Just monitor the traffic cameras at the exits. If anything looks jagged, let me know."

"Who are you talking to?" she demanded.

"Some people. Springing you, getting a new ride, all on short notice, that had to be a team effort, y'know? And I'm still waiting for some gratitude." He pointed. "There's some clothes in the back, nothing fancy though. Better ditch the romper suit soon-as, yeah?"

She reached the car and sagged against the hood. "Temple. It's Ron Temple, he's the leak. The son-of-a-bitch was giving the Tyrants all they needed."

D-Bar nodded gravely. "Okay. Well, look, don't sweat it. We know it's him now, so there are other approaches we can make. And with your help—"

Anna shook her head. "I'm not in this to help you, I'm doing this for me. For Matt." She tore off the prison garb and threw it into the bushes, ignoring D-Bar as he gawked at her. From the backseat she recovered a track suit and sweatshirt. "He has a contact, he must have. I'm going to make him give it to me." She climbed into the car and started the engine.

Abruptly, D-Bar realized that she wasn't going to take him with her. "What about me? You're just gonna leave me out here on the highway?"

"I don't trust you!" she snapped, stamping on the accelerator. The Falcon peeled out into the main lane with a snarl of engine noise that smothered the hacker's string of curses. She aimed for the next exit, already plotting the route in her head that would take her back toward the D.C. suburbs.

Romeo Airport—Michigan—United States of America

The helo extended its rotor-rings and turned them this way and that, running through the last of the preflight checks. Saxon watched, his fist tapping absently against his thigh. It seemed like they had been here for hours, primed and ready to go, watching the clock. Waiting for the word from the forward waypoint. Once or twice he had seen Hardesty and Barrett in quiet conversation, talking animatedly in low tones that didn't carry. Saxon found himself wishing he had an aural booster implant, or maybe one of those lip-reader software upgrades for his optics. He looked away, unable to ease the tension knotting in his chest. After the fight room, after that night in London, he'd expected this feeling to drop away—but it was still there. Saxon could not shake it, no matter how hard he tried. He still felt like an *outsider*—what he had thought were the first inklings of comradeship were ghosts, illusions. The reality was that the bond of brotherhood, of shared purpose he'd felt in the service and then again with Strike Six, was absent here. He wondered if he was fooling himself, holding on to some mawkish ideal of esprit de corps. Perhaps there was no place for something like that in the Tyrants.

His train of thought stalled as Namir emerged from the hatch of the transport plane, stepping quickly down the ramp. The other man had been called back aboard by the pilot; Saxon had caught the tail end of the conversation, something about an urgent signal from "the group." Now the commander's face was furrowed with irritation; whatever he had been told, Namir wasn't happy about it.

"We're going?" Hermann asked, gathering up his rifle. He couldn't keep the eagerness from his voice.

Namir ignored him and beckoned Federova closer as he approached Barrett and Hardesty. "There's been a change of plan," he said, his tone terse. He glanced at the big American. "Lawrence, it seems you'll have the chance to put your boasts to the test. We're proceeding with the Sarif exfiltration at reduced capacity. I expect you to compensate, yes?"

Barrett gave a nod. "Not a problem."

Namir nodded to Federova. "Yelena, you and I will accompany him."

"You're benching us?" said Hardesty. "What the hell for?"

"Close your mouth and listen, Scott." Namir's reply was sharp. "There's been a development. Apparently, one of our North American assets has been compromised and there's a very real danger of some serious blowback. The situation needs to be dealt with immediately." His gaze bored into the other man. "A scorched-earth protocol is now in effect. You will lead a team to expedite immediately." He nodded toward Saxon and the German.

Hardesty's expression changed. If anything, he seemed reassured. "Well. That's different."

"Sir," insisted Hermann, "we have an objective here, in Detroit. We've planned and prepared for it."

"And now you have a new one. Adaptability is something I require from all my operatives, Gunther. Circumstances on the ground are always fluid. We meet the mission needs as they occur." Namir's tone made it clear he would brook no questioning of these orders. He offered Hardesty a data slate. "This isn't something we can trust to hired hands. Details are here. Transport has already been dispatched for the rest of us. The helo is at your disposal."

Hardesty nodded, scanning the data. "It'll be tight. We'll have to do this quick and dirty."

"I made that clear to the group," Namir replied. "It's not an issue."

"Fine." Hardesty passed the slate to Hermann and walked away to brief the pilot of the flyer.

Saxon broke his silence. "This...asset. You want a straight recovery?"

Namir shook his head. "No. Locate, terminate, and sanitize the area."

Terminate and sanitize. He had just handed them an assassination mission. Hermann passed Saxon the slate and asked another question. "There's little suggestion of what kind of resistance we can expect."

"Minor," Namir replied. "Nonlethal embedded security. Perhaps one or two threat vectors, including the target himself. The primary concern is that the asset does not escape and no materials are left behind in any recoverable state."

Saxon read, and he kept his expression neutral. The location was an expensive gated community, part of a suburb of Washington, D.C., called Great Falls. In the helo, flying full tilt, he estimated they could reach it in less than ninety minutes. The target's residence was a large home set in grounds and woodland; he ran his finger over the surface of the slate to reveal the next page, and found the face of the person Namir wanted them to kill looking back at him. He read on, and his eyes narrowed. "This man is a federal agent."

Namir came closer. He nodded, making no attempt to show any disquiet over Saxon's concern. "Correct. As such, he may be armed. He's certain to be on alert, given the situation."

"Which is what?" Saxon insisted. "I'd like to know what requires the murder of a ranking officer of the United States Secret Service."

"Ben," said Namir, his human and synthetic eyes measuring him carefully. "You need to believe me when I tell you that this is necessary. You have to trust me. The Tyrants have a mission, and sometimes that mission requires that we make choices that are difficult, ugly... *bloody*. But I know you understand that."

"Why does this man need to die?" He didn't flinch from Namir's gaze. "What's the reason behind all this, Jaron? I've followed your orders... the *group's* orders without question now for months. But blind faith in your CO only goes so far."

Namir nodded. "I respect your honesty. It's part of the reason I recruited you. So I'll give an answer, but it will be the last time, know that. Because I cannot afford to have men under my command who continually question me at every turn."

The ghost of a threat hung in the air between them, the Israeli face-to-face with him. Saxon tensed, feeling the edges of ready menace coming off the other man; once again he found himself wondering who would prevail if they went against each other. He didn't like the odds.

"The group has been observing a... situation. This man has been classified as a liability," Namir went on. "He can expose us to our enemies. What he knows could severely impede our objectives if it were to be revealed to the wrong people. Ronald Temple is a serious threat to stability."

"And we can't have that," said Saxon, without weight.

Namir gave the slightest of smiles. "I knew you'd understand."

Great Falls—Virginia—United States of America

Configured for stealth and speed, the helo flashed over the countryside at treetop level, ducted blades chopping the air in a low, droning thrum. The pilot kept them off the line of any major population centers or highways, following power lines or river courses as they raced eastward. The radar-transparent polymers and sleek, blended lines of the hull gave the craft the detection footprint of a bumblebee, and in tandem with infrared and ultraviolet baffles cloaking the engines, the flyer was virtually invisible.

"*Two minutes,*" said the pilot, the words resonating through Saxon's head over the mastoid comm. He began his final premission ritual, losing himself in the simple, robotic motions, trying not to think about the job he had been sent to do.

Weapons. Equipment. Armor. All secure. He zipped open a gear pouch to check the contents and hesitated; something inside was emitting a soft glow. Hardesty and Hermann were busy with their own checks, so Saxon reached inside. His gloved fingers found the lozenge shape of the disposable phone; the morning they had left London, he had stuffed it into his kit and thought no more about it. He was certain he had deactivated it. Turning the device to conceal it from the others, Saxon tapped the screen.

An error display told him the vu-phone's digital mailbox was full. He scrolled down and found hundreds and hundreds of text messages, all of them sent from the number he had seen on the side of the advertisement blimp, all of them the same five words: *What master do you serve?*

Uneasy, he hit the mass delete tab, opened the phone's case, and disconnected the battery before concealing it once again.

"Will we need electronic support for this engagement?" Hermann was asking, loading heavy-gauge rounds into the magazine of a Widowmaker tactical shotgun.

Hardesty's tone was dismissive. "Namir said digital interdiction is being handled by other assets, so don't fret about getting caught on camera. Just do what I tell you." He sensed Saxon looking at him and met his gaze. "You got a question, too? Make it fast."

"Ninety seconds to deployment," called the pilot. *"Thermograph can't get an accurate read... At least ten-foot mobiles inside target structure."*

Saxon glanced out the window and saw the flicker of lights below, the soft glow of streetlamps amid patches of darkness. He looked back. "We can do this without collaterals. Cut the power, go in quiet, hit the mark, and extract."

"Like a ghost, huh?" Hardesty snorted. "It's funny. You bitched to me that I didn't have the stones to get my hands dirty in Moscow, but here I am going in at the sharp end and suddenly you wanna soft-pedal it?" He gathered up his FR-27 assault rifle, securing the ammo magazine in place. "How about that. All of a sudden, you're gun-shy."

"This is different. There are civilians in there." The helo dropped into the low grass with a bump and the engine note fell as the rotors went to idle. Through a stand of trees Saxon could make out the house.

Hardesty shook his head. "There's only targets." He pulled a lever to let the hatch slide open and thumped Hermann on the back. The German vaulted out into the darkness. Hardesty went next and Saxon followed him, but he'd barely taken a step before the other man placed the flat of his palm on his chest. "Where you going?"

"Namir—"

"Is not in command of this engagement," Hardesty replied. "I am. And I'm telling you to wait here and hold the landing zone. Y'know, in case a troop of Girl Scouts tries to sneak up behind us, yeah?" He gave a snort and set off.

Saxon stood there, watching the two men melt away into the shadows, his hands tense around the grip of his rifle, a nerve jumping in his jaw. For a second, his finger rested on the FR-27's trigger. *A single three-round burst would put that son-of-a-bitch down...*

Then the moment faded, and the lights in the house went dark. He caught the faint sound of breaking glass and what might have been a woman's scream.

Kelso left the Falcon at the side of the road and crossed a stretch of scrubland to the wall of the estate; she'd been to Temple's place once before, back when he'd just taken the job as department head. It was after the Anselmo case had broken, and in celebration their new boss had held a barbecue to toast the team's success. It seemed like a century ago, a warm summer day with good food and a few beers, Matt there with Jenny...Back before the first time Anna's career had gone off the rails.

She shrugged off the memory and scrambled up over the wall, concentrating on the moment. Temple would have security, she decided, some kind of alarm system—

Anna caught sight of the house as her head came level with the top of the wall, and in that moment she saw every light in the building die. Her fingertips touched a sensor strip on the top of the bricks, but no alarm sounded. Whatever had killed the power had given her a way in. She took the opportunity and scrambled the rest of the distance, dropping to the gravel drive. There were a few cars parked outside the three-story house, mostly high-end sedans and a couple of SUVs. The house belonged to Temple's second wife and she was old money; Anna recalled office talk about how she liked to play the hostess, gathering movers and shakers from the D.C. community. The whole city ran on that kind of networking; Anna was disgusted that Temple could send her off to be disappeared, then stroll home for some overpriced wine with his spouse's cronies without breaking stride.

She moved closer, using the cars as cover. Her hand strayed to where her service weapon would have been holstered and she grimaced. After the van crash, she hadn't thought to steal Agent Tyler's firearm or stun gun. Going in unarmed made her feel naked and supremely vulnerable.

She caught the sound of glass breaking and froze. Something wasn't right; a power outage should not have lasted more than a few seconds. Anna glanced over her shoulder, and in the distance she could see the next house over, the lights still on.

Her head snapped back as she heard gunshots, twice in quick succession. She guessed they were 10 mm rounds from a pistol. The gun sounded again, and this time she saw the reflection of a muzzle flash through a ground-floor window. A woman screamed and a shotgun answered.

She blinked her optics to low-light mode; they had the Eye-See vision-enhancement package, the law enforcement variant, and while they were not as powerful as military-grade cybernetics, they were enough to throw the view of the house into an ashen pattern of green and white. Anna kept to her cover as two figures burst out the front door, stumbling in panic as they tried to flee—a woman in an evening dress and a man in a sports jacket. They raced across the drive, the gravel crunching under their feet.

A shimmering thread, invisible to the naked eye, fell from a first-floor window and drew swiftly across the ground until it crossed the woman's back. There was a hissing snap and a cloud of ink-dark mist blew from her chest. The man turned in fright and took a second round in the sternum. Both of them were dead before they hit the ground.

Anna dared to peer over the wheel well and saw a shadow move away from the window, a rifle slung in a casual carry.

For a moment she considered turning tail, heading back to the car; but she was too deep in now to give up. Anna waited as long as she dared, and then stole toward the house, staying low as she threaded her way in through the front door the dead couple had left open.

Inside, the horribly familiar smells of spent cordite and blood reached her nostrils. A man in a suit lay against the staircase leading upward, his eyes staring sightlessly at the ceiling. Anna felt for a pulse; there was nothing.

She moved on, hugging the walls, finding her way into the open lounge. More of Temple's guests were here, some of them caught still sitting in chairs with glasses of wine in their hands, others shot in the back as they tried to run. Anna saw the telltale patterning of close-range shotgun blasts.

On the floor above, a floorboard creaked and she froze. She very clearly heard a shuffling footstep; then in the next second, a strangled, pained gurgle and the heavy fall of a body.

Cold certainty gathered in her thoughts. An assassin—or more than likely, a team of them—were stalking through Temple's home, systematically executing everyone they found. It could only have been the Tyrants; the brutality and precision of the attack bore all their hallmarks. Above, she heard the creaking again. They were sweeping the house, floor by floor. She had little time; once they had completed their search, they'd double back and look for stragglers.

She scanned the corpses again; he wasn't among them, and if Ron Temple was anything like the man she thought she knew, he would have had a plan for something like this. He was methodical to the last.

The house hadn't changed much since she had visited it, and she concentrated, pulling up her memories of that day. Temple had shown Matt around; she remembered him mentioning something about the basement...

Anna found a doorway in an alcove, behind a privacy curtain. In the dark, it would be easy to miss. Slipping inside, she followed the weakest sliver of light her optics could detect, and with care, descended a shallow set of steps. She blinked back to a normal vision mode. There, half hidden behind a few wine racks reaching from the concrete floor to the low ceiling, was a work area. A desk, a monitor, a rudimentary office. It was cool down here, and the carnage above seemed miles away.

She was two steps into the room when she heard a faint breath. "Temple," she whispered. "I know you're here."

There was a gasp of surprise, and he gingerly emerged from behind the desk, a small pistol in his trembling hand. "You... he whispered. "Are you...Was this a test?" Temple's face was a mess of conflicting emotions. "Did...Did I fail?"

"What the hell are you talking about?" she hissed, throwing a worried look at the stairs. If the hit team heard them, it would be all over.

He kept muttering to himself, thinking aloud. "No... No, it's not that. It's you. It's all your fault!" Temple rose up and aimed the gun at her. "You should be dead! How did you get away?"

"I had help," she admitted, holding her hands open to show she was unarmed.

"That's why they're here...Because of *you*, you stupid bitch! They know! You compromised me and they know it! I'm worth nothing now! Nothing... " He choked off in a sob. "Oh god. Everyone is dead. They're coming for me... They're cleaning house."

Temple's self-pity grated on her and she stepped toward him. "This is the price you pay for betrayal. I'd kill you myself if I could, but that would let you off easy!"

"You can't know what it was like..." Temple looked down at the pistol and studied it, turning it toward himself. "They'll find me..."

"No!" Anna lunged at him and backhanded the man across the face. For a moment they wrestled, and then she knocked the gun away, sending it skittering out of reach under the wine racks. "I need you alive, you bastard. We have to get out of here!"

"And go where?" He met her gaze and Kelso saw a side of the man she'd never seen before. He was falling apart before her eyes. "You can't run. You can't hide." Temple snorted. "What do you think is going to happen, Kelso? That you'll get your day in court like all good citizens? They won't let the Killing Floor be exposed!"

"The what?" She'd never heard the term before.

He wasn't listening. "We are already dead!"

"Not yet," she said. "You're my proof."

He went to the desk and tore through the papers scattered across it. "You want proof? Here. You came back for it, so *take it*!" Temple thrust something into her hands, and she realized it was the flash drive he had taken from her back at the office. "See how far you get!" He was blinking back tears.

Somewhere above them, she heard the crunch of broken glass. Anna grabbed Temple's arm and twisted it. "I don't give a damn what you say. You're coming with me. *Move!*"

She went back to low-light mode as they emerged into the kitchen. Temple gasped at the carnage and she saw him lurch toward a knife block. He pulled out a butcher's blade and cradled it in his hands, his breathing fast and shallow.

Across the room, a door opened onto the garden beyond. Anna heard movement in the lounge and she made for the exit. Her hand closed around the latch and she tested it: *locked.*

From the other room came a metallic click and an egg-shaped object rolled over the threshold, rattling as it came to a spinning halt on the tiled floor of the kitchen.

"*No—!*" Temple cried out just as Anna's mind caught up to what she was seeing; she rocked off her feet and slammed her shoulder into the door, wood splintering around the lock and frame. It came open as the grenade detonated with a shriek of combustion. A churning wall of heat and gas picked her up and threw her the rest of the way, sending Anna spinning into the soft, damp grass outside. She rolled as a torrent of glass and splinters rained down on her. Smoke and flame gushed from broken windows and the cracked doorway. Temple was still in there. Too late now.

Anna pulled herself to her feet, the hot stink of the fire choking the air around her; the blast had to have ruptured a gas line. Without looking back, she took off toward the trees flanking the house. As she sprinted away, two figures in matte black combat gear emerged from the smoke, panning their weapons this way and that.

Saxon swore as the explosion from the house caused his night vision to flare out, and he switched modes to ultraviolet. Crouching on one knee a short distance from the silent helo, he peered down the sight atop his rifle and tapped his comm pad. "White, this is Gray. Respond."

"Don't get your panties in a bunch," came the terse reply. *"We're on the way out. Prep for dust off."*

"That's your take on covert action? Blow the shit out of something?"

Hardesty ignored the comment. *"If I want your opinion, I'll give it to you. Meantime, keep your eyes open. We got a possible runner, heading your way. Intercept and execute, if you can handle that."*

Saxon cut the channel without bothering to answer. Rising from the ground he came forward, the rifle at his shoulder, sweeping back and forth. He heard the woman before he saw her, a moment before she emerged from the tree line. She was running across open ground, the last stretch before the rear wall of the Temple estate. On reflex, Saxon pulled the FR-27 tight to his shoulder and flicked the fire selector to single shot; at this range, he couldn't miss. The assault rifle would put a titanium-tipped flechette round directly on target, enough to tear open an unarmored human body.

Then she saw him and stumbled, staggered, almost lost her balance. Saxon's finger was on the trigger. The smallest application of pressure and she would be dead; an unarmed woman, a civilian, executed in cold blood.

She stood, frozen, waiting for the kill shot to come.

Ben Saxon was not an innocent. There were more than enough deaths that could be laid at his feet, kills he had made in the heat of battle and through cold, calculating aggression. Lives he had ended from afar, and some so close he heard the escape of their final breath. But then he was a soldier, and that had been war. *But this...*

The realization crystallized for him. What he was doing now went against every moral code Saxon believed in.

He let the rifle barrel drop slightly, and the woman saw the motion. In a few moments, she was at the wall and scrambling up over it. Conflicted, he watched her disappear out of sight.

As he got back to the helo, the aircraft's rotors were humming up to full power. Beneath the sound, he could hear the skirl of approaching sirens.

Hermann was already on board, and Hardesty stood waiting. "You get her?" he demanded.

"Nothing out there," Saxon replied. "If you missed one, they're long gone."

"What?" the American grabbed him by the collar, his eyes wide with anger. "I gave you one simple order—"

Saxon said nothing, shook himself free, and climbed into the flyer.

EIGHT

After the helo returned to the barren, isolated airstrip, the rest of the night passed in sullen silence. Hardesty boarded the parked jet in the hangar for what he said would be his "debrief," but until Namir and the others returned from the operation in Detroit, there was little any of them could do but wait.

The thought of getting back on the jet made Saxon feel claustrophobic, and he walked the apron of the airport, turning over his doubts and his fears, unable to make peace with the disquiet that continued to grow inside him like a cancer.

The unrest he felt was reaching critical mass—he could sense it. All the small details, all the little things he had let pass over the last few months, now they accreted into a mass of contradictions and challenges he could no longer turn away from. He had tried to convince himself that Namir had been right, back in the field hospital—that what the Tyrants were doing was making a difference to the world, holding back a rising tide of chaos; but the longer he went on, the less he believed it. Namir had assured him that they would find the men responsible for the failure of Operation Rainbird, the terrorists who planted the false data that led Strike Six to their doom. But aside from vague promises, nothing had been resolved.

Have I been played for a fool all along? It frustrated Saxon that he could not be certain of the answer to that question.

There was an annex at the side of the hangar building, a line of rooms. He went inside, fatigue dogging him. He felt it rise up; he wanted to rest, to close his eyes and make all of it go away, if only for a short time. But instead of solace he found Gunther Hermann, seated at a plain table with ordered lines of weapon components spread out in front of him. He recognized parts of a Widowmaker, still blackened from being fired hours earlier. A pistol, yet to be dismantled, sat within the German's reach.

"Where have you been?" he asked.

"Taking the air," Saxon replied irritably. He studied Hermann for a few moments, trying to take the measure of him; but it was impossible to get a read from those eyes. They were dead, like a shark's.

"You have something to say to me?" said the younger man. The challenge was clear in his manner.

The question came before he could stop himself. "How many people died in that house tonight?"

"All of them." Hermann didn't show the slightest flicker of concern.

"And you don't have a problem with that?"

"Why should I?" He put down the cleaning rod in his hand and studied Saxon. "You heard what Hardesty said. They were targets. They were in the wrong place at the wrong time. Collateral damage."

Saxon's jaw set at the man's matter-of-fact tone. "That's

how you see it, yeah? Black and white? Hardesty says kill and you do it, like a good little dog?"

A tiny flicker of emotion crossed Hermann's face. "I am a soldier. I follow orders."

Saxon shook his head. "I didn't sign up for this. Not to butcher civvies."

"What did you expect?" Hermann replied, confusion in his tone. "Did you come to the Tyrants expecting to keep your hands clean? That is not what we do." He tapped the table with an iron finger. "I had thought a man of your experience would have no illusions, Saxon. We do the worst of deeds in order to protect the world from itself. Because no one else can."

"And who gets to decide?" he shot back. "Don't you ever wonder about that? About who calls the shots?" Saxon leaned closer. "You were GSG-9, right? German police, antiterror unit. When you followed orders then, you were following the law—"

Hermann snorted softly. "When I was with them, the law was a rope around our necks. It kept us from making any progress." He shook his head. "Do you know what Namir said when he recruited me in Berlin, what made me decide to go with him? He told me that the Tyrants did not concern themselves with laws. Only *justice*. The group erased all my connections to the police force and I was happy they did." He nodded. "What we are doing is right. The ends are justified."

Saxon tried to find an answer that didn't stick in his throat, but before he could frame a reply the door opened and Barrett entered. He shrugged off his combat armor and gave them both a level look. "Miss me?"

"It's done, then?" said Hermann, his conversation with Saxon dismissed. The other man was almost eager to hear what had taken place in Detroit. "Were there any complications?"

"Nothing we couldn't take in stride," said the big man. He glanced at Saxon. "That cop you were so worried about? Namir broke him in two." Barrett helped himself to a beer from a cooler and drained it in a single pull.

"What about the people being held there? By Sarif?" said Saxon.

Barrett smiled thinly. "Oh, we handled them." He paused, massaging a contusion on the side of his skull. "They weren't that pleased to see us, though... " He made a face. "Some folks, huh? No goddamn gratitude."

Saxon glanced out into the hangar. "Where's Federova?"

The other man folded his arms. "Well, now. Would have been back here with me and the boss, but 'stead she's still out in the field." He aimed a finger at Saxon. "Cleaning up *your* mess."

"What the hell is that supposed to mean?"

Barrett gave a shrug of his shoulders. "You tell me. Barely got our cargo secured from Sarif before Hardesty is on the horn to Namir, bitchin' a blue streak."

"We achieved our objective," Hermann insisted. "Temple was terminated."

Barrett kept his eyes on Saxon. "Heard you let one get away."

"Bullshit," Saxon insisted. "Hardesty's just covering his own arse."

"Whatever you say, man." Barrett shrugged again and walked away.

Silver Springs—Maryland—United States of America

Kelso knew even as she did it that she was making a mistake. How many times had she seen criminals caught in the very same situation she was in now, and for the same reason? She knew better. The smart play was to fade away, get out of the city, and keep on going.

That wasn't what she had done. Anna kept her head down and walked in the places where the streetlights didn't shine too brightly, staying to the shadows. Instead of fleeing, she followed a basic, animal instinct to return to where she felt safest. *Home.*

Maybe now she understood those criminals a little better than she had when she was on the other side of the badge. For most people, it was counterintuitive to just cut and run. She understood that impulse; the raw need to go to ground. She tried to convince herself she was being smart—after all, no one would expect her to go back to her apartment—but she knew that wasn't it at all. She couldn't just *leave*. Not yet.

From the road she had glimpsed the spherical shape of a police monitor drone squatting on the lawn, the clusters of eyes on the robot ceaselessly scanning the area. The device's face-matching and body-mapping software would be programmed with her biometric profile, and she'd be made in a moment if she strayed too close. Instead, Anna detoured around the back and got in through a damaged window near the trash bins on the ground floor. For once, she was pleased that her landlord had reacted with his characteristic slowness in fixing the problem.

She took the stairs to the fourth floor. Another sensor,

this one the size of her fist, was attached to her front door. A built-in holograph projected *Police Line—Do Not Cross* across the threshold.

Anna's luck was holding; she recognized the security sensor as a model the Secret Service also used. She frowned as she thought of Matt Ryan. He had been the one who showed her how to spoof them. From her pocket, Anna pulled a piece of foil paper taken from a discarded cigarette packet and a vu-phone she had picked from the pocket of a man at the metro station. She gently plastered the foil over the sensor's antenna and worked at the phone, cycling its on-off function. After a few moments, the sensor went dark; Ryan had explained to her that the devices could be put into a reset mode if they were swamped with microwave signals, like those from a cellular telephone—it was a hit-and-miss hack, though. She unlocked the door and had it shut behind her just as the sensor reactivated. Moving slowly so as not to disturb it, Anna advanced into her apartment.

The lights came on automatically, dim enough for her to see her way around but not so much they would be seen from the street; the television chirped as it activated, casting a blue glow across the open-plan apartment.

Anna's gut tightened. The place had been turned over, likely by the agency, and while they hadn't wrecked it, it was still in great disarray. It seemed as if they had opened every cabinet, every drawer and box, searching for... *what*? Some evidence to back up the accusation that she was colluding with terrorists?

The light from the screen illuminated the open door to her bedroom. Even from here, she could see they had got into the wardrobe and found the safe. Her files were gone, just as she had known they would be. Anna thought about the flash drive in her pocket, the one Temple had pressed into her hands. That was all she had now, every other piece of her painstaking secret investigation now lost. She hoped it would be enough, if only she could find someone to entrust it to.

A part of her wanted to fall into her bed and give herself over to sleep. She was exhausted, and the shock and fatigue from the day's events were threatening to overwhelm her. Anna's gaze was drawn to the dark rectangle of the open bathroom door. For a long moment, she fought to ignore the thoughts of what was inside the mirrored cabinet over the sink. She tasted earth in the back of her throat and swallowed hard.

It took a lot of effort to go straight to the bedroom. From the closet, she took a sturdy daypack and circled the bed, gathering up items of clothing from where they had been piled, filling the bag with everything she would need to leave and not look back. Returning to the living room, she finally allowed herself a look into the bathroom. In the reflection of the mirrored cabinet she saw the frosted glass window over the bath, the light from the street shining through it.

Anna turned away and went to the desk until she found what she was looking for. The brass disc was right there where she had left it, and with hesitation, she picked it up, turning it over in her fingers. Suddenly she realized that the sobriety coin had been what really brought her back here. Everything else, the clothes and the bag, all that she could have found elsewhere. The coin she could not have surrendered; it was the last link to the person she used to be, to the person Matt Ryan had always believed in. She swallowed a sob and allowed herself a moment to give in to the emotion inside her, just a brief instant before she forced it away.

Then Anna realized she was looking at something she didn't recognize. She didn't get a lot of paper correspondence, maybe the odd circular or item of junk mail, but there on the desk was a pile of items, doubtless placed there by one of the investigators Temple had sent to search the apartment. The largest was a plastic box, postmarked from the city that day, but with no return address details. She shook it gingerly, and then, with care, used her thumbnail to peel back the wrapping. Inside was a courier case with simple print lock. Anna tapped it with her index finger and it opened with a click; the noise seemed like a gunshot in the quiet of the apartment, and it made her flinch.

Inside there was a commercial data card, coded with a one-way rail ticket from Washington, D.C., across the border to Quebec. She found a Canadian passport with it, a high-grade fake using her face and a name she'd never heard before. The rest of the box was taken up with a flat, slab-sided device that resembled a rifle magazine; a Pulsar electromagnetic pulse grenade. She drew out the weapon and weighed it in her hand. It was a military-grade item, and possession of it alone was a felony... but that was hardly a concern for her now. Who had left her this gift, she wondered? Was it some contingency plan by D-Bar and his Juggernaut comrades, or a clever trap left behind by the Tyrants? She put the grenade back down and sighed.

For a moment, she thought the fatigue was playing tricks on her, but when it happened a second time, Kelso was certain she had heard someone say her name. She gave a start when she realized it was Eliza Cassan, the Picus network's ever-present anchorwoman, voicing a breaking report on the Nightly World News. Anna fumbled for the television's remote and turned up the volume. She saw her own face there on the thinscreen, a still from the agency's press file. A line of text ticked past at the bottom of the image, the words talking about a multiple murder in Grand Falls, a manhunt getting under way...

"...at this hour. *The Picus News Network had learned from sources within the Department of Justice that Agent Kelso was on suspension pending an investigation relating to an incident several months ago, when Senator Jane Skyler of Southern California was injured during an assassination attempt by members of the ruthless Red Arrow triad.*" The picture was replaced with quick clips of Skyler, then FBI agents raiding the home of the senator's maid. Cassan's face reappeared, growing concerned. "*Some viewers may find the following footage disturbing. We have just obtained security recordings of the events at the Temple house that appear to incriminate Agent Anna Kelso in the brutal attack that took place earlier this evening.*"

Anna felt the blood drain from her face as grainy white-and-green images unfolded before her. She saw herself stalking through the halls of Temple's home, a heavy weapon cradled in her arms. She gasped as the figure on the screen entered a room full of people and gunned them down with quick, callous motions. The image froze and zoomed in; the face looking back was very much her own.

"No..." she muttered. "That's not me...They faked it..." She trailed off as the weight of her own words bore down. It made terrible, perfect sense. All the way back to the apartment, she had wondered why the Tyrant soldier who saw her hadn't opened fire and gunned her down. She couldn't understand why he had let her flee, but now she understood. It had to be part of this! They let her go so she could be framed for the killings, and she had played the part for them perfectly. Anna reeled with the sense of it; no one would believe her claims of conspiracy now. To the rest of the world, she would be seen as a violent criminal. A murderer and a traitor.

The screen showed the file photo of her face once more, this time captioned with the words *Anna Kelso—Wanted Fugitive.*

Panic boiled at the edge of her thoughts as she snatched up the daypack, the ticket, and the passport. She grabbed the EMP grenade and thrust it into the bag. Anna took two steps toward the front door and froze. A sense, an impression that years of training and expertise had instilled in her, pushed through the web of fear clouding her thoughts. A cool breath of air brushed her bare neck, and she turned slowly to look through into the dimly lit bathroom. Reflected in the mirror, she saw that the frosted window in there was open. *It was closed,* she told herself, trying to be sure of her own thoughts. *I know it. I'm sure of it. When I came in here, it was closed—*

Static prickled the hairs on her arms and Anna had the sudden, immediate knowledge that she was no longer alone. She spun, pulling the bag off her shoulder to swing it like a weapon, in time to see a lithe figure emerge from thin air, sketched in by ripples of silvery light, like oil on water. A woman, made of glass, becoming real.

Anna saw her face, the dark doll's eyes and the predator's smile on her lips; then she was coming at her, a wicked blade flashing though the air.

Romeo Airport—Michigan—United States of America

Saxon crossed underneath the fuselage of the jet, looking back and forth across the open space of the hangar. He should have known that Hardesty wouldn't let the incident at the house pass without trying to turn it to his advantage; if the sniper had decided to use Saxon's apparent insolence against him, there was no knowing how Namir might react to the situation.

As he reached the pools of shadow at the far edge of the hangar, he heard someone say his name, very clearly; the voice was unmistakably Hardesty's. A moment later, Namir's low tones reached him; the two men were outside on the apron. Saxon caught the familiar scent of Hardesty's acrid cigarettes.

By reflex, Saxon shrank into the gloom, placing himself behind the bulk of a low-slung aircraft tractor—the dense construction of the service vehicle would hide his heat signature if either of the men chose to sweep the area with his optics. Dropping into a crouch, Saxon forced himself to slow his breathing and become as silent as possible. After a moment, their voices came to him on the faint breeze. He strained to hear what was being said.

Hardesty was speaking again. "I'm not trying to second-guess you, Namir. I know you got your reasons."

He turned away to exhale and Saxon lost the next few words. "...Don't trust the limey, *period*. He's a liability."

"So you keep saying," Namir replied, his voice level. "But your personal aversion is not my concern."

"This isn't personal!" Hardesty insisted hotly. There was a moment's pause. "Okay, screw it. Yeah, it *is* personal. The son-of-a-bitch walks around like his shit don't stink, with all that noble-soldier, honor-of-the-regiment crap. I've seen his kind before. I don't like Saxon because he thinks he's better than the rest of us."

"He's good at what he does. More than a match for you."

Hardesty was silent for long seconds, and Saxon wondered if he had been spotted; but then the American went on. "That's not the problem. It's not that he's a threat. He's weak inside. I know what happened in the fight room. When push comes to shove, he's going to fold. Believe me."

Saxon's lips thinned, but he kept his silence.

"We'll see," offered Namir.

But the next words Hardesty uttered froze Saxon's blood in his veins. "You should have let me deal with him after Rainbird." Just hearing him say the name of the grisly failure made Saxon's gut twist with anger and sick dread. Namir's reply was lost as the wind dropped for a moment, but Hardesty's answer was clear. "We don't need them both. Gunther's the better choice. I say we put Saxon down. He's never gonna be a cold-eyed stone killer. He just doesn't have it in him."

When Namir replied, Saxon heard the steel in his tone. "As I said, that choice has never been yours to make. I recruit operatives with potential, men and women whom I consider worthwhile. If the group is endangered, then the decision will be made. No one is bulletproof, Scott. Not Ben, not you, not even me. Never forget that." Footsteps scraped on the asphalt; they were coming back.

Saxon glanced around; if he left his place of concealment, there was no way he could make it to other cover before Namir and Hardesty entered the hangar. He had no choice but to stay where he was and remain silent. He had little doubt now that if they found him, Hardesty would make him answer for it with a bullet.

His mind still racing, Saxon went as low as he could, pressing into the wheel well of the tractor vehicle.

"You're certain that Temple was killed?" asked Namir as he passed.

"Burned to a crisp," Hardesty replied. "Incendiary grenade will do that for you. The cops will be sifting through the ashes of that place for weeks."

"The more important question remains to be answered, however." Namir reached the access ramp at the rear of the jet. "Was the Killing Floor compromised?"

"I don't think so—"

"But you don't *know*," Namir cut him off. He paused, then shook his head. "We can't let that possibility deflect us. Put these concerns to one side, let me deal with the fallout. In the meantime, concentrate on the preparations for the next operation. On that, we can have no margin for error. Clear?"

"Clear." Hardesty stood unmoving, his gaze turned inward as Namir boarded the aircraft.

From his hiding place, Saxon glared at the other man.

More than anything at this moment, he wanted to know what Hardesty knew about Operation Rainbird. He wanted to beat it out of him—the old, familiar anger ran through him, setting his teeth on edge. And that phrase, this Killing Floor...When he had confronted Kontarsky in Moscow, the hacker Janus had mentioned the same thing...

Finally, Hardesty turned and walked away across the hangar. Saxon watched him go, suddenly unsure of his next move. The chill fear that had been lingering at the base of his thoughts for so long was now in sharp, icy focus. He felt the same sensation at the pit of his gut as he had the night Strike Six had set off across the Grey Range.

He was in enemy territory.

In a secure room aboard the jet, Namir shrugged off his combat jacket and settled into a chair. The console in front of him unfolded into panes of holographic imagery, a global map displaying lines of communication spiderwebbing the world. Bright nodes of light sparkled into life in place over cities spanning a dozen nations; the group was giving him a moment of their precious time, and he was contrite. He understood how important they were; to even consider directly interfacing with the Tyrants...that was something that happened only in the most pressing of circumstances.

"Let's cut to the meat of this," said the voice from New York. *"What effect will there be with the loss of the Temple asset?"*

"None, sir," Namir said immediately. "We have what we

needed from him. We've had a contingency for his removal in place since day one. This only brought that forward."

"That was held off because there was a chance the asset might have had more value down the line." The woman in Hengsha made the point. *"We couldn't have foreseen this development with the Kelso woman."*

"Random factors are always the most troublesome," offered another voice, this one transmitting from Singapore.

Namir glanced at a tertiary screen. As he watched, he realized it was footage from a security camera equipped with low-light capability. He saw a woman entering a wide hallway, approaching a man sprawled at the base of a staircase. She touched his neck, and then moved on.

"This was obtained by our associate in Montreal, from the estate's security server," said the man in New York. *"The footage has already been repurposed for our needs."*

Namir cleared his throat. "I have an operative tasked for deployment in the Washington, D.C., area in connection with the primary mission. I took the liberty of activating her early. She may be able to isolate the Kelso woman, if she did indeed escape the Temple hit..."

"Keep us informed, Namir," said the woman. *"Whatever happens, Anna Kelso has gone from being a minor irritant to a potential threat. If she raises her head again, she'll be dealt with. But it is imperative you understand she is only of secondary importance. Stay on-mission."*

Then as quickly as they had come to him, the ghostly avatars of the group vanished and Namir was plunged back into gloom, his masters gone like gods passing beyond the affairs of mortals.

Silver Springs—Maryland—United States of America

Kelso hauled the daypack around on its strap and put all the force she could into swinging it at her assailant. Part of her mind was reeling at what she saw; Anna knew that advanced augmentations like optical camouflage existed, but she had never dreamed she'd see it this close, on someone intent on killing her. The name flashed through her thoughts; *the Tyrants*. They had set her up, and now they would destroy her.

The fractal-edged combat blade whispered through the air and slashed through the material of bag without stopping, opening it along the whole length. The contents spilled out and scattered over the floor. Anna tried to fall back beyond the reach of the dark-skinned woman, but instead she put herself in the open. The woman pivoted on her long, machined legs of carbon steel and plastic, swinging one up to strike Anna across the side of the ribs. The blow connected with a solid smack of metal on flesh and Kelso choked out a lungful of air; the impact vibrated through her bones with such force that it threw her down, and she had to swallow the urge to vomit. Pain lit fires all down her side as she collided with a low stool and crashed to the living-room floor.

She was barely able to blink before she saw the blade coming down again, the shining point aimed at her throat. Anna's off hand shot out to deflect the weapon and she grabbed the assassin's wrist, struggling against her. The woman made a negative noise at the back of her throat and followed through, putting her weight into it. Anna winced as new pain blossomed; her attacker put a steel-capped knee into her stomach and pressed hard.

Anna coughed, tasting blood. She couldn't take her eyes off the tip of the blade as it came inexorably downward toward the bare skin of her neck. The woman had gravity and training on her side; it would only be a matter of moments before Anna could no longer resist, and then she would cut her throat.

Her other hand flailed at the air, scraping across the rug, and her fingers brushed something smooth. Reflexively, she grabbed the object—a heavy coffee mug stenciled with an image of the Lincoln Memorial—and swung it with all the power she could muster. The ceramic broke as she clubbed the assassin with it, smashing it across her cheekbone. The woman gave an angry snarl and reeled backward. Anna kicked and rolled, getting out from under her attacker before the killer could react. She dragged herself away, almost on all fours, toward the scattered contents of the daypack, clutching at the torn clothes, searching.

She heard the woman coming back at her just as she found what she was looking for. Anna tore the activator tag-strip from the top of the EMP grenade and spun, hurling it blindly in the direction of the Tyrant assassin. She scrambled toward the door and made it to the middle of the room before the device went off.

With a low, humming snarl, the electromagnetic pulse lit the apartment with actinic blue lightning. Immediately, the lamps fizzed and went dark, the television screen dying with them. Anna glanced over her shoulder as the woman howled and stumbled, crashing to the wooden floor as her perfectly sculpted cybernetic legs became inert and unresponsive; and in the same moment Anna felt a spike of migrainelike pain lance through her head as the pulse struck the delicate electronics in her optical augmentations. Her vision lost all coherence, dissolving into a wall of featureless gray static.

The literal blind panic she had felt awakening in the hospital six months ago returned with punishing force, and Kelso staggered, her hands sweeping through the air; but then she walled off the pain and the fear, just like they had taught her in training. The effect of the localized EMP would last for sixty seconds, perhaps less—she had that long a head start to escape before the killer came after her. Anna was blind...but she had lived in this building long enough to know her way around it with her eyes shut.

Staying low, moving as swiftly as she dared, she found the door and shouldered it open, feeling along the walls toward the stairwell. As she got outside, feeling faint traces of rain on her skin, her optics began to stutter through the restart cycle, her vision returning by agonizingly slow degrees. She broke into a loping run, and behind her she heard the strident whoop of a siren as the dormant police drone caught her silhouette. She ignored it, picking up speed, and by the time she reached the street, she could see again.

Romeo Airport—Michigan—United States of America

The sun was coming up, the line of orange light at the horizon growing brighter with every passing minute. Saxon walked the edge of the runway, threading the points between the shallow domes of the embedded lights that flanked the long expanse of cracked asphalt.

His hands were buried in the pockets of his tactical

overjacket, his head hunched forward. Saxon tried to lose himself in the simple motion of step after step, but it didn't work. The questions and the conflicts churning around inside him refused to be silenced. He had the very real sense that he was standing on the edge of an abyss, at a point of no return. Looking up, Saxon saw the distant chain-link fence. If he broke into a sprint, he could be there in less than a minute. He could be over it and down to the highway in another five. If luck was on his side, Saxon would be miles from the airstrip before any of the Tyrants knew he had absconded.

He could turn his back on them and go. Leave all the questions and distrust behind, ditch this identity and start anew. He could do it; he still had contacts from the old days, people who might help him disappear.

But what would that get him? A lifetime of doubts and looking over his shoulder? Namir had never said the words, but Saxon knew that the Tyrants and their masters in "the group" were not the kind of people you could just walk away from. The federal agent, Temple, had been a minor player for them and he had been wiped out just on the *suspicion* of being a problem. The Tyrants would not turn their backs and allow one of their number to walk away; Namir would see him killed first. Hardesty would do it and enjoy it.

But how could he stay? How could he look Namir in the eye and not wonder? What did he really know about Operation Rainbird?

Saxon turned back to face the hangar at the far end of the airfield. Wan light spilled from the open doors. He wanted to draw the Diamondback from its holster, bury the muzzle in Namir's neck, and demand he spill everything. He let himself ride on that moment of high emotion, seeing the faces of Sam, Kano, and the others. Remembering the promises he had made to those men, and to himself.

And then he remembered the vu-phone. Saxon opened the rip-tab on the gear pocket where he had stuffed the disposable. Gingerly, he replaced the battery pack and touched the activation button. The phone blinked on and buzzed in his gloved hand. A single message was waiting. He drew it up; it was an embedded video file, what appeared to be a clip from a local affiliate of the global Picus News Network. The footage unfolded, a voice-over explaining that police in Virginia had been called to the site of a fire in Great Falls. On the handheld's screen he saw the woman he had confronted in the grounds rendered in grainy, colorless video. She entered a room full of people and started shooting. White flares of light spat from a shotgun—a Widowmaker Tactical—in her grip, and panicking figures fell like puppets with their strings cut. The footage paused and a close-up gave a better view of the woman. *Anna Kelso,* read the caption, *Wanted Fugitive.*

The lie of what he was seeing made Saxon's hand tighten around the vu-phone. For a moment he tensed, ready to dash the device to pieces against the ground; but then it rang with a soft, persistent hum.

Saxon raised it to his ear. "Yeah?"

"Hello again. Will you speak to me now?"

It was unmistakably the same synthetic, digitally masked voice he had heard in the Hotel Novoe Rostov; the ghost-hacker Janus.

He glanced around. There was no one in sight in any

direction. "What do you want from me? The video...Why did you show me that?"

"*I want you to understand. This is what they do. These are the people that you work for, Benjamin. I want to be certain you have no illusions as to what they are capable of.*"

"How do you know—"

"*Who you are? I know all about Ben Saxon. And Anna Kelso. And Jaron Namir, Ronald Temple, Yelena Federova, Scott Hardesty—*"

"Then what do you want with me?" he demanded.

"*I want to help you,*" said the flat, toneless voice. "*I want to open your eyes. Because when you know the truth, you will be able to help me.*"

"You're a terrorist. You and your Juggernaut mates."

He could almost hear a shake of the head. "*That word is meaningless. Terrorism is the use of violence to achieve radical political or social change. Is that not what the Tyrants are doing, Benjamin? Do you know what master you serve?*"

"Leave me alone!" he snarled. "I'm through with you!"

"*No!*" shouted Janus, with the first glimmer of what seemed like an emotional response. "*Do not hang up. That would be a mistake. Listen to me. You are cutting into the reality behind the lie of the Tyrants and their shadow masters. You know it. You know there are secrets beneath the surface. I want the same thing you do. To be free of their lies. You want the truth about Operation Rainbird. I want to find and expose the Killing Floor. Together, we can succeed.*"

"I don't know what this...Killing Floor is."

"Jaron Namir controls access to a private server on board your transport aircraft. In the files it holds are details of what you and I seek. The truth, Benjamin. The facts about the deaths of your men, and the location data I require. But the server is isolated, protected. It is impossible to access it by anything but direct physical means."

Saxon frowned. The wind carried the sound of gears to him, and he looked back to see the doors of the aircraft hangar shudder and slowly grind open. "You're asking me to risk my life for you," he said. "For a faceless phantom."

"Untrue," said Janus. *"All I am doing is providing you with the means. It is your choice, Benjamin. I cannot force you into this."* There was a pause, and he heard the whisper of encryption software flattening out the texture of the voice on the other end of the line. *"Listen carefully. When Jaron Namir was nineteen years old, his sister Melina was killed in a road accident in Haifa. Psychological profiling conducted several years later, after his recruitment into Mossad, indicated a deep-seated guilt over the death of his sister; he later named his daughter after her. The likelihood of his personal pass code relating directly to Melina Namir is over eighty-seven percent, plus or minus five percent. I have transmitted the four most likely code strings to your vu-phone. Use them to access the server."*

In spite of himself, Saxon laughed. "Just like that?"

"Yes. Just like that." There was no trace of sarcasm in the reply. *"Once you have access, use the wireless link to download the data you find to the vu-phone's memory. But be careful. If you are discovered, they will kill you."*

Saxon considered the offer. "And what if I don't? What if I smash this phone to bits right now?"

The reply was instant. *"You will never hear from me again. But one day, very soon, you will be so driven by your personal sense of anger and despair that you will attack Jaron Namir. And you will be killed."* There was a pause. *"I have also read your psychological profile, Benjamin."*

"I'll think about it," he said, and switched off the phone before Janus could reply.

When he reached the hangar, the jet's engines were already turning, a low mutter of noise resonating through the open space. The hatches were cycling closed along the cargo bay where the helo was stored, and the robot forklifts had all retreated to the corners of the building, clearing the route to the taxiway. Hardesty was there, and he gave Saxon a withering look as he climbed the boarding ramp.

"Where the hell have you been? You turned off your damned comm!"

"I was taking some air," he shot back. "I got sick of the sight of you."

"Oh, yeah?" Hardesty came closer, crowding him. "You weren't thinking about going AWOL, were you? Because it would be my absolute pleasure to show you the error of that way of thinking." His body language was aggressive, daring Saxon to take a swing at him.

"Hey!" Barrett called down to the pair of them from the top of the ramp. "If you two ladies are done kissin', get your asses on board! We're on a clock here!"

Saxon pushed past and sprinted up the ramp, Hardesty a heartbeat behind him. The ramp was already lifting shut as the jet began to move, the engine noise building.

Namir came back from the forward compartment. Around the dermal ports of his augmentations, the commander's face was red with annoyance.

"We are not waiting for Federova?" said Hermann, from a seat by the windows.

Namir shook his head. "She has her own directives."

"The Kelso woman?"

That seemed to touch a nerve, and Namir looked back at the German, his eyes narrowing. "As much as it disappoints me to say it, that target slipped the net a second time."

"Shoulda sent me," Barrett opined. "I'd have dealt with her."

Namir ignored the comment. "It doesn't matter. Yelena is returning to her primary. She'll shadow our main target and we'll regroup on-site."

"On-site *where*?" said Saxon, working hard to keep his voice level. "What target? I thought we were done."

"With this, here? For now, yes." Namir gave a terse nod. "But the mission in Detroit was only one element of a larger operation. We're moving to the next phase. That's all you need to know, for the moment." He paused, scanning their faces. "I'd advise all of you to get some rest. It's another twelve hours to our destination."

NINE

Kelso did her best to sink deeper into her seat, turning her body slightly so that her face was concealed from anyone who might walk past. The rocking motion of the express train's passenger carriage tried to lull her toward sleep, but she was caught in a strange kind of middle state between exhaustion and alertness—unable to truly rest or to stay fully awake.

Each time the train clattered over a set of points she looked up to make sure the noise wasn't the sound of the doors at the far end of the carriage opening; but she need not have worried. There were few other passengers, and most of them had chosen seats on the upper deck, where the view was better. Here on the lower level, it was a noisier and less pleasant place to ride the rails. The express from Washington, D.C., out to Boston was the first leg of the journey to Quebec paid into her ticket; Kelso was scheduled to change trains at Penn Station in New York for the northbound Adirondack route, but she had no intentions of doing so. There were a dozen stops between here and there, and she was already formulating a loose plan based on jumping trains in Philadelphia. She'd wait until the very last second, and vault through the automatic doors as they closed...

Using the ticket was a calculated risk. If she was being tracked, it was likely they'd have people watching the main stations, maybe even someone on the train already—but it was clear that whoever had supplied the ticket, the passport, and the grenade had nothing to do with the Tyrants. Still, until she knew for sure who her benefactors were or what they wanted, Anna decided to treat everyone with the same level of distrust. Right now, that seemed to be the only thing keeping her alive.

There were small screens set in the back of the seats in front of her, and they blinked into life as the train started to slow, the Baltimore suburbs blurring past on the other side of the rain-slicked windows. After the requisite information displays, the screens automatically switched to a feed from a local news affiliate, the ubiquitous Picus News logo framing image loops of global, national, and local events. Anna held her breath as she saw a portion of the same report that had been playing in her house, in the seconds before the assassin had appeared—the same hazy video replay of what appeared to be her indiscriminately killing dozens of civilians. Angrily, she reached forward and stabbed at the screen, darkening it, but the images were all over the carriage, on other displays here and there. Scowling, she drew into the oversize microfleece jacket, letting it swamp her.

Anna's eyes darted back and forth, scanning the area. She couldn't shake the sense of creeping dread that at any second, some citizen might recognize her, some transport cop would make the connection, some camera might get a good look at her face and flag it. *They could be waiting for me in Baltimore, she told herself. Snipers and a takedown unit, ready to swarm onto the train the moment it rolls in. That's how I would play it.*

Anna shook off the moment of burgeoning fear and looked around. There was a restroom at the end of the carriage; it could be a bolt hole if she saw police officers or agents boarding to search for her—

"What the hell am I doing?" It was a moment before she realized the words were her own, the question falling from her lips. The answer was clear, she was running— but where was she running *to*? Even if she made it to Philadelphia, what then? She wouldn't go to ground there. She'd have to keep moving. *But to where?* Panic darkened the edges of her thoughts. Anna had no plan for what was going on right now, and that terrified her. She hated the thought of being out of control, caught by fate and chance; and she knew, through long years of serving the law, that sooner or later a criminal ran out of road. *How much more of* mine *is left?*

A sudden jolt went through the floor of the carriage and Kelso lurched forward as the train decelerated abruptly with a shriek of brakes. Somewhere on the upper deck, she heard a child cry out in alarm and the thud of dislodged luggage. Immediately, a red icon flashed into life on the seat-screens and over the animated advertisements along the walls of the cabin. An automated announcement requested that all passengers remain in their seats, but Anna was already up, propelled by nervous energy. Outside, the lights of the communities on Baltimore's southern outskirts were lost as the train rolled into a tunnel, continuing to slow with every passing second. The screech of the brakes dropped in pitch in time to the deceleration, and with a juddering lurch, the train came to a halt. The lamps inside the carriage blinked for a moment, but Anna was already making her way forward, crouching slightly. She passed an elderly couple who were muttering to each other about the sudden happening, pushed her way to the restroom door—and halted. She thought about being trapped in there and her gut tightened.

Anna reached into her pocket, found the ticket and passport, and tossed them both into the toilet before setting off again. If they were tracking the arfid chips in the data cards, they would already be zeroing in.

Part of her wondered if she was overreacting—anything could have happened, some mechanical fault, a delayed train on the rails ahead of them, any one of a number of nondangerous reasons why they had stopped—but Kelso knew her own instincts. Throughout her career, every time she had ignored them she had regretted it.

Opening the door to the connecting alcove at the end of the carriage, Anna found herself at the foot of the stairwell leading to the upper deck. On either side, doors at platform level looked out at the blank gray tunnel. She flattened herself into the wall and tried to peer down along the length of the train.

Faint illumination from glow strips cast flat shadows around the tunnel floor, but there was motion in the distance—flashlights, bobbing as they came closer.

Anna forced the door, but it refused to open, mag-locked until the train reached the next station. Without hesitating, she braced herself in the crook of the door and kicked out with her feet, aiming her heel at the corner of the glass. After three or four hard impacts, the window webbed and fractured. Scraping her fingers on the bent frame and sharp edges, Anna put all her bodyweight behind it and the glass finally gave, shattering into blunt fragments.

It was a longer drop to the rail bed than she had expected it to be, and Kelso landed poorly, hissing with pain as her ankle twisted. Cold, rain-damp air filled her lungs and she scrambled across the opposite track, crunching over the gravel between the rails. The lights were coming her way, and now she heard voices. The only escape route was back along the length of the train in the opposite direction. Anna hugged the side of the carriages and stole forward, as quickly as she dared.

She was only a few steps from the mouth of the tunnel when she heard a voice call her name. She ignored it and broke into a run, wincing with the ache from her ankle. A halo of white glared around her as she fell into the beam of one of the flashlights, and she threw up a hand to shield her eyes. Anna stumbled backward, and she was looking for another means of escape when she heard the voice again.

"*Kelso!* Damn it, where the hell are you going?"

She squinted into the light. "D-Bar?"

The young hacker became visible, flanked by a couple of thuggish men who had the watchful, grim manner of career leg-breakers. They had machine pistols as well as the flashlights. "You are a real pain in the ass to pin down, do you know that?" D-Bar beckoned her to follow him. "C'mon. We don't have long until the railroad signals reset, and then this will not be a safe place to stand."

Anna hesitated. "You left the package."

That got her a nod. "You're predictable, Agent Kelso. Juggernaut ran your psych profile, figured where you'd most likely go. 'Course, the Tyrants figured the same thing, didn't they?"

She returned his nod. "I suppose I should thank you, then." Anna followed them toward the far side of the tunnel, where an archway led to a branching conduit.

He grinned wolfishly. "That's twice now I saved your pretty little backside. Honestly, being your white knight is getting to be a habit."

"Don't get a swelled head over it..." Anna halted. "Because I'm not going anywhere with you until I know where we're heading."

One of the thugs, a tall Hispanic man with acres of tattoos and chromed augmented hands, stepped toward her in an obvious gesture of threat, but D-Bar waved him away. "No, no. Agent Kelso's got a point. If she wants to stay here and chance it with the cops, she can do that." He leaned in. "Or, you can come with us and finally get a freakin' clue. What's it gonna be?"

Her first instinct was to cut and run. Trust had never come easily to Anna, and after everything that had happened, it was harder still to find that conviction inside herself; but she knew that she wouldn't make it another day without some kind of help. "I guess when you put it like tha...I don't have a lot of options, do I?"

D-Bar gave a smug smile. "About time you caught on."

Aerial Transit Corridor—Northeastern Sector—United States of America

The transport jet settled into its heading, angling into a course that would follow the Eastern Seaboard all the way up to Newfoundland before turning to strike out across the Atlantic. Once they were at stable altitude, all the members of the Tyrant team had taken Namir's orders to heart and returned to their cramped cabins in the aircraft's midsection. The lighting dimmed to night-flight levels; they would not see day again until they reached the airspace of the European Union.

Saxon waited twenty minutes, listening at the wall to be certain of no other movement out in the corridor. Then, with care, he eased open the door to his cabin and slipped back out, moving forward with all the stealth he could muster. The only weapon he had on him was a Buzzkill stun gun, although he wondered if the tazer pistol would be enough to put down any of the Tyrants. He was on a mission of his own making now; discovery would mean failure, and worse.

In another pocket he had the disposable vu-phone. Waiting in the cabin, he had read and reread the message sent by Janus, committing it to memory before erasing the text.

Melina; he turned the name over in his thoughts. Saxon tried to imagine a younger Jaron Namir, a man and not the lethal cyborg that he knew. He tried to picture that young Namir dealing with the death of someone close to him. Had it hardened him, he wondered? Made him callous to the suffering of others, put him on the path to who he had become? Saxon frowned and dismissed the thought. Whatever secrets Namir had, if this worked, he would learn them soon enough.

He threaded his way along the length of the jet, to the stairs dropping to the lower level. Crouching, Saxon carefully placed each silent footfall, keeping in the lines of shadow along the main corridor. Blinks of light, from the wingtip navigation indicators on the jet's wings, cast faint halos of color over his shoulders through the oval windows. Saxon knelt in the lee of a support frame and cycled through the variant modes of his optics. Through the partition walls, he picked out the faint heat-blobs of the two-man flight crew up toward the cockpit area, while at the aft, in the operations center, the only colors were the dull green-blue glow of the idling computer systems.

Saxon entered the ops room and closed the door behind him. Keeping low, he threaded his way to Namir's console and tapped the glassy surface. The panel came to life, immediately demanding a pass code. He let out a breath to steady himself, and tapped out the first string of symbols. *Melina's date of birth.*

The panel chimed a warning; the code was wrong. The sound seemed like a shout in the quiet of the dormant room, among the low murmur of the computers. Saxon waited for a moment, one hand on the stun gun, but no one came to investigate. He went on; the second code string was also incorrect. A fail on the third attempt would lock down the console and doubtless trigger some kind of alert—but the list of potential passwords Janus had provided had more than three variations. He ran them through his thoughts again.

Namir's sister. His daughter. A simple code. It would not be complex, Saxon realized. Namir wasn't that kind of man, not one to waste time on needless subterfuge. He was direct. There were no shades of gray to him.

Saxon thought about people he had lost, people he had felt responsible for; and then he typed in the name of the dead woman as it might have appeared on her gravestone, plain and unaltered.

The console unlocked and bloomed with new display windows, welcoming him into the main lines of its data store. Saxon's eyes narrowed as he saw line after line of files, labeled with places, dates, names...

Targets. There were hundreds of people listed here, and they were all objectives for the Tyrants. He scrolled through the names, looking for points of commonality, struggling to understand. There were men like Mikhail Kontarsky, high-profile figures linked to criminal groups like the Hong Kong Triads and the Russian Bratva, others tagged as in collusion with terrorists and activists— Juggernaut, L'Ombre, Purity First, and others. On the surface, people who looked like bad guys, up to their necks in illegality.

But Saxon had only to scratch the surface to find lists of action orders ranged against the names of civilians, politicians, scientists—people the Tyrants had no business going against. Some of the orders were straight kill commands, others ghosted under setups that would appear as suicides, robberies gone wrong, accidents. A few were tagged as "coercive"—no deaths there, instead the application of violence and intimidation.

Saxon felt betrayed. The mission of the Tyrants, the reason he had allowed himself to be recruited by Namir, was a lie. The faceless men of the group giving the orders were not using them to help maintain global stability— they were using them as enforcers, eradicating anyone who might prove dangerous to them, killing or intimidating all across the planet.

He picked a handful of files at random and opened them. *June Sellers, Department of Homeland Security—terminated; Donald Teague, advisory staffer on the United Nations science council—terminated; Martine Delancourt, founder of the French Bioethics Association—terminated; Garrett Dansky, CEO of Cadin Global—terminated; Ryu Takahanada, cybernetics research scientist at Isolay—terminated…*The list went on and on, and among it all, Saxon found the data on the men he had surveilled in Glasgow and Bucharest; one was a technology researcher on the payroll of the British government, the other a politician. Both files had additional information beyond what he had turned over to Namir; there were still images, digital shots of a body in an alleyway, throat slit and pale, another of a car on fire. Neither man had been a criminal, but clearly, someone had considered them a threat. Now they were both dead. Both killed by the Tyrants. He saw expedited code tags on the files, bearing the idents "Green" and "Red." *Scott Hardesty. Yelena Federova.*

Saxon closed the files and sat in the dimness and silence, musing on what he had seen, silently cursing his own stupidity. At first, he hadn't wanted to think too hard about what he was doing, about what the meaning of the Tyrants might be. It was only as time had passed that the nagging disquiet in the back of his thoughts had grown to a ceaseless churn—and now that he had an idea of the truth, it made his blood run cold. He thought about Janus's repeated question, and nodded grimly. *Do you know what master you serve?* He was beginning to build a picture, and he didn't like what he saw. This was what the Tyrants did. This is who they were, and he was a part of it.

With a quick glance over his shoulder to make sure he was still alone, Saxon brought up a search function and keyed in the phrase "killing floor." He wasn't sure what he had expected to see—the name drew up ideas of some kind of arena, perhaps something like the fight room in Namir's home. Why the members of Juggernaut were so eager to find it was beyond him; but instead of opening a file, the computer showed a new set of data panes. It took Saxon a few seconds to realize what he was seeing; the console launched an interface protocol via an encrypted tight-beam signal to an orbiting communications satellite, and then on into the global web of data net connections.

On the screen, the Killing Floor unfolded; a virtual space existing in a realm of pure information. Shielded by layers of smart attack barrier programs, firewalls, and baffles, the non-place was a shifting island in a sea of data. Program nodes contained files at levels of encryption so powerful that the console read them as impregnable, spiked spheres—but there were other panels of text that were clearly visible, doubtless open for Namir or anyone with the same access level. Saxon read them, but in isolation there was little he could glean. He saw references to Federova's current mission, to the "primary target" Namir had mentioned in passing—but who or where that person was did not make itself clear. He frowned, activating the vu-phone's wireless link, starting the process to copy the contact protocols from the jet's mainframe.

It was clear that the Killing Floor had no true physical reality to it; it was a synthetic server construct, a clever agglomeration of computer programs moving through the data net in a chaotic, unpredictable pattern that no outsider, no hacker, could ever hope to calculate. Without the locational key to gain access, there was no other way in—how could you break into a fortress you couldn't find? It was an encrypted virtual space, reachable in seconds from any location on earth if one was granted clearance, a place where the group could exchange target information with the Tyrants without fear of ever being overheard. It was the digital equivalent of a piece of espionage tradecraft over a hundred years old—the "dead drop."

The vu-phone chimed, signaling the conclusion of the data transfer. Saxon wasn't willing to risk using the device to contact Janus, not yet at least. After they landed in Europe, maybe then…But before that, there was still one more thing he had to do.

He entered two words into the search protocol and waited. Instantly, a file tagged with numerous security flags unfolded before him. There, laid out in stark text, in emotionless, clipped terms, was the reality of what had happened during Operation Rainbird. A dark, fearful impulse made Saxon hesitate; part of him didn't want to know. He wanted to disconnect, to erase the file and bury the memories of that night deep.

But that would be a betrayal, of Sam and Kano and the other members of Strike Six, of himself, of *the truth*.

Saxon began to read, and as he did he felt himself detach from the moment, losing all sense of where he was. In his ears, he heard the rattle of gunfire and the howling of torn metal; he felt the heat of fuel fires on his bare skin, and the sting of burning plastic and spent cordite in his nostrils. It was as if no time had passed, and he was there again on the Grey Range, fighting to stay alive.

What he read on the screen hollowed him out. He saw the reports from the Belltower recon, the intelligence profiles of enemy strength and numbers, the warnings of sleeper drones; and with them, he saw mirrors of the same data, only with all threat and nuance carefully bled out of them. Fabricated reports showing the area of operations for the Rainbird mission clear of enemy contact. Lies and more lies, dressed up like truth.

A truth Ben Saxon had accepted without question. A truth that had cost his men their lives. He heard the crunch of metal and glanced down; his augmented hand had fractured the arm of the seat he was sitting in. Sucking in a breath, he released his grip and glared back at the screen. *Where has this false data come from? How long has Namir had it in his possession?* Saxon's jaw set hard, and his thoughts turned toward darker places.

When he heard Namir's voice call his name, it didn't come as a surprise.

Dundalk—Maryland—United States of America

Passing a network of accessways leading from the rail tunnel, Anna let herself be led by D-Bar and his two minders along a maze of featureless concrete corridors, until they finally emerged in a parking garage. The hacker brought her to a van with blacked-out windows that was uncomfortably similar to the prisoner transport she'd escaped from less than a day earlier, and once inside they set off. The trip was brief; the next thing she knew, the van was halting and the doors were opened once again.

Kelso stepped out into a decrepit warehouse that was little more than a vast box made of bricks, girders, and aged glass. The smell of concrete, rust, and water reached her nose; she guessed that they were in Baltimore's old docklands. The area was a warren of derelict buildings left to rot and crumble, now that the cargo ships entering the city's port were largely automated.

And for someone who needed space and privacy, a place off the grid, it was a good locale. Glancing around she saw that the old building had been retrofitted with converted cargo containers, military surplus tents, and bubbledomes—but it was unkempt and random, here a wide satellite dish, there a cook pit near a pair of armored SUVs. The place was a peculiar mix, like an army's forward command post by way of a rock festival. The eclectic look reminded her of the same chaotic community she'd seen on board the *Intrepid* in New York.

D-Bar saw her looking around. "Don't sweat it, you're safe here." He pointed upward and Anna followed his gesture. High over their heads, vast sheets of silvery material carpeted the ceiling; her first impression was of a giant mosquito net. "Electronic camo screen," explained the hacker. "Blocks orbital scopes, smothers our EM footprint, that kinda thing. We could have the mother of all barbecues in here and this place would still look dead and empty." He beckoned her to follow him. "C'mon, you'll wanna meet the big cheese."

As they walked, Anna caught sight of a circle of screens and a group of young men and women working at computer consoles. "Is this your hideout? Are they... Juggernaut?"

D-Bar snorted loudly. "Ha! They *wish*!" He grinned. "You don't just ask to join Juggernaut, Agent Kelso. You gotta earn it. They come to you, through the 'net. Hell, most of us have never even seen each other. Well, not for real, anyhow."

One of the screens showed a replay of the footage from the Picus News report and she scowled when she saw it.

The hacker gave a solemn nod. "That's pretty good work, if I do say so myself."

"I never—"

He shook his head. "The compositing, I mean. The fakery. It's not easy to pull off something of that quality that quickly." D-Bar gave her a level look. "It's okay, Agent Kelso. No one here thinks you're a killer."

"Stop calling me that," she muttered, walking away. "I'm not an agent anymore. I don't know what I am."

"Perhaps I can change that." Anna glanced up as someone approached. The man was a few years her senior, with an easy smile and immaculate brown hair. She couldn't place his origin just from a first look; Anna guessed that by the tone of his skin and the accent he was of mixed Hispanic extraction. "We're always on the lookout for new recruits. You seem eminently qualified."

She looked him up and down. He wore a tailored Highman leather coat in rich brown that hung to his ankles, and a gold Rolex peeked out from under the cuff; the man was wearing clothes worth more than her apartment. "Don't get me wrong, but you seem a little out of place here."

The man smiled. "Rebels wear a lot of faces." He offered her his hand. "I have you at a disadvantage, Ms. Kelso. Allow me to introduce myself. My name is Juan Ivanovich Lebedev."

Lebedev. The name tripped a memory and she reached for it. "I know who you are," she replied. "Your family are some big shots in shipping. I've seen the name on the side of airships." If anything, she was making an understatement. Lebedev Global was worth billions of dollars and carried all manner of cargo across the planet via air, sea, and land.

"Sky freight is one of the company's core businesses, that's right. But I assure you, that's not my sole interest."

Anna took a step closer. She was aware of other men, clearly Lebedev's security detail, watching her for any hint of danger. "What would someone like you be doing with a group of militants and infoterrorists?"

He chuckled. "We both know that's just a convenient label for the world governments to hang around the necks of the people who disagree with them."

"Still... " She paused, looking around again. "You're running a real risk, aren't you? Being here? Talking to me?"

Lebedev's calm manner turned cooler. "This is not a game, Ms. Kelso. A long time ago, I decided that there was work to be done to preserve our freedoms, and if our nations would not do it, then men like me... Men with the money and the influence to do something about it... We could either serve, or resist. I chose the latter." He smiled without humor. "And as for risk? That van you were inside is packed with mobile screening gear. If we had found any recording devices or suspicious implants, D-Bar would have dumped you on the steps of the federal building and left you to their tender mercies."

"He told me there would be answers." She folded her arms. "So if you're the main event, why don't you start with what the hell is going on?"

Lebedev glanced at D-Bar, and then nodded. "All right. But first, I must know I have your trust, Ms. Kelso."

Anna frowned. "That's pretty thin on the ground right now."

"Indeed. That's why I'll start by confiding a secret in you." He walked to a table and poured coffee for both of them. "In your briefings from the Department of Justice, I'm sure you must have come across an organization called the New Sons of Freedom."

She nodded. "Yeah. A coalition of independent militia groups. Idaho, Utah, Arizona, a few other places. Noise-makers mostly, throwbacks to the 1990s. They're on some domestic terror watch lists, but they're not red-flagged."

"Good," Lebedev replied. "That's exactly how I want it." He smiled as she took his meaning. "The New Sons are my creation. We're one of many groups banding together across this nation with an eye to the future. Preparing. Waiting for the day when we'll be able to secede from the corrupt government running this country." He saluted her with his cup. "We're playing a long game, Ms. Kelso. We're getting ready for the fall."

She eyed him. "Are you serious? You're telling me Lebedev Global is backing the New Sons?"

"Yeah, it's a trip, isn't it?" offered D-Bar. Lebedev shot him a look and he fell silent again.

He pointed at the hacker. "My people have mutually

beneficial relationships with a number of other, shall we say, *extra-legal* groups? And Juggernaut is one of them. We've worked together very closely in the past. That's one of the reasons we've stayed off the radar of the FBI, the ATF, and all the other agencies."

"You're building an army, is that it?"

He shrugged. "It might be that one day. But not today. No, right now we're too small to be a serious threat to those with the real power. So we have to play the game carefully."

"Why are you telling me all this?" she demanded.

"Because all of us, you included, have a common enemy. The Tyrants and the shadow cabal they call master."

Despite herself, Anna tensed. "What do you know about the Tyrants?"

"Bits and pieces," Lebedev went on, glancing at his watch. "We know they're the attack dogs in this particular arena. We know that you are right about them, Ms. Kelso. Your colleague, Agent Ryan. Garret Dansky. Donald Teague. They were all killed by Tyrant operatives."

She felt her cheeks flush red. "So the hit on Skyler was—"

"Cover," said Lebedev. "Two birds with one stone. Dansky was murdered, and Skyler intimidated. Have you seen the senator's most recent public statements? It's quite a reversal from her previous position."

"I've been a little busy," Anna snapped. "You have proof of all this?"

"Of course not. They're very good at what they do, Ms. Kelso. They'd never leave us a smoking gun. And the fact is, the Tyrants have been taking lives and enforcing the will of their masters all over the world, not just here in the United States. Everything they have done has been according to a plan."

"What plan?" Lebedev sat and Anna did the same, staring at him across the table. "I want to know the reason why Matt Ryan died!" He hand was in her pocket, her fingers touching the coin.

Lebedev pulled out a wallet; he drew a paper banknote—a rarity these days—and smoothed it out before him. "The one-dollar bill," he announced, turning it over. "You see this?" He indicated the symbol of the great seal. "The design of the pyramid, here? And the eye in the capstone, looking out? Some people call it the 'Eye of Providence.' But it's more than that." He tapped the banknote. "It's a representation of something that has infiltrated our lives, something lurking in the shadows. Something that has been around for a very long time."

Anna's lips thinned. "Yeah, I've heard that conspiracy theory. Freemasons and flying saucers and Knights Templar, all that kinda stuff. You honestly expect me to believe the Tyrants are part of that?"

"They call themselves the Illuminati." Lebedev became grave, and his manner gave Kelso a moment's pause. "The Tyrants are just their blunt instrument, one of many of their tools. The Illuminati are pulling their strings. A group of powerful men and women who believe that they alone have the will and the right to govern the future of our world."

She shook her head. "What you're talking about doesn't exist. It's the creation of a paranoid mind."

"Is it?" Lebedev paused. "Tell me, wasn't the very

same charge leveled at *you* very recently?" He leaned closer. "If nothing else, I would think that the events of the last twenty-four hours would have taught you that the line between fact and fiction is not as well defined as you thought."

She was quiet for a long moment. "All right. Say I buy that. But what the hell does a group of rich people carving up the world have to do with Matt's death, him and all the others? Not just Dansky, but the other ones I found."

"And there's more where that came from," offered D-Bar, hovering nearby. "A lot more."

Lebedev pointed at her face. "You're augmented. Those lovely eyes of yours. Because of that, you represent something to the Illuminati. You, and everyone else who has chosen to augment themselves. You're a *threat*." He gestured at the air. "New eyes, new arms. Faster reflexes, quicker thinking. But where does that end? When humans have the capacity to change the course of their own evolution, where does that lead?"

Anna struggled with the thought. "It... it gives people control."

He nodded slowly. "Control of their destiny. And a human race with that capacity is one beyond the influence of the Illuminati. That makes for an unstable world, and they can't have that." Lebedev's tone turned cold. "We mustn't be allowed to take charge."

D-Bar came closer. "The United Nations are coming under pressure. They're being pushed toward a referendum on worldwide regulation of aug technology. That's what this is all about. Senator Skyler, all the rest? That's the Tyrants moving the pieces on the game board for their bosses. Setting up the dominoes. Your pal Ryan was just caught in the cross fire."

It made a horrible, chilling kind of sense. The Tyrants were working on lines of influence, removing people who might act as impediments to a greater plan, or intimidating those they needed to use. The coin cut the palm of Anna's hand as she gripped it hard.

"Human history turns on the smallest of moments, Ms. Kelso, and one of those moments is almost here," said Lebedev. "If the UN go to a ballot... " He frowned. "Whoever controls the direction of that vote will be able to manipulate the future of mankind." After a moment, he put down his cup and beckoned Anna to her feet. "I know it's a lot to take in. Come with me, I want you to meet someone. They might be able to make things clearer for you."

D-Bar had already taken the flash drive Anna got from Temple's house, and he gestured with it as he walked away. "I'm gonna get started on analyzing this. See what we got. Tell Janus I said hi, yeah?"

"Who is 'Janus'?" asked Anna.

"I'll introduce you," said Lebedev.

Aerial Transit Corridor—Northeastern Sector—United States of America

"You're a very good soldier, Ben," said Namir, from the ops room doorway. "But there's something you lack."

Saxon saw the other man in the computer screen, a warped reflection of those hard eyes and that scarred face. "Enlighten me."

"You can't see where the line is. You don't know how to compartmentalize yourself. You're not willing to make that sacrifice." Namir took a casual step into the ops room. "That's what we have to do. Put up walls around the parts of our souls we want to keep sacrosanct. Barriers to protect our humanity."

Saxon tensed. "Is that what you do?" He thought of the man in the photo at the house, the father and husband. "You're one man in here, with us. Out there, you're someone else?" He rose slowly, his fury building. "That's not something to be proud of. That's a pattern of psychosis!"

Namir shook his head slowly. "You're very good at what you do, Ben. But inside, you're weak. You can't let go. I thought that might change after what happened in Queensland. I had hopes."

"Were you a part of that?" Saxon pointed at the screen and his voice rose. "Is this about those bastards holding your bloody leash?"

Namir's tone never altered. "I want you to think very carefully about what you say next. Because this is the most important choice you will ever make. What happened in Moscow, then in the house in London... Those things were not the tests of your character, or your loyalty." He gestured to the monitor. "This is the test, Ben. This is what will define who you are, and your future with the Tyrants. Do you understand? I need to know if you can be like me. Like the rest of us."

Saxon's gorge rose; he was sickened by the other man's words, revolted by the thought of what black and poisonous truth lay behind them. "Like you?" he husked.

"You don't hide your humanity away, Namir. You only tell yourself that you do. The truth is, you're not human anymore. You've lost that, you and Hardesty, Federova, and the others. You're a weapon that thinks like a man."

The other man gave a weary sigh. "That's a shame. I really wanted you to understand. I hate to see great potential wasted."

"Tell me what you did... " Saxon spat, his voice rising to a shout. *"Tell me!"*

Namir's gaze never wavered as his metallic hand curled into a fist. "Do you know what real strength is, Ben? *Sacrifice.*"

TEN

It was as if the blood had been drained from him; Saxon was suddenly an empty vessel, echoing and cold. In all the years of battle in conflict zones across the globe, in those moments when death had been a heartbeat away from claiming him, he had never felt the same slow, sickening shock that swept about him now. Carefully, he gathered up the vu-phone and pocketed it, moving slowly to keep one of the ops room consoles between him and Namir.

"I'll give you the truth, if you want it," said the Tyrant commander. "There's little point in being coy about it now."

"Operation Rainbird." Saxon ground out the words like pieces of broken glass. "What did you do?"

Namir sighed. "I wish I could make it clear to you how lucky you are, Ben. Recruitment into the Tyrants is not a reward that just anyone is given. You need to be superlative. You need to be more than just a fool with a gun." He walked a little farther into the room, and Saxon stiffened as he felt the floor shift slightly beneath their feet; the jet was banking, turning eastward. Namir went on. "You were on the radar a long time before I came to you in Queensland. We have ongoing dossiers on many potentials. Our missions have a high level of attrition. Fatalities like Joe Wexler are a regular occurrence."

"Get to the point!" snapped Saxon.

"Oh, I will. But you have to see the big picture first." Namir nodded to himself and pointed. "You were in the prime percentile, Ben. All that was stopping you were your... shortcomings. We freed you from that."

"What?" He could feel the dark answer coming; on some level, he already knew and he didn't want to hear it. He didn't want it to be true.

"Wexler... It took his wife's death to bring him into the fold. Now, Gunther Hermann, he was a very different subject. Much more direct. The group made certain problems he had in Germany go away, and in return he was in our debt. Not that what he owed mattered. He came to the Tyrants willingly, eyes open. But you?" Namir cocked his head, weighing Saxon up. "The man I wanted for my team, the man I know you can be, he was being held back." He nodded again. "Throughout your entire military service, first to King and Country, then to Belltower, you've been shackled to some kind of outdated moral compass. You have a dream of being the 'good soldier.' And while other men have had that beaten from them by harsh reality, you hold on to it, Ben. Against all odds, you hold on. That's why you never rose in rank. We've both been leaders of men. And that means sometimes you have to send men to die, and do it without flinching."

"I'd never make my men take a risk I wouldn't take myself!" he shot back.

"Indeed," Namir allowed. "That's your failure. You've

been abandoned by every family you had. Your parents, your nation, your army, your employer... And yet still you refuse to see the callous truth. You're blinded by your own hope." He smiled. "I took that from you. I broke those bonds because I thought it would make you stronger."

"The falsified data for the mission...You had it substituted for the real thing!" Saxon's muscles tensed. He wanted to strike out, but he had to know the full dimensions of the betrayal. "How?"

"We have assets inside the Belltower corporation. It wasn't difficult." He sighed. "Those men, they were a hindrance to you. They had to be sacrificed. It was a test. If you perished there in the desert alongside them, then you had no place with us. But if you came out alone..."

"I tried to save them!" Saxon shouted. "Duarte...I could have saved his life!"

"He was expendable," Namir countered. "They all were. I gave Hardesty the order to break Rainbird because I needed to know. I wanted to see if you were willing to live, Ben. If you had the courage to *survive*."

Saxon's voice was low and hard. "You heartless fucking bastard..." His hand slipped toward the pocket where the Buzzkill was concealed; but the weapon would be barely an insect bite to the Tyrant commander, with dermal armor sheathing what there was of his flesh.

"Survivor's guilt. That, and your instinct to be loyal to a man who saved your life." Namir studied him. "The psych profile said that was all I needed to control you. But these things are so hard to determine. The human mind is a chaotic system. And as much as men are exactly the animals you expect them to be, sometimes they are not."

He frowned. "I don't need to ask you to choose. I can see the answer in your eyes. You can't let go. Hardesty was right. You don't have the strength to kill cold. "

"I'm pleased I can prove you wrong." With a blink, Saxon shifted vision modes, getting ready.

Namir drew a wicked-looking combat blade from a sheath on his belt. "You are going to fight for it, aren't you?" he asked. "At least show me that courage. Let me know my faith in you wasn't entirely misplaced." Saxon drew the stun gun and thumbed off the safety catch. The other man laughed. "Oh, that's a choice you'll regret," he sneered.

Saxon met his gaze. "I'm not going to use it on you." The reflex booster kicked in and he brought up the nonlethal weapon, firing two rounds into the flat, glassy surface of the main display console. The stun darts, thick shells the size of a shotgun cartridge, discharged a powerful surge of voltage on impact; the console erupted in a violent shower of sparks and acrid smoke. Surge buffers in the ops room tripped, plunging it into darkness, but Saxon was already seeing the space in low-light mode.

Namir reacted, sweeping in with a lunging, lethal attack that Saxon dodged by a hair, the blade cutting the air near his face.

The stink of burnt plastic reached the fire sensors in the ceiling and immediately triggered a carillon of buzzing alarms. Saxon snatched at a monitor screen and tore it from a desk, with a snake nest of cables trailing behind it. As puffs of fire-retardant powder began to rain from safety nozzles overhead, he slammed the display into Namir's head with such force that the screen shattered and the Tyrant commander staggered back under the blow.

Saxon took the moment and vaulted over a workstation and into the corridor beyond. As he ran, the familiar itch in his jawbone arose, Namir's voice issuing out of his mastoid comm. *"All call signs, ignore the alarms,"* he snarled, *"Gray is rogue. Intercept and terminate!"*

Dundalk—Maryland—United States of America

"Hello," said the voice, bereft of anything that could make it possibly seem human. *"I'm pleased to see you are unharmed."*

Anna glanced at the videoscreen set up inside the army tent, and then back at Lebedev, who stood near the door flap, watching her reaction. "What's this? More games?"

"Some of the people we work with prefer to keep their identities a secret," he noted. "Isn't that right, Janus?"

"I'm afraid so, Juan," said the voice. *"It would compromise not only me, and Juggernaut, but also your lives if I were to tell you who I am."*

Anna folded her arms and gave the hazy shape on the display a level stare. "After all that stuff about conspiracies and distrust, you're playing the need-to-know card?" She shook her head. "If I know anything, it's that the less truth you have, the less trust follows. You could be anyone. You could be working with the Tyrants or the... their masters."

"You find it hard to say the name, don't you?" On the screen, the digital shadow shifted slightly. *"Illuminati. A layered word, heavy with meaning and counter-meaning. You don't want to believe. It's an understandable reaction."*

"Our colleague here has been opposing them for a long time," said Lebedev.

"How did you get mixed up in all this?" Anna demanded. "What's your angle? Are you in it for the kicks, like D-Bar, or for the greater good like him?" She inclined her head toward Lebedev.

"*Neither,*" came the reply, and for a moment Anna thought she sensed something like melancholy under the words. "*I found Juggernaut and became one of their circle. I'm doing this for the same reason as you, Anna. Because they killed someone who was important to me.*"

It didn't sound like a lie; but then with all the layers of digital masking in place, she wondered if she could ever read anything about the ghost-hacker.

"*Trust is a rare commodity these days. But you can only accumulate it by spending it. An ironic fact, in present circumstances.*" There was a pause. "*You have questions. I'll answer them if I can.*"

Anna frowned. "This... vote. The United Nations. You're telling me that all the assassinations have been to set that up to fall one way?"

"*Yes.*" The screen blinked and became a map of the world. As Janus spoke, dots of red appeared across the span of nations, each briefly displaying a data window with death certificates, accident reports, security camera footage, and other information sources. "*What you're seeing are the targets of the Tyrants. Hundreds of people, all of whom have lines of influence that can be drawn back to the proposed regulation vote, and how it will play out.*"

Over the map, a matrix of connections formed, a web bringing each person together, showing the human effect of the targeted individuals. Anna was suddenly reminded of a stone dropped in a lake, the ripples radiating outward;

only here, the ripples were being guided, controlled—and in many cases, erased.

One thread through the complex knot of effect was highlighted. *"Consider this,"* said Janus, displaying an image of a smiling middle-aged man and his family. *"A midlevel minister in the Italian government, with many friends in the Euro-Parliament. His son was cured of debilitating brain damage because of a neural implant. He is well disposed toward the spread of human augmentation technology. The recommendations he makes carry weight. A committee of United Nations representatives are currently entertaining a suggestion from certain groups to call for a vote on the regulation of H.E. development..."*

Lebedev nodded slowly. "But before the minister can be consulted on behalf of his country, his wife is suddenly diagnosed with a variant neo-SARS strain. His family comes first. He's unable to fulfill his duties. Instead, the man who replaces him on Italy's technology advisory board is a known associate of William Taggart, the pro-humanist...and now that country is supporting the push for the ballot." He spread his hands. "That's just one story. You saw another, more violent approach firsthand, with Skyler and Dansky."

Anna's eyes narrowed. "What happened to the minister's wife?"

"She died from complications. The minister has been suspended on medical grounds and is currently undergoing treatment for depression." The map returned. *"This is how they work, Anna. Hundreds and hundreds of tiny actions, individually small, collectively gigantic, all working in concert. Every person they have exerted control over has*

been a part of a plan to dominate a vote that has yet to happen. And even this is only one element of an even greater schema."

"The Illuminati are working in tandem with one of their satellite groups, a faction called Majestic 12 born out of the Cold War era, a technology division of sorts... Together, they're in the process of securing a power base for something beyond the scope of the UN vote. Something much bigger."

Anna was reeling from the import of what she was hearing, caught between incredulity and acceptance. "Bigger than regulating the most radical science ever created?"

"We can see only the edges of the conspiracy," Janus told her. *"But what we can be sure of is that the Illuminati's goal is and always has been command over the future of humanity. A New World Order, without freedoms, without questions. Without end."*

She turned away, shaking her head. "No...No! It's too much! I've come here looking for a murderer and you're telling me that the world is turning on all this?" Anna looked toward Lebedev. "Listen to me. I don't care about your damned conspiracy theories! I don't care about who else they've killed! I've thrown away everything I have because I want just one, single thing—*justice*, for Matt Ryan." Her voice caught. "He saved my life. I couldn't save him. So I am going to find the person who killed him and make them pay. If you won't help me do that, then I'll be better off alone." Furious, she stormed out of the tent and strode away over the uneven concrete floor.

Aerial Transit Corridor—Gulf of St. Lawrence—North Atlantic

Saxon tried to think of a worse tactical situation he had been in, and came up empty. Trapped on board an airborne jet with four heavily augmented mercenaries and no means of escape, armed only with a couple of rounds of stun-dart ammo that was nearly useless against these adversaries... *Yeah, it's pretty grim,* he told himself. About the only positive point he could find was that without Federova among them, at least he would see the other Tyrants coming. He wondered how much good that would do him.

Despite Namir's commands, the fire alarms were still in full effect, but retardants had only been triggered inside the ops room. Saxon moved quickly through the galley area, panning the Buzzkill this way and that, going forward.

His mind raced through the tactical options open to him. He had to make a choice; he needed a better weapon, something lethal, and he needed it fast. He could set up a quick-and-dirty ambush, try to kill one of the others when they came for him, and take their gun—but that would cost him time. The second option would be to get into the cockpit, lock himself in there, and force the crew to land the jet on the nearest piece of ground, maybe Newfoundland or Nova Scotia. Without at least one pilot, he'd have to handle the aircraft alone, and Saxon wasn't willing to trust himself on that score. With his rudimentary understanding of piloting, the best he could do in that case was ditch in the coastal shallows and hope he survived.

Every second he spent deliberating, they were getting farther and farther away from land. He nodded to himself. *Take the plane, then,* he thought. *Figure the rest out later.*

He could hear noises behind him. Namir hadn't come back on the mastoid comm after his first announcement, and Saxon imagined he'd be passing a new channel assignment to each of the others by hand. Another reason to move fast; once they were ready, they'd box him in and that would be that.

He thought about weapons again; at least it cut both ways. None of the standard-issue firearms used by the Tyrants could be discharged inside the jet, not without taking the risk of overpenetration. A 10 mm round could pass right through flesh and punch a hole in the fuselage, causing a catastrophic depressurization.

Saxon grimaced. Back down the length of the aircraft there was a weapons locker stocked with all he needed—*a crossbow, maybe? A pulse gun?* But he was thinking like Namir, and Namir would have posted someone there already. He'd have to make do.

Saxon checked his pockets for anything he could use, and his fingers touched the vu-phone. He drew it out and considered it for a second before hitting the redial key. There was a good chance he wasn't going to get out of this alive; if he could make his last few minutes count, maybe contact the hacker—

Movement from the corner of his eye spun him around, and he forgot the phone, coming up with the Buzzkill. He saw a flash of spiked blond hair and a figure in black combat gear burst from the shadow of a storage cabinet. Gunther Hermann collided with Saxon with such force that they were both propelled across the galley and through a folding partition into the next anteroom.

"This time it will be different," Hermann snarled. "I think I will enjoy this." He struck out with a storm of blows that made Saxon's skull ring, lighting flares of pain behind his eyes. Blood hazed his vision and he threw a punch that cut empty air but little else. Hermann came in and hit him again; each shot to the head was like taking a hit from a sledgehammer. Saxon's body possessed a base level of subdermal armor, the Rhino-class augmentation commonplace on Belltower spec-ops soldiers, but it wouldn't be enough to prevent the German's rain of punches pushing him into a concussion. He had to stop the mercenary, and he had to do it quickly.

Hermann had learned his lesson from their brief battle in the fight room, moving constantly, using his nerve-jacked speed to stay outside the swings from Saxon's cyberarm. He punched at air, drawing a sneer from the German.

He feinted into another haymaker that the younger man easily sidestepped; but while Saxon's other arm was only meat and bone, it was still deadly. His attention fixed on his opponent's augmentations, Hermann stepped into Saxon's range and he rushed him. He slammed the heel of his palm upward, breaking the other man's nose, and rode the momentum of the attack. Saxon's augmented legs powered him back across the cabin, with Hermann shoved out before him.

The mercenary slammed into a glass-fronted refrigerator and crumpled with a cry of pain. Saxon punched him hard in the chest, feeling the satisfying crunch of bone breaking beneath the blow. But Hermann would not submit, and he scrambled to extract himself from the debris, cursing in his native language.

Saxon drew the Buzzkill and fired a single, close-range shot. The electro-dart punctured Hermann's right eye, the discharge wreathing his head in a brief flash of lighting. Howling, he fell to the deck, wisps of smoke rising from burnt skin and hair.

"Stay down," Saxon warned, and left him there, heading forward.

Hardesty was waiting in the corridor leading to the cockpit. He announced himself with the crash from a Widowmaker. Saxon dove for cover, bracing himself for the inevitable tornado of depressurization; but instead he caught the edges of a spatter of gooey matter that chugged into the air. Specks of it touched his bare skin and burned; the sniper was firing crowd-buster rounds, saboted cartridges that burst in the air and coated targets with a sticky mess of contact irritants. Saxon resisted the urge to tear at his inflamed skin and swore; the fluid wasn't lethal, but it hurt like hell.

And right on cue, Hardesty called out to him. "They say this crap can kill a man, if he takes a shot to the face. Makes your throat swell up, chokes the air from you." He snorted. "Always wanted to see if that was true. Let me try it out."

Saxon checked the stun gun. One round remaining. At this range, he'd do as much damage with harsh language. Gingerly, he peered out from cover. Hardesty was blocking the entrance to the cockpit, and behind him a door of reinforced steel and plastic closed off the path to the flight deck. If Hardesty had made it up here ahead of him, then Saxon knew his entry code to get that door open was now null and void. Any hope of taking the plane was lost. Now he had to worry about staying alive; somewhere behind or below him, Namir and Barrett were still in the game.

Across the corridor there was a stairwell leading to the other deck, but to reach it he would pass right in front of Hardesty, and give him ample time to unload the rest of the auto-shotgun loads into him.

Think fast. He ducked back just as Hardesty poked the Widowmaker's muzzle out and let off a triple-shot salvo. Saxon tasted vaporized capsicum in the air and winced at the acid tang in his throat. Above him, a portable fire extinguisher the size of a wine bottle sat in a recessed alcove. He snatched it from the clip securing it in place and held it like a club, bringing it down on the arm of a chair at the point where the discharge nozzle joined the foam canister. It bent on the first hit, and he repeated the action.

"What the hell are you doing?" Hardesty called. "Trying to dig your way out?"

On the second strike the joint dented and a hiss of escaping gasses puffed white spray into the air. The third hit dislodged the nozzle and suddenly the canister was a fountain of cold, smothering vapor. Saxon hurled it down the corridor and heard Hardesty cry out in surprise as the makeshift gas bomb filled the enclosed space with choking mist.

Saxon vaulted toward the stairwell under cover of the distraction, even as Hardesty fired blindly, fluid-filled shells splattering all around him. He mistimed the jump and stumbled on the metal staircase, almost tumbling headlong. Recovering, he broke into a run back down the length of the jet, kicking open the door to the main cargo bay; beyond it was the rearmost compartment and the stowed helo. There were weapons on board the flyer. If he could reach them—

Something caught his ankle; for a second he thought the aircraft was banking, but then he was spinning around and the deck came up to slam him in the face. Saxon scrambled to get up.

"Watch your step." Barrett emerged from behind a cargo pod, pausing to bring down a heavy boot on the stun gun, lying where it had fallen from Saxon's pocket. He crushed the plastic-ceramic weapon with a grunt and eyed him. "Namir?" he said to the air. "I got him. Cargo deck, toward the tail section." Saxon never heard the reply, but the grin that blossomed on Barrett's scarred face made it clear what was said. "Got it. Be a pleasure."

The big man came forward, and like a complex mechanical toy, his right arm unfolded to allow a tri-barreled minigun to emerge.

"Go ahead, arsehole," Saxon taunted. "One shot from that cannon and you'll rip the hull open."

Barrett gave a thoughtful nod. "Good point, Benny-boy. In all the excitement, I kinda forgot myself there." He laid his Missouri accent on thick, drawing out the moment as the weapon retracted; it was something Saxon had learned early on about the mercenary. Barrett liked to play up his brutish image, but he was more than just a thug. He liked people to underestimate him. "Guess I'll just rip you limb from limb, then," he added, striding forward. "Shame. I kinda liked you... "

Saxon backed off, eyes darting around for a weapon. Barrett had come ready for anything, wearing the heavy antiblast vest that was his signature operations kit. Nothing short of an armor-piercing round would cut through it.

Barrett made a mock-sad face. "Aw, what's wrong? You don't wanna dance?" He stalked forward, grabbing a metal spacer rod from atop one of the cargo racks. The big man made a couple of lazy practice swings. "We'll try somethin' else, then. Batter up!"

Saxon dodged as Barrett attacked, sweeping the rod though the air; he was running out of room, his opponent backing him into the curved wall of the fuselage. "Namir's lying to you!" he shouted. "He killed my last crew just to get me here! You can't trust him!"

"Gee, you're right. Maybe we should team up, kick his ass. How about that?" Barrett snorted, nostrils flaring around the bull-ring through his nose. His expression became cold and hard. "You don't get it. We're on the winning side here. Anyone else... You're just little people." He snarled and attacked again, this time bringing down the steel rod in a falling overhead blow.

Saxon threw up his augmented arm and blocked the strike, the impact singing through the metal right down to the meat interface at his shoulder joint, fragments of carbon-plastic cracking under the force of the blow. He followed through with a hard punch to the chest, but the strike might have been a love tap for all the effect it had. Barrett hit him with the near end of the rod and Saxon staggered; first the fight with Hermann and now this. The pain was dragging on him. He couldn't keep this up for too long; even his iron stamina had its limits.

Barrett discarded his makeshift weapon and grabbed Saxon with both hands, snatching at fistfuls of his jacket. He picked up the other man and roared with effort as he slammed him to one side, into a cargo rack and then back again. Barrett had maybe Saxon's body mass and half as much again, and most of it was cybernetics. The man was a tank.

Dizzy, his vision blurring, it was all Saxon could do to keep conscious. Barrett's arms drew tight and dragged him into a bear hug. The breath left his lungs in a wheeze and he tasted blood in his mouth. He was going to black out; it was only a matter of seconds.

"My daddy was a mean son-of-a-bitch, but he was right about one thing," Barrett laughed. "He used to tell me, *Mess with the bull, son, and you get the horns*—"

Saxon channeled the last of his effort into resisting the crushing embrace. "Shut the fuck up!" He snapped, jerking his head forward and down, butting the other man on the bridge of the nose. Barrett cried out in pain and for a fraction of a moment, his grip loosened.

That was all Saxon needed. He got his hands free and snatched at the twin bandoliers over Barrett's shoulders. His fingers found the pull-rings on the yellow-and-black Shok-Tac concussion grenades hanging there, and he yanked hard.

"You stupid... " Barrett immediately released him and staggered backward, clawing at the live grenades. Saxon let himself fall and rolled toward one of the cargo racks.

A massive, earsplitting blast of light and noise tore through the confined space, deadening Saxon's hearing into a painful, humming whine. Barrett was on his back, blown into a collapsed pile of storage panniers, coughing up blood. Trails of red oozed from his ears, nostrils, and the corners of his eyes.

Saxon forced himself to stagger away, breathing hard, lurching toward the tail section. It was hard to focus. He had to reach the helo. The weapons locker. And then... *And then what?* His plan was sand, crumbling, falling though his fingers. There was nowhere he could go.

A shadow shifted in front of him, caught by the light cast from the glow strips on the low ceiling. Saxon half turned; the endless shriek in his ears stopped him hearing the approach of a new attack.

Half-blind and enraged, Barrett came at him, grabbing Saxon from behind and locking his hands behind his head. He applied agonizing force, pressing into the bones of Saxon's neck. The American shouted, and Saxon heard the words more than he felt them. "You think that'll stop me? You think *you* can stop me?"

Saxon hit back with elbow strikes, but the viselike pressure was unceasing. He cast around, knowing that death was close. *Not here. Not like this. Not yet.*

Fitted into the curve of the wall was a cargo hatch, used for loading when the jet was on the ground. It was just within his reach. Ignoring his better instincts, Saxon kicked out and broke open the control cover with the heel of his combat boot. Barrett saw what he was doing and pressed tighter, but Saxon was committed now. This was how it would end.

He kicked again and struck the hatch release panel. Immediately, red strobes and a warning Klaxon activated as the door's mechanism stirred into life; but in the next second all sound was lost as a screaming thunder of air tore across the cargo bay. The hatch began a slow march open, revealing a growing sliver of fathomless black sky beyond.

The jet shivered and the nose dropped abruptly; up in the cockpit, the aircraft's autoflight system would have detected the loss of cabin pressure and immediately attempted to compensate by descending to a lower altitude. Barrett lost his grip and flailed, colliding with a support pillar. Saxon fell against a stowed cargo net and grabbed on to it, the polar cold through the hatch ripping at the skin of his face. Across the threshold, a dash of moonlight glittered off the surface of the Atlantic Ocean.

How high are we? How far from land? It was impossible to know.

"*Ben.*" Namir's voice hummed through his skull. "*You can't escape. I'm not going to let that happen.*" As he said the words, the hatch juddered to a halt, half open, and then reversed, sliding toward closure.

If he stayed here, he would die. Saxon knew it with utter certainty, the same pure clarity of thinking that had come to him in the Australian wilderness. He would die, this would end, and there would be no justice for Sam and Kano and the others.

Saxon threw himself at the gap and leapt into the darkness.

Dundalk—Maryland—United States of America

When Lebedev returned to the communications tent, the videoscreen was still active, the same display of smoky digital mist hazing a vaguely human shape. Not for the first time, he wondered what Janus really looked like—if he or she was someone he knew out in the real world. Part of him was always disappointed that the shady hacker could not trust the New Sons enough to drop the mask; but then, these were difficult times, and not everyone had millions of dollars at hand to ensure their own security.

"How is our new recruit?" asked the nonvoice.

Lebedev sighed. "We shouldn't have pushed her so hard, so fast. She's having trouble assimilating it all."

"Anna will come around," said Janus. *"She's resilient. She just needs to see it for herself. Let her process."*

"We need her." He ran a hand through his hair. "God knows, we need every ally we can get."

A moment passed before Janus replied. *"Her skills will be of great use to the cause, Juan..."*

He frowned. The hacker sounded distracted. "Is something wrong?"

There was another pause. *"Forgive me. I'm monitoring another...situation at the moment. Go on."*

"We're running out of time," Lebedev went on. "If we're going to disrupt this thing, it needs to be soon."

"Agreed. I'm working on another approach to access the Killing Floor as we speak. But it's risky."

Lebedev smiled ruefully. "We have to try, my friend. And we can't fail. If we do, the future will never forgive us."

"You're wrong," Janus replied. *"If we fail, our enemies will make sure no one will ever know we existed."*

* * *

Thirteen Kilometers East of Newfoundland—North Atlantic

He never felt the impact when he hit the rolling surface of the sea. It was the only mercy he had; perhaps it was the shock of the fall, perhaps his battered body shutting down for a brief moment in some attempt to protect him from greater trauma.

At first, Saxon saw only flashes. The silver of the moon on the wave tops below him. A flicker of light from the jet as he spiraled away from it, the navigation lights in the dark.

Then he was in the cradle of the shouting winds, snared by gravity. He couldn't see the ocean rushing up to meet him, and for long moments Saxon felt himself disconnect from the real. He could have been floating in the roaring darkness, lost in the starless space.

The cold embrace leached the heat from his bones; Saxon squinted through the windburn and made out what he thought was the surface of the water, coming up fast, dappled by the moon's glow.

He extended his arms like they had taught him in parachute training, making his whole body an aerofoil, trying to slow himself as much as he could. And then, when he couldn't chance it any longer, he triggered the high-fall augmentation implanted in the base of his spine.

The device stuttered into life and cast a writhing sphere of electromagnetic energy about him, lightninglike sparks flashing where the field interacted with the air molecules. The implant ran past its tolerance limit, but Saxon retriggered it, cycling the device over and over. He felt it go hot, smoldering and heavy like a block of newly forged iron embedded in his back. The high-fall was never designed to do the job of a parachute; it was a short-span, low-duration technology, a mechanism spun off from safety implants for racing drivers, firefighters, steeplejacks.

He screamed as it burned into him, and the blackness engulfed everything. For a moment, at least.

Then he was in the frigid rise and fall of the waters, the salt brine smothering him with every new wave. He spun and turned, numb from the waist down. Warning telltales displayed in the corners of his optic field, function indicators for his cyberlegs showing red. He choked and shivered, feeling the weight of the augmented limbs pulling on him, robbing him of all buoyancy.

The ocean toyed with him, and then grew bored. Saxon began to sink, and he couldn't find the strength to fight the icy embrace of the waters. All his defiance, his determination... it was bleeding away, second by second.

Then he saw the lights below, rising. The waters parting as something as large as a truck broke the surface. He saw a shiny, beetlelike carapace, an arch of what might be shell. Just beneath the water, ropes of steel moved past his damaged legs, ensnaring him.

Saxon's mind filled in the gaps; he imagined a massive nautilus coming up from the seabed to gather him into its tentacles, the giant monstrous thing festooned with glaring, sodium-bright lamps.

He blacked out for the second time as it pulled him toward it.

ELEVEN

Dundalk—Maryland—United States of America

Through the dirty glass of the window, Kelso watched the lights of Baltimore turn dim as the sky grew lighter, losing herself in the passage of the clouds overhead and the never-ending wash of the water against the concrete pilings out on the old, abandoned docks.

Sleep, when she'd been able to snatch a little of it, was a fitful and troubled thing. Anna couldn't settle. She dreamed about skies full of squawking ravens, and vast black wings that wheeled and turned in the sky, blotting out the watery glow of a sullen sun. In the end, Anna stayed awake, keeping to the margins of Lebedev's compound while the men from the New Sons worked at tasks she could only guess at, and D-Bar's hackers pored over the sealed files in the stolen flash drive. The inside of the warehouse looked exactly like what it was—a staging area for an antigovernmental terror group—and it ground against all Kelso's training as a federal agent to stand among it and do nothing.

So she went to the windows and watched the march of the morning approaching. Looking out at the distant city, Anna wondered who was out there, looking for her. Drake would be leading the capture team, she imagined.

He would have considered it a personal slight that her escape had happened on his watch. Sorrow crossed her face. *What are they saying about me?* She didn't want to know the answer, didn't want to imagine the looks in the eyes of the men and women who had served with her. All of them would believe the lie about the death of Ron Temple and the murders at his home. They would hate her.

She wanted so much to run, to give in to the base impulse that tensed in the muscles of her hands. But out there, she would be prey. If Lebedev's stories were true, she had nowhere to go. Even if they were not, the fact did not change. Anna Kelso was alone, and she had been forced into a single choice she did not want to make.

Trust or distrust.

But that was the corrosive nature of any conspiracy; it played on the fears inherent in all human beings, the terror of having your secrets known by the unknown, the vicarious thrill of keeping a sinister secret yourself. These people, this group Lebedev called *the Illuminati...* What they were doing lived in darkness, and the part of Anna that was still an officer of the law wanted to see them dragged screaming into the light.

She found herself back at the army tent, and ducked beneath the door flap. The place was empty, but the comms gear and the big screen were as live as they had been hours earlier. The snow of static on the monitor shifted slightly as she came closer, as if her presence were a breeze disturbing a scattering of leaves.

"I know you can hear me," she said. "I want to ask you something."

After a few seconds, the static settled into the familiar

pattern of dispersion she'd seen before, the phantom no-face. *"I will help you if I can, Anna,"* said Janus. *"But please understand that I don't have all the answers."*

"These people...the Illuminati. The Tyrants. Back in D.C. there was something that D-Bar said to me, a phrase that I couldn't get out of my head." She sighed. "He talked about something called 'the Icarus Effect.'"

"Ah, yes. A sociological construct, originally conceived in 2019 by Doctor Malcolm Bonner of the University of Texas. It's a very interesting theory, a societal echo of something that occurs in nature. Imagine a pack of animals, among which is a single individual exhibiting signs of nascent evolutionary superiority. Not common superiority, that is, but a marked difference from the norm. A rare excessive." The ghost-face shimmered. *"The individual's renegade nature threatens the stability of the pack. The others close ranks against it. Expunge or terminate it. Stability returns, and the pace of evolution is slowed to a more manageable scale."*

"We're not talking about animals here," Anna insisted. "This is about people."

"Indeed. But the principle is the same. Like brave but foolhardy Icarus, those who dare to go beyond the boundaries will fall to their deaths."

"But who gets to choose where those boundaries are?" she asked. "This group Lebedev talked about. I thought the Illuminati were just a historical curiosity, some kind of pre-millennium modern myth. But you expect me to believe that they're still around, and they've set themselves up as the...the stewards of humanity?"

"I couldn't have put it better myself," Janus allowed.

"They have been here for a very long time, Anna. They believe that gives them the right to run the world, and so they do not wait for the Icarus Effect to play itself out. They induce it wherever and whenever they deem it suitable. The Tyrants are one of the tools they use."

A chill passed over her. "How...how many times have they done this?"

"You mean, is this the first time they have manipulated global events to their own design? Oh, no. As I said before, the Illuminati have actively taken control of human history in this manner on many occasions. They have a long, long reach. World wars, disasters, famine, assassinations, cover-ups...ll have been set in motion to deliberately retard the advancement of society when it threatened to go too far beyond the borders they created. We can't be allowed to fly too close to the sun, do you see?" Anna thought she detected bitterness in the artificially distorted voice. "Imagine a vast steel hand enveloping the world. We must wear the invisible chains they have fashioned for us, because they believe only they have the right to judge when humanity can step from the cradle."

The screen flickered and began to display a mosaic of images, video, and still photographs from the last hundred years. She saw soldiers on the battlegrounds of the Great War, Vietnam, the Pacific, Europe, the Persian Gulf. Grainy footage of a space shuttle blossoming into a fireball. A clip from the Zapruder film. The Berlin Wall midcollapse. Waves of dark oil across the Louisiana coastline. Gas attacks on the Tokyo subway. Diagrams of what looked like a flying saucer. Blurry news camera shots of an airliner striking the second tower. Tanks rolling through the burning streets of Jerusalem; and there was more, but she couldn't recognize every fractional moment.

Anna thought about Janus's words and looked down at her hands, very aware that she was seeing them not through the eyes she had been born with, but through augmentations that made her more than human. *Transhuman.* The word resonated with cold possibility; it felt a million miles away from Anna's very ordinary existence.

The hacker seemed to sense her train of thought. "*A society that can augment itself at will, a human race capable of exceeding its physical limits through the application of technology... Can you imagine what kind of threat such a thing would be to those who want to control us?*"

"We're flying too close to the sun," she said to herself.

"*The Illuminati see themselves as an intellectual elite. If we are Icarus, they think of themselves as Daedalus, his father. The guiding hand of the parent. The creator and mentor.*"

Anna's lip curled. "I studied Greek mythology in college, and I remember that Daedalus was an arrogant bastard. The man built a maze of death, and killed his nephew when he thought he might be smarter than him."

"*And the Illuminati have killed, and worse. But the truth is, what you have seen is only one thread in the whole. What is taking place right now, the assassinations that claimed the life of your friend and all the others, these things are only the precursor. This is just one battle in a greater campaign they plan to win. At any cost.*"

Her mouth went dry as the scope of that statement settled in her thoughts. "What do you mean?"

When Janus replied, she felt a stab of fear deep in her

gut. *"Would you like me to show you, Anna? I've been building a model of all the potentials. It is incomplete, but there is truth there. You could consider it...a glimpse of our tomorrows."*

And then she heard herself answering. "Show me."

The hacker Janus did as Anna asked. The screen rippled, and the cascade of images returned—but this time they were almost too fast for her to register, a barrage of light and color and sound that washed over her with hypnotic force. She couldn't look away, and across her scalp she felt her skin crawl. The image-storm stuttered and blinked like an old analog television signal, hazing as it tried to tune itself into her. Anna suddenly became aware of the augmented optics in her eye sockets, for the first time feeling them as if they were spheres of hard, heavy steel. Something was happening; Janus's images were moving in synchrony with the digital processors built into her artificial eyes.

It was like a switch flipping inside her mind; and she saw—

—*the skyline of a city made of tiers, fires raging, and weapons discharges sparkling in the twilight, chaos, and disorder rising like a tide*—

—*crowds of panicked people desperately trying to flee hordes of crazed rioters, all of them augmented, all of them mad with wild fury*—

—*a wall of video screens filled with a storm of screaming, hissing static, and before them an enhancile woman collapsing to her knees, tearing at herself in crazed agony*—

—*orbiting above the Earth, a communications satellite shutting down, lights dimming, dish antenna*

*retracting. Then video screens, holograms, advertising
billboards, cell phones, televisions, computer monitors,
all of them showing the same message in bright red
letters—*

—NO SIGNAL NO SIGNAL NO SIGNAL—

*—a field of crosses, made from machine parts and
cybernetic limbs, behind a sunrise over barren grassland.
In the distance, a string of fallen power lines—*

—a ghost town of fallen buildings and empty streets—

—a dead future—

It ended as quickly as it had started, and Anna stumbled,
suddenly robbed of her balance. Her eyes throbbed and
her skull ached. The woman rubbed at the skin of her face
and it was hot to the touch. She glared up at the screen,
which had returned to its neutral aspect.

"What the hell...id you do to me?" Kelso was familiar
with strobe-effect crowd-control systems, and she
wondered if Janus had used something similar on her, the
pulse-image stream casting some kind of soporific effect
through her optics. She felt weak and nauseated.

"*I'm sorry. I didn't mean to disorient you,*" came
the reply. "*But the data is only sketchy. It is only the
impression of a possibility. It's difficult to comprehend in
a more linear fashion. Try to breathe deeply. Normalize
your heartbeat. You're not injured, believe me.*"

Anna glared at the screen. "You're lucky you're not
standing right here in front of me..." She trailed off, her
stomach tightening.

"*I'm sorry,*" Janus repeated. "*But do you understand
now? Did you see?*"

She took a shuddering breath. "I'm starting to, I think."

There was movement behind her, and she turned to see Lebedev enter the tent. He had a curious look on his face, as if he realized he had intruded on something private. "Is everything all right?"

"Fine," Anna bit out. "Are you looking for me?"

He nodded, sparing Janus's screen a quick look. "We have a problem. D-Bar and my people have gone through the contents of the flash drive you brought to us. There's a lot of material there, but what we really want exists in a subpartition that we cannot access. The key to the Killing Floor is inside that thing, if only we can crack it open. But it is protected with multiple-layer firewalls and a kill-switch. If we try to brute-force it, the drive will erase itself."

Anna folded her arms. "I can't help you with that. Ron Temple was the only one who knew the codes for his subnet, and the Tyrants killed him right in front of me." She turned to the screen. "Can't you do something? I thought Juggernaut's hackers were the best of the best?"

"Even we have our limits," admitted Janus. *"I've been watching D-Bar's attempts to crack the device. He won't be successful. To penetrate the subpartition, we need a connection to an active Tyrant computer server. It is as if the first lock nestles inside a second. Without both, it won't open."*

"Then we're no better off than we were a day ago..." Lebedev said, his expression turning stormy.

"There has to be some way!" Anna retorted. "After everything I went through for those damn files, we can't just write this off!"

The ghost-image in the screen shifted slightly. *"There's another solution,"* said the hacker, after a few long moments of silence.

"Explain," said Lebedev.

"It will be here within the hour."

They waited at the dockside, and Kelso scanned the surface of the shipping channel. The water was murky, patched with rainbows of fuel oil and slicks of floating trash. Out in the middle of the vast canal, huge robot cargo ships without conning towers or portholes sailed silently toward the docks, icebergs of steel emblazoned with the names of the corporations that owned them.

Beneath the turgid waters, something stirred, coming closer, making ripples into waves as it rose up from the gloom.

"There!" Powell called out, pointing with a slender cyberarm. He was one of the New Sons, and from what Anna had been able to gather from watching him interact with Lebedev, the man had some degree of authority in the group. He carried himself with a swagger, and she saw prison tattoos peeking out from under the collar of his body armor. His men came quickly to the quay and took up firing positions; they were armed with an assortment of rifles, everything from twenty-year-old Heckler & Koch assault weapons, through to the modern MAO submachine guns that had supplanted the old AK-47 as the signature firearm of rebellions the world over.

Lebedev frowned at the river as the water churned and a shape broke the surface. Anna saw a steel spine and plates of anechoic polymer as the vessel rose into the sunlight.

D-Bar craned his neck to get a better look. "It's an autonomous trawler sub...Like, the little brother of the big computer-controlled cargo barges." Fleets of similar unmanned ships, deployed from carriers in the Atlantic, plumbed the depths for shoals of fish driven from the higher waters by the effects of pollution. "Our buddy Janus must have reprogrammed this one, split it off, and sent it here."

A hatch opened on the dorsal hull, the plates retracting backward, and the stink of wet, rotting fish billowed out to assail them.

Powell nodded to one of his men. "Check it."

Gingerly, the man dropped from the concrete dock onto the top of the bobbing trawler and approached the opening. It was dark inside, and Anna couldn't make out anything. Powell's man snapped on a flashlight clipped beneath the barrel of his rifle and aimed it inside. "What am I looking for?" He stepped into the open hatch, grimacing at the smell. "I don't—"

Without a moment to cry out, the man suddenly vanished, pulled from sight by something inside the trawler. Anna heard a rattling thud from within, and a moment later, Powell's man was thrown back out of the open hatch, arms pinwheeling as he fell into the dirty water. D-Bar swore and backed away from the canal's edge.

The upper torso of a stocky, muscular figure emerged from the hatch, aiming the rifle back at the dock. Anna caught a glimpse of a grimy, weary face glaring down the weapon's iron sights.

Powell and the others all immediately took aim. Lebedev shook his head. "No, no!" he cried. "Put your guns down!

Put them down!"

Anna could see that Powell wasn't convinced, but he lowered his assault rifle and his men did the same; still, they kept their fingers close to the triggers, ready to snap back to a firing stance in a heartbeat.

"Where is this?" called the man on the trawler. His accent was rough, British.

"Port of Baltimore," Lebedev replied. "We were told to expect you. We have a mutual friend."

"Let me guess, a ghost named Janus, yeah?" He let the rifle's muzzle fall a little. "Hell of a thing."

That was when Anna got her first good look at the man, and she gasped. "I know him! He's one of them, a Tyrant! I saw him at Temple's house—"

Suddenly the guns were coming back up. "What is this?" Powell demanded.

"Stop!" Lebedev took a step forward. "We were told—"

"You might sign a lot of checks for us, but I have the military authority," Powell snapped, cutting him off. "Pardon me if I don't take the promises of a phantom hacker as gospel. This smells like a setup."

"I'm not one of them anymore," said the man on the boat. "We had a...parting of the ways." Anna heard the pain and the cold in his voice. She watched him carefully, remembering the moment when he could have ended her life. He had let her live. She wondered if she should return the favor.

Finally, he shrugged and tossed the rifle away, onto the deck of the trawler. He raised his hands. "If you're gonna shoot me, then shoot me. Because I have had a day like you would not believe."

Powell's aim didn't waver. "What reason is there to keep you alive?"

The man pulled a vu-phone from his pocket. "Our mutual friend Janus sent me a message. Tells me this thing has data on it you need. For the Killing Floor." The name brought a moment of silence with it. "That got your attention? I have the access code. So at the very least, you want to keep me breathing until I give that up."

"He works for them," Powell said, glaring at Lebedev. "First off you bring her in"—he jerked a thumb at Anna— "and now this?"

"Waifs and strays... muttered D-Bar.

Lebedev ignored the other man and stepped up to the bobbing trawler. "Who are you?"

"Ben Saxon. I'm just...a soldier." He let out a ragged breath. "I know who you people are. I'm in the same fight as you now."

Lebedev held out his hand and said nothing. After a long moment, Saxon sighed and tossed the phone to him. "Now give me the code."

"I do that, laughing boy there will slot me." He inclined his head toward Powell.

"You want us to trust you?" Anna asked. "Do as he says."

Saxon met her gaze and gave her a long, measuring look; then finally he nodded. "All right. But someone get me off this tub first? I busted both my legs and it stinks in here."

A year ago, it was the kind of gamble he would never have considered making; but a lot had changed since then, and nothing had made it more clear to him than the events of the last few days that his life was turning into one long roll of the dice.

He gave up the sister's name and waited for the one called Powell to put a round in his head. The guy wanted to do it, that was plain as day all over his face; but instead the other guy, the one called Lebedev, had a couple of blokes help him inside a nearby warehouse. Behind the derelict look of the place it was a regular staging post. They dumped him in a hospital tent and left him to the ministrations of a severe-looking medic.

Fatigue held him in tight coils, tighter than the metal nets that the robo-trawler had used to snag him from the ocean. In the grip of the steel wire, dragged under the frigid waves, Saxon had been certain that death was upon him.

It was only when he awoke inside the wet, reeking, meat-locker chill of the trawler's intake bay that he started to piece together what had happened. His attempt to contact Janus from the Tyrant jet had been at least partially successful, enough for the hacker to pinpoint where he was and track the vu-phone. After his explosive midair exit, Janus had retasked the nearby trawler as an ersatz lifeboat.

In the cold and the dark, Saxon fought all the way to stay free of hypothermia and unconsciousness. His augmentations had kept him alive, although the high-fall unit was burned out and would never function again; and as for the Tai Yong–manufactured cyberlegs, his impact with the sea had severely damaged them both.

The medic dosed him with a pan-spectrum restorative, hooked up a nutrient drip, and disconnected his legs beneath the knees with a sparking beam tool; then he left Saxon alone.

As he lay there, hobbled, Saxon felt more isolated than he ever had before. After the crash in Queensland, during recovery at the field hospital, he'd always had something to hold on to, to drive him...the need to find justice for Sam and the others. But now, even that was lost to him. Saxon felt dead inside, as if the energy to live on, to fight back, had been sapped from him by the icy waters of the Atlantic.

As far as Namir and the Tyrants were concerned, he was a dead man. He was compelled to agree with them.

There was movement at the tent flap and the woman from the docks entered, carrying a plastic hard case. She gave him a level stare. "You remember me." It wasn't a question.

He nodded. "You're Anna Kelso. U.S. Secret Service."

"Not anymore," she said bitterly. "No thanks to your friends."

"I had nothing to do with that," he insisted, shifting on his gurney. "I wasn't part of it... " Saxon's words died in his throat. *That wasn't true, was it?* A nagging voice in the back of his head demanded an answer. *You were in all the way. You were just too bloody thick to see what was going on. Or maybe you did see, but you were too gutless to face up to it.*

"Why did you let me live?" she asked. "At the house. You had the shot. You could have killed me."

He glared at her, and an ember of the old rage flickered deep inside him. "I'm a soldier! I don't kill unarmed civilians!"

Kelso seized on his words. "But the Tyrants do. They don't have principles or compunction. They're assassins.

And you're one of them."

"Not anymore," he repeated back to her. "I don't think I ever really was. I couldn't... couldn't stop being the man that I was. Before."

She saw something honest in his expression and her manner softened a little. "Why were you working with them?"

"I could ask you the same," he noted. "I know who these jokers are." He gestured around. "I recognize the hardware, the weapons, the setup. Juggernaut. New Sons of Freedom. They're all on the most-wanted list. That's a long way from the Secret Service."

She offered him the hard case. "I'll tell you what. A trade. You tell me how you ended up on Janus's radar and I'll give you these." Kelso cracked open the case to reveal a pair of replacement legs. "Caidin make. They're compatible with the TYM chassis you got."

He nodded and took them. "Fair deal." Saxon had extensive field training in augmentation repair, and he set quickly to work on his limbs. As he spoke, he let it spill out of him; from the incident in the Grey Range to Namir's recruitment pitch, the events in Moscow and Janus's first challenge, to the moment in the grounds outside Temple's house. "I suppose that's when I knew it," he concluded. "When I couldn't stay silent anymore. I thought I was going to make a difference in the world. But all we did was exercise someone else's power."

He sealed up the last of the connections and pushed off the gurney. Saxon stumbled a little as the gyros in the replacement modules ran through start routines and synchronized.

Kelso nodded at the legs. "You can consider that repayment for not shooting me."

He jerked his chin at the door flap and the warehouse beyond. "And the rest of this raggedy lot? What's their take?"

"Half of them think you're a security risk and want you killed. They found an inert tracer in your damaged leg. The other half want to interrogate you. Pull out everything you know about the Tyrants."

Saxon snorted. "Hell, I'll give you that for nothing. I'll sing like a bloody canary, as long as you promise me I get to be there when the Tyrants are taken down." He looked away. "I got no loyalty to them. Once, maybe... I thought I did. But right now, the only thing I want to do is *break* them."

The woman gave a nod. "Well, we got that in common, then."

The tent flap opened and a young guy peered in. His face was flushed with excitement. "Kelso! We got the uplink! Looks like our new pal here was on the money."

Saxon stepped forward, limping slightly. "This I wanna see. Show me."

Kelso followed D-Bar back to the hacker's work pit. In the center of the warehouse was a section of the building that had probably been a cluster of bathrooms; now all that was left was a square patch of yellowed, cracked tiles and the brick roots of partition walls demolished in the name of some refurbishment project that had never come. There were ragged holes in the tiled floor, from which snaked thick knots of cabling; the Juggernaut hackers had helped the New Sons set up their base here by drilling directly into the municipal power lines running from the city, snatching watts from the raw feed.

A ring of consoles, server units, and eclectic computing hardware circled the cable trunk. Every one of the decks was alive with screens and holos showing complex, overlapping panes of data. D-Bar dropped into a canvas chair and set to work. Lebedev and Powell watched like a pair of sentinels, faces grim.

Anna saw the flash drive, the case broken open and festooned with jury-rigged connectors. Nearby, another of D-Bar's team had Saxon's vu-phone wired up to a console, which in turn was cabled to a collapsible satellite antenna.

"Here we go," D-Bar said, cracking his knuckles. "Data sources are linked in parallel. All we need to do is ping the main Tyrant server and the rest is easy."

Lebedev folded his arms. "How much risk is there to us? We're opening a live connection to the Tyrants. What's to stop them backtracking it to this location?"

"Agreed," Powell added. "We could be calling an air strike down on ourselves."

D-Bar made a face, as if those were the dumbest questions he'd ever been asked. "Okay, forgetting the fact that I'm bouncing our signal through a hundred other locational IPs around the country before we even send it, forgetting the copious layers of active subnet masks being run in real time by my troop of monkeys here"—he threw a wave at his team—"not to mention nigh-invulnerable firewalls written by yours truly, there's this." The hacker laid his hand on a black box lined with glowing indicators. "It's a speed-imager. I need to get only a couple milliseconds of access to duplicate what we need from the Tyrant server. Then we can disconnect and run a virtual analog of it right here, without them ever knowing we were there."

"So there's no chance we'll be detected?" Saxon asked.

D-Bar grinned. "I never said that. But if I screw up, the last thing we'll see is the sky going white as some orbital laser array burns us off the face of the earth. So why worry, yeah?"

"Yeah," Saxon replied flatly.

Lebedev sighed. "Do it."

Anna stood back and watched. She really didn't know what to expect; on the screens, timer windows opened as a web of virtual system nodes unfolded, depicting a representation of the connection, the servers, the target. D-Bar's face became a study in calm as he plunged into the lines of code. His augmented hands were a blur across the keyboard in front of him, and flashes strobed down the connector cables that wound from a terminal behind his ear to the console.

Saxon looked up at the grimy skylights over their heads. "Nothing yet."

Rods of data reached from node to node across the screen, the alarm timer falling with each passing moment. At zero, the network would go into lockdown and the tiny window of opportunity to invade the server would slam shut. It would be the virtual equivalent of sending up a flare in front of the Tyrants.

Nodes turned green where the hacker team had been successful, others blinked red where the invading code was not taking root. Anna realized that D-Bar and the others here in the warehouse were not the only members of Juggernaut working on this digital attack; other inputs from across the globe were leading their own assaults. But of Janus, there was no sign.

"Ten seconds," Powell said, reading off the time. "Can you do this or not?"

"Do it?" D-Bar sniggered. "It's already done!" With a flash, all the nodes went green, and the hacker lolled back in his chair, jerking the connectors from his skull socket. "Piece of cake." The film of sweat over his pale face put the lie to his words.

With five seconds left on the clock, the connection was severed; but now a new construct was blossoming on the holographic screens. A meshing of three complex clusters of information—the flash drive, the vu-phone's memory core, and the duplicate server.

D-Bar saw her staring into the display. "We still gotta work fast," he said. "The ghost copy of the Tyrant server won't maintain parity for long. It's like trying to catch an echo. Longer you hold on to it, faster it degrades."

"Open it up," said Saxon. "Let's see what I almost died for."

A fourth data node emerged from the shared flux and blossomed like a flower made of newsprint, petal-pages spilling out. "The Killing Floor," said Lebedev. "This is the means through which the Illuminati commune with the Tyrants, the method they use to give them their targets and their missions."

Anna glimpsed vast libraries of files as they swept past. On some of them were names she had seen from her own investigations, but many were unknown to her. "We have to get a drop on them," she said, thinking aloud. "We need to know the name of their next target *before* they attack it."

"Exactly," agreed Lebedev. "Find us a face and a name," he told D-Bar.

"Look for something connected to an operative named Yelena Federova, code name 'Red.'" Saxon pointed at the display. "She was deployed separately from the rest of the Tyrants. That has to mean something."

Anna tensed with a moment of memory. "I think... she was the one who tried to murder me."

"Likely," Saxon agreed, with a grim nod. "She enjoys the close-up work."

"Got something," D-Bar announced. On the screen, a single blue-haloed file moved to fill the image. The image seemed grainy and hazed. "Parity is starting to drop quicker than I expected. Better make this fast."

Powell stepped closer to read the data presented before them. "Operative ident 'Red' tasked to shadow target-designate 'Alpha,'" he read aloud. "Action: terminate with extreme prejudice."

"That's it," said Lebedev. "But who is Alpha?"

"Gimme a second..." D-Bar typed in a few commands, and on a tertiary screen a new image appeared; a publicity still of a man in his sixties, with gray hair and glasses. He wore a dark suit and an expression of patrician earnestness, both of which were impeccably tailored.

Anna had seen him before, from a skybox balcony in downtown Washington. "That's William Taggart. He's the founder of the Humanity Front."

Saxon raised an eyebrow. "What, that anti-augmentation bunch? The ones always whining about 'science gone too far'?"

"Why would the Tyrants be targeting him?" She turned to Lebedev. "He wants the same thing as the ones holding their leashes! Restriction and regulation of human augmentation technology. Why kill him?"

"More important," Powell broke in, "why haven't they done it already?" He glanced at Saxon. "This Federova woman. If she's already shadowing Taggart, could she ice him?"

He nodded. "In a heartbeat. She's a phantom. Could make it look like natural death and no one would ever know she'd been there."

Anna saw something on Saxon's face as he said the words. "What is it?"

"Powell's got a good point. If Taggart's the next mark, why isn't he a corpse?"

She studied the image for a moment, thinking back to what she recalled from the last series of briefings she'd had at the agency. "Search for a connection between Taggart and the United Nations," she told D-Bar.

New data unfolded before them. Anna saw images of the Palais des Nations, the foundation and European headquarters of the UN in Geneva. "There's stuff here from a sealed memo to the Secret Service from the U.S. State Department," said the hacker. "Designating Taggart as a citizen of note. He's going to be part of the American delegation in a meeting with some of the movers and shakers at the UN."

"The vote," Lebedev muttered. "Taggart's going to the United Nations to spearhead the push for a ballot on augmentation control."

Saxon gave a dry chuckle. "*Huh*. Oh, yeah, now I get it. Makes sense." He glanced at Anna. "You want to know why Taggart is still breathing? Because they don't want to kill him quietlike. They want to do it out in the open, in front of people. They want an *event*."

"The founder of the Humanity Front, murdered by an augmented killer in full view of the global media, on the steps of the Palais des Nations..." Powell shook his head. "Can you imagine the fallout from that? Taggart becomes a martyr to his cause. His organization already has a lot of momentum. They lead the charge and do the work of the Illuminati for them. It's brilliant."

"Who?" Saxon asked, catching on the word, but Lebedev spoke over him.

"It's what they do. They find others and manipulate them into following their agenda." He frowned. "How long until Taggart arrives in Geneva?"

"His flight lands in Switzerland around midday our time," said D-Bar. "According to this, eighteen hours later he's at the UN to give his speech. We got less than a day before they waste him."

Powell drew himself up. "We've got to stop the kill from going down."

Lebedev nodded. "I'll contact our colleagues in France, get them to mobilize."

"That won't be enough," Powell insisted. "We need to be there. I'll assemble a unit. You get us some transport."

Anna watched the other man mulling it over. "All right," he said after a moment. "It can be done."

Powell gestured toward Saxon. "I want him to come with us."

Saxon snorted. "You trust me now, all of a sudden?"

Powell ignored the question. "He can provide visual

identification of any Tyrant operatives."

"Fine by me," grunted the soldier.

Lebedev nodded again. "Agreed." He turned to the hacker. "D-Bar, gather your gear. You're going along as well."

D-Bar's pale face flushed red and he blinked. "What? Why? *No!*" He shook his head. "I can do this from—"

"No arguments!" insisted Lebedev. "We can't go in without an information warfare specialist. You're always telling me how good you are—now you can prove it."

D-Bar jabbed a finger at the screens. "What, this wasn't enough for you?"

"Cheer up, son," Saxon offered. "You'll get to see it from the sharp end for a change, yeah?"

Anna listened to the interchange and it was as if she were falling away from it all, being left behind with every passing moment. When she spoke, the words came of their own accord, without her conscious control. "I'm going, too." Anna searched herself for a good, convincing reason, but she came up empty. All she could grasp was the distant, undying anger deep in her chest.

Powell shot her a look. "No. We don't need you."

"How about she goes and I stay?" offered D-Bar.

"I *have* to!" she insisted, with a force that came from nowhere. Anna went on, her voice rising. "I've been chasing the Tyrants for months! I've thrown away everything—"

"Kelso is right," Saxon broke in abruptly. "She should be part of the team. We can use her."

"How, exactly?" Powell demanded.

Saxon made a *look-see* gesture. "She saw the faces of the Tyrants. Two sets of eyes, mate." He gave Anna a look that was unreadable. "Right?" he asked her.

"Right," she repeated. "Yes."

Powell seemed as if he was about to argue, but Saxon gave him a look and tapped his wristwatch. "We don't really have time to waste arguing, do we?"

"Get the veetol and head for the shore," said Lebedev, ending the debate. "I'll contact you with the details once you're airborne."

TWELVE

The veetol was an old air-ambulance model stripped to the bare metal, a bulky and ungainly thing like a fat gull borne up on bright thruster nozzles that spat exhaust from the wingtips. They flew fast and low, following the line of the canal from Baltimore, until the river mouth opened up before them. Saxon felt it in the pit of his gut as the veetol rose up in a near-vertical ascent, trading altitude for thrust. He made an attempt to glance out the porthole; along with the Kelso woman and the hacker, Saxon was crammed into the rear of the flyer with Powell and four of his men from the New Sons. None of them looked like soldiers of any stripe he thought worthy of the name; they had a different air to them, which reminded him of the feral intensity of the gang kids he'd grown up with on the streets of North London. He pegged them for ex-cons or militia types. Kelso sat with her head down, lost in her own thoughts.

D-Bar gave him a smile that was all fake bravado. "What's wrong? Don't like flying?"

Saxon didn't allow himself to dwell on the similarity between this veetol and the one he'd rode into the wilderness six months ago. "Something like that," he offered. It was a tight fit in here, and he was starting to get tired of it. "Hey, Powell!" He had to shout to the other man to make himself heard over the roar of the engines.

Powell had the distracted look of someone using a comm implant. He glanced at Saxon but said nothing.

He nodded at the FR-27 rifle slung over the man's chest. "Do I get a weapon?"

"I only give guns to people I trust."

"What are we doing?" Saxon went on. "As cozy as this is, we can't fly to Switzerland in this thing."

Powell smiled thinly, reacting to something only he heard. "Don't sweat it," he called back. "Our ride is here." He jerked his thumb at the porthole.

For a moment, Saxon couldn't see what he was talking about; then his perception caught up with what he was looking at, and the shape he'd thought was just another churn of storm clouds took on a different aspect.

From out of the easterly front emerged a massive, elongated ellipse. Lined with fins and stabilators, great hoops hung from its flanks, the centers of them blurred by the motion of wide, fluted rotor blades. Along the flank of the aircraft he saw a blue-on-blue livery and the name: LEBEDEV AIRCARGO.

"Whoa!" said D-Bar, crowding in to take a look, "Cargo zep...Good cover." He trailed off as he thought it through. "But...how are we gonna get on board?"

Powell was getting to his feet. "Not the easy way."

The veetol's deck dipped and the hull of the airship rose to fill the window. The other men were securing their gear, checking straps and gear pockets. Kelso met Saxon's gaze with a questioning look and he gave her a shrug as a reply.

D-Bar turned to him, catching on. "He's not serious—"

A red light flashed and along the side of the veetol, a seam opened to peel back a long drop-hatch. Cold air howled into the cargo space and Saxon felt his gut tighten. He closed his eyes and for a moment he was remembering blackness and the shriek of wind.

The dorsal hull of the airship drifted past below them, a curved stretch of ridged aluminum as wide as a football field. He saw guide rails set into the metal and thick maintenance cables. The veetol dropped, almost bumping into the hull of the cargo carrier as a gust of wind pulled at the wings.

Two of Powell's men went first, the gale-force airstream catching them. Before Saxon could stop him, Powell went forward and shouldered D-Bar out through the open hatch. The hacker screamed as he fell, but the men on the hull were there to grab him.

Powell turned on Kelso and shouted, "You should stay behind. Go back with the flyer."

Saxon saw the shift of emotions on her face and she shoved the man out of her way. She dropped from the veetol, a flash of panic on her face—and then she was down and safe, clinging to the guides.

"You next," Powell ordered.

Saxon frowned and made the drop; it was less than a meter and a half of open air, but a sudden burst of wind shear hit him like a punch in the gut. He felt his foot touch the curve of the hull and slip out from under. His balance wasn't there and he was falling.

Suddenly, slender but strong fingers were gripping his wrist tightly. It gave him the moment he needed, and Saxon's cyberarm snagged a cable and held fast. He turned his head to see Kelso holding him steady with no little effort.

Saxon nodded his thanks and scrambled back up the curve of the hull. Powell and the last of his men dropped to the deck as the veetol curved away, and he led them forward to a windbreak and a hatch set flush with the hull. D-Bar barged his way to the front and made sure he was first in. The rest of them followed suit. The hatch slammed shut as he dropped into the airship's maintenance bay, cutting out the roaring cold. He frowned; his face was raw with windburn.

"You okay?" Kelso asked.

He nodded and gestured to his cyberlegs. "It's these new pins. Still working out the gyro synch. Thanks for the assist, though. Hope you didn't strain anything."

"It was just reflex," she snapped, suddenly terse.

"One suh-skydive without a chute is enough f-for anyone," said D-Bar, fighting back the shivers.

"Can't argue with you there," Saxon replied, with feeling.

"Okay, listen up," Powell ordered. "The zep crew know the drill. They don't ask, we don't tell. The ship'll make a speed-run over the Greenland-Iceland-UK gap and then on down to Switzerland." He looked at them all in turn. "We need to be ready to go the moment we reach Geneva, so I advise you all to get some rest, because the moment we touch down, we don't stop until the Tyrants are dealt with, you read me?"

The other men gave a chorus of nods, and Saxon glanced at D-Bar. The young hacker was quivering and wiping tears from his ruddy face. "Wow," he managed, crack-throated, "that was some rush, huh?"

"Get below," said Powell, cutting off any reply.

Geneva International Airport—Grand-Saconnex—Switzerland

It was late evening, and a light drizzle was falling in desultory waves across the gray runway and the aircraft apron. Namir listened to the rattle of the raindrops off the apex of the open hangar cowling overhead; the wide, low metal shed was dimly lit so as not to draw attention from the civilian traffic passing only a few hundred meters from the nose cone of the Tyrant aircraft parked within. Once again, the jet's livery had been reprogrammed and reconfigured to conceal its true nature. Currently it wore the black and gold of the private military contractor Belltower. The PMC had a long-standing relationship with the Swiss government that proved a useful cover for the Tyrants. They would be left to their own devices.

Namir walked the length of the aircraft, casting a glance across the darkened hangar to where Hermann and Barrett were working at the back of an unmarked commercial van. The ruin of the German's right eye was hidden under an adhesive patch, but he showed no signs of suffering for the injury. Namir didn't intervene; they knew their jobs, and after the recent incident on board the plane, they knew better than to do anything that might be considered a further failure of their duties. He reached the jet's cargo hatch and halted, studying the door. The seal was undamaged, but there were clear signs of surface damage around the hinges and opening mechanism. It had never been designed to be operated while airborne.

He sensed someone approaching and turned. Federova walked toward him, folding down a hood from her dark hair, flicking rain from her shoulders. Her expression was unreadable, but Namir knew her well enough to see the irritation lurking there. She didn't enjoy the surveillance operations; she liked the hunt and the kill better than the stalking.

"You're late," he said.

She looked up and saw the same scarring on the hull, and cast a questioning look at him. He smiled slightly. Yelena loved the sound of her own silence; sometimes it seemed as if he had never known her to speak at all.

"It's nothing of concern," he noted. "I'm afraid Ben Saxon made a decision to part company with us. He chose the time and place rather poorly."

Her eyes narrowed and she made a throat-cutting gesture.

"Likely." He held out a hand, changing the subject. "So. Give it to me."

Federova produced a small digital slate from her pocket and handed it over. Namir tapped the screen and scrolled through the images in the memory. The display was full of shots of the Metropol Grande, one of the more opulent of Geneva's great hotels. The footage highlighted locations for monitor cameras and security posts around the front entrance and throughout the underground garage beneath the building; others showed corridors on the executive penthouse level, accessways, and the like. The last image was at an angle, a surreptitious shot captured in a moment of opportunity. In the frame was an older man flanked by a coterie of bodyguards and personal assistants. The profile of William Taggart's face was unmistakable. He scanned the other people in the frame, measuring them against himself, looking for anything that could be a threat. Some of the faces he was already familiar with from the files that Temple had supplied to the Tyrants; there was Isaias Sandoval, the Humanity Front's right-hand man and chief of staff alongside Taggart's personal assistant Elaine Peller, and a few others. Not one of them possessed even the most basic of augmentations. Namir wasn't foolish enough to believe that his implants made him invulnerable, but they did make him *superior*. Quite how these people believed they could ever hope to protect themselves from the threats of this world—threats like the Tyrants—was beyond him.

"Good work," he told her. The rest of the slate's memory was filled with copies of itinerary files and route maps, but the majority of that data had already been in the hands of the unit for some time. "Take this to Gunther. Make sure there are no last-minute variables, then help him secure the payload."

She walked off, casting a sideways look as she crossed paths with Hardesty coming the other way. The operative ran a hand over his bald pate. "Ice queen's back, huh?" He watched her traverse the hangar. "So, I guess that means we still have a green light?"

"We still have a green light," Namir repeated. "Gunther can function, despite his injury. This sanction is too critical to the group for postponement. It must go ahead." Hardesty nodded, but he didn't leave. After a moment, Namir spoke again. "Was there something else you wanted to say, Scott?"

The other man folded his thin arms over his chest. "I was right about Saxon."

"Yes, you were." Namir met his gaze and waited for the rest of it.

Hardesty didn't disappoint. "He was weak. He never had the steel for this work. You made the wrong call—"

"Enough," Namir silenced him. "What do you want from me? An apology?"

"You misread him, and it almost cost us the operation!" Hardesty was emboldened by Namir's admission of error, and he was pushing it.

"Do you know why I wanted him to join us?" said Namir. The ice in his tone chilled the air between them. "It's because he had a code of conduct, Scott. Unlike you. Because this unit needs balance."

Hardesty was on the verge of launching into an argument, but he caught himself before he said something he might have regretted. As much as he was a braggart, Hardesty wasn't foolish enough to cross swords with Jaron Namir. Instead, he allowed himself a belligerent smile. "Balance, huh?" He glanced up at the scarred hull of the jet. "Look what that got you," he said, walking away.

Aerial Transit Corridor—Maury Sea Channel—North Atlantic

It was cold inside the airship's cavernous cargo bay. Faint layers of frost gathered on the sides of the container pods filling the length of the compartment. Breath emerged from Saxon's mouth in streams of white vapor as he walked the length of the companionway; the Caidin replacements for his lower legs were starting to bed in at last, and he'd used the downtime to get himself back into fighting condition. He didn't want a repeat of what happened when they boarded.

Powell and his men kept close to the aft service bay, where noisy electric motors fed the airships rotors and kept the area a little warmer than the rest of the cargo spaces. Without comment, he crossed into the group and helped himself to a couple of cheap YouLike self-heating coffee cans and power bars.

He found Kelso on her own, huddled inside a solar foil blanket. She was miles away, her gaze fixed on a brass coin as she turned it over and over in her fingers. She looked up as he approached and palmed the coin, as if she'd been caught doing something wrong. He held out a can and she took it, striking the base on the deck to get the thermal tab working.

Saxon dropped into a lotus settle and did the same, tossing her one of the bars. She unwrapped it with her teeth, waiting for him to speak; he tried to frame the question the right way, then finally gave up.

He nodded at her hand, where she had the coin. "How long have you been clean?" When she didn't answer straight away, he went on. "S'okay. I know what the chip is for... " He drifted off, frowning at himself.

Kelso studied him. "You were in the program?"

He shook his head. "Not me. My old man." He made a drinking motion with the can. "He didn't do that well with it."

"Stims. For a while." Her eyes narrowed; she was

taking this as a challenge. "It doesn't make me weak," she told him.

"Of course not," he replied. "If anything, they give you the chip, it means you're stronger, yeah?"

"Yeah." She didn't sound convinced by her reply.

He swigged at the coffee and made a face. It tasted like someone had stubbed a cigarette out in it; but it was hot, and that was what counted. Saxon leaned forward. "You don't think you can trust me." He jerked a thumb over his shoulder. "Like Powell and the rest. You think I'm marked."

"After everything that's happened to me over the past few months, I'd question my own family." She grimaced as she took a pull from the can, then shot him a look. "Why'd you lie to Powell?"

"About what?"

"When I said I wanted to come. You told him I'd seen the faces of the Tyrants. That's stretching the truth."

"You saw Federova and lived to talk about it. Trust me, love, there's not a lot of folks can say that."

Her eyes narrowed. "Her and one other." Kelso's lips thinned. "I need you to tell me something. Washington, D.C., the hit on Skyler. Were you one of them?"

The question came out of nowhere and he took a second to follow it through. "When?" Kelso told him the date and he shook his head, his gut tightening as an old, hateful memory made itself known. "No. I was halfway around the world that day, trying not to die. Namir recruited me afterward. He was a man down, he said." He eyed her. "Were you responsible for that?" He thought about Wexler, the man he had replaced, and the lines of invisible influence that had brought him to this place at this moment.

She ignored the question. "Why did you lie?" she repeated.

He gestured at his eyes. "You got the same look I see in the mirror. You're like me. You're looking for someone to pay a butcher's bill."

"They killed a man who saved my life," she said, her gaze becoming distant. "Did it right in front of me. And I couldn't do a damn thing. Then the Illuminati's proxies covered it up and buried him under the lies." Kelso shook her head. "I couldn't let that stand."

"*Illuminati.*" Saxon turned the word over, sounding it out, connecting it with what he knew. "Namir called them 'the group,' like he was afraid to say any more. They're the ones pulling the strings, signing the death warrants, fronting the cash... " He sneered. "I've heard the name. Some bullshit secret society, something outta trashy thrillers... only *not*." The soldier considered it. "Makes a cold kinda sense, when you think about it. Ghost orders and missions that never were... men and women sacrificed for the sake of keeping the shadows long."

"If what Janus says is true, these people are positioning themselves to manipulate... *everything*. The future of humanity. The creation of a new world order."

"Maybe so." Saxon looked back at her. "But you want to know something?"

"Go on." Kelso clasped the heated coffee can, drinking in the scant warmth from it.

"I don't give a fuck about all that shit." He shook his head. "I'm a blunt instrument, me, I'm not a clever bastard like the kid or Lebedev." Saxon nodded toward the others. "I've got a very simple need, and it's the same as yours. I want some bloody payback."

She looked away. "I... I'll tell you what I need, what I want. I want my life back. I want to go home. I don't want to have to know any of this!" Her voice rose suddenly. "Because now I can't walk away!"

"Ignorance is bliss, isn't it?" said another voice. Saxon looked up as D-Bar approached. He looked pale and sweaty.

"Anyone ever tell you it's rude to eavesdrop?" Saxon retorted.

"Please," said the young hacker, "I spend my life finding out other people's secrets." But almost as soon as he said the words, his bravado disintegrated; and suddenly Saxon remembered that he was looking at a boy still in his teens, just a scared, cocky kid who was only now waking up to the fact that he was in way over his head. "Makes you wish you could just erase the data in your brain, right?" he was saying. "Search and replace 'Illuminati.' Go back to being one of the happy cattle."

"You really mean that?" asked the woman.

The more he watched D-Bar, the more Saxon saw how shaken he was. "I... I've been going through the files we got, the fragments we could salvage. You wouldn't believe the stuff in there. Hints about the things they got planned. The things they've already done. We're not just talking JFK and Roswell here, I mean this is big... " His eyes lost focus and his voice dropped to a whisper. "Majestic 12, the United Nations, the WTO... They're so *big*. Every time you think you've seen the top, but it's all just layers and other layers!" D-Bar caught himself and blinked. "I mean, how can we fight that?"

"We break up their game." Saxon's reply was iron hard. "They think they got a clear hit on Taggart? Not today." He got to his feet. "Today *we* got the edge."

"How's that?" asked Kelso.

He smiled wolfishly. "They think you're hiding in fear. They think I'm a dead man. So they'll be looking the other way when we stick a knife in them."

The Rhône—Peney-Dessus—Switzerland

The countryside was dark and shrouded by heavy storm clouds, masking the approach of the airship. The transfer was swift, the massive craft moving low with all running lights extinguished, drifting along the center of the river to match pace with a long cargo barge steaming north toward the Swiss capital. On descenders, Powell and his men led the group to the deck of the vessel, and Anna looked up as her feet touched the rain-slick metal. In the night's gloom, it seemed an impossible sight; the airship a featureless black cloud among gray companions, rising in silence amid the wind. In a few moments it merged with the overcast skies and was gone as if it had never been there. The rain came harder, and she pulled her hood tight over her head, hurrying below.

Inside the barge were five more men; they all had the same aura as the New Sons, the same wound-tight aggression simmering just beneath the surface, the same eternally alert manner of the career renegade. All of them were armed and showed off augmentations to a greater or lesser degree. Powell shook hands with their leader, a rail-thin man with unkempt, greasy hair and a ragged beard. He had implants covering his eyes, like frameless glasses. They were dark and reflected no color.

He extended a hand to Kelso and she shook it. "Welcome to Switzerland," he said. The accent was French, but she picked up inflections that suggested he'd been educated in the States. "I'm Croix. You've brought us something interesting. The information on the hit is confirmed?"

"It's solid," said Powell, looking around. "Where's the rest of your people?"

"Standing right in front of you," said the Frenchman. Before Powell could argue he went on. "We have our own operations in progress. And this is extremely short notice."

"You understand how important this is?" A nerve jumped in Powell's jaw. "The reason we're moving so fast on this is precisely because we have an unparalleled opportunity here. A chance to get the drop on the Tyrants!"

"*D'accord,*" said Croix, stepping closer to Saxon, "but we don't have the manpower or the money that you do, my friend. We have to pick our fights."

"You're members of L'Ombre," said Saxon. "I read the file on you guys when I was at Belltower."

The name rang a bell with Anna; L'Ombre was on Interpol's watch list as a known militant activist group in mainland Europe, linked to a number of incidents with an antiglobalization agenda. But given what she knew now of a clear connection between them and the New Sons of Freedom, she wondered how accurate that intelligence really was.

Croix allowed a smile. "Do we get good press?"

"Not really," he admitted. "They wrote you off as day-players."

The other man's smile vanished. "Their mistake. We're in this fight for the duration, believe me." He looked Saxon up and down. "So you're the turncoat, then? Lebedev told me you'd be joining us. Should I trust you?" His hand slipped to the revolver holstered at his belt.

"Your call, mate," Saxon offered. "But I don't think Lebedev would have shipped me halfway around the world just for you to kill me."

"True," said Croix.

"He helped us get the data on the Taggart hit," said Anna, uncertain why she felt compelled to defend the man.

Croix glanced at her. "And you. You're the fugitive. Interesting choice of recruits, Powell."

"That's one way of putting it," said the other man. "So, can we cut to the chase here? What do you have for us?"

Croix snapped his fingers and one of his men produced a laptop. D-Bar immediately crowded in, studying the device. "As I said, we lack manpower but we make up for it in other areas. L'Ombre has access to certain sources of electronic intelligence."

"What do you mean?"

D-Bar sniggered. "According to this, the Swiss sat-comm network has more holes than... well, you know, the cheese."

"We exploit them," said Croix. "As such, we've been able to track two distinct encrypted communications nodes that have appeared in the Geneva area."

"They match what we have on record," said the hacker. "It's the Tyrants. They're here, all right."

Anna felt her pulse quicken, and she stepped closer to look at the laptop. "You're telling me you can read their communications?"

"Of course they can't," D-Bar snapped irritably. "Quantum coding crypto? Don't be stupid!"

"But we can recognize their presence. It's a fingerprint," said Powell.

Croix's smile returned. "Oh, we've done better. We have locations."

"How'd you manage that?" Saxon raised an eyebrow. "Namir's team don't make mistakes."

"People get lucky sometimes, Saxon," D-Bar broke in.

Croix nodded to the man with the laptop, who brought up a series of digital maps. "One of the communication nodes remains static at the airport."

"Must be the jet," said Saxon. "Namir uses it as a command post."

"The second," Croix went on, "is mobile." He said something in French and the other man used the computer to show grainy footage from what appeared to be a traffic camera. "A delivery vehicle. It's been making a circuit of the city."

"Cleaning the route," said Anna. "Making sure he's not being tailed, before... "

"Before what?" asked Saxon.

Powell folded his arms. "That's what we need to find out." He was silent for a second. "All right. We need to do this right now. Take the vehicle and the jet at the same time. We don't know what we're dealing with, and we can't afford to wait and watch."

Anna saw something on the video footage that sparked

a cold tremor of recognition within her. She moved closer, peering at the images.

"Taggart does not speak until midday," Croix was saying. "They won't move against him until then."

"Are you sure? Do you want to take that risk?" Powell insisted.

"The plane will be the harder target, though, right?" said D-Bar. "And if Saxon is right, if that's the control..." He swallowed. "Look, with this setup I can monitor the van from here—"

"No," said Powell. "It has to be a simultaneous takedown."

"The kid's right, though," offered Saxon. "That aircraft will be heavily defended. You try to storm it with anything less than a full team and the Tyrants will cut you to ribbons."

"Croix." Powell turned to the Frenchman, considering the other man's words. "Get us an entry into the airport. Then set up a vehicle so we can at least tail the mobile. I'll lead the team against the jet. Saxon will come with us."

Anna heard him talking but she registered what he was saying only peripherally. "I'll take the van," she said. "Get me close and I'll take him."

Saxon's brow furrowed as he heard the raw fury bubbling up inside her words. "Kelso, what is it?"

She pointed at the screen. "You know him?" On the monitor, the blurry image of a man's face had been captured by one of the traffic cameras. He wore a bandage over one eye and a cap.

Saxon gave a wary nod. "He's German, former GSG-9. Gunther Hermann."

The name echoed in her mind. Hate, cold and hard like black diamond, grew solid in Anna's chest. It was the same man from that horrific day in Georgetown. The killer who had left her for dead, who shot Byrne and Dansky... and Matt Ryan.

Geneva International Airport—Grand-Saconnex—Switzerland

"There," said Saxon, pointing into the gloom. "Hangar four."

Beside him, Powell squinted down the eyepiece of a monocular. "That's a Belltower aircraft."

"It's *them*," Saxon insisted, studying the shape of the parked jet. "I'm not seeing any movement, though. They have to be inside."

Powell spoke over the general comm channel. "All right, listen up. Two entrances, one gangway at the forward hatch, another drop-ramp at the aft. You know the drill. Move in, neutralize any threats. Fast and efficient." He glanced at Saxon. "Stay where I can see you. Croix may want to give you the benefit of the doubt, but he's not me."

Saxon shrugged. "Whatever you say."

"All units," Powell said to the air, "take the plane. Go, *go!*"

They covered the distance to the far hangar in a few seconds, veering from shadow to shadow, avoiding the footprints of security cameras. Saxon had to admit, for a group of irregulars, the New Sons had the makings of a good spec ops team; but he wasn't convinced they'd be enough to deal with the Tyrants.

Not that survivability was foremost in his mind at this

very second. All he cared about was finding Jaron Namir, and ending his life.

There were active boxguard robots scanning from the corners of the hangar interior, and Powell's men went after them with Pulsar grenades, shutting them down with flashes of electromagnetic discharge. Saxon hesitated at the foot of the gangway, glancing back down the line of the plane to where the cargo bay doors were wide open. He toggled his mastoid comm. "Any unit at the rear: is the helo in place, over?"

He got a reply immediately. *"What helo, over?"*

"There should be a small veetol flyer stowed back there—"

"Saxon!" Powell snarled, coming up behind him. "Stay off the channel unless it's important!"

He frowned and climbed up the staircase, staying low.

Avenue de l'Ain—Geneva—Switzerland

The highway traffic coming into the city across the Rhône from Lancy was mostly commercial at this hour, and there was a moment of uncomfortable recollection when Anna watched a massive automated truck thunder past them. She'd insisted on taking the shotgun seat, kneading the grip of the Zenith automatic Croix had given her while the Frenchman sat behind the wheel of their black sedan. He had a connector running from one of his augmented arms into the dashboard, and he scanned the road ahead, his face set in concentration.

The interior of the car was dark, but in the backseat, D-Bar was lit by the glow of the laptop computer; the screen's pale light gave his face a corpselike pallor.

"I see him," said Croix. "Five hundred meters ahead. Confirm?" He threw the question over his shoulder.

When D-Bar didn't reply, Anna turned in her seat. The hacker blinked and looked at her. There was a mix of emotions on his face that she couldn't read. "Oh. Yeah," he managed. "Confirm."

"He's turning off the motorway," Croix noted as the van slipped into a feed lane. "Heading into the city. We need to know where he's going."

Anna listened, but she was watching the glow of the taillights from the target vehicle with almost feral intensity. In her mind's eye she could see only the face of Gunther Hermann, that and the moment of Matt Ryan's murder, over and over.

Geneva International Airport—Grand-Saconnex—Switzerland

"We're in," said the other team leader. *"Tail section clear. Moving to secure lower deck."*

"Copy," whispered Powell. "We're moving aft."

Saxon pressed himself into the wall and strained to listen. They had found no one in the cockpit, nothing but the jet's controls set in standby mode. It rang a wrong note in his mind, and he hesitated, frowning.

"Something's not right," he said as Powell came to his side.

"What, that we got the drop on your Tyrant buddies?" he husked. "Keep moving." He gestured with the silenced FR-27 in his grip.

With Powell and another two of his men following on behind him, Saxon moved down past the galley to the doors of the ops room. He felt an unpleasant chill on his skin. Walking the halls of the jet so soon after having nearly died there did not sit well with him.

On a three-count, he tore open the door and fell into the room, looking for a target.

The ops center was empty, the consoles working quietly, screens showing a steady train of data as it scrolled past. He moved carefully into the middle of the room, a cold sweat forming between his shoulder blades.

"Clear," said Powell, a note of disbelief in his voice. He tapped his comm. "Unit two. Move to the cabins. They could be sleeping. Execute whoever you find."

"They're not sleeping," Saxon muttered. Something caught his eye and he moved to one of the control panels. It was part of the jet's encrypted communications suite. The screen showed a series of active broadcast nodes. The first was highlighted on a map, moving through the Geneva suburbs. *Hermann in the van,* he thought.

Over the radio, he heard the voice from before report in. *"Sir, got something here in the cargo bay... Looks like chemical drums. Commercial-grade ammonium nitrate. Accelerants. Everything you'd need to build a backyard IED."*

Powell's brow furrowed. "Why the hell would they need that crap? We know the Tyrants have access to military-grade explosives... " He turned to the soldier with him. "Cooper, check everything in this room. We don't want any surprises... "

Saxon's attention was still on the comm system. He found a second node display; this one was a stream of encryption, shifting and moving. The location was static.

He realized he was looking at a virtual icon for the jet and the ops room.

"*Sir,*" said the operative on the lower deck, "*whatever they were making here, they built it already. All we got is leftovers.*"

The color drained from Powell's face. "A truck bomb..." He tapped his comm bead again. "Patch me in to Croix, right now!"

Saxon distantly registered the conversation, hearing Powell shouting an urgent warning to the L'Ombre field commander. He didn't hear the words, instead tracing the line of the signals between the first and second Tyrant communication nodes; and beneath them both, he found a *third*.

It was isolated, away from either of the others. Saxon frowned, trying to interpret the complex web of signal and encoding; and then with a sudden, cold clarity, he understood what he was seeing.

None of the communications to Hermann had originated from the jet. All of them were coming from the third, concealed comm node, the identity and location displayed only as a single codeword—*Icarus*.

Wherever Namir and the Tyrants were, it wasn't *here*. They were broadcasting to the jet, then letting the automated systems on the aircraft relay the signal to the van. Namir had to know that the Tyrants were being monitored.

They had never been here.

"We've been set up!" he shouted.

Rue de Lyon—Geneva—Switzerland

Powell's voice sounded from Croix's hand radio as they passed the Parc Geisendorf, heading east. *"The vehicle Hermann is driving has explosives on board. The Tyrants have put together a fertilizer bomb... They're going to detonate it in the city!"*

Croix swore. "That's perfect. They blow up a piece of Geneva and then fake a claim from some transhumanist radicals; they get what they want and Taggart dies... "

"Where's Taggart now?" Anna asked D-Bar.

The hacker hesitated again before he answered. "The, uh, hotel. The Metropol Grande, downtown."

"The Grande has a large underground parking garage," Croix went on. "A big enough explosion in there could collapse the whole building."

"We've got to stop him now!" Anna snapped, working the slide of the Zenith.

But Croix was already pointing down the road ahead. "He's making a run for it!"

Anna saw the van's lights flare as it leapt away at high speed, jumping a stop signal, tires squealing as it veered past a car crossing the highway. Croix flattened the accelerator and the sedan surged forward.

"Floor it," Anna snapped. "Get us closer!"

Geneva International Airport—Grand-Saconnex—Switzerland

"What the hell are you talking about?" demanded Powell.

"We've got to get off this plane, right fucking now!" Saxon told him. "Namir and the others are somewhere else, bouncing the signal off the comm gear on board!"

"Why?" Powell shot back.

"They knew we were coming!" he roared.

Powell's rifle was coming up, his face split with an angry snarl. "Did you—?"

But in the next second another voice was speaking over both of them. "Sir?" They both turned as Cooper backed away, his face pale. "Saxon's right."

The other man had bent down to open an access panel; concealed behind it was a fat brick of gray, claylike material, with a series of silver detonator pins wired into it.

Powell shouted into the radio. "All units, disengage, disengage, *disengage*—!"

The first of the remotely triggered charges went off at that moment, blowing the jet's tail into a cloud of metal shrapnel.

A gust of hot gas and smoke came rolling down the length of the aircraft toward them as they ran. Inside the spaces of the fuselage, a second charge detonated, then a third. The churning inferno blossomed into a deadly flower.

Rue de Chantepoulet—Geneva—Switzerland

The two vehicles roared across the junction and cut through the sparse traffic, jockeying for position as they turned back toward the river. Taggart's hotel was across the Mont Blanc bridge, less then five minutes away.

Anna shouted "Closer!" and dropped the passenger-side window. Her actions were dislocated somehow; it was as if she were watching herself from a long way away. She shrugged off her seat belt and dragged herself out the window as Croix brought the sedan alongside the van. Anna got a quick look at Hermann's incredulous expression in the wing-mirror before she raised the Zenith and unloaded four rounds into the vehicle, aiming for the engine block.

The van skidded and recovered, turning as the feed lane to the Pont du Mont Blanc opened up before it.

The next thing she did was a moment of pure instinct, without conscious thought; Anna kicked off and threw herself at the van as the two vehicles bumped. Her foot found the running board and her free hand snagged the mirror. She ignored the winds battering at her and fired blind, shooting out the glass and firing into the driver's side of the van.

Hermann shot back with a burst from a Hurricane machine pistol, spraying bullets into the air. His shots were wide; despite all his augmentations, driving the wounded vehicle, aiming, and firing at the same time were beyond him.

Her neurovestibular implant went hot and she felt the rush of new focus shiver through her; the feed-forward system augmentation tightened her aim to the point between the muzzle of the Zenith and her target. Anna let the ice-cold flood of her anger take over, let it ride the aim point.

Time slowed as the van hurtled across the bridge. Anna brought up the pistol and fired again. The shots struck Hermann in the head, carving across the front of his skull, ripping flesh and breaking bone. The impact trauma was massive, throwing him off the steering wheel.

The van skidded again and this time there was no one to stop it. Anna's grip was torn away by the hard pull of gravity and she instinctively fell into a roll as she struck the highway. The pain was breathtaking; Anna screamed as the road tore at her, her forward velocity shed in agonizing impacts as she tumbled.

The van veered into the guide rail and cut straight through it, bouncing over the pedestrian path to slice through the side barrier. Engine roaring, the vehicle plummeted toward the Rhône river and clipped the rear quarter of a barge passing below.

As the van hit the water, something in the makeshift bomb broke. Perhaps a connector damaged by Kelso's gunshots or a vital component short-circuited by the force of impact; the effect was the same.

The bomb went off in a howling, thunderous discharge of water and air, tearing the vehicle apart with the force of concussion.

Blood streaming down her face, Anna lurched to her feet as Croix came running. In the light from the streetlamps she saw the remains of the van spin into the froth of the river and vanish from sight.

Geneva International Airport—Grand-Saconnex—Switzerland

Saxon heard Powell die as the last detonation took him off his feet and threw him across the hangar and out onto the runway. Powell's scream was torn away by the roar of the fire and then Saxon's world spun around him.

He landed hard, scraping his skin across the tarmac, pain lighting him up all over. The great ball of fire ejected a rain of steel fragments and burning debris, and Saxon dragged himself to his feet, trying to get clear. The heat rolled over him and he coughed, smoke and the stench of burning jet fuel searing his lungs.

He cast around, and his heart sank. *Again... Not again...*

No one else moved among the devastation and the flames; he cursed himself for being the survivor once more. Powell and his team were gone, the jet and any chance of finding Namir and the Tyrants obliterated...

Saxon stumbled and collapsed on the grassy verge across the runway. In the distance he could see the flash of lights from approaching fire tenders and police vehicles. He had to run. He had to get away...

His legs refused to move. *How?* The question thundered in his head, robbing him of all motion, all power. *How did they know we were coming?*

Kelso's face blurred through his thoughts and he tensed. He had to warn her.

Saxon's blackened, pained fingers found the spot on his jaw that toggled his comm implant. "Kelso... " His voice was a crackling, painful wheeze. "Kelso, do you read me? This is Saxon! We've been set up!"

For a long moment there was nothing but static; and when the reply came it was like a knife between his ribs.

"Ah, Benjamin," said Jaron Namir. *"I'm afraid it's worse than you think."*

THIRTEEN

A nna hobbled to the edge of the bridge and steadied herself with one hand on a piece of the broken guide rail. A layer of smoke and fumes hung over the Rhône, shrouding the damaged barge as it listed in the shallow swell. Small fires were burning where patches of oil on the surface had caught fire, and she saw indistinct shapes bobbing in a slick of wreckage. The damp air was cloying.

She glared at the river, willing it to give up what she wanted to see; but there was no sign of anything that looked like a human body. Her fingers dug into the palm of her hand. It had all happened so fast; the car catching up to the van, the gunshots, the crash.

She wanted Hermann to see her face, to know who she was. She wanted him to understand what she was feeling, the need, the hard, sharp darkness of her anger. It wasn't enough for him to just die. *It wasn't enough.*

Anna's rage boiled out of her in a cry. *"Bastard!"* She snatched up the Zenith automatic from where it had fallen and emptied the rest of the clip into the water, firing rounds at random into the murk, as if that would force the German's corpse to rise from the swell; but the river gave her nothing. Part of her wanted to throw herself in after the crashed van, trigger the rebreather implant in her chest cavity, and go deep, until she found Hermann's body.

Then Croix was at her side, wrestling the gun away from her bloodied fingers. She shook him off and stumbled back a few steps, pain sharp in her legs. "Get away from me... " she grated, swallowing a sob.

Croix peered over the split in the barrier. *"Il est mort,"* he muttered. "Come on. We can't stay here. Something is wrong. I've lost contact with Powell and the others." He grabbed at her arm, but Anna shrugged him off.

"I want to see his face," she snarled, her voice rising into a scream. "I want him to know what this was for!"

The Frenchman's expression shifted as understanding came to him. "Ah. Vengeance, for someone close to you?" He saw the look in her eyes and nodded to himself. "It does not follow the path you lay out for it, *cherie.*"

"It's not *enough*," Anna hissed.

"It never is," agreed Croix. He took her arm and this time she let him. "Come on."

Limping painfully, she followed him back to where the black sedan was parked on the outside lane, the engine idling. She strained to listen for the sound of sirens, but heard nothing; Anna wondered what remnants of Hermann would be dragged from the river when the emergency services came to investigate. Was he really dead? The detonation of the improvised bomb had been attenuated by the river, but the ball of fire and the torrent of currents beneath the surface would have been enough to tear anyone to pieces.

She looked to the sedan and saw D-Bar getting out of the backseat. Croix called out to him, but the hacker's face was set in a dogged glower.

D-Bar's hand emerged from behind the car door with a small, slab-sided pistol in his grip. He fired twice, without hesitation; Anna heard the snap of the rounds cut the air.

The shots struck Croix in the chest and stomach. He let out a choking wail and stumbled backward, collapsing to the road. She saw the whites of his eyes and he gasped, flecks of foam gathering at the corners of his lips. "What the hell?"

"Shut up, bitch!" D-Bar's retort was full of venom. "Just fucking shut up!" He advanced. "You stay right there and you... you don't move!" He was breathing hard. "Do you realize what you just did? You have no idea!"

Anna cradled Croix's head and found a thready pulse at his neck. "Patrick," she said, "tell me—"

The youth exploded with ferocity. "Don't you talk to me like you know me!" He came closer, aiming the pistol squarely at her head. "I didn't want any part of this! I didn't want to come here!" He gestured to the radio clipped to Croix's tac vest. "Give me that! Slide it over!"

She did as he told her. "What are you trying to do?" she asked, feeling for a read on D-Bar's emotions. He was confused and angry, fearful and brimming with energy, all at once. With the gun on her, she knew that any move she made would cause him to shoot.

D-Bar grabbed the radio and stuffed it into a pocket. "You're so stupid," he retorted. "You really think you were *lucky*? They don't make mistakes!"

Anna felt sick inside. "You've betrayed us."

"*Us?*" D-Bar shouted the word at her. "You're not one of *us*! You never were, you're just a tool, that's all you ever were. Juggernaut used you, I used you... "

"For what?" she demanded.

But he went on as if she had never spoken, the gun's muzzle drifting back and forth. "I didn't know... I didn't *see* it! I thought we could win, but we can't. Kept trying to tell myself it was a game... But it's not." He shot her a wild glare. "The files, Kelso. You never saw what was in those files, did you? Not the whole thing. Not all the things they've done... " He blinked, and in the depths of his throat D-Bar made a noise that was almost a moan. "All the things. What they're capable of. We can't fight them." Then the hacker shook off the moment and straightened. "Juggernaut, the New Sons, L'Ombre... Sarif and Caidin and the rest, all on the losing side! It's like a raindrop fighting the ocean, there's no way to win!"

On the breeze, Anna thought she heard the hum of rotors coming closer; but she kept her eyes on the hacker. "When did they turn you?"

"On the zep." He gave a brittle, bitter laugh. "Or maybe before, but I just didn't want to admit it. They'd tried once or twice. Always laughed it off. But that's because I never understood. Not until you brought us the flash drive. Then I got it. I got it all." D-Bar's eyes flared with hate once again. "Why couldn't you have lost that thing? I didn't want to know all this! I wish I never knew!" He shot a look up into the air, then back at her. "I called them. And they made me a better offer. Juggernaut's days are numbered. The Illuminati have already taken all the people they need. They're going to win." He shook his head, grim faced. "I want to be on their side."

"The jet was an ambush." Anna thought it through. "But they never expected us to go after the van, not like this... " Saxon's face rose in her mind and her breath caught in her throat. "Are the others... ?"

"You fucked it all up!" D-Bar was about to go on, but the hum of rotor noise grew loud and Anna looked up, shielding her eyes as a black shape angled in to land on the bridge. She saw the spinning discs of lifter rings and a compact armored fuselage with no markings of any kind.

A man dropped from the open compartment behind the black helicopter's cockpit and strode toward them, glancing around, taking the measure of the situation. He reminded Anna of Saxon in manner, sharing the same wolfish stride, the same trained economy of motion in everything he did. Muscular cyberarms made of dull steel bones and bunches of dark crimson muscles caught the streetlights. He cradled an assault rifle in a deceptively casual carry across his torso.

"This isn't what you promised," he called, irritation flaring. "You've made a very poor start to our working relationship, Mr. Couture. Do you have any idea how much effort went into this operation?"

"It was Kelso!" shouted the hacker. "She killed your man, Namir, not me!"

"That remains to be seen," said the Tyrant leader, sparing Anna a passing look. "What matters now is that we employ a contingency." He frowned. "We need to reassess the situation and deal with this mess. Yelena?"

Anna felt the air shift behind her and she half turned. The woman from the apartment was suddenly *there*, right at her back, looming over her. Anna tried to scramble to her feet, but a gloved fist backhanded her and she spun away, new pain cascading through her skull.

She blinked as Namir nodded toward Croix. "Leave him for the *gendarmerie*. Secure the woman."

In one fluid move, the assassin bent down and snapped the unconscious Frenchman's neck; then she stalked toward Anna on her slender, silent machine legs.

"Wh-what about me?" D-Bar managed, trying to keep the fear from his voice as he watched Federova drag Anna to her feet. "We had an agreement... "

"Contingent on your continued value to the group," Namir replied coldly. "Care to prove that?"

Before the hacker could reply, a hiss of static rattled from the radio in his pocket, and he gathered it up. Then there was a voice, wracked with pain *"Kelso... "*

Namir stormed forward and snatched the radio from D-Bar's hand, meeting Federova's gaze. "The jet... "

"Kelso, do you read me?" said the voice. *"This is Saxon! We've been set up!"*

"You... said they'd be gone," D-Bar replied.

"Be quiet," Namir told him, looking into the distance for a moment. Then he turned his attention to Anna and raised the radio to his lips. "Ah, Benjamin," he began, "I'm afraid it's worse than you think."

"Saxon, *no*—!" Federova's hand shot out like a striking cobra and clamped tight around Anna's throat, silencing her.

Geneva International Airport—Grand-Saconnex—Switzerland

"Namir." Saxon moved away as fast as he could, dropping into the shadows cast behind a dormant runway service robot. "You're getting sloppy, mate. I'm still breathing."

"I admire your tenacity, Ben." The reply resonated through the bones of his skull, making his teeth itch. *"It's*

one of the things that drew me to you. I'm only sorry I couldn't find a way to make better use of it."

"You're welcome to try and kill me again," Saxon retorted. "Let's have a face-to-face and talk about it over a pint, yeah?"

There was a long pause before Namir came back on. *"Be realistic, Ben. You don't have a play here. Even if you make it outside the airport perimeter, where can you go? Geneva belongs to our people. By dawn, all this mess you've made will be glossed over and done with."*

Saxon listened to the other man's words, feeling for a lie beneath them. He'd heard Anna Kelso's voice, just for a moment, so he knew she was still alive. But there was something else, something in Namir's manner, the same thing he'd heard when the mission in Detroit had been disrupted. The van... the bomb... If it had gone right, Namir's tone would have told the tale.

He decided to take a chance. "I'm not the one who just blew his objective. Taggart will be spooked. He won't show. You'll never get to him."

Namir's reply was all the confirmation he needed. *"I beg to differ. Our friend in the Humanity Front has more courage than you credit him for. Believe me, he will speak tomorrow. We'll make certain of it. Too much has been invested in this for an irritant like you to derail things now."*

Flashlight beams danced on the ground nearby, and Saxon shifted, stealthily making his way around the rear of the robot garage. Across a service road, he could see a chain-link fence and the shapes of cargo warehouses beyond. He sprinted from shadow to shadow.

Namir's voice dogged him all the way. *"I have the woman, Kelso. Your fellow fugitive. I want your full and complete attention, Ben, or she dies. And it won't be quick. I'll give her to Barrett to toy with, do you understand?"*

"Kill her," Saxon bit out the bluff, ice forming in his gut. "She's nothing to me."

Namir chuckled. *"You really are a very poor liar. You won't let Kelso perish, not while there's a chance to save her. Let me tell you how I know that."*

Saxon gripped a section of the fence and ripped it open, ducking under. In a moment, he was inside the darkened warehouse, moving away from the airport proper.

"You're guilty." The ghost-voice echoed through his thoughts. *"Guilty about the men you lost during Operation Rainbird. Guilty about those who lost their lives tonight while you didn't. You're guilty because you didn't keep your promises. Am I close?"*

"Piss off." The words slipped from him before he could stop himself.

Namir laughed again. *"Survivor's guilt, Ben. It's what makes you weak. It's how I controlled you when you were one of us and it's how I'm going to control you now."* There was a pause, and when Namir spoke again, he was firm and commanding. *"You and this little group of troublemakers are responsible for disrupting my line of attack against the target, but the plan is adaptable. You're going to help me put it back on track."*

"Not bloody likely." Saxon halted at a window, peering out. A police car raced past and he ducked back into cover.

"I'm not giving you the choice," Namir grated. *"When William Taggart walks out onto the steps of the*

Palais des Nations at midday, he's going to be shot dead by an augmented killer. Can you see where I'm going with this, Ben?"

A sense of grim inevitability settled on him. "Taggart's life for the woman."

"I knew you'd understand. Be at the grounds of the Palais one hour before. If you try anything foolish, I'll make sure Barrett transmits every last second of what he does to Kelso, so that the only way to silence it will be to dig that comm implant out of your skull. Are we clear?"

"As crystal... "

A click echoed in his head as the line went dead. Saxon sat in the dark and the quiet, the promises he had made turning over and over in his thoughts. Sam and Kano, Anna...

Damn Namir, but the bastard was right. He knew Saxon couldn't walk away, not now, not after everything that had happened—because for every second he was still alive, there was still a chance he could get Kelso out of there, still a chance he could find Jaron Namir and *end* him.

He had broken a vow to Sam Duarte, a promise to get him home again. He wouldn't let Anna down the same way.

Saxon found a door and forced it open, slipping out to the road. A tram terminal, empty this early in the morning, glittered in the dark. He climbed to the platform, finding a shaded corner to wait for the next train into the city.

When he was sure he was alone, Saxon reached for the cracked and scratched vu-phone in his pocket, and dialed a number.

The call was answered instantly by a voice made of echoes and phantoms. *"Hello, Ben. Are you all right? I feared the worst."*

"I need help, Janus."

"What can I do?"

Saxon thought about the communications display he'd seen on board the Tyrants jet, and the Icarus ghost-node. "I need you to help me find something."

Route de Ferny—Geneva—Switzerland

He found a restroom at the terminal where he could clean himself up and take stock of his options. When Saxon was ready, he picked the pocket of an unwary night-shift worker and used her pass to ride the tram to the Nations station.

When he got there, he found a confusion of crowds strung out along the line of the open plaza, leading to the southern gate of the Palais. They clustered around the base of the Broken Chair, a twelve-meter-tall sculpture of a wooden seat with one shattered leg—a symbol for the victims of land mines and cluster bombs. There were two groups, each as loud as the other, each sporting banners and placards in English and French. The first were pro-augmentation, transhumanist activists, rallying around the sculpture as if they could use it as an image to underline their desire for freedom to control the human body; the other, larger group were against them, calling for the regulation of cybernetic enhancements. Their banners read *Stop Playing God, Protect Mankind* and other familiar slogans. He saw the symbols of Taggart's movement, the

Humanity Front, at every turn.

The tension in the air was palpable, and between the two opposing sides news crews from SNN, Picus, and the BBC moved back and forth while the Swiss police did their best to remain a discreet but obvious presence.

Confrontations over the controversial science of human augmentation technology were happening more and more. Saxon had seen the reports of angry demonstrations in Washington, D.C., Tokyo, and Mombasa, incidents where the vociferous clashes had turned ugly in the blink of an eye. He pulled his jacket closer to conceal his own cyberarm, unwilling to have either group figure him for one of their camp, and studied the lines of opposition. He wondered how much of this and all the other global protests had been stimulated by the Illuminati, surrogate fights staged to manipulate media coverage and public opinion. So much bloodshed over something so abstract... At first the thought of it sickened him; but then Saxon found himself wondering about the truth. How many other flashpoints in human history had begun like this? How many had the Illuminati turned to their design?

Hovering low over the plaza, a drone blimp drifted across the morning sky. The underside was festooned with cameras, while two thinscreens showed the Picus Nightly World News feed. Saxon glanced up and saw the elegant aspect of Eliza Cassan. The Picus anchor was one of the best-known celebrities on the planet, a face trusted by millions to be the voice of truth. The mere idea of that now seemed childish and naïve to the soldier.

A speaker grille broadcast her voice across the square. *"A spokesperson for the Swiss cantonal police has informed*

Nightly World News that the crash of a light aircraft at Geneva International Airport was a tragic accident and in no way connected to today's sensitive meeting of the United Nations science advisory board." Behind Cassan, images of fire tenders working on the runway unfolded. *"The meeting, which has been called to determine if UN involvement in human augmentation technology is warranted, will be attended by controversial figures such as pro-humanity advocate William Taggart—"*

Mention of Taggart's name brought a brief surge of cheers and catcalls from both sides, and Cassan's voice was lost in the sound of the crowds. Saxon watched the drone blimp continue on its way. The report made no mention of what happened to Gunther and the vehicle bomb; he reflected on what Namir had said before. *By dawn, all this mess you've made will be glossed over and done with.*

He frowned, burying his hands in his jacket pockets. Head down, he threaded his way through the jeering protesters, who were now taunting one another across the closed-off length of the Avenue de la Paix. Beyond lay Ariana Park, the wide commons once open to the public but now heavily patrolled and cordoned by Swiss law enforcement agencies and the private security contractors in the employ of the delegates. Saxon spotted a cluster of Belltower grunts in lightweight ballistic tunics and bascinet helmets with polarized gold visors. They were armed with flechette-firing assault rifles and urban-duty tactical shotguns, more than enough to cut him down if he tried to break the security line.

In the middle of the park was his target, the Palais des Nations. The meeting Taggart was attending would take place there, in the Assembly Hall. Saxon began to think like the assassin Namir wanted him to be, evaluating points of entry and approaches. Once Taggart was inside the Palais, he would be insulated from any attack. The man would have to be killed on the steps of the building, or not at all.

Saxon's eyes narrowed as he turned the thought over in his mind. In the SAS, this was a mission he had performed on more than one occasion; but then it had been in defense of King and Country, to stop conflicts rather than to start them. Here and now, he truly was no more than a blunt instrument, wielded by men in the shadows for a cause beyond his understanding.

From out of nowhere, a gruff voice cut through his thoughts. *"Keep walking. Past the tram halt. Fourth streetlight."*

He crossed the plaza to the road that paralleled it, and as he approached the lamp pole, a black SUV pulled in and halted. Saxon stepped closer as the driver's-side window dropped. "Hands where I can see them," said the voice. Hardesty's glowering face appeared, eyes narrowed behind dark glasses. "Well," he muttered, "it's true, then. You really *are* too fucking stupid to die."

Saxon obeyed and dropped his arms to his sides. He wasted no time with preamble. "This is a no-go. I can't get in there, let alone get close to Taggart." He stood stock-still, taking in the man, the vehicle, anything that might give him a clue about where Namir might be. A tag on the dashboard caught his eye; it looked like a security tab, similar to the arfid discs used by the Belltower grunts.

Hardesty shifted in the seat and Saxon's attention was drawn away. The other man had a Diamondback revolver resting across his folded arms. The muzzle was aimed right at Saxon's chest. "You have no idea how much I want to pull this trigger," said Hardesty, ignoring his comments. "Put a round into you, blow your lungs across the goddamn plaza... " He grinned coldly. "You almost cost us this op. I had an instinct about you from day one, limey. I should have fragged you in Queensland along with the rest of your squad."

A calm kind of anger settled on Saxon. "Then do it, if you got the balls. Either that or be Namir's errand boy, like he told you to. I don't have all day."

For a long second, Saxon thought Hardesty might actually shoot, as his expression tightened into a rictus; but then he sniffed and let the gun drop. "You're right. You don't. So listen up, 'cos I'm not going to repeat myself." He reached for a small bag and threw it at Saxon. "There's an armor jacket in there for you. Follow the avenue around toward the next gate. A public-works crew are laying some new blacktop in the near lane. You got cover there to hop the wall, get inside. The Swiss cops got two-man teams on patrol, so don't get caught before you get to the target."

"You expect me to walk right up to Taggart and break his neck?"

Hardesty sniggered and opened the revolver's chamber, shaking the gun so all six bullets fell out. Then he handed the empty weapon to Saxon, who quickly stuffed it into the bag before anyone spotted him. "Here," he said, holding up a single round between his thumb and forefinger. "You're supposed to be good. So this should be more than enough."

He tossed the bullet and Saxon caught it out of the air. "What about Kelso? I don't even know if she's still alive."

"That's right, slick, you *don't*," snarled the other man. "Now, go be a good dog and do as you're told, and maybe the bitch lives." He leaned forward, lowering his voice, showing teeth. "Personally? I'm hoping you try something. I want you to refuse, Saxon. I *want* the excuse to put you out of my misery." Hardesty spat on the ground. "You talk like you're a soldier, but you're nothing, limey. I know your kind, bleeding-heart warrior, all about the good and the noble, but you got no idea how the real world works. You got no steel in you."

Saxon met his gaze, looking through the dark lenses to the dead eyes beneath. He saw nothing there, nothing but a cold machine soul driven by anger. "You're right," he admitted. "Because if being strong means turning into a heartless fucker like you, I'll stick to being human."

Hardesty laughed. "Good luck with that," he retorted as the SUV surged away in a growl of acceleration.

Location Unknown

Anna clawed her way back to a waking state as if she were buried in wet sand, digging herself out inch by inch. She felt the chemical drag of sedatives in her bloodstream; her last conscious memory was of Federova bundling her into the back of the black helo before something sharp and metallic nipped at the flesh of her neck. After that had come a turbulent dream filled with scattershot images of burning cities, crazed cyborgs, chaos, and conspiracy, rising up from the recall of the vision Janus had put in her head.

She was in a small room with metal walls, the only decoration a perfunctory cot bolted to the floor, a lamp set in the ceiling, and a steel toilet in the far corner. Anna rolled to a seated position and the room swayed around her. The floor seemed unsteady, and her stomach turned over. The fog of drug haze made it difficult to move; her legs were like lead.

She wasn't secured by handcuffs or any kind of tether; clearly the Tyrants didn't consider her enough of a threat, which was insulting in its own way.

Beyond the door to the cell she heard movement, and held her breath, straining to listen.

"...with Hardesty," said Namir's voice, as he came closer. "Once it is done, we'll need to recover and proceed to the extraction point."

"Got it," said another man, this one gruff and hard-edged. "What about the li'l punk?"

"We've got what we need from him."

"This one, too?" Anna knew they had to be talking about her.

"We will see," said Namir. "If not, the Hyron Project can always use new materials." She heard him come closer. "Open it."

Anna scrambled back into the far corner of the cell as the door opened to admit the mercenary. She caught a glimpse of a thickset bull of a man hovering behind him, his face scarred by old burns down one side. He gave her a callous wink and walked away.

Namir stepped in and closed the door. "Anna Kelso."

"Jaron Namir," she replied. "Yeah, I know who you are."

That got her a moment of irritation, but it vanished just as quickly. "Ben should learn when to keep his mouth shut. It gets him into trouble."

"Are you here to kill me?" she asked.

He shook his head. "Not yet. For the moment, you're required intact. For purposes of leverage."

She snorted. "Against Saxon? I hardly know him. You think he's going to risk his life for a complete stranger?"

Namir nodded. "Of course he will. If you did know him, you'd know he *will* risk his life for you." He folded his arms over his chest. "It's a character flaw. Despite everything that has happened to him, every loss and disappointment, under it all Ben Saxon wants to be the good man. The hero." Namir smiled coldly. "Others would have had that beaten out of them by now. But not him."

"Lucky for me," she offered, with more defiance in her tone than she felt.

"Not really." Namir stood opposite her. "I'm intrigued by you, Anna. Your tenacity. It's quite impressive for someone with such personal failings to overcome." He cocked his head. "When was the last time you had a dose? It must be difficult going cold all over again."

"Bite me," she snarled.

He smiled thinly. "I know this is difficult for you to understand, but you have to realize that you are fulfilling a purpose here. We all are. For a greater good."

"A greater good?" She spat the words back at him. "Your Illuminati are a cancer! You kill and threaten and ruin lives all because some faceless cabal of old men want to play God with the world? *What gives you the right?*"

"There is no God," Namir told her. "That's why these

things need to be done. That's why the group exists." He sighed. "The Illuminati were created for that very reason. The future of humanity is too delicate to be left to the whims of passing kings and despots. It's too complex to be decided by the greater mass of mankind. It is the burden of the elite to be fit to rule, to take the reins of the world, and to guide it toward a stable unity."

"They teach you that little speech?" she replied. "The cowards who ordered the deaths of my friend and countless others?" She shook her head. "I've heard the conspiracy theories, but until now I never thought they could be true. But that's how they want it, right? They stay in the dark, pull the strings, and no one knows it. They decide what wars are going to happen, who gets elected... And now they want to control the right to evolve!"

Namir studied his cybernetic hand. "Is that so wrong? Think about it, Anna. Think of how the free spread of augmentations has changed the face of our species, the divide it has created between 'cog' and 'natch,' the metal and the meat. Think of how it has changed *you*. Anyone can make themselves into a killing machine with the right hardware and enough money. Wouldn't things be better if there were controls, boundaries, regulations?" He leaned closer. "You know that rules exist for the good of society." Namir opened his hands. "All we're doing is putting them into place."

For a moment, his words cut deeply; but then she pushed them away. "And it doesn't matter how many freedoms you have to kill to get there, does it? Because you believe you're right."

He frowned at her tone. "Your young friend Patrick

came around, once he had an understanding. I hoped you might, too, I really did. Saxon... he won't change... I thought you were smarter than him."

"I'm glad to disappoint you," she spat.

Namir watched her for a moment, before he spoke again. "You wonder why you're still alive. It's more than just Saxon. There's something I want to know." When she didn't answer he took her chin in his hand. "Who is Janus? What did he show you?"

Palais des Nations—Geneva—Switzerland

The limousine swung around Building C, where the council chambers were located, and pulled to a halt on the gravel drive in front of the United Nations Assembly Hall, the white pillars rising up across the entranceway behind it. A handful of Swiss security staff stood on the upper steps, while Belltower guards waited at the drive. Standing in a line before the nearby library, a group of reporters trained their camera drones on the vehicle as one of the guards opened the rear door, allowing Elaine Peller to exit; the Humanity Front's media relations staffer and personal assistant to the founder stepped clear and addressed the hovering cameras.

"Mr. Taggart will make a short statement. He will take no questions."

As she finished speaking, Isaias Sandoval was the next to step out; his thin Hispanic features were perpetually set in a nervous frown, and today was no exception. Despite what they had been told by the authorities, Isaias had been awakened in the predawn light by what could only have been an explosion out on the bridge near their hotel. He was still smarting that his employer had outright refused to take his advice about postponing the meeting with the UN science board.

William Taggart followed him out into the bright light of the day, smiling warmly and sparing the cameras a fatherly nod and a wave. The face of the largest pro-humanist movement on earth appeared, as ever, impeccably groomed and perfectly at ease; and yet he never seemed to lose the cool sense of intent, the quiet, scholarly charisma that made so many people listen to him.

Taggart stepped around to the front of the limo and nodded again. "My friends," he began, "it fills me with hope to be here today, to talk to these good people and present our point of view to them. At no other time in human history have we found ourselves at so delicate a juncture, when the very nature of what we are is under threat by scientific avarice ungoverned by any moral code or—"

It happened with unnatural speed and violence, with a fierce, controlled power that could have come only from the union between human will and machine strength. A muscular figure in a security officer's jacket slipped out from behind one of the Belltower patrol vehicles and punched the closest guard with such force that he spun and bounced off the hood of the car. The man swept in, pivoting on one leg to kick away a second Belltower trooper, the heel of his boot smashing the gold visor across his face. He dropped, blocking the falling blow from a crackling electro-prod as a third man tried to tackle him; the attacker rose back just as quickly, brutally snapping the man's arm against the direction of the joint, putting him down in a screaming heap.

All this in less than a few seconds, every motion and attack powered by nerve-jacked, hyperaccelerated reflexes and brute-force cybernetics.

"Get back in the car!" Sandoval was shouting, grabbing at Taggart's suit jacket, pulling him toward the rear of the vehicle. On the steps, the Swiss police officers were rushing forward, pistols out. Taggart stumbled against the limo, panic in his eyes, catching sight of Peller as she fumbled at the door handle.

Taggart's personal guards were two thickset men, both of them ex-military, trained and strong with it; but they were still only men, neither of them with a single augmentation, as the Humanity Front's founder demanded of his staff. For all they could do, they could not match the speed of their attacker.

He put them down as they blocked him, both bodyguards striking together, trying to split his focus. In one hand he had a heavy-frame revolver, and he used it like a club, shattering the nose of one man in a gout of bright blood. The other of Taggart's guards took a shattering strike to the knee that broke bone. His gun didn't clear its holster; instead, a following hit spun him into the dirt.

Taggart was at the door, Sandoval's hands on his back, shoving him toward the armored safety of the limo's interior.

Isaias turned and the killer was there, his face twisted in a grimace, cold augmented eyes that still held a spark of very human anger. "No, please don't!"

Kicking the door shut, the assassin threw Sandoval to the

ground and leveled the revolver at William Taggart's head.

The target raised his hands in a gesture of self-protection.

All around there was screaming and shouting, the buzz of the drones, the clatter of weapons snapping into fire mode—but Saxon didn't hear that. The only thing that reached him was Taggart's question.

"D-did they send you?" he stuttered. "Was it them? Did they send you?"

The Diamondback's hammer clicked to the ready and he held the aim. The moment stretched like tallow, becoming long and fluid, extending away. All it would take would be the slightest pressure on the trigger. One shot and one kill, and it would be done.

He had no reason to care about William Taggart's life. Men like him detested what Saxon was, thought him to be less than human. How much pain had the Humanity Front and their radical cohorts in Purity First caused for people like him?

And how much more blood would be shed if he did this? How much more persecution and death would come from this one man's murder, here and now? Was that a fair trade for Anna Kelso's life?

"Fuck!" Saxon's curse exploded from his lips and he let the gun drop. He couldn't do it. He could not let himself be Namir's weapon in the Illuminati's secret war.

Confusion flooded Taggart's face. "Who... Who are you?"

And then another voice echoed in his skull. *"You gutless prick. I knew you'd choke when the time came."*

From the corner of his eye, Saxon saw a shimmer of

sunlight off the lens of a rifle scope, up on the roof of the library building. "Sniper!" he roared, grabbing a handful of Taggart's jacket and pulling him down behind the limousine. His cry was drowned out by the crack of a heavy-caliber shot.

Taggart fell out of the sight line, the hum of the round buzzing scant centimeters from Saxon's cheek; in the next moment he heard a wet thud and a strangled cry.

Turning, he found the Peller woman on her back, a blossom of red growing on her chest, blood staining the white gravel beneath her. Her sightless eyes stared up into the cloudy sky.

Saxon spun and aimed his gun toward the rooftop, but Hardesty was already moving, vanishing into the library. Amid the confusion and the chaos, he vaulted the hood of the car and ran for the windows of the building, scattering the reporters like panicked birds.

FOURTEEN

Building B was the library, the archive, and the League of Nations Museum, closed today because of security concerns over the meeting and as such empty of visitors. Saxon broke in through a ground-floor window and blinked his cyberoptics through their scan modes, sweeping the big chamber for motion. Lines of high bookshelves formed shadowed lanes running the length of the building, and above a balconied area contained the glass cases of the museum exhibits and the interactive hologram tour guides.

Hardesty and Saxon found each other at the same moment; the sniper was moving with the Longsword rifle at his hip, and in one fluid movement he swung it up to his shoulder and fired.

Saxon vaulted to the floor, landing in a tuck and roll as a heavy rack of books exploded into confetti. He was in the worst place he could have been. Hardesty had the height advantage, looking down from the second floor, and the range to make the high-powered rifle work for him; Saxon had a revolver with a single bullet.

It wasn't just the lay of the land that was working against him. Outside, the Swiss police were gathering their wits and he had maybe a minute before they would pile into the library, mob-handed. And he knew one thing for certain; if he was going to find Anna Kelso, he would have to go through Scott Hardesty to do it.

As if on cue, the sniper called out to him. "Hey, limey! Thanks for the help, man. No matter how this plays out now, you've done the job for us! I'm gonna ice you, leave you here for the cops...Namir gets the group to finesse things a little, and by the evening news cycle, it'll be like you pulled the trigger yourself."

He edged along one of the shelves. "You reckon? You missed the mark, mate. Taggart's still breathing!"

"Doesn't matter!" he shot back. "We got a contingency for everything, Saxon. Don't you get that? The plan goes ahead, no matter how much the little people try to screw with it... "

Another bullet ripped through the shelves close to Saxon's head and he ducked. The son-of-a-bitch had a T-wave scope, peering through the cover. Unless he could get out from under, close the distance, nothing the soldier could do would keep the sniper from making the hit sooner or later.

He glanced up. The balcony overhead was a few feet from the top of the tallest bookshelf; he could make it, but the moment he moved, Hardesty would cut him down. He needed a distraction.

Saxon leapt up onto the top of a study desk and the sniper saw him, swinging his rifle around to draw a bead. Saxon raised the Diamondback and squeezed the trigger; as good a shot as he was, even with the aim point enhancements in his optics, Hardesty was in three-quarter cover and essentially untouchable.

The massive crystal chandelier above him was a far larger, far easier target to hit. A great bowl of frosted glass and brass workings suspended from a metal chain, it dated back to the opening of the Palais almost a century earlier. Saxon's shot destroyed it utterly, the fragile antique exploding under the impact. Hardesty cried out in alarm as the chandelier came apart and crashed down around him.

Glass pealed as it shattered and collapsed, and Saxon used the moment to his advantage. Discarding the spent, useless revolver, he rocked back on his augmented legs and applied power to a sprinting leap that took him scrambling up the bookcase, careworn old volumes tumbling to the tiled floor as he kicked them free. Reaching the top of the stack, he swung for the rail running the length of the balcony and snagged it with his cyberarm. The metal fingers locked on and he hauled himself up with a hissing grunt of effort. He was rolling over and down as a bullet strike cut a divot of marble from the balcony at his side, sending chips of stone scattering like shrapnel.

Hardesty dashed from his cover, changing position, seeking a better angle. The long sniper rifle wavered at his hip, a spear made of black iron.

It was exactly the move Saxon knew he would make; the man wasn't one to take a fight on the terms that were offered to him, that was his weakness. Hardesty always wanted an engagement his way, and sometimes that wasn't how things worked out. Saxon, by contrast, had learned through hard experience how to play the hand he was dealt.

He gave a book cart a savage kick and it spun across the floor, cutting off Hardesty's escape route; then he mantled a desk and came diving down on the man, leading with his augmented arm.

Hardesty brought up the sniper rifle to block him and Saxon punched the gun in the breech, hearing a satisfying crunch as the mechanism inside broke under the impact. He followed through and brought the other man to the ground, sweeping in with a punch that knocked Hardesty's sunglasses from his narrow, hairless face.

Saxon forced the weight of his forearm across Hardesty's throat and pressed down with all the power he could muster. He heard a strangled yelp die in the other man's mouth, and the sniper flailed, bringing up his hands in what for a second looked like a gesture of surrender, palms open, fingers spread.

Then the shape of Hardesty's right hand bifurcated and reassembled itself, little finger and thumb sliding back, middle fingers opening in a fan until the hand resembled some kind of strange insect; at the same moment, a slot across the palm of Hardesty's left hand grew a wide, flat dagger-tip of sharpened steel.

He slammed the palm-blade into Saxon's gut, but the jacket protecting him deflected the first few stabs, the tip skipping off the articulated panels of armor embedded in it. Hardesty snapped the spider-hand around Saxon's throat and contracted it. He stabbed again, and this time the blade plunged through into the flesh of Saxon's belly.

Pain shot through the soldier in a hot, burning surge, and he let it drive him. Saxon's free hand scrambled for purchase and caught Hardesty as he tried to twist the blade. The sniper pushed back and the men shifted, staggering, caught in a lethal embrace.

Saxon's fingers slipped on the palm-blade, his own blood preventing him from getting a solid grip; at the same time, Hardesty was inexorably tightening his own hold on the soldier. Warning icons flicked into view at the corner of his cone of vision, projected directly onto his retina by his implanted health monitor. Oxygen levels were dropping; he was getting dizzy. Had he still had organic eyes, Saxon would have been on the verge of a gray-out.

"You won't win," spat his opponent. "I will fucking gut you!"

Holding on to Hardesty was like trying to keep his hands on a snake, the other man writhing and shifting, doing everything he could to break free of the soldier's grip. Saxon had the strength but not the agility to match him; and if the sniper disengaged, he wouldn't be able to close to combat range again.

Finish it now, he told himself, *before it's too late.*

With a roar of effort, Saxon dropped his cyberarm and snagged Hardesty's wrist. Twisting his grip violently, he bent the other man back and yanked the hand with the palm-blade against the direction of the joint. The ball socket squealed and snapped back, forcing the dagger-tip up and away.

Hardesty's dead eyes widened as he suddenly understood what Saxon was going to do. For a moment, they pressed against each other, strength against strength; but it was a fight that the American was never going to win. Saxon had the weight, the power, the stamina.

Ignoring the pain singing from his knife wound, Saxon locked his gaze with the other man and slowly, relentlessly, forced the blade into the base of Hardesty's jaw, jamming it up though the roof of his mouth in a spatter of blood. The spider-hand juddered and snapped open, and a flood of air filled Saxon's starved lungs.

Hardesty tried to speak, but all he could do was emit a froth of pink fluid from his lips. With a last grunt of exertion, Saxon shoved him away and the sniper spun backward, clipping the edge of the balcony. His body tumbled over the rail and fell to the marble below, landing in a heap.

At the far end of the library, the main doors slammed open and smoke grenades entered the space, trailing mist behind them. Figures in combat armor moved behind the smokescreen, the thin red threads of targeting lasers sweeping ahead of them. Saxon heard voices calling out commands in French.

He grimaced at the pain from the cut and ran for the window; beyond were the grounds and a mission as yet incomplete.

Location Unknown

When the cell door opened again, Anna vowed she would be ready; but to her horror it wasn't Jaron Namir who slid open the metal hatch. She found herself staring at the bigger man she'd seen in the corridor before, the one with the buzz cut and the thuggish swagger. He surveyed the small chamber with a predatory eye; Anna saw that the scarring down one side of his face was the puckered tracery of burn damage. His jawline seemed off somehow—until she realized that his jaw was actually a prosthetic of plastic pseudoflesh. She wondered what could have damaged a man so brutally; but he carried his ugliness like a badge of honor. The mercenary *wanted* people to see the mutilation, as if it were an act of defiance.

His nostrils flared around the brass bull-ring through his nose, and he grinned, ducking slightly as he entered the room. "Lawrence Barrett, at your service," he said in a mocking tone, spinning out his drawl in parody of a Southern gentleman. "Pardon me if I'm the bearer of some bad news."

It was all Anna could do not to back away as he approached. She still felt woozy and unsteady on her feet. Her hands gathered behind her back and she watched him come closer, waiting for the right moment, fighting down her panic.

Barrett cocked his head. "Your value has taken a dive. Seems your pal Saxon didn't hold up his end of the deal." He grunted in amusement. "He gave you up. How about that?"

Despite herself, Anna felt a sudden, sharp jolt of emotion. She tried to ignore it. She was on her own here; she'd been on her own all along, from the very start...

"I know you," Barrett said, studying her. "Yeah. Washington. The Dansky kill. You were there, right?"

Anna's blood ran cold, her thoughts snapping back through the reports she'd read and reread about the incident in Georgetown, the data on the faceless figures who had ambushed the limo. *He was one of the killers, part of the same team as Hermann.*

Barrett kept talking. "Couldn't let it go, could you? Why'd you women always do that, huh? Never leave well enough alone?" He was looming over her now, close enough that she could smell his breath.

"What...do you want?" she managed.

He showed her a cruel smile. "Namir reckons you know some things. You wouldn't talk to him." Anna swallowed, her throat tight with the pain where the other Tyrant had held her as he questioned her about Janus. "I'll bet you're gonna talk to me, though," Barrett went on. "Once we get better acquainted, 'course."

She knew what would come next. Barrett bent down slightly, reaching up with the heavy, thick digits of his cyberarm, closing the distance between their faces; and that was when she hit him.

Anna put every ounce of force she could muster into the swing from her balled fist, bringing it around in a fast haymaker. Even as she threw the punch, she was stepping into him, snatching at the bull-head belt buckle at his waist. She had only once chance to strike; with Barrett's heavily muscled, augmented frame, if he landed any kind of return blow on her she would be done.

Her fist hit him on the cheekbone and slid up to strike Barrett in the eye. The brass sobriety coin, held between her index and forefinger, ripped across his skin and dug into him, the blunt edge ripping at the scarred flesh. Pain ignited in a dull, burning shock through her knuckles, and the force of the landed punch was so much that she felt her thumb dislocate behind the coin. Anna followed through by slamming her kneecap into Barrett's crotch; she was rewarded by a concussive grunt from the big man.

He flailed, clawing at his face and the blood streaming from his eye. "Damn, bitch!" Barrett struck out blindly and she was almost felled by a black metal hand that snatched at empty air near her head.

Anna threw herself past the mercenary toward the still-open door to the cell, but Barrett was faster than she had anticipated, and he was turning, reaching for her.

He grabbed the trailing hood of her top and snagged it, pulling hard. For a second, Anna was yanked off balance, but then she wriggled free and slipped out of the hoodie, half running, half stumbling out of the cell.

Barrett made a wordless noise of anger and came after her, his face lit with fury. She caught a glimpse of his expression and knew that the man would beat her to broken if he got hold of her.

Anna slammed the heel of her fist into the door control, and it slid shut—but not fast enough to prevent Barrett from getting his forearm through after her. The cyberlimb thrashed right and left, bending in angles that would have been unnatural for a human arm. "I'm gonna make you pay for that, you cop whore!" he shouted. The hatch jammed in place, and she could hear Barrett snarling as he tried to force it open. "You got nowhere to go!"

She ignored him and broke into a run down the narrow, windowless corridor, frantically searching for anything that could tell her where she was, and more important, how to get away. The corridor split, and one branch ended in a steep metal staircase. Anna took it, two steps at a time, and felt a faint vibration through the frame, like humming engines.

Then she was emerging on the next level, a wider corridor lit by bright daylight through wide rectangular windows. Anna lurched toward the windows, shaking her head to force herself to concentrate, fighting off the last dregs of the sedative in her system.

The floor shifted slightly beneath Anna's feet, and the abrupt understanding of exactly where she was hit her like a shock of cold water. Out the windows, she could see the blue-green of Lake Geneva ranging away, on the far shore the Rue de Lausanne highway and the suburbs north of the city. She was on a boat, racing away from Geneva at a steady rate of knots.

Anna glanced around, desperately trying to map this new information onto her current predicament. The vessel was a large one, an opulent three-hundred-foot megayacht, one of the many that circled the lake in the employ of the wealthy who made the resorts between here and Montreux their homes. The smoky-colored sandalwood paneling and elegant brass details all around conflicted sharply with the stark steel and gray of the lower decks where the Tyrants had been holding her.

If she stayed here, they would kill her. Perhaps not at first, not until they had been able to wring every last morsel of information from her, no matter how trivial; but her death was certain if she did not escape. With the boat, they could take her anywhere, north to some isolated location in the Swiss mountains, south into France, or perhaps nowhere, adrift on the lake and isolated from any prying eyes until they decided to pitch her overboard...

Clutching her injured hand, Anna hurried toward the stern of the yacht, alert for any sign of danger. She still had the brass coin, gripped in her clawed, bloody hand.

A sound from belowdeck reached her as she moved away; a howling snarl of effort and the shriek of a mechanism forced open against its tolerances.

She broke into a run.

Ariana Park—Geneva—Switzerland

A four-wheel ATV veered off the pathway as Saxon reached the Space Memorial, the Swiss civil police officer in the saddle leaning into the turn to bring the quad bike back toward his target. Riding in the jump seat behind him, a second lawman brought up a pump-action MAO shotgun and fired twice at the fleeing mercenary.

Saxon heard the low hum of the thick tangler gel-rounds as they passed near him. The semifluid was a biodegradable hyperglue compound, a nonlethal man-stopper that adhered to anything, and a single hit would be enough to arrest any plans of escape he might have.

He dove into a deliberate tumble, letting the curve of the shallow hill roll him down and away from the metal spar of the memorial sculpture. The ATV came after him, the rider following Saxon over the blind rise.

The Swiss officer met a strike from nowhere as Saxon suddenly reversed his motion and came running back to meet them as they crested the hill. His powerful cyberleg hit the rider in the chest and took him from the saddle. Uncontrolled, the quad bike spun out and pitched the cop with the shotgun into the grass.

Saxon grabbed the rider and dragged him into a sleeper hold. Using his knee to pressure the man against his grip, in seconds his target had blacked out and Saxon was running again.

The other policeman was on his feet, working the slide to pump a new round into the shotgun; Saxon heard him calling out over the police band, requesting backup. He was on him before he could fire, the two men colliding in a crunch of impact that drew a howl of pain from the other man. For a moment, they wrestled over command of the shotgun, but then Saxon got the angle and shoved hard, slamming the butt of the weapon into the officer's faceplate. It shattered and he cried out again.

Saxon snatched the shotgun and used the gel-round to put him down; the fat plug of bright pink resin frothed and foamed, expanding into a gooey, stringy mass that only a tailored solvent could dissolve. The lawman swore in a torrent of violent, gutter French to Saxon's back as he made for the stuttering ATV, where it lay upended on the lawns.

The quad bike was still operational, and Saxon flipped it, gunning the motor. As he set off down the slope, the vu-phone in his tac vest buzzed. He slapped at the device, opening the channel. "What have you got, Janus?"

The reply was relayed to the mastoid comm. "*A possibility. You must understand, the situation is fluid and there's a lot of virtual traffic in this quadrant—*"

"Save it," he snapped, leaning into the handlebars, fighting to control the pain from the wound in his gut. "The Swiss cops are throwing a net over this city and I don't have long before they take me down. I need answers now!"

"*I understand,*" said the hacker. "*Cross-referencing the code name 'Icarus' with known Illuminati holdings and surrogates yielded a large number of returns, but only one of consequence. Statistically, it's your best shot at locating Anna Kelso, if she's still alive.*"

Saxon took the ATV across a service road and out across the railroad running parallel with the parkland. "Go on."

In the distance, he could hear the rattle of approaching police helicopters.

"*A vessel, registered to the DeBeers Foundation, a private yacht owned by a corporate interest Juggernaut has long suspected to be an Illuminati front.*"

"*Icarus* is a boat? Namir must be using it as a secondary command post... "

"*Exactly. And it's currently five miles from your present location, heading northeast at four knots. I'm sending you an image now.*"

Saxon toggled the brake and the quad bike skidded to a halt. "How the hell am I going to get out there?"

When Janus spoke again, there was a hard edge under the hacker's words. "*Listen to me. I can't help you with this anymore. I've already gone well beyond my own... limits in order to assist you. There's a marina on the far side of the botanical gardens, close to your location. I suggest you appropriate some waterborne transport there and attempt to intercept the* Icarus.*"

"What limits?" Saxon demanded, with a wince. "You know who these people are, Janus. You know what they are capable of. You can't back off now. You're in too deep. We *all* are."

The line was silent for a long moment, and Saxon began to wonder if the hacker had cut the connection and gone dark for the last time; but then the response came again. "*I have done questionable things.*" The strange non-voice wavered, static lacing the tones, pushing them back and forth between male and female, high and low. "*It's disturbing.*"

"I know what you mean," said Saxon with feeling.

"I'm trying to make amends. I don't know if I can do any more... "

"You can. Help me," he insisted. "Help Kelso. Help me save at least one life today."

The reply was firm. *"This will be the last time. I'm tapping into the civil police network. I'm going to flag the* Icarus *with an Interpol stop-and-search warrant, alert the Swiss. But I can't do any more to disrupt whatever plans the Tyrants have. That's up to you."*

"Thanks." He hesitated. "Look, Janus... "

"No," said the hacker, anticipating the question forming in his mind. *"You're never going to know me. I'm not ready to reveal myself yet. Good luck, Ben."*

Saxon frowned. "Yeah. You too," he replied; but the line had already been severed.

M V Icarus—*Lake Geneva—Switzerland*

The yacht's name was emblazoned on a brass plaque near the sundeck, between a spray of crystal ornaments and antique loungers. She frowned and kept moving aft, shouldering open a slatted door that led into the boat's tender garage.

The small bay extended across the width of the *Icarus*'s hull; scuba gear, water skis, and a compact motor-launch hung from a complex set of lifting gears and equipment racks over her head, while a curved staircase led to the passenger decks above. One wall was a retractable gate for deploying the smaller craft, and inset in the wooden decking there was a circular dive hatch made of heavy-gauge polyglass, looking down a drop tube to the frothy waters of the lake. She hesitated over it. The rebreather implant in her chest was capable of keeping a human being going for several minutes without the need to take air, but could she risk exiting the boat this way? Through the glass she saw a churning chop of dark blue and white foam. The dive hatch was never designed to be used while the yacht was in motion—the second she hit the water, Anna would be exposed to the riptide from the powerful hydrojet motors propelling the *Icarus*. She had to find another escape route.

Skirting the patches of seawater on the slatted wooden deck, Anna scanned the space for anything she could use. With her elbow, she broke open the emergency case on the dash of the motor-launch, and greedily snatched up the flare launcher inside. The device was shaped like a pistol grip with no barrel; it was hardly a weapon, but she was in no position to be choosy.

Anna stuffed the flare gun into her pocket and pulled at a heavy duffel that lay discarded along the launch's keel, hoping that the contents might be something more useful. She pulled at the rope ties and the bag opened up to her.

Inside, D-Bar stared blankly into nothing, his face ashen. A purple-black contusion discolored the flesh around his throat where his neck had been twisted and broken.

She swore and jerked back. Dive weights clattered out of the duffel and onto the deck. For an instant, Anna's anger at the young hacker boiled over and she allowed herself to hate him for his betrayal; but then the emotion bled away and all she could see before her was the corpse of a frightened youth who had got in over his head.

He was not long dead, she guessed, examining the body.

Only a matter of hours had passed since the double cross on the Mont Blanc bridge, and while Anna had been left to ride out her dreamless chemical sleep, Namir and the others had doubtless put D-Bar to the harshest of questions. Looking him over, she found more bruising and contusions; she tried to imagine what he had gone through, perhaps believing himself the equal of the Tyrants for the dispatch of Croix and the gift of her as his prisoner, believing that right up until the moment they decided to torture him.

The hacker would not have lasted long, and for all that he told Namir, all the secrets he gave up, the killer would have hurt him all the same, just to be certain he had not lied. *What did he tell them?* she wondered. *The names of his Juggernaut cohorts? The locations of the New Sons of Freedom?* It was troubling to think what could be done with such information.

"Patrick," she said, gently closing his eyes, "you stupid kid."

The words left her mouth as a ripple shimmered on one of the puddles across the deck, in the corner of her sight; and a coldly familiar sense of no longer being alone raced through her. Anna reached into the launch and her hand tightened around the shaft of a boathook.

Without warning, she spun in place and swung the wooden rod out in a fast arc. It swept through the air and collided with something invisible, splintering. In the next second, a ghost formed out of nothing and Federova batted the boathook away, sneering as she came in to attack the other woman.

Federova was *so fast*; in the apartment, the EMP charge had leveled the ground between the two of them, but here and now Anna Kelso was totally outclassed.

Out of blind fury and raw fear, Anna grabbed the gear rack above her head and hauled herself up. She kicked out to meet Federova as the other woman came in, and her heel connected with the assassin's face, knocking her aside. Before Federova could recover, Anna was running for the stairs, crashing up toward the main deck.

The assassin was directly on her heels as she emerged into the middle of an observation space, walled in on three sides by elegant glass windows. Velvet couches and master-crafted faux-Elizabethan tables were side by side with minimalist holographs and inset data consoles.

Anna grabbed at a footstool and hurled it behind her, trying to slow Federova down, but she missed and stumbled. The Tyrant woman was suddenly on her and she heard the soft hiss of augmented muscles. Anna came off her feet and Federova pitched her into the air.

She spun and crashed through a glass lamp, bouncing off the half-moon bar at the back of the room. Pain flared along her side as she plowed through an arrangement of glasses and liquor bottles. Air blasted out of her lungs in a croaking howl and she tipped over and down.

Dizzy, blood wet on her face where her earlier wound had reopened, Anna struggled into a crouch. There was broken glass everywhere she laid her hands. Blinking owlishly, she saw a bottle of bourbon lying on its side, and she grabbed it by the neck.

Anna rose as Federova came in to hurt her again, and brought down the bottle like a club. The assassin tried to deflect the hit away, but the glass shattered on her arm and she hissed in pain.

Despite herself, Anna showed teeth in a feral grin; to get something from the silent woman, even the smallest of utterances, was a little victory in itself.

The rich, brown liquid spattered across Federova and the curved bar, and she staggered back a step. That was all the time Anna needed to yank the flare launcher from her pocket.

She squeezed the trigger bar and a smoking dart chugged out into the air, skipping off the bar in a blare of sputtering phosphorous. Federova went for cover as the flare ignited the bourbon spills and carried on across the room, battering itself against the inside of the windows. Orange smoke, acrid and cloying, choked the air.

Coughing, Anna fired off another shot and clipped the Tyrant woman with it. Federova's bolero jacket instantly caught alight, red flames leaping up at her face.

Through the thickening haze and shrieking of the trapped flares, Anna stumbled blindly toward the windows, desperate to escape. Behind her, she heard the tinkle of breaking glass and the crackling chugs of a fire taking hold, as one of the couches became a torch.

Federova came out of the roiling smoke ahead of her, a furious revenant blocking her path. Her skin seared and her face twisted in hate, the Tyrant looked like something spat from the fangs of hell.

The stolen jet ski rode low and fast over the wave tops, leaving the water in skipping blasts of power as it skimmed across the wake of the *Icarus*. The stern of the yacht loomed high before Saxon, just as a glint of bright light flashed along the mid-deck. For a moment, he thought it was a reflection from the sun, but then it happened again, and this time thin plumes of orange smoke coiled from the cracked windows.

Saxon twisted the throttle and gunned the motor, bringing the jet ski around to approach from the near side, where the haze would hide his approach.

The voice on the radio repeated itself in French, English, and Mandarin, warning the *Icarus* to cut power and heave to, by the authority of the Swiss civil police.

Namir's lip curled and he silenced the speaker, shooting an angry glare across the yacht's flying bridge as Barrett entered.

The big man's face was thunderous, and his scarred cheek was red with lines of blood, spilled like tear tracks from his eye. "What the hell is going on down there?" he demanded, jerking a thumb toward the aft. "The fire alarms are going crazy! Kelso wasn't on the mid-deck, so—"

"Yelena has her," Namir snapped. "She's cleaning up your mess."

"The bitch got the drop on me!" Barrett roared.

"Imbecile!" Namir shot back, with such force that the other man fell silent. "You underestimated the woman and she made you pay for it!"

Coils of smoke, black threads joining the flare fumes, drifted past on the wind. Fire-suppressor lights blinked across the control boards and Namir could hear an alarm bell ringing somewhere beneath them. He advanced to the helm control and pulled the throttle levers back to the zero mark.

"What are you doin'?" said Barrett. "Where's the pilot?"

Namir nodded toward the rearward sky deck where the unmarked Tyrant veetol was waiting. "He's warming up the helo. We're abandoning ship." He ground out the words in annoyance. "This operation is turning into a clusterfuck! We have to extract now, while we can still salvage something." He glared out of the bridge's canopy. "Police launches are on the way. Our mission security has been compromised. Apparently someone alerted them as to our extralegal status."

"Saxon?"

"Does it matter?" he snarled. "Our objective was achieved, even if Taggart didn't die. The Humanity Front is in disarray, the media will report what we want them to say. We are done here."

"We're just gonna cut and run?" Barrett replied. "First we lose the jet and now this tub?"

"Let it burn," Namir told him. "The cost is nothing against the gains. We'll be across the border before the Swiss realize what has happened, and by the time they've doused the flames, the group will spin the truth to whatever best suits their needs."

Federova's fingers were like iron rods where they bored into Anna's flesh through the smoke-dirtied sleeves of her blouse, and each motion of her pushing and shoving her across the decks was a new flash of pain. The assassin worked a nerve point in her arm and it was like her skin had been doused in acid.

She gasped and kept moving, tasting blood in her mouth. Anna caught a brief glimpse of herself in the curve of the *Icarus*'s gray glass windows as she passed; once upon a time she would have loved to find herself walking the decks of an elegant vessel like this, but now she looked like an apparition, some walking wounded left behind by the passing of a war.

Federova marched her to the upper tier and shoved her forward. The wind across the open sky deck caught her and she staggered. Across the flat space, the unmarked black flyer that had gathered her up from the Mont Blanc bridge was poised, ready for takeoff, rotor rings humming at idle. Namir and Barrett were waiting, and the big man's face lit up with a dark, hateful smile as he saw her approach. He took a step forward, flexing the thick, heavy digits of his machine hands.

Anna tried to back away, but there was nothing behind her but a curved line of steel rail and the slope of the flying bridge. The silhouette of the yacht angled away down to the main deck and the prow, the profile like a knife blade edge-on. Smoke wreathed the drifting vessel.

Namir held up a hand to halt Barrett before he could tear his payback from her. "I want Kelso intact," she heard him say, over the drone of the rotors. "If we can't interrogate her here, we'll do it at a black site."

"No... " She struggled again as Barrett grabbed her and pulled her along until she was almost off her feet. *"No!"* Anna threw punches and kicks, but they battered off the other man without effect.

A dark pit of terror opened up inside her chest. Until this moment, Anna had been able to hold on to the thinnest thread of hope, the slimmest chance that she could still find a way to escape from the Tyrants and survive. That hope disintegrated as she was dragged toward the helo, the hard, unflinching certainty falling down upon her that she would have no future, no respite, no escape—

"Hey!" Ahead, Namir rapped on the cockpit hatch, calling to the pilot. "Answer me!" He tugged at the handle and the canopy opened; the pilot's lifeless body shifted and spilled out onto the helipad. The dead man's neck was canted at an unnatural angle.

Anna saw a figure drop from the cover of the tail fin and jam a shotgun barrel into the meat of Namir's neck.

"Where the fuck do you think you're going?" said Saxon.

FIFTEEN

Namir froze, the weapon resting at the base of his skull; even with the nonlethal rounds loaded in the shotgun, a blast from point-blank range would still be enough to put him down.

"Benjamin…" He let out a sigh. "I take it Scott won't be making the rendezvous, then?"

"You'll see him soon enough." Saxon's finger tightened on the trigger. Adrenaline and pain coursed through him, and he had to work to keep himself in check; all he wanted was to kill the man in front of him. But he had come this far, and across the sky deck he saw Barrett hoist Kelso off her feet, holding her in front of him like a human shield.

"Do you really want to do this now?" Namir asked him, his tone almost reasonable. "You can't win this."

Saxon's eyes narrowed. "Your wife. Your kids. Do they know what kind of man you are, Namir?" he snarled. "Do they know how much blood there is on your hands?"

Namir's voice was ice cold. "If you were a smarter man, you would understand. Every life I've taken has been to make theirs better. You and the woman? That's a cost I'll pay without even a moment of doubt."

The stink of smoke was everywhere. Belowdecks,

the fire was taking hold, overwhelming the automatic suppression systems—but no one was leaving the *Icarus* until Saxon had what he came for.

"Ben," Kelso cried out a warning. "Federova—!" Barrett silenced her with a jerk of his wrist.

Crouched behind the helo, Saxon hadn't seen the Russian assassin. She did her ghost trick again, shifting visibility as the EM aura of her cloak hazed the air around her. In a split second, he sensed the prickle of the stealth augmentation's field as she came at him. He shoved Namir away and turned the shotgun before Federova could plunge a fractal-edged combat blade into his chest. The weapon boomed twice and glutinous plugs of tangler-gel hit the assassin in the gut and sternum. The impact force was enough to blow her back off her feet and send the woman skidding over the polished deck.

Spitting like an angry cat, Federova tore at the sticky mess, downed and for the moment out of the fight.

Namir didn't hesitate to use the assassin's distraction and whirled on Saxon, the crimson musculature of his augmented arms bunching as he threw a blow at the other man. The joints pivoted in unnatural ways and he swept down two high-low arcs, the first fist clipping Saxon's temple, the second knocking the police-issue shotgun from his grip. The weapon rattled away and vanished over the side.

Saxon recoiled, trying to fall back before Namir forced him off balance. He heard the snap and click of machined parts and saw Barrett's face set in a feral grin as his cyberarm reconfigured, growing a length of cannon barrel, rising up to aim at him.

"No," Namir ordered. "I'll finish this." The Tyrant commander's face turned to fix Saxon with a cold, determined glare. "The responsibility is mine. As it always was."

Namir snarled and surged forward.

Anna struggled in Barrett's grip, but he was inflexible, inescapable. She strained to breathe, watching Namir lead into his attack on the soldier. The mercenary moved with unnatural speed, his limbs twisting on hydraulic shocks that made him more agile than anyone she had ever seen; Saxon seemed lumbering and slow by comparison.

Namir went low and threw out his legs in a blur, sweeping around in a swift spin-kick that almost took Saxon off his feet, but the soldier did not allow the attack to put him on the reactive. Instead, Saxon launched himself at his opponent as Namir regained his balance, charging into him.

Legs pounding, Saxon gathered up Namir and shunted him bodily across the sky deck in a fast tackle, driving him into a support stanchion with a heavy crash.

Anna heard the grind of fracturing bone and the dense thuds of metal fists on human flesh as Namir struck at Saxon's neck and torso, his hands blurring as the apparatus in his arms went into machine-fast retaliation. He punched at the bloody patch on Saxon's belly, drawing a howl from his opponent.

Fluid spattered from the soldier's mouth as he let the mercenary commander drop, and Saxon engaged him with a flurry of punches and kicks. Strikes went back and forth between the two men, some blocked and parried, others hitting home.

The two opponents seemed evenly matched—at least at first sight. But Jaron Namir had come fresh to this fight and possessed some of the most advanced combat augmentations in the world; Ben Saxon was already on his reserves, his stamina running raw, fatigue poisons turning his bloodstream into acid, the knife wound in his gut weeping red.

Momentarily dazed by a snap-punch, Saxon shook it off and threw a heavy blow that knocked Namir back. The Tyrant turned with the strike and pivoted on one leg, whipping up the other limb to plant a heavy combat boot in Saxon's jaw.

Anna saw the blow flash home, but at the last possible second, Saxon snagged his former commander's leg and twisted it, arresting the momentum. He pulled Namir in with all his might and dragged the other man off-kilter.

Namir stumbled and Saxon snatched at him, arms curving up around his shoulders to lock behind his neck. In a heartbeat, he had the Tyrant in a breaker hold, and he squeezed, drawing a howl of pain from the other man. "I never should have trusted you," Saxon grunted, applying lethal pressure.

"I was about... to say the same thing... " managed Namir.

Saxon felt the other man's augmented arms squirming in his grip, and it was all he could do to hold on. *Just a few more seconds, and he could end this—*

Namir's arms went rigid and turned forward. Before Saxon could recognize what was happening, the limbs shifted and moved against the balls of their joints, twisting opposite the true and folding back against the lines of flexion. Dislocating the cybernetic arms, Namir swiftly inverted the chokehold and tore himself free, snapping his head back to crack Saxon across the bridge of the nose.

He felt a hard shock of pain and blood gushed from his nostrils. Namir snaked away and snapped his arms back to a more human mode, lashing out with a cross-handed blow. Saxon tried to block him, but Namir pushed in and caught his left arm—his *human* arm—in a steely vise.

Saxon cried out as the humerus bone snapped with a wet crunch, agony tearing up his nerves in a burning wave. With a savage wrench, Namir pulled him aside and threw Saxon at the fuselage of the flyer. Unable to arrest his motion, the soldier slammed into the blunt prow of the black helo and collapsed to the deck near the body of the dead pilot. The pain was blinding, and the impacts from the storm of punches had cast scatters of static across the vision field of Saxon's optic implants. He dug deep, reaching for a last reserve of strength even as he knew he had little left to give.

The attack at the airport, the fight with Hardesty, and now this... Saxon was tapped out, running on vapors.

He heard Namir coming up behind him. "Time to end this," said the Tyrant commander. "No more distractions."

And then he saw his last chance, lying there before him. He reached for it.

Anna choked back a gasp as Saxon struggled to his knees, trying to bring himself back up from the deck. Namir stood over him, and cast a quick, frosty glare toward her and the other Tyrants. "We fix our own mistakes," he told them.

He turned back to meet Saxon as the soldier came up on one knee, releasing a roar of pain and effort. Something metallic glittered in his hand and he cracked it across Namir's face with brutal intent; a pistol, torn from the holster of the dead pilot.

The mercenary was knocked away, blood streaming across his face. Saxon rose, the gun in his machine arm, and he fired three bullets into Namir's chest from close range. The shots would have killed a normal man, but the Tyrant commander wore a tac vest lined with armor inserts, and beneath that he carried dermal shell implants capable of stopping any low-caliber rounds that made it through; still, Anna felt a ripple of pain-memory as she recalled a bullet from a similar gun that had cut into her.

Barrett was shouting as Saxon raised the pistol's muzzle a degree higher and laid his aim on Jaron Namir's head.

The big man's grip on her neck tightened again, enough to draw a strangled scream from her lips.

"Saxon!" bellowed Barrett. "You kill him and the woman dies next!"

Namir lay in a heap on the deck, scarred and wheezing. He looked up, one eye gummed shut, the other the bright lens of an augmented optic. "Go on, then," he panted. "That was a very clever recovery, Ben... It's one of your best skills... The ability to evaluate and exploit a tactical opportunity. You're quick that way." He coughed up a string of bloody spittle. "So do it. Kill shot." He tapped at his cheekbone, under the undamaged eye. "Right here. I'll die, and you'll have what you want. Your payback." On the lower tiers of the yacht, glass portholes shattered as the fire continued to spread, waves of heat radiating up through the floor of the sky deck. "*Icarus* burns," said Namir, chuckling painfully at his own joke. "And so will all of us, one way or another. What's it to be?"

"Drop the gun!" Barrett shouted. Pushing Federova aside, he dragged Kelso to the front of the upper deck and shoved the woman until she was half over the guide rail. "You test me and I swear to you, I'll drop her into the fire!"

The muzzle of the pistol wavered. He thought of Sam and his men, the ghosts he had seen in the gloom of the field hospital. He owed them this, this last bullet. *This measure of justice.*

"Shoot me," Namir demanded, "or save Anna." He shifted, dragging himself to his feet with slow, agonized motions. Blood was streaming from the wounds in his chest, but he never broke eye contact with Saxon. "You're aggrieved. You've been lied to and used. But that's the world we fight in. That's *who we are.*"

"Not me," Saxon bit out. "I'm not like you. I never was."

"Then you have to decide." Namir gave a shrug. "Is your need for revenge worth another innocent life?"

He would never be this close again. Saxon knew it with ironclad certainty—if he did not pull the trigger, Namir would slip away, the Tyrants would vanish into the shadows cast by the Illuminati, and all the deeds they had done would go unpunished...

And the cost would be only one innocent life. Just one single person. Another name on the endless roll of sacrifices laid down for the ideal of the Illuminati's draconian one world order. Anna Kelso's death in exchange for Jaron Namir's, a man whose soul had to be black with all the horrors he was responsible for.

He could *not* let him live. It wasn't right that such a man should have a life, a family, a *purpose,* while all Ben Saxon had turned to ashes around him.

It is not right!

With a sudden snarl of fury, he flung the pistol away into the waters of the lake, turning to Barrett. "Let her go, you son-of-a-bitch."

Barrett grinned through bloodstained teeth. "Sure, whatever you say." He opened his hand and Kelso screamed as she went over the edge of the sky deck and into the churning black smoke.

Saxon heard him laughing as he exploded into a full-tilt run, racing toward the far side of the boat. Barrett brought up his gun-arm and let rip with a screaming hail of rounds that chopped up the decking all around him, shredding wood and plastic.

Without halting, Saxon reached the lip of the rail and threw himself over it, Barrett's shots hissing through the air around him.

One moment, her world was a fog of pain, consciousness hanging by a thin thread, and the next—

Anna was falling into the mouth of hell, gasping as black smoke filled her lungs, the heat of an inferno beating at her. She landed badly on the slant of the hull, a glass-and-steel slope that ranged away down to the main deck. Anna flipped over and tumbled. She threw out her hands to arrest her plunge, but she couldn't find anything to grab on to. The smooth, polished glass resisted all attempts to grip it. She slid inexorably toward the flames gathering below.

Above, gunfire rattled, and through the smoke she saw another figure vault over the edge and come down toward her. Fear lanced through Anna; someone was coming down to finish the job. But then she saw Saxon's blood-streaked face.

He punched his machine-fist into the hull and found a moment's purchase. Anna grabbed for his outstretched arm and heard him cry out in agony as she pulled on the broken limb. Her shoes scraping over the hull, she shoved herself up, feeling plumes of heat from the fires searing her back.

A shape hazed into view through the smoke. Barrett leaned over the edge of the sky deck and sneered, pointing his gun-arm toward the two of them. The tri-barrel cannon spun up to firing speed and spat a line of stark, yellow-white tracer, shredding the paneling.

"Hold on!" shouted Saxon, as the glass window beneath them shattered under the salvo, opening up into a void of hot vapors. The two of them tumbled into the interior of the burning yacht, vanishing from sight.

Barrett spat over the rail and turned away in disgust, cordite vapor coiling from the maw of his gun. He kicked away the spent brass casings at his feet and moved toward the idling helo. Federova, her ice-cool glower now sullen and silent in its fury, shot him a hard look. She'd managed to extricate herself from most of the tangler rounds, but she was angry that none of Saxon's blood had ended up on her blade.

Namir ordered her into the flyer with a sharp gesture, and he climbed into the empty pilot's chair. "Is it done?" he asked.

"Lost them in the smoke—" Barrett's explanation was interrupted by a dull concussion from deep inside the *Icarus*'s engine room. The yacht shuddered and listed alarmingly, tilting so far to port that the lake waters broke over the main deck and swamped it.

"Get in," Namir told him. "The police launches are a few minutes away. We're not going to be here when they arrive."

Barrett threw one last look over his shoulder, listening to the death-throes of the boat as the *Icarus* was consumed by fire and water. "See you in hell, Saxon," he muttered, pulling himself into the flyer.

The rotors became shrill, spinning the smoke into twisting columns; then the aircraft lifted off and rose vertically, pivoting to survey the burning boat as a raptor would hover over the corpse of a fresh kill.

Anna crouched close to the carpeted decking and did her best to draw what little untainted air remained into her chest. She cast around, finding Saxon in a heap on top of a broken table. They had crashed through the roof into the forward gallery of the yacht, a richly appointed dining room. Small fires had taken hold here, crawling slowly along the support stanchions. The floor was gritty with a layer of extinguisher powder that had proven ineffectual. She moved to him, staying low, her breathing ragged and painful.

Above, a rent in the glass ceiling looked out into a blackened sky. The smoke filled it like a chimney, the hot haze billowing around her. She blinked, her eyes stinging. "Saxon?" She could hardly speak; the call came out like the bark of an animal.

He stirred and rolled off the table, hissing with pain. Shards of shattered glass were buried in the meat of his damaged arm, and Saxon pulled at them, tossing the blood-stained fragments away. "We... We have to get off this deathtrap."

Toward the bow, the *Icarus* was already a quarter submerged, a wide slick of burning oil spread out across it. Water lapped in through breaks in the forward doors, but a fallen stanchion blocked any hope of getting them open. They couldn't go back the way they had come in, and the metal staircase leading to the deck above was searing hot to the touch. Anna chanced a look up the stairwell and saw nothing but flames.

She turned back to Saxon. "Down," she told him, a plan forming in her thoughts. "We've got to go down. There's no other escape route." The risk of what she was suggesting made her blood run cold; but at the same time she knew there was no other option open to them.

"This boat's sinking, or hadn't you noticed?" he retorted. "Those decks will be full of water."

"I don't plan on burning or drowning," Anna snapped back. "Saxon, you have to trust me. I know a way out! Come on!"

He nodded, with effort. "Go, then," he said, and limped after her, deeper into the dying vessel.

The corridor to the aft canted at a forty-five-degree angle and the cold water of the lake was at Saxon's waist. All around them, the *Icarus* was dying, electrical systems firing blasts of sparks over their heads, the hull moaning as it buckled.

At the door to the tender garage, Saxon and Kelso had to put their full weight behind the hatchway to swing it open against the pressure of the water. The pain in his arm and his belly were numbing fires.

The small bay was a mess, debris scattered across the room floating in drifts and the yacht's launch already overturned and knotted in its own guide ropes. Water was pouring in from the port side, and what space they had to breathe was thick with suffocating smoke.

"This is your way off?" Saxon asked.

Anna didn't answer him; instead she dropped beneath the surface and vanished into a cloud of bubbles. A moment later, she broke through again and pulled at his arm. "You can swim, right?"

"Of course I can bloody swim."

"There's a dive hatch set in the deck. We get it open, we can get out into open water."

He shook his head. "This wreck is on fire! We're surrounded by burning fuel, we try to surface out there and we'll die!"

Anna shook her head. "That's not what I said. I told you to trust me, so *trust me*!" She grabbed his other arm and pulled him.

A crash of fire and heat rippled down the corridor behind them, ending any more argument from him. Taking as deep a breath as he could, Saxon followed her into the water. His hands brushed the deck beneath them and found the edges of the hatch.

Together, they pulled at the latches as the water around them churned and boiled.

Namir turned the helo in a tight orbit over the *Icarus,* but it was difficult to make out anything. Thermals from the raging fires buffeted the flyer, and he didn't dare venture too low, as gas tanks in the midsection began to combust one by one, lashes of orange flame jetting into the air as the heat broke them open.

The yacht's bow crumpled and fractured down the length of it. The craft was taking on water as fast as it was burning, and it would be a race to see which would claim it first.

He looked over his shoulder at Federova, who scanned the blazing wreck down the sights of a heavy battle rifle. "Anything?"

She gave a curt shake of her head, and Namir knew she was itching to rake the craft with a hail of 5.56 mm rounds, just to make certain that the *Icarus* was Ben Saxon's grave.

"Company!" Barrett called out to him and pointed across the lake.

Namir glanced back and saw the blue-and-white hulls of the police patrol boats cutting through the wave tops toward them. "Time to go," he said, and grabbed the helo's throttle, pushing it forward to maximum. The flyer's nose dipped down and Namir guided it through the clouds of fire smoke, and away toward the far coastline.

Under cover of destruction, the Tyrants vanished.

The *Icarus* perished with a final, spasming explosion as the diesel fuel reached combustion point and flashed into fire.

The blast took the yacht apart and rained fragments down in a cascade of shards and flaming debris. Anyone caught on board would have been killed instantly, ripped apart or burned to ashes.

Beneath the surface of the lake, the concussion resonated through the water and beat at Saxon and Kelso, a heavy hammer of force battering them down into the depths.

Saxon lost control and tumbled; blue-water ops had never been his thing, and now the pain and the hurt and the fatigue all combined with the blast to rob him of his last breaths, the oxygen in his lungs streaming from his mouth in a gush of bubbles. He was going to drown, and there was nothing he could do to stop it.

Then Anna was there, her arms snaking around his back, pulling herself close to him, fighting the undertow to draw them together into an almost intimate embrace.

Through his clouded vision he saw her face, milk-pale like some ghost come to claim him. Over her shoulder he saw other shadows, other men. The dead and the gone, the true ghosts beckoning him to join them. He reached out, and tried to speak. *I'm sorry,* he wanted to say, *I let you down.*

Anna's face closed in and she pressed her lips to his, cupping the back of his skull, pushing them together.

The kiss was like an electric shock; and then from it new breath flooded into his mouth and his lungs, trickles of bubbles escaping as Kelso gave up her air for him.

Pressed to him, he felt something flutter against his chest, something beneath the flesh of Anna's breast; a rebreather implant. She turned her head away, peering through the murk as they drifted there, gently exhaling, breathing without breathing before she turned back and gave him another moment of life. The implant could act like a small reservoir of air if needed, increasing lung capacity against gas effect, suffocation...and drowning. He had trusted her, and now in turn she saved him.

Saxon saw her face, saw the pain hiding beneath the surface, the scars that didn't see the light of day. They were alike, the two of them. Both damaged by the same lies, both survivors of it. Both *haunted*.

Beneath the shroud of flame across the surface of the water, between the shafts of light and the fall of the wreckage, they held on to life, and to each other.

Eiffel Tower—Paris—France

The private elevator took him to the second tier of the tower, which, as he had expected, was closed to the public for the duration. The restaurant Jules Verne was equally empty, the only figures moving between the tables a discreet pair of young waiters who doubtless had been thoroughly vetted for their reliability.

DeBeers dismissed his men with a glance and they found themselves somewhere to stand, out of his sight line. He crossed to the table where his colleague was waiting. Morgan Everett got up, extending a hand and warm smile, framed against the windows and the view of the Champs de Mars beyond.

"Lucius," he began. "It's good of you to come. It's been a while."

"Since we were face-to-face? Indeed." DeBeers took his hand and shook it. "You look well, Morgan. Paris agrees with you."

That got him a smile in return. "This city has always been important to the group. And the truth is, a lot of things here agree with me." Everett gestured to the chair across from his and they sat.

DeBeers found the glass of Les Forts de Latour waiting for him and considered it. "How *is* Elizabeth, by the way?"

"She sends her best," said the other man. "She has other obligations." He nodded toward the waiters. "I hope you don't mind, but I took the liberty of ordering for you."

"I trust your judgment," he replied. "So, this is just the two of us, then?"

Everett sipped his wine and leaned forward. "You're not going to pretend you thought it would be anything else?"

"I suppose not," DeBeers allowed. "I'm concerned that the council might be dismayed at the thought of us meeting in secret."

"To conspire?" Everett chuckled. "Lucius, you've been an excellent teacher all these years, and one lesson I learned very early on was that there is an elite within the elite."

"Some believe that," he agreed. "Page and Dowd."

"Bob Page has enough to do with the biochip initiative and his projects at Majestic 12." DeBeers detected a note of irritation in his old friend's voice, but chose not to comment on it. "And dear old Stanton won't leave New York for anyone."

"True enough. Still, it's a rare occurrence for any of us to meet in the flesh. It's simply not done."

Everett laughed again. "I know, it's almost reckless, isn't it? I quite enjoy the thrill." He sobered. "But the Illuminati own Paris. We have nothing to fear here." He took another taste of his wine. "Speaking of which. The events in Geneva—"

DeBeers waved him into silence. "I have a considerable amount of influence in that city. I've made sure the blame was laid firmly at the feet of L'Ombre. The explosions at the airport and the bridge, the assassination attempt, the sinking of the yacht... "

"Yes, such a pity about the *Icarus*."

"I have others. The vessel was a liability, anyway. It might have been connected to me eventually."

"Of course." The appetizers arrived and they ate for a moment before Everett spoke again. "I asked you here, Lucius, because I wanted to discuss the juncture we find ourselves at, without the... the distraction of other voices. We've recruited so many people to the group recently and I miss the clarity of our more direct discussions." He gestured airily. "It's not just Page and all his ambitions. Our lady friend from China, the scientist... "

"I concur," said DeBeers. "We have so many endeavors. Sometimes it is difficult to juggle them all."

Everett nodded. "Exactly. Some of the group forget that the current undertaking is only one of many lines of influence in development. Let's not forget the work on the HIV cure, the D-project, and the fault-line venture in California... "

"All equally important, I grant you," he replied. "But the biochip is where our focus should be."

"And we are on course?"

DeBeers nodded. "Obviously, there was a need for some compartmentalization of events from certain subordinate members of the council. But you can rest assured that the pattern of influence fell more or less exactly where we wanted it to. As always."

"The United Nations have agreed on the need for a referendum, then?"

He nodded again. "I was informed of that fact just before I left Switzerland. The attempted murder of Taggart was enough to push them over the edge. That, along with our other vectors of influence and the recent decision by Senator Skyler to come around to our way of thinking, brought us the desired result."

Everett cocked his head. "What happened at the Palais... Did you really intend that to succeed?"

DeBeers allowed himself a smile. "Either way, it would have been win-win, Morgan."

"I see. That explains your, shall I say, prudence?"

He went on, paraphrasing the report that Jaron Namir had given him in the weeks after the incident in Geneva; although the Tyrants had lost half their agents, they had still been able to complete their mission objectives. The mistake of recruiting Saxon had been erased and Hardesty, while useful, was not irreplaceable. Remarkably, Gunther Hermann had been recovered alive—although severely injured—from the waters of the Rhone by MJ12 operatives. It was a testament to the German's strength of will that he had survived a bomb blast, but the detonation had rendered him physically crippled and heavily burned. DeBeers was aware that Page had already co-opted Hermann, for extensive reconstructive surgery and induction into a cybernetic mech-augmentation program. Perhaps, in time, he would be ready to be redeployed.

"The fact is," DeBeers concluded, "the question of the

global regulation of human augmentation technology is now unavoidable, and we have positioned ourselves to take full advantage of the situation. The result will be a forgone conclusion."

"The best kind," said Everett, saluting him with his glass. "And our larger plans move on with only minor alterations. Excellent." He paused. "Still. There are issues yet to be resolved. Those children in the Juggernaut Collective, for example."

DeBeers shook his head. "We've dismantled that little gang of data thugs. Those who aren't dead are on our payroll. And as for their friends in that separatist rabble... We'll keep them around. Use them for our own purposes."

"The operative with the attack of conscience, Saxon? And the Kelso woman?"

"They haven't resurfaced, both figuratively and literally. But then, Lake Geneva is quite deep."

Everett accepted this and studied his mentor for a long moment. "You've yet to mention the hacker. What does he call himself—Janus?"

DeBeers frowned. "Gone. Silent. None of our concern, for the moment." He drew himself up, dropping the mannerisms of a friend in conversation with his best student, and his behavior became more authoritative. "There are other matters of more importance to attend to. Like the work of Reed and the team from Sarif Industries."

"Of course, Lucius," said the other man. "I appreciate the opportunity for... clarity." He looked up as the waiters returned with the main course, and with a nod he had the server pour a fresh measure of wine into each of their glasses. Everett raised his and smiled. "To the future, then?"

"The future," said DeBeers, savoring the moment.

Santa Lucia—Guanacaste Province—Costa Rica

The hamlet was a small place a few miles past the outskirts of the main township, little more than a collection of homes and buildings clustered around the road in the lee of greenery and the encroaching edges of the jungle. Aside from the gray discs of satellite antennas and snarls of telephone cables webbing the redbrick buildings together, the scene was as it would have been twenty, maybe even forty years ago. It was basic and unhurried, and a long way off the grid.

The man and the woman who arrived were not locals, and some of the children who played in the street took it upon themselves to follow the pair of them, measuring these *blancos* and wondering who they were. The big man was an *hombre de la máquina* like they saw in the action vids, and they were wary of coming too close. The braver of the boys told the others that they heard men like him had chips in their heads that could read your thoughts and arms that could rip apart a car. The woman, she was different, her blond hair pulled back tight in a ponytail, the color turning back to brunette at the roots where the dye job was fading. She wore mirrored sunglasses and a wide-brimmed bush hat that did its best to hide her face from the world.

At the Duarte house, the two new arrivals were greeted with a strange mixture of emotions. The big man was welcomed like a cousin, with a tearful hug from the mother and a sad, knowing nod from the father. Samuel Duarte's parents both wept a little, but they thanked the big man and brought him inside, the woman following a few steps behind.

The children who asked questions about the couple in the earshot of adults were told to be quiet and speak no more of them. These people were friends, and that was all that mattered. They had come here to be away from the questions of others, and everyone in the village understood that.

Anna sat on the balcony as the sun set and stared out into the green; in the distance the color bled away to a gray-brown haze where the jungle ended in the maws of the mammoth logging camps, in the shadow of the mountainside. One hand she kept balled in a fist, resting on her lap. It was as if she couldn't remember how to unclench it.

She looked away and found Saxon, offering her a brown bottle of some nondescript local beer.

"Thanks." She took a long pull. "Are we good?"

He sat next to her, making a face as he pulled on the sutures in his belly. "We're good. This place is not on anybody's radar, you can be sure of that. It's... " He smiled ruefully. "It's just a barrio rattrap. No one knows who you are down here." The smile faded. "We're outta their reach. That's what you wanted, yeah?"

She nodded. Fleeing from Europe, there had been many places they could have gone to ground, but something dark and potent inside Anna Kelso had driven her to seek sanctuary as far away as she could go. Somewhere off the map, far from cities and the threats of what she saw when she dreamed.

He was watching her. "You'll be okay here."

Anna put down the bottle. Something in his tone rang a wrong note. "I will? And what about you?" When he didn't answer she glared at him. "You're not going to stay?"

He shook his head. "Job's not done, Anna. Namir and those bastards he works for are still out there, still playing their games... I can't look Sam's family in the eye and know that I let Namir keep breathing after I let their son down."

She moved closer to him. "Redemption, that's what you want, isn't it?" Anna sighed. "So do I, for Matt. But I want it for myself as well... "

"Yeah... " He drained the beer. "Haven't found it yet."

"You're wrong." She took his hand. "You saved my life, Ben. You came to save me when you could have just gone on with the fight. Then I did the same thing. I saved you. We... we redeemed each other." At last, she opened her hand and showed him the brass coin, its surface blackened and scratched.

"It's not enough... " he muttered, looking away. "After all we've seen, it's not enough." He went to the balcony. "They won, Anna. After everything we did to burn those bastards, they still won!"

She shook her head. "Not yet. Not until they silence us. This game isn't over." Anna followed him to the veranda. "Stay here," she said. "Please tell me you will stay here."

"You don't need me," said Saxon.

"It's not about need," she replied. "It's about what's going to happen. I don't want you to die out there... "

Anna heard the fear and pain in her own words, rising up from deep inside.

"What do you mean?"

Anna told him about what Janus had shown her, the torrent of images and sights the hacker had pulled from the depths of the Illuminati's dark schemes; things she couldn't comprehend, half-formed pictures that lurked in her subconscious and tainted the patterns of her dreams. She hadn't slept well since that day; the specter of what Janus had revealed was always there when she closed her eyes.

"There's one thing I remember very clearly," she said. "It's burned in my memories like a brand. An image, an impression, of every city in the world." Anna shivered as she spoke, despite the heat of the fading day. "All of them engulfed in fire and fury. That's what they're planning."

Saxon watched her carefully, struck by the strength of her certainty, and her fear. "What are you saying? There's gonna be a war?"

She looked up at him. "A change is coming, Ben. And we can't fight it. We can't stop it. The wheels are already in motion. The only thing we can do is ride it out, and wait."

"For what?"

"For a new future." Anna took his hand again and looked up as the day passed into darkness.

Out across the sky, night fell on the world they knew.

ACKNOWLEDGMENTS

Much respect is due to the creators of the original *Deus Ex* games and their compelling fictional world— Warren Spector, Harvey Smith, Sheldon Pacotti, Austin Grossman, Chris Todd, and everyone who was part of the Ion Storm team.

My appreciation to my colleagues at Eidos-Montreal for making my work on *Deus Ex: Human Revolution* such a great experience—Mary DeMarle, Taras Stasiuk, Mark Cecere, Lucien Soulban, Jean-Francois Dugas, Jonathan Jacques-Belletête, Antoine Thisdale, Francois Lapikas, Jim Murray, David Anfossi, and Stéphane D'Astous; tips of the hat also to André Vu and René Valen.

Thanks to my editors, Tricia Pasternak and Michael Braff, at Del Rey Books.

Lastly, my gratitude to William C. Dietz and Karen Traviss for their advice; my fellow narrative paramedics Rhianna Pratchett and Andrew S. Walsh; and much appreciation to Chris Bateman for the nod.

ABOUT THE AUTHOR

James Swallow is a writer on *Deus Ex: Human Revolution*—the third incarnation of the *Deus Ex* videogame series—and the *New York Times* bestselling author of more than twenty-five books, including the Scribe Award-winner *Day of the Vipers*, *Nemesis*, *The Flight of the Eisenstein*, *Jade Dragon*, the *Sundowners* series of steampunk Westerns, *The Butterfly Effect*, and fiction from the worlds of *Warhammer 40,000*, *Star Trek*, *Doctor Who*, *Stargate*, and *Judge Dredd*. Swallow's other credits include the critically acclaimed nonfiction work *Dark Eye: The Films of David Fincher* and scriptwriting for *Star Trek Voyager*, videogames, and audio dramas.

He lives in London, and is currently working on his next book.

ABOUT THE TYPE

This book was set in Sabon, a typeface designed by the well-known German typographer Jan Tschichold (1902–74). Sabon's design is based on the original letterforms of Claude Garamond and was created specifically to be used for three sources: foundry type for hand composition, Linotype, and Monotype. Tschichold named his typeface for the famous Frankfurt typefounder Jacques Sabon, who died in 1580.

For more fantastic fiction from Titan Books check out our website: www.titanbooks.com where you'll find details of all our exciting titles, including:

Novels based on hit games, TV shows and movies:

Dragon Age: The Stolen Throne by David Gaider
Dragon Age: The Calling by David Gaider

The Infernal City: An Elder Scrolls Novel by Greg Keyes

God of War by Matthew Stover and Robert E. Vardeman

RuneScape: Betrayal at Falador by T.S. Church
RuneScape: Return to Canifis by T.S. Church

Primeval: Shadow of the Jaguar by Steven Savile
Primeval: The Lost Island by Paul Kearney
Primeval: Extinction Event by Dan Abnett
Primeval: Fire and Water by Simon Guerrier

Supernatural: Nevermore by Keith R. A. DeCandido
Supernatural: Witch's Canyon by Jeff Mariotte
Supernatural: Bone Key by Keith R. A. DeCandido
Supernatural: The Heart of the Dragon by Keith R.A. DeCandido
Supernatural: The Unholy Cause by Joe Schreiber
Supernatural: War of the Sons by Rebecca Dessertine & David Reed

Terminator Salvation: From the Ashes by Timothy Zahn
Terminator Salvation: The Official Movie Novel by Alan Dean Foster
Terminator Salvation: Cold War by Greg Cox
Terminator Salvation: Trial By Fire by Timothy Zahn

WWW.TITANBOOKS.COM